Usually to be
mug of black
her jacket po
local café.

Jenny combines her past experiences as an archae...
tutor, cheese seller, newsagent, hat maker, Robin Hood obsessive and
date ... with the sights and sounds of everyday life, to weave tales
of ... relatable romance.

... 'other Cup of . . .' series has been a consistent bestseller,
yo... *Cornish Escape* hit the Amazon Kindle top 10 and stayed
... many months.

... ical mysteries under the name of Jennifer Ash.

... more at www.jennykane.co.uk

Praise for Jenny Kane:

'... fan of Jenny Kane' Katie Fforde

'... read as scrumptious as its Cornish backdrop. Brilliant!'
... May

'... this frothy cappuccino of a book!' Christina Jones

'... of escapism. Great and truly lovable characters to root for
... ful descriptions of Cornwall' ***** Reader review

'... put this book down! I warmed to the characters immediately
... desperate to see how things worked out for them' *****
... view

'... read, heartwarming and funny' ***** Reader review

'... this story from start to finish. The perfect read for a weekend
... noon, with a cuppa and your feet up' ***** Reader review

'One of the best books I have read' ***** Reader review

Also by Jenny Kane

Another Cup of Coffee
Another Glass of Champagne
Jenny Kane's Christmas Collection
Romancing Robin Hood
A Cornish Escape (*previously published as* Abi's House)

Ebook Only
Christmas at the Castle
Christmas in the Cotswolds
Another Cup of Christmas

Children's Fiction
There's a Cow in the Flat
Ben's Biscuit Tin Adventure

Writing as Jennifer Ash
The Outlaw's Ransom
The Winter Outlaw
Edward's Outlaw
The Meeting Place

A
Cornish
Wedding

JENNY KANE

ACCENT

First published in 2017, previously titled *Abi's Neighbour,*
by Accent Press

First published in this edition in 2020 by Headline Accent
An imprint of HEADLINE PUBLISHING GROUP

1

Cataloguing in Publication Data is available from the British Library

ISBN 978 1 7861 5784 3

Offset in 11.87/15.15 pt Times New Roman by Jouve (UK), Milton Keynes

Printed and bound in Great Britain by Clays Ltd, Elcograf S.p.A.

HEADLINE PUBLISHING GROUP
An Hachette UK Company
Carmelite House
50 Victoria Embankment
London
EC4Y 0DZ

www.headline.co.uk
www.hachette.co.uk

For my wonderful parents

Chapter One

Cassandra stared at the 'For Sale' sign in the front garden. A fresh slogan had been pasted proudly across it, proclaiming *Another House Sold!*

She frowned. The estate agents must have made a mistake. Justin had talked about renting the cottage, this poky little two-bed terrace in some Cornish backwater, but he'd never once suggested *buying* it.

Sitting on the low stone wall that ran in front of the row of cottages, with her back to the sold sign, she let out a string of vehemently whispered expletives. Resisting the temptation to throw a pebble at the seagulls which were squawking their hearts out on the roof behind her, she steadied her breathing, like she did when faced with a particularly demanding client.

Shrugging off her suit jacket in deference to the early summer sunshine that poured from a cloud-free sky, Cassandra tried to focus, but doubts continued to assail her. She hadn't misunderstood Justin, had she?

They'd been laughing over the breakfast table at one of the most exclusive hotels in London when the subject of Cornwall had first come up. Making plans for their future life together, they'd celebrated in grand style the fact that Justin had, after six years of secret trysts and stolen nights together, decided to leave his wife, the dreadful Jacinta.

1

Excitedly they'd plotted and planned over plates of eggs Benedict and smoked salmon, raising their glasses of Buck's Fizz to Justin's promotion to senior partner at the law firm. A promotion which meant that, providing they merged their finances, Justin could afford to get a divorce without being catapulted into penury.

There was only one snag.

The legal company Justin now worked for, Family Values, prided itself on its moral integrity. There was no way he could risk a scandal after securing the promotion he'd coveted for so long. It would be bad enough when he explained to his colleagues that he was getting a divorce – suddenly producing a long-term mistress would be too much for them to accept in one go.

So Justin had asked Cassandra to move away for a while. He'd suggested they use this short diplomatic period of separation to their advantage, and rent a property to later sublet – at a vast profit – to exhausted executives seeking a spot of relaxation. Cassandra, who could run her own business from anywhere via the Internet, would go and make sure the property was up to date, arrange any decorating that was required, and then rejoin Justin in London once things had died down.

Thinking back, Cassandra realised she should have asked a lot more questions about exactly how much research Justin had already done into this move. But under the influence of the early-morning alcohol, not to mention the triumph she felt at having *finally* succeeded in persuading Justin to leave his wife, she had suppressed all her instincts and agreed to everything he'd said.

The untidy, clipboard-wielding woman started talking as soon as she climbed out of her Mini. 'Hello, my name's Maggie, and I'm from –'

Cassandra cut impatiently across the formalities. 'Sennen Agents, obviously. It's written across your car.'

'Oh, yes. So it is.' Maggie paused. 'Anyway, I'm sorry I'm late, I got stuck behind a tractor down the lane.' She jingled a keyring in front of her. 'I have your keys, Miss Pinkerton.'

'No, you don't.'

'I don't?' The estate agent frowned, looking away from the woman that stood before her in expensive couture with crossed arms and a far from happy expression. Flicking through the papers on her clipboard, Maggie said, 'I was instructed by a Mr Justin Smythe that you would be accepting the keys on his behalf?'

'I *meant*, no, my name is *not* Miss Pinkerton. It is *Ms* Henley-Pinkerton.'

'Oh. I see.' Maggie refrained from further comment as she clutched the keys a little tighter.

Determined to make sure the situation was clearly understood, Cassandra pulled her jacket on, turning herself back into the sharp-suited businesswoman she was. 'In addition to your error regarding my name, there appears to have been a further mistake.'

'There has?'

'Mr Smythe has *not* purchased this property. He has merely rented it, with an additional agreement to sublet it as a holiday home. I am here for two months to make the place suitable.' Cassandra ran a disdainful eye over the beautiful exterior stonework. 'It would seem that my work

3

is going to be well and truly cut out.'

'This is a much sought-after street, Ms Henley-Pinkerton. And this particular property is in excellent period condition.' Feeling defensive on behalf of the old miner's cottage, Maggie bit her tongue and flicked through her paperwork faster. Extracting a copy of the bill of sale, she passed it to the slim, angular blonde. 'I think the misunderstanding must be yours. Mr Smythe has purchased number two Miners Row outright. It was a cash sale.'

Snatching the papers from Maggie's fingers, Cassandra's shoulders tensed into painful knots. Why hadn't Justin told her he'd done this? She was convinced she was right. And anyway, he'd never deliberately make her appear foolish in front of a country bumpkin estate agent…

Yet as Cassandra scanned the document before her, she could see there'd been no mistake. Closing her eyes, she counted to ten, before opening them again to regard the badly dressed woman before her, who was once again holding out the offending set of keys.

Failing to take them, Cassandra gestured towards the little house. 'Perhaps you would show me around, after I've made a call to Mr Smythe?'

Maggie, already feeling sorry for this unpleasant woman's future neighbours, took unprofessional pleasure in saying, 'Good luck with that call. The phone signal here is unpredictable to say the least.'

It had taken a ten-minute walk towards Sennen village to get a decent reception on her mobile phone, and then,

4

when she'd been able to connect the call, Justin's line was engaged. When she'd finally got through, she was more than ready to explode.

'Justin! How could you have done this to me without a word? You've made me look a total idiot.'

Clearly thrilled that he'd managed to buy the terrace for a knock-down price – which, he'd claimed, was a far more economic use of their funds, an investment that would make them a fortune to enjoy in their retirement – he'd sounded so excited about what it meant for their future together that Cassandra had found it hard to remain cross.

Assuring her that the situation remained the same, and that she was still only expected to stay in Cornwall while he secured his new position and got the wheels of the divorce in motion, Justin told Cassandra he loved her and would be with her very soon.

Returning to the terrace reassured, if lacking some of her earlier dignity, Cassandra swallowed back all the words she'd have liked to say as she opened the door and the gloom of the dark and narrow hallway enveloped her. She was sure that awful Maggie woman had been laughing at her. The agent had taken clear pleasure in telling her that if she hadn't stormed off so quickly she'd have found out that the phone reception was excellent if you sat on the bench in the back garden.

Vowing to never drink champagne in any form ever again, as it clearly caused her to agree to things far too readily, Cassandra saw the next two months stretching out before her like a lifetime.

5

Letting out some of the tension which had been simmering inside her since she'd first seen the for sale sign, she picked up a stone and threw it at the back fence, hard.

Maggie had gone, leaving her reluctant client sitting on an old weathered bench in the narrow rectangular plot at the back of the house. Playing her phone through her fingers, Cassandra saw that there was enough reception to make calls if she sat in this spot – but only in this spot. One step in either direction killed the signal dead, which was probably why the previous owners had placed a bench here. *And probably why they left this Godforsaken place!*

The Internet simply didn't exist here. When she'd swallowed her pride and asked Maggie about the strength of the local broadband coverage, the agent had actually had the audacity to laugh, before informing Cassandra with obvious satisfaction that people came to Sennen for their holidays to leave the world of emails and work behind them.

In short, there *was* Wi-Fi in the village – but only sometimes. It was becoming clearer to Cassandra by the minute why Justin had secured this place for such a bargain price.

Breathing slowly, she pulled her shoulders back, pushed her long, perfectly straight blonde hair behind her ears, and took a pen and paper out of her bag. It looked as if she was going to have to tackle this, old school. First she would make a list of what she considered necessary to make the house habitable for holidaymakers, then she would locate the nearest library or Internet café so she could source decorators and builders to get the work

6

underway. The sooner she got everything done, and herself back to the hustle and bustle of London, the better.

Deciding there was no way she could sleep in this house, which Maggie had proudly described as 'comfortable', 'sought-after', and 'ready to be made absolutely perfect', Cassandra hooked her handbag onto her shoulder and headed back into the whitewashed stone house. Shivering in the chill of the hallway, despite the heat of the June day, she jumped in the silence when the doorbell rang just as she bent to pick up her overnight bag.

For a second she froze. It had been years since she'd heard a doorbell ring. In her block of flats back home she buzzed people in via an intercom, and anyway, people never just dropped by. She hoped it wasn't that dreadful Maggie back with some other piece of unwanted advice.

It wasn't Maggie. It was a petite woman in paint-spattered clothes, with a large shaggy dog at her side. Cassandra's unwanted visitor wore a wide smile and held a bunch of flowers in one hand and some bedding in the other.

'Hello. My name's Abi, I live next door. Welcome to Miners Row. I hope you'll be very happy here.'

Gesturing to the contents of her hands, the woman continued, 'I picked you up a little something to brighten the house up before you get your own things in place, and I thought some fresh bedclothes could be handy if you haven't got any unpacked yet. I know how damp these places can get if they're left empty for long!'

Chapter Two

'What happened next?'

Abi took a mug of tea from Beth's outstretched hand. 'She looked me straight in the eye, pushed away the flowers, and told me, in no uncertain terms, that the idea that a mere bunch of flowers could brighten that hideous place up enough to make someone happy was unthinkable. Especially in a ropey little backwater like this.'

'You have got to be joking.'

Abi sighed. 'I wish I was. Then she ripped into Maggie for having told other people her business.'

'But surely Maggie was being kind? She probably thought a friendly face might cheer up her client, as she obviously didn't want to be there.'

Abi shrugged in her best friend's direction. 'I don't think the woman I encountered is the type of person who would ever admit to needing help. Unless she was paying for it, maybe. And even that would only be help from the *very best* professionals, of course.'

After a few seconds spent statue-still on the doorstep of number two Miners Row, staring in disbelief at her new neighbour's rapidly disappearing back, Abi had left to put the flowers in a vase in her own kitchen. She couldn't believe how unnerved she'd felt when she'd been left holding her welcome gift in one hand, and the evidence of her thoughtfulness in the other. Her head had suddenly been full of images of her late husband, Luke, who'd treated her in a similarly dismissive way for the majority of their married life.

Glad that it was nearly half past three, which meant that Beth would be home from the village school where she worked as the nursery teacher, Abi set off for her friend's flat. She badly needed Beth to put her fears into perspective. Could the depressing London life she'd escaped just under a year ago have followed her all the way to Cornwall?

Beth's flat was the top floor of her grandfather's old shop, and sat above her gallery, where Abi also worked, as resident artist and general helper-out. Now, lounging back against the sofa, Abi took a sustaining gulp of tea.

'Women like my new neighbour made my life in London miserable. I thought I'd left them all behind after Luke died, and now one's moved in next door – or at least sort of has. I think it was the linen that offended her the most. She went on about "how dare I think she'd come so unprepared", then with a tiny overnight holdall in her hand, which can't possibly have contained any bedding, she slammed the door and marched towards the village to find a hotel room.'

Incensed on Abi's behalf, Beth said, 'Well, I hope she can't find one, and ends up back at the cottage sleeping on damp sheets!'

'The cottage has been empty and unaired for so long that the sheets could well be damp and mildewed too. Especially after such a cold winter.' Abi took a biscuit from the tin that

10

Beth was holding out to her. 'Half of me hopes she can't find one as well, but the other half hopes she does. The less time she spends next door, the better, as far as I'm concerned.'

Beth sank down onto the sofa next to her friend. Putting the open biscuit tin between them, she proceeded to munch her way through a cookie as she said, 'If she's as high-powered as you suspect, then she'll probably get a taxi to take her to one of the big hotels in Penzance.'

'Possibly. When I spoke to Maggie, she said she couldn't say much because her boss was listening, but from what I gathered it's not so weird that she doesn't seem keen to live there. She's been sent by someone else to get the place ready as a holiday let. So at least I'll be spared her actually moving in permanently.'

Abi sighed again. 'I honestly can't decide if that's better or worse. The last thing I want is a constant stream of City types moving in and out, all thinking they want to escape the pressures of London while simultaneously complaining that the Internet doesn't work.' She grabbed another biscuit. 'Although I suppose that's better than having a woman who reminds me of that dreadful local wives' group Luke forced me to join. They were all perfect and sterile and made me feel inadequate with just one pursing of their expensively glossed lips.'

Crunching her ginger nut, Beth was thoughtful. 'It does sound a bit strange though. You said Maggie told you the woman was under the impression that the house had been rented, not bought.'

'She didn't come across as the sort of woman who makes mistakes.' Abi put her mug on the table in front of them. 'Come to think of it, she didn't come across like the

11

sort of person you'd send to do up a house either. I can't imagine her rolling up her sleeves and grabbing the soda crystals and a pair of rubber gloves.'

'She could be the sort of person to write a list, though, and then get other people in to scrub the walls and repaint the ceilings.'

'You may well be right.'

'Talking of decorating, how's Max? I haven't seen him this week.'

Abi's frown instantly gave way to a smile as she thought about her boyfriend. 'He's great, thanks. Working on a bathroom over in St Ives. The guy employing him is on a deadline to get his place done up before the summer season, so Max is working long hours, and then crashing out in one of the guest rooms there until he's finished. It's saving him a fortune in petrol, but the phone signal is crap. It's weird not talking to him all the time, but he'll be back in Sennen soon. How's Jacob? Any luck finding a new studio?'

Beth's partner, Jacob, had been searching for a suitable new pottery studio ever since he'd officially moved in with her four months earlier, although he had more or less lived in Beth's flat since the day they'd got together the previous August.

Pulling a face, Beth fished for a second biscuit. 'Not so far. We've seen a few, but they're all too far away. He might as well keep using the one in Hayle until the lease is up in October. Ideally we want to find a place around here before then.'

'I'll keep asking the artists that are booked into the gallery, not to mention those who phone up for future bookings. You never know, someone might know of somewhere suitable.'

'Thanks, Abi.' Beth stood up and brushed her crumb-covered fingers down her jeans. 'Fancy a pizza? I'm starving.'

'It's only 4.30!'

'I know. It's end-of-term syndrome. The kids are either hyper at the thought of moving on to big school after the holidays, or they're totally knackered after a term of preparing for the same thing. Jollying them along, calming them down, and reassuring them all at once can take it out of me sometimes – and makes me hungry!'

'I bet!' Abi pushed herself off the comfort of the sofa. 'I can't stay, though. I'm having dinner with Stan tonight. It's time for our fortnightly dinner date.'

'Crikey, have two weeks passed already? How's he doing in the old folks' home?'

Abi laughed. 'Well, apart from hating that people call it a home when it's a set of independent apartments, Stan told me on our last catch-up that, and I quote, he's as "happy as a sandboy".'

'That's good.'

'I think the only thing he misses is having Sadie around.'

'I'm not surprised. The dog was the only company he had for years. Are you taking her with you tonight?'

'Stan would kill me if I didn't!'

Abi and Sadie waited patiently for Stan to open the door to his flat for their dinner date. They had first met when Abi had given into her curiosity and knocked on

13

the door of Stan's home, Abbey's House, which had been the house of her dreams for over twenty years – ever since she'd seen its prophetic name on a family holiday when she was eight. Abi and Stan had formed a firm friendship, and she'd ended up buying Stan's home from him the previous September.

As the front door opened, Sadie pushed her nose against her former owner's legs, and Stan beamed his ever-ready smile at his visitors as he affectionately ruffled the golden retriever's fur.

'How are two of my favourite girls then?'

'Well, Sadie here is just fine.' Abi unfastened Sadie's lead and followed Stan through the hallway into his small open-plan living and dining room. 'But I'm...'

About to tell Stan about her new neighbour, Abi abruptly stopped talking as she realised they weren't alone.

Stan's grin became even broader, as he turned from Abi to the lady on the sofa, and back again. 'Dora, may I introduce you to my very dear friend, Abi Carter. Abi, this is Dora Henry. And this beautiful creature is Sadie.'

Temporarily silent, Abi quickly came to her senses. 'Hello, Dora, I'm very pleased to meet you. You're Stan's bridge partner, isn't that right?'

'I'm a bit more than that, I hope.' Dora winked at Stan, and Abi felt discomfort ripple up her spine as she noticed that the table was laid for three and not two as usual.

Abi was spared from saying anything for a moment, as Dora said, 'I've heard so much about you. I've been dying to meet you. I hope you're OK with me gatecrashing your dinner?'

'Of course!' Abi wasn't sure if she minded or not, but her inbuilt politeness had automatically engaged, and anyway, she wouldn't want to upset Stan for the world. Right now he was looking more proud than she'd ever seen him. 'I've heard plenty about you, too. I believe you're the terror of the bridge club!'

'Dora is something of a card shark,' Stan said with a twinkle in his eye.

Dora laughed. 'I shall overlook that dubious accusation, seeing as you're being so generous as to feed me, Stanley Abbey.' Then, speaking more seriously, she said, 'I'm very pleased to meet you, Abi, but if you object to me stealing some of your alone time with Stan, then I'm more than happy to disappear.'

'Not at all.' Abi found her natural curiosity kicking in about this small, elegant woman in Stan's living room. 'Shall I put the kettle on, Stan?'

'It's already on, Abi my girl. I tell you what, I'll leave you two chatting, and I'll make the tea and get Sadie some water.'

Watching Stan disappear into the kitchen, Abi sat next to Dora. 'I'm pleased to have the chance to meet some of Stan's friends.'

'As am I.' Dora focused her pale green eyes on Abi kindly. 'Stan always keeps you all to himself. He's very protective of you, Abi.'

Abi's initial disquiet at Dora's presence eased as Dora received the Sadie seal of approval. The dog, as if sensing Abi needed reassurance, padded across the room, and placed her chin on a delighted Dora's knees.

'You, my lovely,' Dora stroked the retriever's golden

back, 'are also at the top of Stan's list to talk about. And who can blame him? Not many blokes his age have two beautiful females as regular visitors.'

Abi wasn't sure what to say as she looked at Dora, who, although almost as old as Stan himself, retained the air of a classic beauty. The tone of her words was gentle, and Abi detected no sarcasm or jealousy, but there was something... something Abi couldn't put her finger on, that was hanging unsaid in the air.

Deciding she was being ridiculous, Abi asked, 'How long have you been living at Chalk Towers, Dora?'

'Five years this coming Christmas.' Dora's warm smile lit up her eyes as Stan walked about in with a tray of tea, and the unease Abi had felt instantly returned.

They aren't... are they?

Hoping she was letting her imagination run away with her, Abi stuck firmly to small talk. 'Do you like it here?'

'I love it. I wasn't sure at first. It was a bit of a gamble for me. Like you, I'm not a local girl, but I had so many happy memories associated with Cornwall that I decided to retire here.'

With one eye on Stan as he sat down and served the tea, knowing he would never have invited Dora to join them if he wasn't very fond of her, Abi said, 'I take it Stan has told you how I ended up living in his house?'

'It's your house now, Abi.' Stan passed her a mug.

'True – but it took ages before I stopped feeling like I'd evicted you.'

Stan regarded his young friend. 'I've said it before, and no doubt I'll have to say it again, but this is the best thing I've done in years. I was so lost after my Mary

16

passed away. You did me a favour, Abi, coming along when you did.'

Abi squeezed his hand, and passed a cup and saucer to Dora. 'Do you take sugar?'

'She's sweet enough without!' Stan said.

Abi was about to laugh at the old cliché, but the expression on Dora's face stopped her. There was no doubt about it – her suspicions had been correct. Wishing that Max was with her, Abi didn't know what to say, but she did know that this wasn't going to be the evening when she shared her fears about the cottage next door.

Dora peered shrewdly at Abi from over the top of her cup as she took a sip of tea. Then, patting the space on the sofa next to her, she beckoned Abi to sit back down. 'We were going to tell you after dinner, but judging by how pale you've gone, I'd say you've already guessed. Stan said you were clever.'

Stan patted his faithful dog's fur for luck and said, 'Abi, I have something very exciting to tell you.'

'You do?'

'Yes.' Reaching out, Stan took hold of his bridge partner's hand. 'Dora and I have decided to get married.'

Chapter Three

Beth slipped the last of the completed school reports into her bag, and smiled across the kitchen table to where Jacob sat with his laptop, ordering a new range of glazes for his ceramics business.

'Have you decided which of your pots you're going to exhibit in the gallery in August?'

'I think so.' Jacob glanced up from the screen. 'That's why I want these new glazes. I thought I'd try a few new colour schemes, with a slightly different style, and see if the tourists go for them. Although,' he lifted up the collection of estate agents' particulars he had on the table next to him, 'if I can't find a new studio soon, then they'll be the last new pieces for a while. I'm going to have to work like stink in order to build up enough stock to tide us over if I can't find anywhere new by October.'

Beth couldn't help feeling guilty. If it hadn't been for her, then Jacob wouldn't have been hunting for a new studio in the first place.

Almost a year ago Beth, with Abi's help, had turned the cobbler's shop she'd inherited from her grandfather into the Art and Sole gallery. Jacob had taken up her invitation to be the first visiting artist for her new enterprise, and it had been lust at first sight. A feeling that had resulted in Jacob never managing to go home for more than a change of clothes. Their lust had quickly grown into a love that had shocked them both with its arrival. He'd been happy potting away at his current place in Hayle for years, building up a stock of stunning ceramics, before that wonderful, fateful day.

'You OK, Beth?' Jacob reached a hand across the table. 'I wasn't complaining about having to move the studio, it's just proving a bit harder to find something suitable than I thought it would.'

'Are you sure you don't mind? I feel bad about you having to leave your lovely studio because of me.'

'It isn't because of you, it's because the drive to work during the tourist season is a nightmare. Anyway, now I've given up my home over there, it seems mad to commute to Hayle if I don't have to.'

Beth pointed at the studio specs on the table. 'Any of those any good?'

'One of them is possible. It's in St Just, which makes it handy distance-wise. I thought I'd go and see it tomorrow.' Jacob pushed the relevant paperwork across the table and went to the fridge to get them both a bottle of lager.

Beth read the specs carefully. 'It looks lovely, but isn't it a bit small on the storage side?'

'It would be a bit of a squeeze if I made the volume of stuff I do now, but I thought, if you didn't mind, that I could keep any overflow in the gallery store downstairs.'

'Of course you could. You could always display your work in the gallery full-time, you know.'

Jacob sighed in his girlfriend's direction; they'd had this discussion more times than he cared to remember.

'Beth, the whole point of your gallery is that Abi works there all the time, so that people can see an artist in action, and then, on the other side of the gallery, you have a turnover of fresh art each month. If my stuff was always there, that freshness would be lost, and people wouldn't come back every four weeks to see what treasures you have for sale this time.'

'I guess you're right. Abi tells me we've started to get regular visitors who always nip by to see what's new.' Beth took a swig of lager. 'Talking of which, when I was checking the schedule of who was booked to come over the next six months, I noticed you've already nabbed August for next year. The main month of the season!'

'Perk of the gallery manager being one of my best friends – and of sleeping with the boss!' Jacob shut down his laptop. 'Talking of which,' he put down his bottle, 'I think it's time I reminded myself of just how good your lips taste…'

'I've just realised something.' Beth sat up in bed the following morning, instantly distracting Jacob as the sheet slipped from her grip.

'Uh?'

Beth laughed, 'Honestly, Jacob, you've seen it all before! I said I've just realised something.'

'Sorry.' Jacob reluctantly dragged his eyes upwards, a teasing expression on his face. 'What have you realised?'

'Next month it will be a year since Abi came to Cornwall. If it hadn't been for her, there'd be no gallery. We should do something to celebrate.'

Pulling himself into his potting overalls, Jacob agreed.

21

'That's a great idea. Do you think we should do something for her, or combine it with some sort of shindig for the first anniversary of Art and Sole?'

'I hadn't even got as far as thinking about that. It's all happened so fast, and yet at the same time it feels as if Abi and the gallery have always been around.'

'Well, I for one am very glad Max found her. If Abi hadn't got lost looking for Sennen the first time she drove down here, and Max hadn't given her directions, then the gallery might never have happened – and I wouldn't be sharing a bedroom with a wantonly dishevelled primary school teacher.'

Beth stuck her tongue out as she got up. 'I'll call Max later. He's bound to want to celebrate as well. We could have a meal out together to mark Abi's anniversary, and then maybe a party at the gallery in September too.'

'Sounds good.' Jacob kissed Beth with enthusiasm before turning to the door. 'I have to get going. I want to get the kiln filled before I go to St Just for the viewing. Do you want me to put some milk on for your porridge before I go?'

'Oh no, thanks.' Beth pulled a face. 'I don't think that lager agreed with me last night. Think I'll give breakfast a miss this morning.'

Jacob frowned; Beth usually had the constitution of an elephant. 'You OK?'

'Fine. It's end-of-year stress. I'm always like this as July approaches and I have to wave my little ones off to turn into proper schoolchildren.' Beth gave him a further reassuring kiss. 'Off you go. Good luck with the studio.'

Beth crossed her fingers as she made her way to the

shower. A studio in St Just, which was only five miles away, would be perfect.

'Max? Where on earth are you?' Beth had to strain her ears to hear her oldest friend. It sounded as though he was answering the phone underwater.

'I was testing that the shower I've just installed works. It's one of those walk-in wet rooms, and it echoes like mad. Hang on.'

Beth could hear clanging in the background, and had the impression that Max was hitting something with a hammer, when suddenly her friend was back.

'Sorry about that. Now, to what do I owe the pleasure of a lunchtime phone call? Aren't you supposed to be on junior crowd control?'

'Just done my half an hour in the playground, and I have the headache to prove it!'

'I'm not surprised. Those kids know how to let off steam! I would have thought you'd be hardened to it by now though.'

'Some things will always be annoying, and the sound of screaming children is one of them!'

'Spoken like a true earth mother.'

'If you say so.' Beth, knowing her lunch break was almost over, got to the point. 'Anyway, I'm calling because next month is the first anniversary of when Abi arrived in Cornwall. We thought we should celebrate somehow. Plan a party or something. What do you think?'

Max sank down onto a deckchair in the back garden of the St Ives house he was working on. Good-natured to the core, he was trying not to be annoyed that Beth had remembered about Abi's anniversary. He'd known it would be too much to hope that the gallery's birthday was overlooked, nor should it be, but Abi's arrival in Cornwall was also the anniversary of the day they'd met. The day that, for the first time since he'd discovered his ex-wife had been having an affair, he had allowed himself to admit there could be another woman out there for him.

He raked one of his large palms through his short ginger hair. He'd been thinking about asking Abi if she was ready for them to move on as a couple. In fact, the thought had been slowly building into an obsession, keeping him awake at night, and causing his concentration to suffer at work. Max was convinced he'd have finished this job two days ago if his mind hadn't kept wandering off into either happy daydreams of him and Abi living happily together in her new home, to nightmare scenarios, of Abi telling him in no uncertain terms that she didn't want to share her dream home with anyone. Ever.

He knew he was being irrational, but Max didn't seem to be able to stop the mad cycle of contradictory thoughts in his head. He had been meaning to ask Beth's advice, but she and Abi were so close, and anyway, Beth didn't seem quite herself at the moment.

Now he came to think about it, Max couldn't remember the last time he'd heard Beth laugh. He frowned. Normally she would have made some sort of silly comment or laughed when he'd called her an earth mother. Today she hadn't. Deciding he'd call her back as soon as the school day ended to see if she and Jacob were alright, Max returned to the shower room.

If Jacob was messing Beth about, he'd better start looking for a new studio in Outer Mongolia, and even then that might not be far enough away if the potter had hurt his childhood friend.

Max was about to get out a syringe of putty to top up the seal he'd placed around the shower's basin, when his phone rang again.

'Abi! You beat me to it. I was going to call as soon as I'd finished this job in about an hour.'

'Do you want me to call back?'

'No way! I miss you. I know it's daft, but not seeing you every day seems weird. I can't believe you've got through to me. This must be the only room in the whole house with a mobile signal.'

Abi wanted to tell Max about the new neighbour in person. She needed him to envelop her tiny frame in his bulky one, and cuddle the unexpectedly mixed up feelings she had about Stan's wedding, out of her. 'Max, is there any chance of you coming home tonight? I need to talk to you.'

'I'm just finishing up. I'll be home by about four with luck.' Alarm bells were ringing in Max's head. This couldn't be anything good. 'You're alright, aren't you?'

'I'm not sure. I think I'm in a state of shock.'

Max packed his tools into the van at top speed, and was about to drive to Abi's house as fast as the narrow lanes would allow, when his phone went again. 'Typical,' he muttered to himself before answering, 'no bloody signal all week, and now I'm leaving, the phone doesn't stop ringing!'

'Max Decorates, how can I help you?'

Chapter Four

The happy community of toadstool-dwelling pixies Abi had been commissioned to draw, as illustrations for a forthcoming picture book, was still without any actual pixies. By four o'clock, after her fifth attempt to make her lead character appear cheeky but loveable had failed, and the gallery's trickle of visitors had dried up, Abi had had enough. Driving herself mad with her thoughts, which had been seesawing between Stan's bombshell and the prospect of London having arrived on her doorstep, she locked up Art and Sole early and headed home.

Greeted by the ever-obliging Sadie, Abi kicked off her shoes, grabbed a cold can of cola from the fridge, and walked into the early evening sunshine of her back garden. Sitting at the patio table where she'd first got to know Stan and Sadie, Abi replayed the previous evening in her head. She knew she'd got through it by floating along with whatever was said, and nodding whenever she felt she was supposed to. It had been as if she was observing Stan and Dora through the wrong end of a very long telescope, from an ethereal plain. There was Stan – so familiar, so friendly – right there within touching distance, and yet he had been so far away from her that Abi wasn't sure she'd be able to feel his arm if she reached across the sofa.

He and Dora were obviously happy and comfortable together. *And why shouldn't they be?* Abi knew she minded, and she was cross with herself for minding. She was half looking forward to having the chance to talk to Max about it, and half dreading him thinking that she begrudged Stan's happiness. Which she didn't. Not for a second.

And yet...

'Oh, Sadie, I'm being silly aren't I!' Abi gave the golden retriever a big hug. 'Is it because I've got used to having Stan all to myself? That I've never had to share him before?' She peered into the dog's big brown eyes. 'Is this how you felt when I came and disturbed your quiet life with Stan?'

Getting nothing but a half-hearted wag of the tail from Sadie, Abi sighed. 'It isn't that I don't like Dora. I'm not sure how much of what she said about her life was true, but I still like her, and I can see why Stan does too. There's so much life in her compared to most of the residents in the flats. You'd never guess she was eighty-five. And to see him so happy and settled is certainly a weight off my mind. I've never really forgiven myself for interrupting your lives here and...'

Abi broke off mid-sentence as she heard a sound behind her, and Max appeared via the kitchen doorway. 'So this is where you're hiding.'

'Max!' Abi got to her feet and ran into her boyfriend's arms, becoming enveloped in his much larger frame. 'I didn't hear you come in.'

'I'm not surprised; you were deep in conversation with this wise old girl here.' Sadie was already on her feet,

28

wagging her tail wholeheartedly at the arrival of the man who took her on the most interesting walks, and always gave her plenty of tasty snacks which were well off the list of sensible foods for dogs.

'You don't have to give me those puppy eyes, Sadie.' Max dug a hand into his overall pocket and pulled out a doggy chew. 'I'd never leave you out.'

'Sadie gets a chew, what do I get?' Abi fluttered her eyelashes at Max, who answered her question by re-engulfing her in one of his bear hugs, instantly making her feel safe as she shuffled her petite frame against his bulky one.

'Better?'

'I'd like to stay here a bit longer actually.'

Kissing the top of her head, Max said, 'So, what's been happening? What was the shock you mentioned? I was worried.'

Abi held him tight as she explained, 'Shocks plural, I'm afraid. I'm sorry; I didn't mean to worry you, Max. So much has happened so fast, and I guess I've got used to talking things out with you. I've missed you not being around.'

'I'm very glad to hear it.' A flicker of hope arose in Max's chest. Perhaps he wasn't so mad to consider asking Abi if she wanted them to live together. Keeping hold of her, he sat Abi on his lap on the garden bench and stroked her blonde ponytail through his fingers. 'Tell me.'

'The first thing is Stan.'

'Oh God, he's not ill is he?'

'Not at all. In fact, I've never seen him look fitter or happier.'

Max frowned. 'So what's the problem then?'

Abi took a deep breath and, twisting around so she could see the reaction on Max's face, said, 'He's getting married.'

'What?' Max couldn't believe it. Was everyone out to steal his thunder? First Beth and Jacob had unwittingly gatecrashed his idea to celebrate the anniversary of Abi's arrival, and now Stan had asked some old biddy to marry him, when he was sure everyone was expecting him to be asking Abi any minute now. Whether they were ready to or not...

'Max? Are you with me?' Abi was looking at him with concern.

'Sorry...yes. I think I might be in shock as well. Are you serious, Abi?'

'Very much so. I went over to St Buryan for my usual fortnightly dinner with Stan last night, but it wasn't only me and Sadie with Stan. At first I thought Dora was just one of his new friends, but the way they looked at each other...it gave them away before they told me they were a couple. I hadn't even got my head around that idea before they dropped the wedding bombshell.'

'So, who is she, this Dora?'

'Stan's bridge partner.'

'Did you like her?'

'Yes, I did. She's a lot of fun. But, Max...I know it sounds mean-spirited of me... and I am pleased Stan's happy...but he's eighty-nine!'

Max held her closer. 'And I have no doubt you said all the right things, and made Stan feel OK about it?'

'I hope so. He's so thrilled by it all. I tried hard to keep

30

the concern out of my eyes, and obviously I'd never want to spoil his joy. But…'

Max thought about Stan, and not for the first time was impressed by the old man's zest for life. He sat up straighter and took Abi's hand. 'Tell me about Dora. I assume you asked her a lot of questions about herself?'

'I didn't ask much, to be honest. I was sort of stunned. I must have come across as a bit manic with my fixed smile by the end. I was like a rabbit in headlights.'

Moving so she was sat against Max's side, Abi stretched her legs out along the bench while attempting to describe Stan's girlfriend. 'I got the impression Dora was a bit of a player in her day. You know I said she was Stan's bridge partner? Well, she's also something of a poker whizz. Stan called her a card shark.'

'He probably didn't mean that literally though.'

'I'm not so sure.'

'Stan's not daft, Abi. His body may not be tip-top any more, but his brain is as sharp as ever. He wouldn't be easily taken in.' Max thought for a moment. His natural inclination was not to be negative about a person he'd never met, yet his protectiveness towards Stan made him say, 'Although I suppose being good at cards would mean she'd be good at bluffing, then?'

'That's what's bothering me.' Abi couldn't stop fidgeting and swung her leg back onto the floor, turning to face Max again. 'You don't think she's conning Stan, do you?'

Max frowned, making the freckles on his face bunch into little lines across his forehead. 'No. Well, I don't think so. I haven't met her though, have I, love,

31

so I can't be sure. But what would be the point of hurting him? If she's as old as Stan, then she isn't going to have that long to enjoy his money if she *is* out to steal it. Unless she has impoverished kids she wants to leave it to?'

'She hasn't got children, and for that matter, Stan hasn't got much money. And what he has got is in trust for his daughter and grandchildren in Australia. He'd never change that arrangement, would he?'

'No, he wouldn't.' Max shrugged. 'It feels wrong even speculating like this. We don't know Dora. And you say Stan is happy, which is the main thing, right?'

'Absolutely.'

'What did Beth say when you told her?'

Abi sighed. 'I haven't told her. I know I usually phone her the instant there's any news, but this feels so big I wanted to talk to you first. Oh, Max, am I a horrible person?'

'You're a concerned friend. Stan has been so good to both of us, it's natural you want to look out for him.'

'Thanks.' Abi kissed him. 'I've missed you.'

'You too.' Max traced a finger around his girlfriend's face. 'I want to hear lots more about Dora, and I am *desperate* for a vast mug of tea, but there is something I want even more than all that.'

Abi smiled knowingly. 'And what would that be?'

'I haven't seen you for a fortnight, woman! My curiosity, *and* my desire for a decent cuppa, come a lot further down the list than seeing if you are as beautiful as I remember – from top to toe.'

* * *

32

Abi placed a mug of tea next to Max's side of the bed, and climbed back in next to him, laying her head on his shoulder. 'Dora told me quite a story. I suspect it was true – mostly – although I'm sure she did get a bit carried away on occasions.'

Lifting his tea to his lips, Max let Abi cuddle into his side. 'Tell me as much as you can. We'll worry about if it's true later.'

Comfortable and safe against Max's side, Abi told him Dora's story. A tale that had made Abi sad at the time, and even as she retold it to Max now, she felt a lump form in her throat.

Dora had explained to Abi how she had married her first love, Gordon Henry, in 1950, when she was only eighteen years old. A Flight Lieutenant in the RAF, Gordon's plane had been shot down during the Korean War. And so by the time she was twenty-one she was already a widow.

It had taken Dora many years to get over the shock, and when she had, she'd explained to Abi, she hadn't seen any point in anything any more, so she'd taken on various dangerous jobs. The sort of jobs that, at the time, would never normally have been given to a woman. Just before she was twenty-five, she was picked for special training, and did secret work for government departments which, Dora had claimed, she wasn't supposed to talk about.

'No wonder she had no children. Poor woman.' Max put his empty mug down. 'She never got remarried?'

'She said she'd never found anyone who was a patch on Gordon until she met Stan. I have to say, they were really sweet together.'

'Do you buy all that "secret work" stuff?'

'That's the bit I suspect is embellished. I've heard people do that sort of thing when they experience grief young. They invent a means of escapism in their lives.'

'Really? How do you –'

'After Luke died I was given more unwanted advice than anyone ever has the right to receive, and…'

Max put his hand up. 'I'm sorry. That was tactless of me.'

Abi kissed him softly. 'You have nothing to be sorry about. Nothing at all. But I love you for being sorry anyway.'

'I love you too.' Max's stomach gave a loud rumble, making them both laugh, 'My belly always did have a well-honed sense of timing! Very sexy, I don't think!'

Abi, stroked his belly affectionately. 'I don't suppose you've been eating more than pub snacks for ages.'

'True.'

'Come on, let's cook.'

Ten minutes later, as he peeled some potatoes for dinner, Max said, 'I think I'd like to meet Dora myself, just to put my mind at rest.'

'Well, that isn't going to be a problem.'

'It won't?'

'As I left Stan, I was called into the new care manager's office; have you met Dan yet? He's nice.'

'Briefly, the last time I went. Sadie liked him, so that's good enough for me. What did Dan want?'

'I think he wanted to reassure me. He told me that Stan and Dora will be able to live together without any problems as far as the home was concerned. There are already some couples in residence, although most of them

34

arrived together. I have to say, Dan did seem genuinely pleased for Stan and Dora. It's good to know they have someone so kind keeping an eye out for them.'

'And?'

'And he wondered if you'd give him a hand helping with moving Dora's stuff into Stan's place. Some of her furniture is antique and quite heavy apparently.'

'I thought you were joking! Seriously? They're going to live together?'

Abi couldn't help but laugh. 'Why does that shock you? You look more put out by that than the idea of them getting married!'

'Well, I guess I didn't think it would actually happen. I mean, these things take years to arrange and they don't exactly have time on their side.'

Abi smiled. 'Then I think you should prepare yourself for another shock, Max.'

'Go on.'

'The wedding is next month.'

Chapter Five

Cassandra could barely contain her frustration and disappointment as she climbed into the taxi that had drawn up outside number two Miners Row.

Half an hour earlier, dressed far too provocatively to have been anything other than freezing cold in the thick-walled cottage, she had rushed to answer her doorbell. Expecting to see a suggestively grinning Justin, she had instead been confronted by an initially beaming, then blushing, delivery man. In one hand, he had the holdall of her clothes which Justin had promised he'd bring with him, and in the other, a huge bunch of flowers.

Muttering her thanks, Cassandra had hastily signed the proffered electronic device, closed the door again, and with her back pressed against the chilly hall wall, she'd read the card attached to the bouquet. Justin hadn't even written it himself, but had got the florist – or worse, his secretary – to type it for him.

My Darling Cassandra, please forgive me. I was so looking forward to our first Cornish night together, but my new job demands me this weekend. I will see you soon, I promise. J xx

Flying upstairs to the room she'd spent a fairly sleepless night in, and determined not to cry, Cassandra had pulled on her only set of already unpacked casual clothes before running into the back garden so she could get a phone signal to call a cab. Then, sitting at the kitchen table while she waited the half an hour until the car was due to arrive, her heart thumping harder than it ever had, she fought the urge to scream.

Despite contacting every hotel and bed and breakfast in Sennen and nearby, she hadn't been able to find an available room for the night in any of them, and had ended up staying in the house after all. Wishing she'd been less hostile to her neighbour, and had accepted the woman's offer of clean linen, Cassandra angrily brushed away the tears that pricked at the corner of her eyes. If she didn't get a grip then she was in danger of feeling sorry for herself.

'But what am I supposed to do? I can't keep myself locked away in here,' she muttered as she stared down at the end of the garden, which she knew could be beautiful if she could be bothered to do anything about it – or, more realistically, if she could be bothered to employ a gardener to do anything about it.

She'd only come to Sennen in the first place because Justin had been so excited about their new start together. Cassandra had never imagined that start would begin with her hundreds of miles away from her lover, in a clapped-out house with none of the comforts and amenities she took for granted in London.

Hating how lonely and out of routine she felt, Cassandra abruptly stood up and began to visit each room in the house. The sooner she pulled herself together and got this place habitable, the sooner Justin would put it up for rent, and they could plan a proper future together.

Telling herself to be realistic, and that it wasn't that unreasonable that Justin was required to work a weekend so soon after his promotion, Cassandra started to make a list of everything that had to be bought for the house. Quickly feeling better for being productive, she soon realised it was going to be a lengthy list despite the fact there were only two tiny bedrooms, one bathroom, a lounge-diner and a kitchen. Top of the list, she wrote, *bed linen*.

An hour later, blindly staring at the Cornish scenery as it disappeared and reappeared between the high hedges that sporadically lined the roads the taxi travelled the long miles to Truro, Cassandra made another list. A private one for her own sanity.

1.   Call Justin
2.   Rent a car
3.   Find a hairdresser

'Are you sure you haven't taken a wrong turn?' Cassandra addressed the cabbie as she glared at her watch accusingly. 'This journey seems to be taking for ever.'

With the patience of someone used to ferrying unrealistic tourists around, the driver replied with steady practicality, 'I've been driving this route for longer than you've been on this earth, me 'andsome. It always takes over an hour to drive to Truro. I'm sure they'd 'ave told 'ee that when 'ee booked the ride.'

'I thought they were joking.'

'This is Cornwall. This is how it is, me 'andsome.'

Cassandra bit her lip, refraining from sharing her own

opinion about Cornwall with a man whose relaxed acceptance was more annoying than if he'd got cross with her for being impatient.

Resting against the car seat, resigning herself to at least another twenty minutes, Cassandra took her notebook from her bag and re-read the list of things that needed doing to the house, and added *Find a cleaner/decorator/gardener* to the top.

It never ceased to amaze Cassandra how a haircut could make her feel better about life. Her previously long blonde hair was now a neat bob, its ends feathered to take away the severity of the cut.

Relaxed with a perfectly crafted latte outside a small Italian coffee shop, with the June sunshine playing around the skin of her newly revealed neck and shoulders, Cassandra let out a slow, and utterly unexpected, mutter of contentment. Perhaps, if she could schedule time here in Truro, then her temporary exile to the foot of England would be much more bearable.

Passing a hand through her hair, getting used to the fact that it stopped six inches shorter than it used to, she wondered what Justin would think of it. For the past six years as his mistress she'd had hair that hung halfway down her back. Would he like her new style? She hoped so; she loved how soft it felt, and so Justin should as well.

Gazing up at the cloudless blue sky, listening to the comforting bustle of shoppers as they passed by, Cassandra found herself smiling for the first time since her arrival. She wouldn't tell him about her hair; it would be a nice surprise for next weekend.

A new optimism took hold. If she could find the help she required to get the house decorated, then she could book into a hotel in Truro, or perhaps Penzance, which wasn't such a distance from Sennen, and leave the house keys with the workmen. Picturing the terrace, mentally scanning the rooms, Cassandra found herself unexpectedly taking pleasure in visualising how each space could look after she'd imposed her will upon it.

Checking her watch and judging that Justin would be having his usual gastropub lunch about now, Cassandra picked up her mobile and dialled his number.

'Darling! Did you like your flowers?'

Justin sounded so delighted to hear from her that any lingering doubts that Cassandra had about him not coming to see her were instantly extinguished. 'I loved them, although I'd rather it had been you holding them, and not some sweaty courier.'

'I know, and I'd rather have been holding you rather than a bunch of flowers, but a last-minute case came onto our books. Now I'm a partner I have to take my turn in dealing with these last-minute situations, and I want the chance to prove myself. You understand, don't you, darling?'

Cassandra could picture Justin so clearly. He'd be wearing a good-quality suit, probably in charcoal grey. His dark blond hair would be neatly gelled into place, and his right hand would be placed flat over the foot of an expensive wine glass which contained expensive wine. There would be a bowl of salad, laced with so much dressing that any of its low-calorie claims would be extinguished before he'd filled his fork for the first mouthful.

'Of course I understand, but I still wish you'd told me about buying the house. I felt such a fool.'

Justin didn't bother to hold in his exasperation. 'Come on, Cassandra, I've explained that already, you're a businesswoman. You can see the purchase of the house made excellent sense. Don't turn into my wife, for God's sake!'

Immediately stung by how quickly he'd become cross, Cassandra felt her easy mood dissolve. Never, in six years of her being his mistress, had he compared her to the dreadful Jacinta. 'Justin, I am here, in the middle of nowhere, precisely because I am *nothing* like your bloody wife. I'm here as part of your escape plan!

'I have put my entire life and my business on hold for you. *For us*. Don't you dare give me a hard time because you made a major decision, using my money as well as yours, without even telling me. And before you say it, it doesn't matter that I would have agreed anyway – what matters is that you didn't consult me.'

There was silence down the line as Cassandra waited for Justin to respond. She was annoyed by the disapproving looks she was getting from passers-by. What the hell was wrong with the people down here? In London no one batted an eyelid if they passed someone having an argument, it was merely white noise, and nobody's business but those involved.

'I'm sorry. You're right. I miss you, Cassandra. It's not very pleasant here right now. I shouldn't take it out on you. I'll make it up to you soon, I promise.'

Taking a sip from her latte, Cassandra relented. 'Has it been as awful as we assumed it would be, telling Jacinta and your boss about the divorce?' She ran a hand through her hair, and without waiting for an answer, added, 'That was a stupid question! I'm sure it has been beyond awful. I'm so used to us being in touch, of knowing what's going on with each other. I feel so cut off.'

Speaking more soothingly, Justin said, 'I have tried to call a few times, but you don't answer.'

'The signal is awful; I have to be in the correct part of the town to get calls and Wi-Fi.'

'There you are then! I'm not ignoring you, I can't reach you. And yes, it has been beyond awful. Jacinta is not going to go quietly.'

'We never thought she would, that's why you hid some of your money in my account.'

'It's just as well we did. And my boss didn't take the news well. Not good for the image of a family orientated company. I'm glad we are drip-feeding him information. If he knew I'd already got a new wife lined up, he'd probably sack me before I'd got my new desk in order.'

'New wife?' Cassandra spoke the words with delight, her heart soaring. All Justin's other words seemed to fade away. 'Really? Are you serious?'

'I am, my darling. I am. But I'd like you to forget I said that for now so I can propose properly at a more romantic opportunity. I wasn't going to say anything at all, but seeing as I've abandoned you for a minute, I thought it was only fair to reassure you that I love you, and this is going to work out for us. Anyway, how's the house?'

43

Accepting his abrupt change of subject, while imagining how he might propose when the time came, Cassandra said, 'It's a mess. You can tell it has been empty for a while, and that the previous occupants were elderly. The smell of damp is so bad in the spare room it would make you gag. I'm in Truro today, sourcing new furnishings and thinking about colour schemes. Do I have a free hand to do what needs doing?'

'You have excellent taste, darling, I can't think of anyone better to attend to the interior design of an executive holiday home.'

'Sennen Cove isn't exactly an executive area, Justin.'

'Which is why it's so perfect. An exquisitely decorated house, with all the mod cons anyone could want, but in a rural retreat which offers the ultimate temporary escape from the pressures of work.'

A flicker of excitement stirred in Cassandra. 'Well, if you put it like that, I'd better go and make a start. It's going to cost a lot to make it perfect though.'

'We'll be earning our money back right from the first rental.'

'Right then! I'd better get started. Love you.'

Having memorised directions from the obliging barista, Cassandra set off in search of a corridor of shops, which he'd described as 'local crafty chic places'.

As soon as Cassandra pushed open the door to the first shop in the row, a place which did up old furniture, she had the strangest feeling: it was like falling in love.

Reconditioned items had, until that moment, been things that happened to other people. Cassandra had never seen the attraction of buying something second hand if you could have something brand new. She'd only gone in because she'd noticed some attractive paint points in the window, boosting themselves to contain vintage colours, as used by many a stately home. The shop smelt inviting, fresh and crisp, and she was entranced. There wasn't a hint of 'oldness' about it anywhere.

'Hello there. Shout if you want some help, or say if you'd rather I left you in peace.'

Cassandra was taken aback by the generous welcome from the woman behind the counter, who was currently wrestling with a chest of drawers. Judging from her fragile build, Cassandra found herself speculating if the chest would win.

'I'm happy browsing, thank you.'

Taking up some sandpaper, the assistant smiled again before returning to her attack on the giant piece of furniture. 'Right you are.'

Running her hand lightly across the top of a butter yellow sideboard, which had three exquisite bumblebees painted in one corner, Cassandra knew that she had to have it. The few items of furniture the previous occupants had left in number two Miners Row were dark wood, and although she had no doubt they were of excellent quality, they made the place feel even more cramped than it was.

The more she explored the TARDIS-styled shop, which was far larger than it had first appeared, the more items Cassandra found to delight her, and soon she realised that the three bumblebee pattern was a theme that was repeated on tables, cabinets, and even a slim dresser.

Wishing she'd had the foresight to measure the space available in the dining half of the living room, not to mention the kitchen, Cassandra checked the price tags on the bee furniture and nearly fell over. While they weren't exactly Bond Street prices, they weren't the cheap option she'd assumed they'd be. Still, Justin had said he respected her judgement, so maybe if she measured them to see if they'd fit in the spaces she had already visualised them in...Especially if she had the walls painted a lighter colour, a warm ivory perhaps...

'Excuse me; I don't suppose you have a tape measure I could borrow?'

'Of course. Would you like a hand? Tape measures are always a bit easier with two, aren't they?'

'Well, yes. Thank you.' Wondering if she'd ever get used to people not only being friendly, but willingly helpful, Cassandra pointed to the sideboard. 'I love this, but I'm not sure it'll fit into the house I'm updating.'

'No problem. I'm glad you like it. I have to confess, out of all of the pieces in the shop today, I spent longer on that one than most of the others put together.'

'You did this?' Cassandra was impressed.

'Yes, the bee is my signature. If you see a bee on a lump of furniture, then it's one of mine. A few friends sell their work in here as well. We all have our own signature.'

'I love that!'

'Thank you. I'm Jo by the way.'

'Cassandra. Umm, I don't suppose I could pick your brains?'

Jo laughed heartily. 'If you can find them, they're all yours.'

Cassandra couldn't help but grin back. Something

about the woman made feeling happy contagious. 'I'm after a decorator, someone I can trust to do a good job even if I'm not around.'

'Whereabouts is the property?'

'Sennen Cove.'

'Oh that's easy then.'

'It is?'

'Sure. You'll be wanting Max Pendale. He's the best down there. No question.'

'Reliable?'

'Very much so. His reputation has reached this far north with good reason. I have his number; I'll fish it out for you once we've measured all you want to measure.'

Gesturing to Abi to pass the pen they'd been using to fill in the newspaper crossword, Max spoke into his mobile. 'Yes, yes, I know the place very well. I can come round and do you a quote first thing Monday morning, if that's convenient?... Excellent. Can I take a name and a mobile number in case of emergency?...You're right, the signal here can be awkward, yet somehow we manage...Nine o'clock on Monday morning will be fine... I will see you the day after tomorrow then. Thank you.'

Scribbling down a name next to the phone number he'd already written on the side of their newspaper, Max looked across the table at Abi. 'There's a coincidence.'

'In what way?'

'The new neighbour you were worried about has just called me and asked if I'd be her decorator, assuming she likes my quote.'

'You're joking!'

'Not at all. The rather efficient-sounding Ms Cassandra Henley-Pinkerton is expecting me on her doorstep at precisely nine o'clock Monday morning. You, my darling, are about to have a spy in the camp!'

Abi groaned out loud, 'Her name is Henley-Pinkerton? Oh God, she sounds exactly like the sort of nightmare women I ran away from. I blame my old neighbours for moving! They were so lovely!'

Holding Abi close, Max said, 'They had the chance to live nearer their grandchildren, we can't blame them for that. Anyway, there is one compensation. If Ms Double-Barrelled takes my quote, then I could stay here while I'm working next door. If you'd like me to, that is.'

Abi's expression blossomed with joy. 'I'd like that. I'd like that very much.'

Chapter Six

Parking the cherry-red Kia she'd rented from a car dealer on the outskirts of Truro in a lay-by, Cassandra suddenly had a sensation of being overwhelmed. At least, she thought that was what she was feeling. She'd never felt out of her depth like this before.

Forcing herself to think clearly, she stroked the little car's steering wheel affectionately. She didn't understand how she felt at all. Free, maybe? To be able to drive a car down any road she liked, when she liked, without some enterprising soul demanding money for cleaning your windscreen as you waited at the lights was as liberating as it was disorientating.

It wasn't just that, though.

Cassandra had spent far longer in the reclaimed furniture shop than she'd intended to. It had seemed perfectly natural to accept an offer of coffee as they chatted, laughed, and she had been genuinely interested when Jo, without a hint of being patronising, had offered to show her how to make the most of the kitchen table and old wooden sink unit that were already in place at the cottage.

Having left the shop with Jo's phone number programmed into her mobile, and details of how to get to the nearest department store to buy linen, and where to find a car rental place, stored in her brain, Cassandra had spent a thoroughly relaxed day wandering around Truro. For the first time since the train had whisked her unwillingly into Cornwall, she began to think she'd be able to survive in the south-west for a few weeks.

Climbing out of the car to take in the view across the fields, towards the sea, a meagre flow of traffic pottering past the lay-by at a thoroughly Cornish pace, Cassandra thought about Justin. The knowledge that he was only working over the weekend so he could hasten his departure from his wife had certainly been a major factor in her more peaceful state, and the thought made her pulse quicken.

Logically, Cassandra knew that if they'd been in London, and Justin had cancelled a meeting due to work issues, she'd have waved away the situation with only a twinge of regret, knowing they'd catch up as soon as they could. 'It's just because I'm down here and I miss him that I feel so muddled,' she told the scenery before her. 'If I was in my flat I'd call a friend and go to the theatre or something, or get some work done.'

Climbing back into the Kia, Cassandra set off towards Sennen, planning as she went. 'If I'm happy enough working in London while I wait for Justin to turn up, then there's no reason why I can't be content doing the same here.'

Loving how easy the unfamiliar car was to drive, Cassandra continued to sort out her immediate routine out loud. 'I'm going to stop at the next available supermarket to get some supplies, drive back to Sennen, measure the furniture, make up the bed, then go to the nearest restaurant for dinner. And the day after tomorrow, after

I've interviewed the decorator, I will drive to Penzance and get some actual work done.'

Negotiating the overtaking of a horsebox, her thoughts turned to the business she'd built up on her own after graduating from business school eight years ago. 'It's high time I checked on my staff to make sure that there are no problems.'

Cassandra smiled as she thought about The Pinkerton Agency. It had been a real challenge, at the age of twenty-two, to build up the company which aimed to provide well-educated, qualified nannies, who had the qualifications to not just look after the children of businessmen and women, but to teach them as well, acting as pre- or after-school tutors.

Word about how good the agency was had spread quickly, and families who'd marked their children for private school before conception welcomed the chance to have their offspring moulded into high achievers from birth by intelligent young men and women.

'Right then,' Cassandra told the car as she pulled into a small supermarket car park near St Just, 'on Monday morning, after we've sorted Mr Pendale, we are going into Penzance to catch up on emails.'

'So, how was the studio?' Beth stretched her legs out on the sofa so that her feet rested on Jacob's lap.

'I think the best word to describe it was poky. There wouldn't be room for me, let along the pots and Oscar.'

'Rats! That place would have been perfect location-wise.' Beth sighed. 'I assume most studio owners would be OK with you having a cat in tow?'

51

'No issues so far with Oscar being an extra tenant. We'll have to see.'

Hastily pushing away the tears that were threatening to escape, glad that Jacob hadn't noticed, Beth said, 'I'll ask Abi to make some calls to the artists she's booked for the gallery in case they know of somewhere suitable. I'm sorry, I meant to do that this morning, but I forgot.'

'Don't worry, love.' Jacob regarded Beth carefully; it wasn't like her to forget anything. 'I've put the word out on the potters' grapevine, so if there is anyone out there who's been thinking of giving up their studio space, they'll know to get in touch with me directly rather than going through an estate agent.'

'Well that would certainly make it a bit cheaper as well, if we didn't have agent's fees to consider.'

Jacob patted his lap, and Beth turned so that her head was lying on a pile of cushions on his lap. As he stroked her hair, Jacob looked down at his partner. 'Are you OK, Beth? You don't seem yourself today?'

'I'm fine, honestly, I told you the other day, it's end-of-term syndrome. Only a few more weeks to go, and then you'll have the normal non-stressed me back.'

Jacob was about to tell her that he didn't mind what she was like as long as she was alright, when his mobile buzzed into life. 'That's probably Max, we said we'd go for a beer once he got back from St Ives…oh no, hang on, it's not Max.' Jacob gently levered up Beth and moved into the kitchen.

Beth could faintly hear him talking through the thin wall that divided the kitchen and living room. Standing up, she stared at her reflection in the mirror over the fireplace opposite the sofa. Groaning softly, she ran her hands through her hair. It felt lank, and as Beth peered harder at her image, she saw the faint signs of wrinkles she was sure hadn't been there last week.

'You're tired. Stop it!' Beth muttered crossly to herself. 'Have an early night, wash your hair in the morning, drink less coffee and more water, and you'll be fine. It's just hormones and the end of term thing.'

Surprised that her personal pep talk hadn't worked as well as it usually did when she was feeling down in the dumps, Beth was about to sit down again, when Jacob reappeared by running across the room and sweeping her up into his arms.

'Well, gorgeous teacher lady, we've had a bit of luck!' Jacob kissed Beth hard, before breaking away.

'We have?'

'That was one of my mates from the aforementioned potters' grapevine.'

For the first time in days Beth's smile felt genuine. 'A studio?'

'Yep! We have one.'

'Just like that?'

'Yep, and the best thing is, not only is Oscar's presence no problem, I already know that it will be perfect, because I've worked there with Frankie – he's the potter that taught me how to make those huge Ali Baba type pots I do – so I've said yes!'

Beth hugged Jacob. 'Where is it? Can I see it? Can we afford it?'

'St Buryan. Yes and yes!'

'St Buryan? That could be perfect. You can pop in and

see Stan when you're waiting for your pots to harden and stuff... I can't believe I forgot to tell you!'

Jacob frowned. 'Tell me what?'

'Unless Max had already told you?'

Grabbing hold of Beth's arms, which were whirling around as if she was some sort of demented wind-up toy, Jacob said, 'I have no idea what you are talking about. Slow down, woman, you're freaking me out.'

'Stan! Abi called me this morning. It went out of my head.'

'What went out of your head?'

'Stan's getting married to his bridge partner.'

Jacob beamed. 'You're kidding? Good ol' Stan! What's the lucky lady's name?'

'Dora. Abi says she's lovely, but prone to weaving the odd tale or two.'

'She sounds fun!'

'Abi's a bit wary about it, but as long as Stan is happy I think it's brilliant. Lovely to think he'll have someone to wake up with in the mornings again.' Beth sank onto the sofa as if she was exhausted after her moment of leaping around. 'I think I'll go and see Stan soon to offer our congratulations.'

'Not to mention Dora.'

'Oh yes, of course. I can't wait to meet her.' Abruptly reenergised again, Beth took Jacob's hands and pulled him onto the sofa, her mind flying back to their previous conversation 'Tell me all about the studio. When can you take it from?'

Laughing, half from relief that Beth appeared her usual chirpy self again, and part from relief that he'd found somewhere local to work from, Jacob allowed himself to be quizzed about Frankie's studio. 'We can take it from August, and it will be Frankie we're paying rent to rather than to an agent, so you were right, it will be a bit cheaper.'

'Why doesn't Frankie want it any more?'

'He's retiring. He's eighty-two.'

'Oh good heavens. He's retiring late, isn't he?'

'I think I should warn you, Beth, potters tend to work until they physically can't. We don't retire. It's an obsession after all.'

Beth was smiling so wide it was beginning to hurt, and yet she couldn't seem to stop. 'You don't say! Shall we go and see it tomorrow? I could see if Abi's planning to see Stan, and we could go together. Would that be OK?'

'Sure. I'll come back from Hayle a bit early.' Jacob looked at his girlfriend quizzically. 'You've gone all hyper.'

'I'm so excited! And it'll be wonderful for you to have such a short commute to work. You'll have to get your stuff packaged up and moved. Do you think Max will lend you his van?'

'I'm sure he will.' Jacob held Beth tight. 'Come on, I think you should get some sleep before you burst from overexcitement, although I'm pleased you're so pleased!'

Standing in the bathroom ten minutes later, tears streamed down Beth's face. *What the hell is the matter with you, woman? Anyone would think you were hitting the menopause…*

As the words crossed her mind she was suddenly

dumbstruck. *I can't be. I'm over-emotional and tired; nothing else.*

Doing some hasty calculations on her fingers, Beth sat on the edge of the bath and tried not to let panic claim her.

'I'm not pregnant. I *can't* be.'

Closing her eyes, Beth took some calming breaths. Now she'd had the thought she knew it was true. Her period was late, she was an emotional powder keg, and she was either hungry or tired all the time.

She pulled out the little diary she kept in the bathroom cabinet next to her monthly supplies. 'Oh, hell.' She had missed two periods, and the third should have been imminent. Beth's breathing snagged in her throat. It wasn't that unusual for her to miss one month, but never two in a row. *How did this happen? How did I not notice?*

'Beth, are you alright in there?' Jacob called through from the bedroom.

Jacob. What will he say? Will he leave me?

'I...I'm fine. Bit daydreamy tonight. Be right there.'

As Beth lay next to Jacob, snuggled against his back, out-of-control thoughts started to spin through her brain. *What about my teaching job? It's a small town – will people be alright about an unmarried teacher having a baby? It's alright in an episode of* Doc Martin, *but this is real life!*

A baby.

Oh my God. I'm going to be a mum!

Grandad, I wish you were here.

Beth closed her eyes, and hoped that the confused tears that began to run silently down her face wouldn't wake Jacob.

Chapter Seven

Feeling enthused by the eight-week plan she'd drawn up that formalised her thoughts of the previous day's journey, Cassandra confidently breezed through her meeting with Max Pendale.

She'd been encouraged to find the decorator, who'd asked her to call him Max, radiating a comforting honesty from his bulky frame. He was as punctual and professional in his approach to his work as any of the tradesmen she'd employed in London. In fact, if she was truthful, Max was better than any of the city decorators she'd encountered, because he smiled, appeared to be genuinely enthusiastic about her ideas, and, like Jo the previous day, was happy to share ideas without expecting them to necessarily be taken up.

Taking a leap of faith and agreeing to his quote without obeying her usual strict rule of getting three quotes first, Cassandra had waved Max off, rolled up her metaphorical sleeves and, checking she had time according to her new rota, had made a start on updating the house before starting on some paid work. After all, the sooner this was all sorted out, the sooner she could get back to Justin and start on the far bigger project of finding a home for the two of them.

Nearly an hour later, she'd made satisfying, if rather

messy, progress. Ripping down curtains, curtain poles, and unscrewing unwanted and rotting shelves from in and around the house had been surprisingly therapeutic. Amazed by how much she was enjoying the physical nature of the work, her mind drifted to Jo, and how happy she was making a living doing the sort of work which Cassandra would traditionally have consigned to a workman without a second thought.

Dumping all the unwanted fixtures and fittings into the front garden for Max to collect when he started work in a couple of days' time, Cassandra experienced a sense of satisfaction at the mild ache of muscles she'd previously only ever used in the gym. Then, after stopping for long enough to shower away the dust, change into her business suit, and grab her laptop, Cassandra climbed into her hired car and headed to Penzance exactly on schedule.

Sat in a secluded corner of Penzance library, with a rising sense of disbelief, Cassandra re-read the email on the screen before her. Every vestige of colour drained from her face.

Even when she took her annual holiday, she always cleared her inbox every other day, but the large volume of messages awaiting her attention had not alarmed her. That was until she'd read the first email in the queue.

By the time she'd read the third email, Cassandra was reaching for her mobile phone, and was about to tap in a number when a firm but friendly nod towards a 'No Mobile Phones' notice from a passing library assistant made her put it down again.

The day's initial optimism was completely wiped away

as Cassandra faced facts. She shouldn't be that surprised that a couple of her governesses had resigned – it happened all the time when you employed young staff – but the resignation of Susie, her longest-serving employee, and the email that had gone with it, had left her reeling.

Susie had stated in her usual to-the-point manner that she was hurt that, after seven years' loyal service, Cassandra hadn't had the decency to inform her that The Pinkerton Agency was in the middle of takeover proceedings. She particularly didn't appreciate having to find out via an impersonal round robin email.

What?

Cassandra started to email Susie back, saying someone had obviously played a cruel joke on her, but then stopped. She owed Susie the chance to talk to her in person. Looking around, she located the library assistant, and explaining it was an emergency, arranged for the woman to keep an eye on her laptop.

She dashed outside, her mobile already attached to her ear.

Thankful for the bench near the library's front door, Cassandra sank down as the call ended. Her legs felt weak. Susie had almost been in tears, and clearly didn't believe Cassandra when she'd explained that she had no intention of letting the agency go.

It was Susie's final sentence that had sent her crashing onto the nearby seat.

'Please don't treat me like a fool, Ms Henley-Pinkerton, the letter was from your solicitor. It was very clear. I will be staying at my present place of work, but I

59

will *not* be a part of your agency. I am fortunate that my employers value my work more than you appear to. Many of your other employees will not be faring so well.'

Susie, who was one of the most good-natured and intelligent women Cassandra had ever met, had hung up the phone without another word, leaving her employer – or ex-employer – in a state of shock.

Cassandra's hands shook as she called Justin, not only for his reassurance, but because he was her solicitor. He had been ever since she'd started the company, it was how they'd met. If he hadn't been, then she wouldn't be in Cornwall in the first place. If the letter Susie had received really was from her lawyer, then it had to have come from Justin.

Swearing under her breath as her partner's mobile went direct to voicemail; Cassandra left a brief message asking him to contact as soon as possible.

Sitting perfectly still, Cassandra tried to remember how to breathe properly. *Think logically. You're a businesswoman. You own the company. No one can just take it away. Someone in Justin's office has made an error. It's as simple as that.*

Thanking the library assistant for her temporary security detail, Cassandra decided she needed an espresso to calm the thumping headache behind her eyes. Gathering up her belongings, she crossed the road to a Costa, and silently praying it had a Wi-Fi connection, settled down to a double-shot espresso. Then, doing her best to ignore the panic building in her throat, Cassandra attempted to call every employee on her books.

All of those who answered their phones told Cassandra the same story. They had each received an official letter saying that the company was closing in its present format. By the time Cassandra had explained to the last employee on her list that this was a dreadful administrative mistake which had only just come to her attention, Cassandra's throat was dry and her temper was short. Many of her staff had already spoken to the families they worked for, and had reached an agreement to be employed directly.

If she was going to save her company, she was going to have to repair the damage to her good name, and find a large number of fresh employees. And fast. The new school term was only ten weeks away.

As her disbelief turned to fury, she tapped in another number on her phone, and got through to Crystal, Justin's PA. Forcing herself not to scream at the messenger, Cassandra ignored the perspiration breaking out on the back of her neck as she listened, trying not to sound as though she hadn't got a clue what was happening to her own business.

Seething into the coffee aroma filled air, as soon as she'd hung up the phone, Cassandra Googled *Solicitors in Penzance*, and within minutes had booked an appointment to see a Mr Clearer that afternoon.

Knowing she had to get as much information from the emails she'd received as she could, Cassandra felt the need for another espresso, along with something extremely unhealthy to eat. Only then would she have the mental wherewithal to design a plan of what to ask Mr Clearer, because right now all she really understood was that, according to Crystal, the correspondence sent to all

61

Pinkerton Agency employees had not been a mistake, but had been on her – Cassandra's – instructions. The PA didn't know which partner had double-checked and processed the instruction; and she wasn't able to put her through to Justin at that moment because he was in a meeting.

Damn. Suddenly Cassandra could see the situation so clearly. This must have come from Justin's new business partner. The Family Values Company obviously wasn't taking his divorce news well, and if they had somehow connected her to him, perhaps they'd done this to sever their connection.

The hours between making the appointment to see Mr Clearer and the time of the actual meeting flew by in a hive of desperate activity. Cassandra had gone over all her contracts, her original legal agreements from when she'd set up The Pinkerton Agency, and every email she'd received from her staff over the past few months. If she wasn't going to appear as stupid as she felt, Cassandra wanted to make sure she knew her business as well as she'd previously thought she did.

She also re-dialled Justin's number every ten minutes for the next three hours.

There was no answer.

Cassandra trusted Donald Clearer on sight. Obviously nearing retirement age, he oozed calm capability without cutthroat ambition. Rather than making her feel embarrassed by what had happened, he had listened carefully, made copious notes, and allowed Cassandra to print out as much information from her own laptop as she wanted, including a copy of the letter that Crystal had sent her, which Family Values had been sending out.

They were soon on first-name terms. A long-serving secretary had delivered tea and biscuits as they talked, and Donald had perched his semi-circular glasses on his nose and read everything at least twice before making a few phone calls.

'Well, Cassandra, I will have to explore this matter further, but my initial thoughts are that Mr Justin Smythe of Family Values has indeed been acting on your behalf. As he is your solicitor, that wouldn't have been difficult for him to do. If you didn't make this instruction yourself, then we will have to ascertain that no verbal order from yourself could have been misinterpreted.

'According to Ms Crystal Andrews, Mr Smythe had someone sign on his behalf, but it appears the initial order was on his request, with the rider that it was your wish.'

'It was Justin? *Not* his business partner?'

Picking up on his client's tone, Donald asked gently, 'Do you know Mr Smythe personally as well as professionally?'

Cassandra nodded slowly, as a nasty suspicion she couldn't quite bring herself to dismiss gripped her.

Was Justin in the process of selling the company from under her?

Pulling into the car park by Marazion beach an hour later, Cassandra let the emotions that had been tightening in her chest for hours go. Tears streamed her face as she rang Justin's number once more as she replayed the last few minutes in Donald's office.

He had re-called the Family Values office, and had spoken to Crystal for a second time, telling her he was a lawyer acting for a client who was employed by The Pinkerton Agency. Donald had been informed, without hesitation, that Mr Smythe was currently on his way to America to attend a conference, and wasn't contactable for the foreseeable future.

In that one moment Cassandra had seen how much of a fool she'd been.

Justin had never had any intention of coming to join her in Cornwall.

Nor did he want her back in his life in London.

It had been her flat they'd rented out to help fund the upgrading of the holiday cottage, and as Justin had always handled her legal affairs, she'd trusted him completely, Cassandra hadn't even argued when he'd said that her flat hadn't been more than a place to sleep for her anyway, so they might as well make money out of it. He'd said it wasn't a home, more a holding place in between the chances to stay with him in hotels, while Cassandra waited for them to move in together. *And I let him!*

Staring over the heads of the people sat on the beach, Cassandra's eyes came to rest on the ebb and flow of the sea, as she faced the unpalatable fact that, just maybe, nothing Justin had ever done for her was as she imagined.

Did Justin insist that I stay down here to keep me out of the way, not so he could arrange our lives together, but so he could steal my business?

Every bone in her body ached with the desire for all this to be a misunderstanding. That Justin had seen a business opportunity for the agency that was too good to miss, and he simply hadn't had the chance to talk to her first. With the phone signal being so poor here, it was possible – but only just… Or maybe she should cling on to the hope that Crystal had been misinformed, and the letters were a genuine mistake down to Justin not wanting to tell his PA the truth about their relationship…

You're grasping at straws.

The image of Donald's kindly round face telling her that he would investigate to his utmost ability came to the front of her mind. He'd told her that she'd be wise to prepare herself for the fact that, even if this was an error – which he didn't consider to be the case – then the damage to her reputation would need addressing quickly.

Cassandra's first instinct had been to get on the next train to London to confront Justin face to face, but if he was travelling to the States, which had been another shock, there was no point. She really didn't want to confront Crystal, and have her over-made-up face silently laughing at her gullibility.

Her throat felt dry and her eyes smarted with the effort of stopping her tears. *There's no point in crying until you know the facts. Go back to the house, get that sorted out, and think. Think very, very hard. You still have a business – just no staff and a shattered reputation…*

Abi stood by the gate that led into her front garden. A feeling of horror filled her as she surveyed the haphazard pile of broken fixtures and fittings which had been heaped forlornly in her neighbour's small front garden.

This was precisely what she'd been worrying about all day at work. Ms Cassandra Henley-Pinkerton was ripping the soul out of number two Miners Row. She was bringing London to Sennen Cove. After so many years of dreaming of escaping the city, Abi had done her best to dismiss her initial fears about her new neighbour as paranoia.

The reassurances Max had given her at lunchtime, that Cassandra only wanted number two to be repainted and updated, now felt horribly inadequate. The woman had obviously played down her intentions to Max.

With a heavy sigh, Abi opened her front door to be greeted by a delighted Sadie, just as her neighbour drew up in the car she'd acquired. Ignoring Abi, she marched up the path and into her house.

Noticing that Cassandra wasn't her usual pristine self, and that she might even have been crying, Abi held back her natural inclination to check if she was alright. If the woman couldn't even take the trouble to say hello, Abi wasn't going to bother about making sure she was alright. Anyway, she was in too much shock at the sight of the debris from her previous neighbours' lives lying, abandoned and unloved, in front of the adjoining terrace to care.

Calling to Sadie, Abi grabbed her handbag and headed to her car.

'Come on, sweetheart. Time we talked to Stan.'

Chapter Eight

Beth wasn't sure how she'd got through the school day. Her young charges had sensed her lack of control. A rare reign of chaos had taken over her classroom, until the noise level had broken through the fog of Beth's brain, and she gathered her wits long enough to get them sorted into drawing groups.

Sat at her desk, watching the village's three- and four-year-olds sketching pictures of what they hoped to do over the forthcoming summer holidays, Beth felt her heart constrict. Would a child of her own be drawing in here in a few years' time?

At lunchtime she'd resisted the urge to call Abi or Max and tell them what she suspected. She badly wanted to talk to her best friends, but what if she wasn't pregnant? She could be coming down with a bug or something and worrying over nothing. And if she was, then Jacob should know first – but what if he hated the idea?

He'd uprooted his life to be with her, but the deal for the local studio wasn't signed and sealed yet. Would he panic and run back to Hayle to renew the rental agreement there when she told him the news?

Rather than make any phone calls to Jacob or her friends, Beth had walked unsteadily into Sennen during her lunch break. She'd got as far as the chemist to buy a pregnancy test, when she'd realised it was a bad idea. If she purchased it there, then the whole of Sennen would know that one of the village's unmarried teachers suspected she was pregnant within half an hour.

Instead, the instant the end of the school day had arrived, Beth had driven to a reassuringly anonymous supermarket in Penzance, and made the most frighteningly exciting purchase of her life.

Now, with her eyes firmly closed, Beth sat on the edge of her bath. The plastic wand in her hands felt oddly heavy, as if it was weighted with her whole future.

Her phone's stopwatch, which had counted down the longest three minutes in history, had gone off at least five minutes ago. Knowing she couldn't put off the moment for ever, biting her bottom lip, she lifted the pregnancy test to eye level, Beth opened her eyes.

Unsure if she was happy or terrified, in a throaty whisper, Beth said, 'Grandad, I hope you can hear me. You're going to be a great-grandad. Oh, God, I miss you so much.'

The tears came then. Tears, because she knew she wanted this baby, because she was scared the man she loved wouldn't want her any more, because she could lose the job she adored, because people might gossip, because she wasn't even sure what being pregnant meant beyond the obvious, and because she was sat in the flat where she had nursed Grandad for many years before he'd died, and because she would have done *anything* to be able to hold his hand just one more time.

Go and see Stan, my darling girl.

Beth felt the words in her chest. Whether she'd

actually heard them, or if her imagination was being fanciful, it didn't matter. She was sure that if her grandad could talk to her, then he would tell her to go to see his friend. Stan would never tell her she was a bad person for having a child out of wedlock. He'd be the perfect person to help get her perspective back.

'Abi!'

As Beth climbed out of her car in the Chalk Towers car park, she saw her friend and Sadie walking towards the entrance to Stan's block of flats.

'Beth, how wonderful! I was going to call you later and…' Abi paused, studying her friend's pale face with more care. 'You alright?'

'Sure, I just thought I'd come and see Stan. I haven't visited him in ages. I don't like the idea of him being on his own too much.' Beth stroked Sadie's fur. 'Anyway, forget about me, you look fit to explode. I'm not used to seeing you cross. Are you OK?'

'Not really, although I guess I might be being a bit petty.'

'That's not like you.'

'I like to think not.' Abi looked at Beth carefully, not convinced her friend was as alright as she was claiming to be. 'That's why I've come to Stan. He always says the right thing.'

Beth gave a half-smile back. 'That's why I'm here too, actually.'

'Beth?'

'I'll tell you both at once.'

Abi watched Sadie affectionately as she snuggled

herself against Beth's legs, as if sensing an extra-special cuddle. 'Although the chances of Stan being alone are slim. I suspect Dora will be there as well.'

'I'm dying to meet her actually. Are they honestly going to get married? Boy, you and I have got to have a proper catch-up. It seems ages since it was only the two of us.'

'Let's do just that. Fancy fish and chips in paper after we've seen Stan?'

Beth felt a surge of love for her friend. 'You have no idea how much I'd like that. Although I wish you hadn't mentioned fish and chips, my stomach's rumbling now!'

Letting Sadie lead the way, they walked towards Stan's home. 'Let's have an hour here before Stan and Dora have their evening meal, and then we'll drive down to the cove? Be like old times.' Abi smiled, trying to hide her concern for her friend. 'I can't believe it's nearly a year since we got to know each other on Marazion beach over fish and chips and coffee.'

Climbing the stairs to Stan behind Abi and Sadie, Beth's smile began to return, and she sent up a silent thank you to her grandfather for telling her to come here. 'So, Abi, quick, tell me before we get there, what's this Dora like?'

Stan couldn't have been more delighted by his unexpected visitors if he'd tried. As offers of tea and coffee were made and accepted, Abi took over the kettle duties, while Stan and Beth settled down at the dining room table. It was clear to the girls that they'd arrived in the midst of a wedding planning day.

Gathering some mugs together, Abi gestured to the

pile of lists. 'I thought Dora might be here making wedding plans. Everything going alright on that front?'

'Yes, thanks.' Stan chuckled. 'Dora's currently chatting up the prison warder. She considers young Dan very dishy.'

Abi laughed. 'Does she indeed! You've got some competition then?'

Beth frowned. 'Dan?'

'He's our new care manager. We call him the prison warder out of love and affection.'

'Naturally.' Beth turned to Abi. 'Have you had the pleasure of meeting Dan, is he young and dishy?'

'I have, and he certainly is. Assuming you consider early thirties young.'

'Speaking as someone in her early thirties, I'm not sure about that!'

'From where I'm sitting, thirty is very young.' Stan picked up his tea and grinned. 'Dora will be here in a minute or two. She'll be so pleased to meet you, Beth. We were only saying last night that we'd love it if you'd both come over for dinner one evening, along with Max and Jacob.'

As Abi got up to make a further cup of tea, so it was ready for Dora's arrival, Beth's phone rang. 'Oh, I'm sorry, it's Jacob. He's been checking out a new studio. Hell! I was supposed to go with him! I totally forgot. I'll take this in the hall.'

As Beth disappeared out of the door, Stan turned to Abi. 'I'm glad Beth's popped out for a minute. I wanted to ask you something.'

Abi frowned as a dark shadow crossed over her

71

friend's face. 'What's wrong?'

Stan reached out and clasped her hand. 'There's something bothering me. Something I can't share with Dora.'

'Go on.'

'Abi, girl, you don't think I'm being a silly old fool for getting married at my age, do you?'

Squeezing Stan's hand gently, Abi said, 'I will admit it was a shock when you told me, but no, Stan, I don't think that. Grasp every minute. You taught me that. So no, I don't think you're silly. Why do you ask?'

'Sally.'

'Ah.' Abi was thoughtful for a moment. It wasn't her place to comment on Stan's daughter. 'Sally hasn't taken the news well then?'

'Not as well as you did.'

'Oh.' Abi didn't know what else to say. She'd always felt a bit awkward about how close she was to Stan, and knew he thought of her as a daughter. Abi had never been sure how Sally felt about that either.

'There's something else as well.' Stan lifted his left hand and began to play with the wedding ring he'd worn for most of his life. 'It's Mary. Do you think she'd be cross with me for getting married again?'

Finding herself loving Stan even more than she already did for asking such a question, Abi looked him in the eye. 'If Mary was even half the woman you have described to me, she'd be pleased for you. Loving Dora doesn't mean you love Mary any less, nor does it mean that Dora has disregarded her love for Gordon.'

Stan nodded, not trusting himself to talk, and filled the moment of silence by cuddling Sadie.

Sensing her friend required a minute, Abi got up from the table. 'I think I'll make sure Beth's OK, she's been a while.'

Slipping quietly into the living area, Abi was alarmed to find that Beth was no longer outside in the hallway on the phone, but was sat on the sofa with Dora, who was giving her a cuddle.

Looking from Beth, who was smiling and crying at the same time, to Dora, Abi said, 'Beth? Dora? What's going on?'

Gently easing Beth up, giving her a firm, 'It'll be OK', Dora spoke to Abi, 'I found Beth outside. I think she could do with a friend right now.'

'Beth?'

'I'm sorry, Abi, I wanted to tell you straight away, but then I thought I should tell Jacob first, and then Grandad said I should come here and talk to Stan. He was right; being here with you, Sadie, and Stan made me feel so much better...' Beth was talking faster and faster, and Abi could see she was shaking '...and then Jacob called and told me he's signed the contract for a studio just up the road from here, and so that's it. He won't be able to escape from me now, and I honestly don't think I'll be able to stand seeing him every day once he's left me. Seeing him with someone else when I love him so much will rip me apart; and I should have been with him at the studio in the first place but I forgot, and now I've cried all over Dora, and we haven't even been introduced yet, and...'

Glancing at Dora, who shrugged, Abi interrupted her friend mid-flow. 'Beth, honey, you aren't making sense. Jacob is crazy about you. He moved in with you after only

73

hours of you being together for goodness' sake.'

Dora raised her eyebrows. 'Really? Go Jacob!'

Smiling weakly, Beth said, 'But he might not want me now.'

'Why not?' Dora frowned. 'Men don't just move in, my darling, not long-term anyway. I know these things. I've lived for ever and seen stuff that would make your hair curl!'

Abi gently pushed a mug of tea in Beth's direction, before sitting next to a concerned Stan, and before Dora got into full flow about her past life asked, 'What's wrong? Please, Beth, I'm worried. We're worried.'

'But I shouldn't tell you first, I should tell Jacob, but I'm scared.'

Now Abi knew exactly what was wrong, and the concerns she'd been planning to share about her neighbour disappeared into insignificance. In fact, there was nothing wrong with Beth at all.

A broad smile swept across Abi's face. 'Beth, are you telling us you're going to have a baby?'

Chapter Nine

'They won't tell Jacob or Max, will they?'

Having insisted they stick to their plan of stopping for fish and chips by the sea on the way home, Abi glanced at Beth's worried face. 'Of course they won't.'

Stretching her legs out across the sand, making the most of the last vestiges of heat from the day's sunshine, Abi popped a chip into her mouth and stared into the horizon for a while before saying, 'Can I ask you a personal question, Beth?'

'You don't normally ask permission; you always dive straight in.'

'True, but this is more important than usual.' Taking a swig from her takeout coffee, Abi said, 'How do you feel about having a baby? Do you want it?'

'What?' Beth was offended, and then she was shocked by how Abi's innocent question had made her feel. 'Yes. I could never... I mean, I'm not a teenager caught out or anything. I want my baby.'

'So what's the problem?'

Beth fiddled with her chips. She'd been starving a minute ago, now she didn't think she'd want to eat ever again. 'I'm frightened. Frightened of what is going to happen to me, and scared of losing Jacob. And, until now, I haven't stopped being scared long enough to think about how I feel.'

Abi put her arm around Beth's shoulders, 'Well, now it's time you started to think more logically. I suspect Jacob will be absolutely thrilled, but if he isn't, then the only question you have to consider is, are you comfortable with being a single mum?'

Beth whispered so softly that Abi had to strain to hear her. 'I don't want to do this on my own.'

'But you won't be on your own. Whatever happens, you won't be alone.'

'I won't?'

'Didn't you see Stan and Dora's faces? Over the moon doesn't even begin to cover it. Stan is going to be a great-grandad-ish, and if the excitement of the wedding hasn't tired him out this evening, then the news he is going to have a mini-person to bounce on his knee will surely have him snoring next to Dora by now.'

Beth giggled through her waves of panic. 'Maybe that's why Grandad sent me to Stan.'

'I'm sorry?'

Scooping up some sand, Beth let it trail through her fingers. 'You'll think I'm daft.'

'I often think you're daft, so give it your best shot!'

'I could have sworn I heard Grandad talking to me earlier. Just after I'd done the test. I felt so alone, and I said aloud how much I missed him, and well…I sort of felt his words, in here.' Beth rubbed her chest. 'It was so clear that he wanted me to visit Stan. I knew I'd feel better for going.'

'And do you feel better? Now the shock is passing?'

Beth pulled her knees up to her chest and wrapped her

arms around them. 'I think so. My brain feels like it's going to explode with "what ifs?" though.'

'I bet.' Abi smiled at Beth. 'Well, if you want to talk, any time, I'm here. Whatever happens. OK?'

'Thanks, Abi.'

'And I know you're worried about Jacob, but honestly, Beth, just the way he looks at you is enough to show that he loves you to pieces. He isn't going to do a bunk. He's going to be a dad!'

'Oh my God! And I'm going to be a mum.'

Abi's smile became a beam. 'Yes you are! And I'm going to be a sort-of auntie.'

Beth felt the first flickers of excitement edge past her fears. 'There are so many practical factors to think about as well. I mean, our home is so small, we'll have to move away from Grandad's flat, and then there's money. I might have to leave the school as I'm unmarried, and potters don't exactly make a mint.'

Abi put a reassuring hand on her friend's arm. 'Beth, love, all those problems will have to be faced in time, but not yet. How did this happen anyway?'

'Seriously?' Beth burst out laughing, 'You may look like the most innocent sweet in the shop, Abi Carter, but I know different.'

Her friend stuck her tongue out. 'You know what I mean!'

'I forgot a pill about ten weeks ago. And then I forgot that I'd forgotten it and didn't make sure we were covered in other ways, if you see what I mean.'

'Ah. Easily done.' Abi nodded. 'Doctor's appointment for you tomorrow, young lady.'

77

Jacob raised a hand in acknowledgement as he saw Max stoop to fit through the door of The Old Success pub.

'Got you a pint of Tribute, mate.' Jacob gestured to the table between them, where two pints of St Austell Brewery's finest sat awaiting their attention.

'Thanks, Jacob.' Max landed with a satisfied thump onto his seat. 'Just what I need.'

'Heavy day?'

'Busy more than heavy. I have a new client who wants me to start work asap, and as it's a big contract, I can't afford not to take it.'

'But that means working above and beyond to get the current job done ahead of schedule?'

'You've got it.' Max wiped the back of his hand over his mouth, savouring the taste of his beer. 'It's bad enough that I haven't seen Abi much lately, what with the conversion in St Ives, but now I'll have to work late this week to get it done ready for the next job. At least the next one is closer to Abi's place though.'

Jacob cradled his own pint. 'I was didn't think you'd be up for a pint tonight, to be honest, I thought you'd be with Abi.'

'She's gone to see Stan. I think the shock of the forthcoming wedding has subsided, and she's gone to see if they want help getting it all sorted.'

'That sounds like Abi.' Jacob stared into the middle distance. 'She'll see Beth there. I found a note on the table when I got home, saying that she was going to see if she could meet the mysterious Dora.'

'In that case, they'll probably be hours. Once those

two get talking there's no stopping them.'

'True.' Jacob was quiet for a minute. 'I don't suppose Beth has said anything to you, has she?'

'About what?'

'That's just it, I'm not sure. I'm probably imagining things, but Beth hasn't been laughing as much as usual lately, and she is a big laugher. And she forgot she was supposed to come to see a studio with me today.'

Max shrugged. 'I haven't noticed anything wrong, but I haven't been around much. Although now I think about it, she didn't laugh on the phone the other day. But she was on her lunch break, so she probably had a small child hanging off her somewhere. Abi hasn't mentioned a problem. If she was worried about Beth I'm pretty confident she'd have said something. I bet it's end of term pressure, and she'll be fine once it's the summer hols.'

'That's what Beth said.'

'Well, there you go then.' Max picked up the menu on the table. 'I'm starving. Steak and chips?'

Abi gazed at her friend. 'I can't get over it. You've got a tiny little life growing inside you. That is so incredible.'

Beth stroked her stomach. 'That is one word for it, although terrifying is another good one.'

'Go home and talk to Jacob. You'll never relax until you've told him.'

'If he flips out can I come and stay with you for a bit?'

'Beth, love, he won't flip out, but yes, if the very worst happens – which it won't – my spare room is yours for as long as you like.' Abi clambered to her feet and brushed sand from her palms. 'Now go home! I'm going to nip back in to reassure Stan you're OK, then I'm going to see how Max got on with the neighbour from hell.'

Beth paused as she climbed into the driver's seat of her car. 'What? Oh I'm sorry, that's what you wanted to talk about, wasn't it? I just took over the whole evening!'

Abi held up a hand. 'Come on, Beth, compared to your news it's nothing! Anyway, it's a long story. I'll tell you all about it tomorrow. Go and talk to Jacob. And then please text me to let me know you and he are alright.'

'I never thought I'd see the day when I'd be attending Stan's wedding.' Jacob squirted a dollop of tomato ketchup onto this plate. 'Yours and Abi's, yes, but not Stan's.'

Max, who'd been struggling with his thoughts on the same matter, said, 'It's very Stan though, isn't it? Living for the day and all that. Do you remember when we took him to London for that auction at Christie's?'

Jacob laughed. 'I sure do. He was like a child on holiday. I hope I have half the energy when I'm his age.'

'Me too.' Max stabbed a forkful of chips. 'I hope I still have Abi with me though, rather than contemplating a new model.'

'God yeah, likewise with Beth. You going to move in with Abi?'

Max, who, even after almost a year of knowing Jacob, still wasn't used to his open conversations, having always been happier coping with problems alone, laid down his fork. 'I don't know. I mean, I want to but... Look, mate, Abi and I need to go slower than you and Beth. Our history is less straightforward, and moving in would be a big deal for us.'

'Sure. I get that. Actually, I thought you'd pop the question first, and then move in. Stan not inspired you in that direction? I see you as doing the decent thing, rather than living in glorious sin like me and a certain primary school teacher.'

Hoping his smile and accompanying roll of his eyes hid how nervous he was about the prospect of ever getting married again, Max said, 'I think we should be there for Stan and Dora before anything else happens. Anyway, I'm planning a night in a hotel for Abi's anniversary. A getaway for the two of us.'

Jacob's eyes twinkled mischievously. 'Sounds good to me!'

Having left a sleepy Sadie lounging in the back of her car, Abi knocked on Stan's door, hoping she wasn't about to wake him up. Only a few seconds later, however, she heard him approaching on the other side, and was struck by how much more confidently he moved these days. When she'd first met Stan, living alone in the home which she now owned, he'd shuffled around with the aid of walking sticks. Now he only used them for trips into the outside world.

'Abi, I'm so glad you came back. How's Beth? We were worried.' Stan ushered her through to the living room, where Dora was sat on the sofa.

'That's why I popped back. I can't stay, I don't like to leave Sadie in the car, but I wanted to let you know Beth's OK. She's in shock. I know she always wanted children, but I think she'd rather assumed it would be after she'd

81

had some sort of discussion with Jacob on the subject.'

Dora nodded. 'Is Beth genuinely worried that Jacob will do a runner once she tells him? From what Stan has told me about him that doesn't seem to be in his character.'

'No, it isn't. Personally, I think he'll be chuffed to bits, but we'll have to wait and see. She's gone home to tell him now.' Abi smiled at her friends. 'Right, I'd better go home as well; Max will be waiting for me.'

Stan and Dora exchanged a glance, which stopped Abi from heading to the door. 'What is it?'

'Well, actually, we wondered if we could ask a favour.'

'You can always ask me for a favour. What is it?'

Stan looked at Dora, who smiled encouragingly. 'Well, Abi my girl, plans for the wedding are moving fast, time not exactly being on our side and all that. The thing is, as I said earlier, Sally is less than thrilled. Would you talk to her, Abi? I know it's a big ask, but would you Skype Australia for me and put her mind at rest?'

Beth couldn't stop pacing. She'd found a note from Jacob, written beneath the one she'd left him, saying he was at the pub with Max. Wishing he'd hurry up and come home, so she could tell him her news before she drove herself mad with worry, she grabbed the keys to the gallery downstairs. Wandering between the quilts that hung on the walls, she stroked a finger over their softness. They were breathtakingly beautiful, and she could see why so many had a little red sticker stuck next to them, signifying that they'd been sold.

Sitting on the chair where Abi spent every weekday drawing illustrations for children's picture books, Beth anxiously listened for the sound of Jacob's key in the front door. Eventually, the scrape of metal against metal told her the moment of truth had arrived. Perspiration coated her palms, and her throat was so dry she wasn't sure any words would be able to come out of her mouth anyway.

'Jacob?' Beth called croakily from the gallery.

'Beth? What are you doing in here at this time of night?' Alarm engulfed Jacob; she wasn't about to leave him, was she? He'd expected to come in and find her curled up on the sofa, laughing at some repeated comedy on the television, a glass of wine in one hand and a packet of crisps in the other.

'Umm, I haven't had time to visit the gallery much lately and these gorgeous quilts will be gone to make room for the next guest artist soon. Mad, really, as we only live upstairs.'

'But you haven't turned the lights on.'

'Oh, no, so I haven't.' Beth looked at her hands in despair.

'Please, love, you're freaking me out. What is it? You're not leaving me, are you? Please speak to me.'

Beth was stunned; it hadn't occurred to her that Jacob could think that. 'No! Never. Never!'

'Are you ill?'

'No. No, I'm fine I'm...' Taking a deep breath, Beth nervously blurted everything out. 'I'm pregnant, and I'm scared. Don't leave me, OK? Please. I know it's my fault, I forgot a pill. It was just once. I wasn't trying to trap you or anything. Don't be angry, I know it's…'

Relief flooded Jacob as he held Beth close, before stepping a little away from her and running his wide green eyes over her body in the pale grey light of the gallery. 'Oh my God, I'm going to be a dad!'

'You aren't angry?'

'Don't be silly! A baby. We're going to have a baby! Wow, oh my God! I'm going to be a daddy!'

Holding on to Jacob, Beth burst into tears all over again, but this time, every drop was one of joy.

84

Chapter Ten

'What did Stan say about Cassandra when you saw him last night?'

Abi bit her lip as she passed Max his packed lunch. She hadn't a clue how she was managing to keep the news about Beth's pregnancy secret. 'I never got round to telling him about her. He and Dora are so excited about the wedding.'

Her grin, which had been firmly in place since she'd had a late night text from Beth telling her Jacob was delighted with the news of his impending fatherhood, was temporarily diminished as Abi remembered the favour that Stan had asked of her. 'Actually, they want me to talk to Sally for them.'

'I assume she isn't very pleased about this latest turn in events?'

'I think wary is the word.'

'I'm not surprised.' Max hooked the straps to his decorator's dungarees over his shoulders as he stood up from Abi's kitchen table. 'I'd be the same if I was thousands of miles away and hadn't met the woman my father wanted to marry.'

'Me too. I'm not sure what I can say to her that might help. It's hardly my place to convince Sally it's all going to be OK, is it? I mean, I can see that Stan and Dora get on well, but that doesn't guarantee they'll be happy, does it? All I can promise Sally is that Dora isn't after Stan's money as she has plenty of her own. In fact, if Dora goes first, Stan will be the one who's better off.'

Max made a face. 'That's all a bit clinical, isn't it?'

'I know. I was rather uncomfortable when they told me about the financial stuff last night, but they think Sally will believe me more than them.'

'Puts you in an awkward position.'

'Tell me about it! I am not looking forward to the call one bit.'

'Do you think Sally will come over for the wedding, assuming she doesn't convince her dad not to go through with it?'

'I honestly wouldn't like to say.' Abi shrugged. 'It's not been a year since she and the children flew over to help Stan move into the flat. They only managed to afford that because Stan used some of the money he made at the auction.'

'I'll help you have a think about what you can say later, if you like.'

'Thanks, Max.' Abi smiled. 'And I want to hear more about my new neighbour! You never did get round to telling me about your trip next door.'

Max pulled on his steel-capped boots. 'There isn't much to tell beyond what I said on the phone. Cassandra wants to get the place redecorated before it goes up as a holiday let. She has a good eye, I'll give her that. Butter yellow throughout, not unlike this.' Max pointed at Abi's kitchen walls. 'She isn't so bad. A bit put out that she's here at all, mind. I got the impression she'd been rather 'dropped in it.'

'That hardly excuses the junkyard in the front garden.'

Max enfolded his partner in a hug. 'It's only rotten shelves, old curtains, and a couple of the original shutters that are beyond repair. I'd have chucked them myself if she hadn't got there first.'

'If you say so.'

'I do say so.' Max kissed Abi's forehead. 'Forget about it. Cassandra will only be here for a few weeks. She has a business to go back to London to, and she obviously doesn't fit here.'

'She has no intention of trying to fit either, does she?'

'Sadly, I don't think she does, no.'

Determined not to let the evidence of Cassandra's rough and ready approach to interior design get to her today, Abi left for the gallery, determined to see Beth before her friend left for work.

The thought of her friend's impending motherhood was enough to temporarily diminish the fears she had about having an endless succession of unknown people living next to her on and off all year.

Jacob opened the door, his expression torn between delight and disbelief. Abi realised she should have asked Beth if Jacob knew she'd already been told the news. Her hesitation, when she didn't quite know if she was supposed to congratulate Jacob or not, was quickly curtailed as he thanked her for taking care of Beth the previous day.

'It was my pleasure. She told you about her wobble then?'

'She did. Daft woman.'

'Congratulations, Jacob. I don't have to ask if you're pleased, you couldn't look prouder if you tried.'

'Proud? God, yes! My Beth is going to have my baby. Can life get more perfect than that?' Jacob calmed down a fraction. 'Just when I thought I'd never find someone who was mad enough to settle down with me I found Beth. And now this! Incredible.'

Beth came into the hallway. She looked tired, but her usual air of control had returned, ready for a new school day. 'Hi, Abi, early start?'

'I wanted to see with my own eyes that you were OK before I got back to my pixies.'

'Still terrified, but not about facing life alone.'

Jacob rolled his eyes, and repeated, 'Daft woman!' as he hooked his holdall onto his shoulder. 'Right, I must love you and leave you for the depths of Hayle. I'll call at lunchtime, Beth.' He hugged his partner, and then turned to Abi. 'Make sure she books a doctor's appointment.'

Abi saluted. 'Will do!'

'Thanks, she has a crazy idea about leaving it until the school holidays.'

'I told you, I'll be fine until then,' Beth protested, but to no effect. Jacob shook his head just as Abi said, 'I'll make sure it gets made today.'

Waving Jacob off, Beth turned to her friend. 'I do have to leave the appointment until the school holidays, you know.'

'Because you're busy, or because if you don't get the official word from the doctor's until after the end of term, you'll be able to put off telling people and avoid the village gossip?'

88

Beth sighed. 'OK, you've seen through me. I don't want to face all that judgemental stuff.'

'This is a friendly place. People that judge aren't worth worrying about, are they? Anyway, everyone local knows you live with Jacob and you aren't married. No one's ever bothered you about it.'

'Logically I know that, but…well, I want to get used to the idea of parenthood myself first.'

'I understand that, but what about the head teacher? Won't they need to know so arrangements can be made for maternity cover next year?'

Beth gulped. 'Do you think they'll sack me?'

'Sack you?'

'I'm not married.'

'Oh for heaven's sake, Beth, it isn't 1950! Come on, I'll help you carry your stuff to school. We'll drop into the surgery on the way to make your appointment. It's a confidential service, and if word gets out, then it's the receptionist who'll be risking getting the sack, not you.'

Secretly glad to give in, Beth passed Abi a bag of exercise books to carry. 'OK, but on one condition. We talk about something else for a little while. I want to pretend everything is normal for a minute.'

Abi laughed. 'Normal? That's pushing it, isn't it? With the eldest of our friends getting remarried, and a double-barrelled businesswoman living next door to my house?'

'You never got around to telling me about the neighbour from hell.'

As they locked the connecting door between Beth's home and Art and Sole, Abi said, 'To be fair, I don't know her. Cassandra could be OK deep down. But I did try to introduce myself, and as you know, my offer of friendship was knocked back, so I've kept quiet since then. Max seems to like her, though.'

'Max?'

'She's hired him to decorate number two before it becomes a holiday let. He hasn't told her that he lives next door, part-time.'

'Ah,' Beth glimpsed sideways at her friend as they walked down the hill towards the village, 'still only part-time?'

'It works for us.' Abi allowed herself a small, silent groan which she hoped had gone unnoticed, before adding, 'Is it wrong of me to wish Max hadn't liked her?'

'Max likes everyone.'

'True. I know I'm being unfair. She just reminds me so much of all those Stepford Wife types I left behind. I wanted to escape the life Luke made me lead, not have it turn up on my doorstep. She's so together and businesslike – and rude!'

'Sounds a lot like Lucinda.'

Abi stopped walking. 'Max's ex-wife?'

'Yeah, she was very much the slick businesswoman. She hated it down here. Thank goodness.'

Pleased that they'd reached the doctor's surgery so she didn't have to voice her sudden concern that Max seemed to like Cassandra – a woman just like his ex-wife – quite a bit, not to mention that it was becoming more obvious that he was never going to ask her to live with him, Abi asked, 'When are you going to tell Max about the baby? He'll be almost as delighted as Jacob was.'

'I thought we could all go out for a meal at the

weekend.'

'I can't keep it quiet for two more days! I'm bursting to tell him already! It's so exciting. Can't you both come over tonight?'

Noticing a cloud of concern pass over Beth's face as they turned into the surgery reception, Abi said, 'It's only an appointment to see a doctor. You don't have to tell the receptionist why you're here.'

'She'll guess. I'm never ill. In fact I don't think I've been to the doctor in five or six years.'

'Sneeze a bit then.'

'What?' Beth looked confused.

'You know, fake-sneeze. Make out like you have a bug or something. Sniffle a bit.'

Beth laughed. 'Abi, you are priceless. I'd have to sneeze on and off all day if I did that.'

'Only when you're in public before and after school.'

Beth's eyebrows rose. 'I never had you down as an arch criminal.'

'I like to think of it as harmlessly sneaky rather than criminal – and only in a good cause.' Abi pushed her friend towards the receptionist.

Watching Beth make the first in a long line of doctor's appointments about her child, Abi felt a tightening in her chest. Would she and Max have kids one day? She hoped so.

She rested against a handy pillar. With each month she lived in Cornwall, a little more of the Abi that she'd suppressed during her marriage to Luke, when she was playing the model executive wife, made its way back to the surface. She didn't think about that London life often

91

now, but every now and then a little bit of her previously squashed personality would pop out and surprise her. The sneezing ploy had been an example of that. A harmless lie to help someone she cared for. Abi wasn't sure if that was a good characteristic or not.

Closing her eyes, she felt tired despite the early hour. She knew if she was going to stay true to herself she couldn't let the Cassandra situation go on. The image of her new neighbour, sad and possibly tear-stained, the previous day kept elbowing its way to the front of her mind, despite all the other stuff cluttering her head.

As Beth, looking happy, and proving that fake-sneezing wasn't her forte, came back from the receptionist clutching a scrap of paper containing an appointment time, Abi knew she was going to have to try and speak to Cassandra again.

Everyone deserved a second chance. Abi had got hers when she'd met Max and Beth. They'd been far kinder to her than any stranger ever had before. *Perhaps Cassandra simply needs someone to be kind to her?* Abi wasn't sure if she'd live to regret it, but she knew she'd be knocking on the door of number two Miners Row as soon as she'd got home from work.

Chapter Eleven

The sunshine was beating through the gallery's picture windows so fiercely that Abi had to pull some of the blinds down to see clearly enough to work. Not that concentration was ever likely to have come easily today. Usually, if anything was playing on her mind, Abi would soon become absorbed in her illustrations, so that real life became temporarily lost in the process of creativity.

Today however she was glad of the steady trickle of early holidaymakers who came in to view the exhibition side of the Art and Sole Gallery. The majority ran curious eyes over her work, and many pointed delightedly at the pixie gang that was taking shape on her latest page. At least interacting with the visitors stopped her obsessing over whether she should check on Cassandra, what she could say to Sally, and if she should ask Max to move in with her.

Abi had flirted with the idea of asking Max to live in her house on and off for the last six months. But she'd had to fight so hard for her own home and her own space that she had decided to keep her cottage her own for a while. Max had always been supportive and happy with that arrangement, and she knew he understood her desire for space after such a suffocating marriage. Over the past few weeks, though, Abi had begun to wonder if they were missing opportunities by not being together all the time.

It's just Stan's wedding and Beth's baby news that's making you think this way. If Max wanted us to live together he'd have asked me by now. He's an old-fashioned guy. I can't ask him, it would make him feel rushed. He'd hate that.

Putting a final sheen to the tip of the chief pixie's hat, Abi laid down her paintbrush and stared across at the gallery. The quilts, which had proved so popular with the past four weeks' worth of visitors, would have to be taken down that evening and replaced by a display of watercolours by local artist Serena Browne first thing in morning.

Serena had proved very popular locally when she'd displayed her work there eight months ago. Abi was looking forward to seeing the artist again, but wasn't sure anyone should have to face Serena's exuberance before eight o'clock in the morning; she *was* rather over the top. Resolving to have an early night, and glad that Max had already agreed to come and help her take down the quilts later, Abi felt her habitual smile return. At least Serena was too busy to attend the exhibition every day, and was leaving any sales to Abi. Occasional visits were fun, but Serena's constant presence in the gallery would put her work back weeks, as the artist rarely stopped talking and Abi herself always felt duty bound to listen.

It was already nearly three o'clock. Beth would be home in an hour. Perhaps she should ask Beth about Max? The idea was appealing, Beth had known Max longer than anyone; and if he'd talked to someone other than Abi about the future, it would have been her. Tempting though it was, Abi quickly dismissed the idea. It was unfair to add to Beth's worries at the moment, especially as her doctor's appointment had been booked for five o'clock that evening.

She was about to put the kettle on when Jacob bounced through the main gallery door.

'Hey, Abi, fancy making that coffee for two?'

'Sure.' Abi grinned in the face of the potter's happiness. 'You're back early.'

'Beth called; she wants me to come to the doctor's with her.'

'Of course she does. Exciting, isn't it?'

Jacob was obviously hyper and restless, but as Abi sensibly reached for the decaf coffee he frowned. 'I can't help wondering though; what if she *isn't* pregnant? The test was positive, of course, but what if it was faulty? I know Beth was worried about telling me, but now we'd both be gutted if she wasn't expecting after all.'

'I'm sure she is. All the signs are there.'

'She isn't being sick though.'

'Then she's either very lucky,' Abi stirred some milk into Jacob's mug, 'or she hasn't reached that stage yet. Beth doesn't know how far gone she is, does she?'

'True.' Jacob blushed with uncharacteristic coyness. 'It's not like she's…regular and stuff. You know.'

'Yes, I know.' Abi laughed. 'Now, why don't you drink this, try and calm down, and tell me all about the new studio you're taking over?'

'I could help you take down the quilts if you like.'

Abi considered how nice it would be not to have to come back to the gallery that evening, but one look at how skittish Jacob was told her it would be a bad idea to let him loose with exhibits worth over two hundred pounds apiece. 'Thanks, Jacob, but I promised the artist they'd be up right until close of work today, just in case we get a random last-minute sale.'

'Probably for the best, I'd hate to catch a thread or something.'

'Max is going to help me take them down later.'

Jacob leaned against the counter and sipped his drink. 'How about you then, Abi? Fancy making Max a daddy one day?'

***

Abi checked her watch for the third time as she walked home from the gallery. It was six minutes past five. Assuming the doctor wasn't running late, Beth would be having her pregnancy confirmed right now. Or, at the very least, would be peeing into a cup so that a final test could be taken.

Up until Jacob had asked her straight, Abi had tried not to picture herself in Beth's position, but now she was finding it increasingly hard not to think about her and Max having children. Luke had never wanted a family. Or rather, he'd told Abi he did – right until after their honeymoon, when suddenly there had been a 'no children' rule, and a myriad of other embargos which had stifled the life out of her.

Max was Luke's polar opposite, and although he'd once told Abi he wanted children, the 'family' conversation had never come up again. Now that Beth was expecting, it seemed to be hovering between them – and he didn't even know yet! She didn't want Max to think she only wanted children now because Beth was

96

going to have one.

Abi gave herself a mental shake. She was being silly even thinking like this. It was a non-problem, she loved Max and he loved her. She was only thirty-three. They had time for all that. If she wanted to worry about something constructive, she should be worrying about what to say to Stan's daughter.

Lost in thought about how to tackle the forthcoming Skype call to Australia as she climbed the hill towards Miners Row, Abi didn't notice Cassandra in her front garden. It was only when she heard a snuffling noise that Abi turned to look at the pile of abandoned bits and pieces, and saw her neighbour sitting on the small remaining patch of grass, her laptop resting on her knees and an expression on her face that was so defeated that, despite their last encounter, Abi had to ask if she was alright. Which clearly, she wasn't.

'Hello? Are you OK?'

Cassandra blushed, her red cheeks glowing against the backdrop of her yellow hair, which looked as though she'd been repeatedly raking a hand through it. 'I'm fine. Thank you.'

Abi watched as her neighbour, clearly angry with herself for being caught crying, rubbed her bloodshot eyes with her wrist and got to her feet.

'Cassandra, isn't it?'

'Yes... how did you know?'

'Max, your decorator; he's my boyfriend.'

Cassandra was about to fire off a blunt comment about client confidentiality, when she remembered where she was and how ridiculous she'd sound saying that to her neighbour if the decorator she'd hired lived next door. 'He never said.'

'Max wouldn't have wanted you to feel obliged to hire him because he stays on your doorstep sometimes.'

Cassandra nodded. 'He seems a good man. You are very lucky.'

'I think so.' Abi felt awkward, she didn't feel she could leave her neighbour so plainly distressed, but at the same time she didn't want to intrude. 'I was going to make tea, would you like to join me for a cuppa?'

Abi wasn't sure if the Londoner was more stunned or upset by the offer.

'But I was horrid to you.' Cassandra stared at the pile of wreckage in front of her. 'You were being thoughtful and I... I'm not used to neighbourly stuff.'

A genuine smile of understanding crossed Abi's face. 'Well, if you live in anything like the part of London that I lived in for so long, then the concept of neighbours means competition, not consideration.'

'That's exactly what it's like.' Cassandra looked confused. 'Forgive me, but you don't come across like you've lived in London. Were you a student there or something?'

'I was, and then I lived there for several years. I've only been in Cornwall for eleven months.'

Cassandra's mouth dropped open. 'But you act like a local.'

'Thank you!' Abi laughed. 'Sorry, I'm not laughing at you. It's just good to know I appear to fit in. I didn't fit properly in either London or Surrey. Although I did try to belong.'

Tapping the lid of her laptop, Cassandra gave Abi a weak grin. 'I'd love that cup of tea, thank you. I can't now, though, I have to sort something out that won't wait.' She glanced at the computer.

'Ah, that's why the front garden. You get a signal here?'

'A bit of one.'

'Well, if you want to chat, just come on over, OK?'

'Thanks, umm?'

'Abi. My name's Abi.'

'Like the house?'

'Just like the house.'

Cassandra tilted her face under the full flow of the shower, letting the water stream through her hair and pound her shoulders. The terrace may have been sorely in need of decorative work, but at least the previous owners had understood the requirement of a good power shower.

The tension that knotted her whole body, however, had stubbornly withstood the heat of the water, and as she got out and draped herself in a towel, Cassandra felt no better than she'd had before she got in.

This really is happening.

Mr Clearer had sent an email, and there was no mistake. It had been a Mr Justin Smythe who'd set the wheels in motion to sell off The Pinkerton Agency to an American company who were intending to expand their nanny business in the UK.

Justin was still not answering his phone, and now Crystal was ignoring her calls as well.

Cassandra felt lost, humiliated, hurt, confused, and

angry all at the same time.

How much else had been a lie? The divorce? The fact he loved her? Had Justin ever seen her as more than a leisure pursuit? A convenient woman to use when lust arose? Someone whose business he coveted – had he merely been using her while he waited for the moment when he could swoop in and steal her business? Justin had even mentioned marriage and she'd believed him.

I am a fool. A totally stupid, bloody fool.

Cassandra scrubbed her body hard, taking out her frustration on the droplets of water that drenched her flesh. *I believed every word he said.* I let him basically run the legal side of my business without ever checking up on him.

Of course you did, you love him. You trust him. Trusted...

Trying not to scream at herself for being so blind, Cassandra pulled on a pair of jeans and a T-shirt. She had to go and find Justin, there was no other answer. 'But first you are going to decide what to say to him, and how you are going to reverse all this. You have to make a plan. Once you have that, then you are going to give the people who have rented out your flat two months' notice and go home.'

Cassandra sat down with a despairing thump. Suddenly she felt very, very tired.

***

Max parked outside Abi's House, and cast an eye over the mess in Cassandra's garden, trying to work out if it would all fit into the back of his van, or if he'd have to move

100

some of his tools out first.

He was picking up an old shutter when he caught a glimpse of his client behind the window at the front of the house. He could have been imagining it, but he'd have sworn she was crying, a fact that did not fit with the together businesswoman he'd encountered so recently.

Quietly, Max put the shutter back down, closed the van doors, and went indoors to find Abi.

'Abi, lass, how about Cassandra helps you to take down the quilts in the gallery while I clear up her garden? I've just seen her, and frankly she needs a friend whether she wants one or not.'

Chapter Twelve

Knocking on the door to number two Miners Row, Abi felt awkward. She couldn't stop Beth's voice echoing in her ears, telling her how much Cassandra sounded like Lucinda, Max's ex. If a shoulder to cry on was required, though, she'd rather it was her shoulder Cassandra cried on, and not Max's.

'Abi? Hello. Again.' Cassandra had changed into less summery clothes, and was rubbing her arms as if she was cold, despite the gorgeous burgundy fleece jumper she wore, which Abi knew would have cost more than the average person's monthly wage. The dark shadows that underlined Cassandra's eyes had almost been hidden by a good concealer, and if she hadn't seen her earlier, Abi might have thought Max had been exaggerating her neighbour's distressed state.

Nor sure where to start, she decided to take a leaf out of Stan's book, and dived straight in with a big smile. 'I hope you don't mind me interrupting, I just wondered if you wanted to escape for a while.'

'Escape?'

'Well, you'd be doing me a favour actually.' Abi found herself rubbing her own arms as if in sympathy with her unseasonably cold neighbour. 'I run the Art and Sole Gallery in the village. This month's display has to be taken down. Max was going to help me, but he wants to get on with clearing your front garden and ordering in your paint so he can crack on with the decorating the minute his current job is done.'

Cassandra was openly amazed. 'You run that gorgeous studio gallery on the corner of the Cove?'

'A little less shock in your voice would be nice, but yes, my friend Beth owns it and I manage it for her. Have you been in?'

'No, I haven't, although I've passed it. I haven't had the chance to go in yet.'

Abi could tell Cassandra was undecided whether to go with her or not, so she pushed her advantage home. 'I know it's an awful cheek to ask you when we don't know each other, but if Max can make a start here…'

Cassandra didn't wait for Abi to finish her sentence. The possibility of being out of Cornwall and back in London even a day sooner was a chance worth taking. 'I'll get my bag. Do I need anything else?'

'Not a thing. Thanks, Cassandra, I appreciate it.'

Stopping just long enough to leave a spare set of keys to number two with Max, and for Cassandra to ask if he'd check whether the larder door should be saved or replaced, the women walked down the lane towards town, each frantically wondering what on earth they could talk about.

Not wanting the silence to become uneasy, Abi adopted what she assumed would be safe conversational ground.

'Beautiful here, isn't it?' She pointed out across the unfurling view as the seascape came into sight.

'Do you think so?' Cassandra sounded far from convinced.

Abi stared at her companion in astonishment. She'd never come across anyone who had to stop and consider whether the sparkling sea and yellow sand, backed by stunningly rugged rocks, was beautiful or not. 'You don't?'

'It's just the seaside, isn't it? I mean, the sand gets everywhere, and it's never terribly relaxing, what with non-private school children being on holiday pretty much all the time these days.'

Abi opened her mouth, and then closed it again. She had absolutely no idea what to say as Cassandra expanded her point.

'I mean, look at those overflowing rubbish bins, and the seagulls fighting over those fish and chip papers. And don't even get me started on the smell.'

'Smell?' Confusion crossed from Abi's expression into her voice.

'Salty air and boat oil.'

Abi took a surreptitious sniff. There was a hint of oil in the air, she supposed, but then, they were near the harbour, so it would have been odd if there wasn't. And of course there was salt in the air. It was the coast!

Cassandra glanced at Abi and started to laugh. It was a sound that fell halfway between genuine amusement and hysteria. 'I'm sorry, Abi. I'm not laughing at you; it's just that I've never seen anyone gobsmacked before. Why does everyone look like that when they meet a person who isn't keen on the seaside? It can't be that rare, surely?'

'Well, I...' Abi shrugged. 'I guess if you choose to

live by the sea, it must always seem odd that other people wouldn't want to live there as well. Especially when so many people can't wait to escape to the coast for a break from everyday life.'

'And that's fine for them. I understand the need for a radical change of scene every now and then, but it isn't the coast that does that for me. I love picturesque villages and little boutiques, antique shops, and galleries. I even found a wonderful shabby chic furniture place in Truro, which I could have spent years in, but the actual seaside…no thanks!'

'So if I said let's go for a sit on the sand after we've finished, the answer would be…?'

'A very loud and clear "no thank you".'

'A walk over the cliffs?'

'More tempting, but only on a sunny day and with the offer of a cup of coffee, or maybe a gin and tonic, at the other end.'

Abi's good humour returned. 'Now you're talking. How about a trip to the outdoor theatre near Penzance sometime?'

Cassandra's smile met her eyes for the first time since Abi had called at her front door. 'The theatre, I love. Even if it's *only* regional. Did you go much when you lived in London?'

Deciding to ignore the gibe, Abi swallowed hard. She had been hoping to avoid talking about her life in London, but now Cassandra had begun to soften, albeit only a little bit, she didn't want to ruin it. It was beginning to appear as if Sennen was to Cassandra what London was to Abi.

'I did, yes, I was very lucky. I was taken to visit the

West End at least once a month.'

'You don't miss it? The West End musicals, the plays, all the restaurants, wine bars, the department stores so nearby, all the museums, the sheer convenience of *everything*?'

'Not at all,' Abi pointed to the seascape, 'but I'd miss that if I went back. You can see a Debenhams anywhere, but that view...it's only here.'

Cassandra nodded. 'I understand that. It isn't my thing, but I totally get it.'

Abi fished the keys to Art and Sole from her jeans pocket. 'Well, let's see if I can't persuade you that there is one good thing about the village. Come inside my arty world.'

Cassandra felt shame flush her cheeks. 'Oh God, I am so bad at this.' She hung back from walking into the gallery. 'I'm not making excuses for seeming all dismissive of this place, Abi, but I've had an awful few days, and well...let's just say if the streets of Sennen were paved with gold then you would still have a hard time selling it to me right now. I'm not anti-Cornwall, I promise – I'm just not at home.'

Breathing an invisible sigh of relief, Abi realised her hands had begun to tremble like they used to when she anticipated her late husband's displeasure. She was about to explain how the gallery worked, when Cassandra got in first.

'Oh, this is wonderful! You work here?'

'Yes. There, in fact.' Abi pointed to her chair by the easel and work station on the studio side of the room, before turning on the lights and pulling down the blinds so

107

that they could take down the display without being watched by strolling tourists and curious locals.

'You're an artist?'

'I'm a children's book illustrator. I could work anywhere, but when I moved down here I had the good fortune to meet Max, and then his best friend, Beth. She inherited this place from her grandfather. It was his cobbler's shop until she converted it last year.'

'Hence "Art and Sole", as in shoes?'

'Exactly. Beth and her partner live upstairs.'

Cassandra drifted over to the quilts. 'These are exquisite. Do they really have to come down?'

Pleased that at least her taste in textiles met with her new neighbour's approval, Abi said, 'I'm afraid so. Each exhibitor rents the space for a month. As you can see from the red stickers by so many of them, they did well with sales.'

Cassandra ran a finger over one of the red spots next to the rectangular card of notes the artists had placed next to each quilt, which explained its source of inspiration and title. 'It's like a real gallery.'

Abi winced. 'Excuse me? I think you'll find this *is* a real gallery.' She put her hands on her hips. 'I'm sorry you're stuck in a place you don't want to be, Cassandra, I know how that feels, and it's horrible, but we aren't keeping you here. You don't come across as if you're exactly poverty-stricken. I'm sure that if you genuinely wanted to leave you could up sticks and flee to the nearest place that suits you. So why don't you?'

Cassandra opened her mouth to fire back that that was

precisely what she wanted to do, but her usual self-righteousness had deserted her. One glimpse at Abi's offended face robbed her of all her indignation. Crashing onto the viewing sofa in the middle of the room, she burst into a new round of tears.

She couldn't believe what was happening. Not even Justin had seen her cry. Not once. She was Cassandra Henley-Pinkerton and she did *not* cry. She was always in control. Always. She was secure in her looks, her abilities, and her intelligence.

Or she had been.

Justin had stolen all of that.

Abi only watched her visitor for a second before her generous heart got the better of her. Picking up the box of tissues she normally used for dabbing at stray runs of paint, she passed them to Cassandra.

Speaking far more calmly than she felt, Abi said, 'You've insulted my home and my gallery. You might as well tell me why. If we're going to be neighbours, even if only for a while, it'll make life a lot easier if I understand why you're being such a bitch.'

Cassandra turned to her host. 'Why haven't you just thrown me out?'

'Because I suffer from chronic niceness. It's a real pain in the arse, but totally incurable.'

The Londoner shook her head in disbelief. 'As you've probably worked out, I suffer from no such ailment. Perhaps it would be better if I did.'

Abi got up again and fetched the emergency bottle of wine she and Beth kept in the small fridge beneath the counter, along with two glasses. 'So, talk to me.'

Feeling so far out of her emotional depth that she wasn't sure where to start, Cassandra gulped and began to tell her story. How she'd met Justin, about their affair, how she had given him joint legal power over her business, and how they'd started to plan a future together. Then she told Abi why they'd got the house in Cornwall, and how she was only supposed to be there to do the place up while he secured his promotion and told his wife he wanted a divorce.

'At least, that's why I thought I was here.'

'Ah. And you are *really* here because?'

'It appears I've been sent here so that Justin could steal my business from under me while I wasn't looking, ruining my life, career, and reputation all in one go.' Cassandra took a large mouthful of wine before adding, 'And yet, I can't quite accept it.'

'Or you don't want to believe it?'

Cassandra rubbed a hand over her temples. 'Only a few days ago he was talking about marriage. Justin can be a money-grabbing toad sometimes, and he is very materialistic, but this…it doesn't seem in character, somehow. It's too cowardly for him.'

'You think if he wanted to break up with you he'd say so, rather than dragging things out?'

'Exactly. I also think if he wanted me to sell my business he'd tell me. He's the biggest shareholder, he'd do very well out of it without having to risk stealing from me. It doesn't make sense.'

'What does Justin have to say about this?'

'He isn't answering my calls or replying to my texts. Apparently he's in the US.'

'You don't sound convinced.'

'I'm not. His PA, Crystal, would do anything to protect him.'

'You think she fancies him?'

'She always has.'

Abi took another gulp of her wine before brushing her hands decisively down her jeans and approaching the first quilt. 'I may regret this. But it's possible I know someone who could help, or at least someone who would know the right person to discover if Justin is still in London or not.'

'*You* do?'

'Less disbelief and more gratitude would be good here, Cassandra.'

'Sorry.' Appearing as contrite as she sounded, Cassandra got up and helped support the first quilt as Abi took it off its wall fixings. 'Ever since I got to Cornwall I've been a bit...I don't know how to describe it.'

'Unpleasant?'

'Um, yes... although I meant overwhelmed. It's so friendly, everyone listens, and no one seems in competition with anyone else. It's taking a bit of getting used to.'

'Yes, I can see that. But if you want us to help you, you're going to have to unbend a bit. Be pleasant. I'm sure you can do that!' Abi softened a little. 'When you don't go all city slicker, you seem quite nice!'

Feeling thoroughly told off, Cassandra said meekly, 'I'll try.'

***

By the time all the quilts were down, secured in their protective bubble-wrap jackets, and those that had been sold were double wrapped in attractive tissue paper ready for the new owners to collect, Abi had explained to Cassandra all about Luke, her life working in London, and her quest to find Abbey's House, as well as peace and quiet, in Cornwall.

'I was so lucky that Stan was the owner. I'm sure no one else would have let me and Max cross the threshold in the first place.'

Cassandra smoothed a hand over the final quilt. 'That was fun. Thanks for asking me to help.'

Abi looked at her. 'Did you really enjoy doing that?'

'Yes, I did. I'm quite surprised at myself to be honest. I had loads of fun at that shop in Truro as well.'

'I think we may have more in common than we think we do.' Abi smiled. 'Would you like me to see if I can make some enquiries in London, then?'

'Do you truly know people who could help?'

'I'm not sure, but I know people who are well connected with the money side of things in the City. I don't like them, but I know them.'

'Who?'

'My former brother-in-law for one.' Abi trembled as she thought about Simon Carter, the man who had tried to convince her to marry him directly after his brother's death just so Luke's money could be kept in the family. 'I can't stand the man, though, and Max hates him.'

'Why would you do that for me?'

'Because I think you are a much better person than you pretend to be.'

Cassandra stood and stared at Abi. She had absolutely no idea what to say.

'But for goodness' sake don't tell Max, he'd go mad if he thought I'd called Simon. And while you're at it, phone Jo in Truro. Her reputation is excellent. Book some lessons in furniture restoration. If you're going to be trapped here for a bit, then take the chance to learn new skills. You never know, we might even convert you to liking sand.'

Cassandra laughed. 'You're very kind, Abi, but that may be one miracle too far.'

Chapter Thirteen

Leaving Cassandra on her own, Abi picked up her mobile and went outside. She took a few gulps of the sea air she loved so much. Just the thought of making contact with Simon was making her feel nauseous.

Why did you offer to do this?

Abi stared across the part of the cove that was just visible at the far edge of the horizon. Was she doing this simply because she wanted Cassandra to love this place as much as she did?

Not for the first time, Abi wished that her craving to make everything OK for everyone wasn't so strong. Max would never understand her risking getting back in touch with Simon; especially for a virtual stranger. The last time they'd seen each other, Max had punched Simon on the jaw, and as Max was the most laid-back man on the planet, it had taken one hell of a lot of provocation for that to happen. Which just went to show what a horrible man Simon was capable of being.

There has to be another way… Abi stared at her phone for a minute, then, taking another deep breath, placed a call she hadn't thought she'd ever make again. Not to Simon, but to Luke's old office. It was already after six o'clock in the evening, but unless things had changed in the last year, Abi was sure the office would still be occupied – and hopefully by Luke's former PA, Sasha, who had always worked until seven, such was her dread of missing something.

'Good evening, Mr Williams' office, how may I help you?'

'Hello, is that Sasha?'

The answering voice was hesitant on hearing the use of her first name. 'Yes, can I help?'

'Umm, Sasha, it's Abi. Abi Carter, I'm not sure if you remember me?'

'Abi! Of course I remember you. Where are you? There's a rumour going round that you've gone native. Slimy Simon was trying to convince everyone you'd been committed through grief at one point, but no one bought that.'

'He did what!' Abi felt anger bubble up, and then brushed it away. He wasn't worth it. 'Yes, that sounds like Simon. I can assure you, I'm perfectly sane. I just didn't want to marry him, that's all.' She relaxed a fraction. 'I love that you call him Slimy Simon. Very suitable!'

'Trust me, you aren't the only trophy he's chased over the years.' Sasha spoke more quietly, presumably aware of the chances of being overheard. 'I did wonder if it was hurt male pride. It was always obvious he coveted his brother's wife.'

The PA's voice was laced far more with curiosity than pleasure, *but at least*, Abi thought, *Sasha hasn't put the phone down on me*. 'Well, I can assure you that I'm not at all deranged, but I am after some information for a friend.'

'Go on?'

'Do you know a lawyer called Justin Smythe? He works for Family Values.'

Sasha didn't even pause. 'The company I've heard of. His name doesn't mean anything though. Can I ask around the office, or is this confidential?'

'Ask away.' Abi crossed her fingers, hoping that Cassandra wouldn't mind.

After a few minutes of hearing muted mumbles down the line, Sasha was back on the phone. 'Do you mean the Justin Smythe who is married to Jacinta?'

'Could be. Why?'

'Well, Jacinta I have heard of, although she uses her maiden name. She's better known as Jacinta Scott-Thomas.'

'Like the actress, Kristin?'

'Yes, although there's no relationship there. Gossip maintains that she likes people to assume there is, though.'

Abi groaned: perfect City wife syndrome, with all its one-upmanship, petty rivalries and gossip, was obviously still alive and well in her absence. 'I'm basically trying to find out if Justin is in the country. A friend has business connections with him, and can't track him down.'

'A friend?'

Abi laughed. 'Ten out of ten for trying, Sasha, but I'm not one of those chattering executive types!'

Sasha laughed down the line. 'Which is one of the reasons we all had time for you, Abi. I'm so sorry about Luke, by the way. I don't think I ever had time to say. You disappeared so fast.'

117

'Thank you.' Not wanting to discuss Luke with someone who had probably worshipped the ground he walked on, and would never believe the truth about his acts of manipulation, Abi said, 'So, is Justin in the country?'

'I don't know, but I'll make a few enquiries for you.'

'Discreetly, and preferably without Simon ever knowing I've been in touch?'

'No problem.'

Cassandra couldn't sit still. Abi had been outside for what felt like ages. It probably hadn't been long at all, but it felt so foreign to let someone else sort out her problems.

Wincing as she mentally played back her conversation with Abi, Cassandra dug her red painted fingernails into her palms. Had she really been so openly callous about the place Abi loved? *No, you were worse than that. You were patronising.*

Cassandra ran a palm over the back of the purple velvet sofa, and watched as the colour changed slightly under the pressure of her hand. It was so much easier in the city. Everyone was independent. Here ... here it was all so interconnected. The rules were different, and she wasn't used to them.

Everyone knew everyone else, and people actually cared. It had been enough of a shock to discover that Justin could have been conning her; she wasn't prepared to accept that was definitely the case yet. To find that she was in a position where she'd have to air her dirty linen in public if she wanted to sort it all out was a humiliation she hadn't expected, and swallowing her pride was proving a bitter pill to take.

She strolled to the illustrator's desk. The second her eyes met the crazy, brightly coloured scene of toadstools and pixies, she found herself smiling. It was so joyous, so innocent. The eyes that would search out every hidden detail in that page of book when it was complete wouldn't have made any of the decisions she'd made, and in that moment, she found herself wishing away half of her life choices.

Cassandra was still trapped in the world of fairy castles and unicorns when Abi pushed the door to the gallery open. Sasha had called her back less than a minute after they'd hung up their original conversation, and suddenly the remaining wine in the bottle on the table didn't seem enough to help her through what she was going to have to tell Cassandra.

Sensing Abi wasn't sure how to say what needed to be said, Cassandra let her off the hook. 'Tell it to me straight. If we were in business suits in an office, in the days before you met your husband, then we wouldn't worry about upsetting each other, we'd just say what had to be said.'

Well, you wouldn't worry, Abi thought to herself, *but I would…*

'I didn't call my brother-in-law in the end. That is something I will leave for an absolute last resort. I called Luke's old PA. She didn't know Justin, but her assistant knows his wife, Jacinta.'

'Really?'

'Jacinta Scott-Thomas rules the company's executive wives with an iron rod apparently.'

'That's her.'

Abi patted the sofa, to indicate Cassandra should stop pacing and sit next to her. 'Right then, there's no easy way to say this. There was a promotion looming for Justin.'

'But?'

'But never a divorce. Not that the gossips have picked up on anyway.'

Cassandra went pale as she whispered, 'What?'

'If he does intend to leave his wife, he either hasn't told her yet, or he has, and Jacinta is having none of it. The word is, and I'm sorry to be the one to tell you, that Jacinta has always known Justin had a mistress. She has been working for some time to get her – you – sidelined.'

Cassandra's complexion went from pale to alabaster white as she whispered, 'She knew?'

'Someone always knows.'

'But Justin travelled a lot; he didn't *have* to be with anyone.'

'But he was always with you. I mean, you always went away with him.'

'Yes, but we never said a word to anyone.'

'Cassandra, love, I suspect that whatever is going on with you and Justin right now has more to do with Jacinta than he'll ever admit.'

'It was his wife who ruined my business?' Suddenly scared, Cassandra found herself shivering, 'It wasn't him, it was her – but how?'

'I haven't a clue. All I do know is that Justin *is* in the UK. He is currently taking some time to adjust to his new promotion by working from his home in Chelsea, where I suspect his wife has him under some sort of weird house arrest.' Abi paused to refill their glasses. 'If Sasha's assistant has the correct information, that is. We're relying on the often exaggerated words of the materialistic mafia here.'

Cassandra felt sick. 'I've been nothing more than a cliché mistress, haven't I? All those years thinking I was *the one*. That he was going to leave her for me… and I've been nothing. Nothing at all. And now? Now I'm less than nothing.'

Feeling decidedly awkward, Abi said, 'We don't know that. Justin may well love you. Jacinta, however, is another matter. By the sounds of things, she's not a woman to trifle with.'

Picking up her glass of wine, Cassandra downed it in one. 'That explanation would make some sort of sense at least. What better revenge than selling out the business connection I have with her husband?'

'It would also tally with what you said about Justin not having anything to gain from stealing the business from you.' Abi though had the feeling there was far more to it than that, and was pretty sure that if she met Justin she would hate him on sight.

'Do you think it was Jacinta behind this? She could have forged Justin's signature on the documents.'

Abi could see how badly Cassandra wanted her to join in with the idea of blaming Justin's wife, but she couldn't bring herself to give false hope. 'I haven't a clue, but I am convinced of two things.'

Cassandra felt as though her face was fixed in a permanent frown. 'Which are?'

'First, whether you love the seaside or hate it, right now you are better off down here. And second, you should smile more often.'

Cassandra wasn't sure how or why she'd allowed Abi to take her to meet her friend Stan. The last thing she felt like was meeting the pensioner and his fiancée, who she'd heard all about during the drive from Sennen to St Buryan. But Abi had been adamant that they'd cheer her up, and that she needed all the friends she could get right now.

Unable to argue with that final bit of logic, and knowing that at least it would put off the dreadful moment when she'd be alone and have no choice but to sort out everything Abi had discovered, Cassandra found herself sat on a very flowery sofa, next to a pair of the liveliest octogenarians she had ever met.

She began to wonder if she'd accidently strolled onto the set of a cosy television drama. Stan and Dora had accepted and welcomed her as Abi's new neighbour, without question. In less than three minutes after walking through the door, she was holding a steaming cup of tea plus a slice of Dora's homemade Victoria sponge cake, which was far too heavy on the cream and jam filling, and found herself marvelling at how brave the pensioners were at organising a wedding at their time of life.

Having been gently but persistently quizzed on her plans for number two Miners Row by Stan, who clearly cared a great deal about the home he'd left behind, not to mention the young woman who lived there, Cassandra found herself volunteering information about her own life without realising she was doing so.

By the time a new round of teas had been poured, Dora had declared she was going to concoct a plan to help Cassandra get her own back on Justin and Jacinta.

Shaking her head, Cassandra grinned at Abi. 'I think these two are a great loss to MI5. I've just shared more with them about my life tonight than I have with anyone in a decade!'

Abi exchanged a glance with Stan as Dora, as if on cue, said, 'Funny you should mention MI5, because once upon a time I did exactly that.'

Cassandra found herself laughing hard as Dora expanded her colourful claims, drawing them an image of her younger self going covertly beyond enemy lines in a way that was hilarious, even though it shouldn't have been. In seconds everyone, including Dora, who was musing out loud if she'd have been better off crawling under barbed wire with her current short blue rinse hairstyle rather than the brunette ponytail she'd had then, was laughing as well.

Cassandra was still chuckling when the doorbell rang, and Stan asked if she could answer it as Abi was doing the washing-up, and he and Dora didn't move at speed so late at night.

Happy to oblige, high on the lightness of unaccustomed laughter after days of worry and confusion, Cassandra threw open the door, still laughing.

'Wow, what a great laugh!'

Cassandra found herself looking up at a tall man, with closely shaved hair and a cute smile, and she instantly blushed. 'Oh, umm, thanks.'

'I'm Dan, I work here. Can I come in?'

'Sure.' Cassandra stood back to let him in, and was stunned to find herself flustered, before sternly telling herself that it was pure coincidence that Dan had found himself on the receiving end of one her best smiles. After all, she'd never smile like that at anyone other than Justin until she knew for sure he'd let her down – especially not at someone with tattoos.

Chapter Fourteen

Cassandra stood before the bathroom mirror berating her reflection. She had actually *blushed* in front of the sheltered housing care manager.

What the hell is happening to you? This is absolutely the worst possible time for you to go soft.

Her sexy black satin and lace night attire, which she'd bought in Truro to wear for Justin, seemed to be mocking her as she stared at her own image. Ripping it off, she pulled on the oversized T-shirt she'd also picked up in Truro. The intention had been to wear it when she was instructing Max what and where to decorate. Now it was going to be her nightshirt.

She tried to picture Justin finding her attractive in a grey T-shirt with a large picture of Little Miss Sunshine splashed across the front, but that leap of the imagination was too great. Such lack of effort on her part would have been interpreted as meaning she didn't care. 'And yet I'm expected to put up with his awful rainbow-striped boxer shorts!'

The thought that Dan wouldn't care what she wore floated through her mind, and caught her by surprise. Cassandra was sure that, whoever he was with, Dan would appreciate the voyage of physical discovery, regardless of the packaging...

She gave herself a shake. 'I'm just very tired. You are with Justin.'

Am I?

'And even if you aren't any more, Dan is very much not your type. He looks like a thug even if he isn't one.'

Not entirely believing what she was telling herself, Cassandra turned away from the mirror, unable to face her usual bedtime beauty care routine. With a quick brush of her newly shortened hair, she dived into bed and prayed for sleep to overtake her before her brain tried to tackle the problems she'd spent the last hour trying to stamp down. As far as she could tell, there were no answers to those problems anyway.

Waking with a jolt, Cassandra squinted towards the sunshine that was streaming through the window she'd forgotten to draw the curtains on the night before. Not only had she slept, but she'd had the most pleasant dream of her life – that she could remember anyway.

There had been laughter, and smiling, and the feeling of being cared for. A sense of being amongst friends...of a muscular tattooed arm holding her...

Cassandra's eyes landed on her laptop, and her brief sense of wellbeing dissolved as a shaft of panic clutched at her chest and reality elbowed its unwelcome way back in.

Closing her eyes again, Cassandra laid her palms over her knees and counted to ten. She badly wanted to believe that it was the evil wife and not the betraying lover who'd conned her.

An abrupt clatter broke through her thoughts, and

Cassandra shot out of bed, dragged on her jeans and threw a jacket over her nightshirt. Her heart thudded fast as she reached the bedroom door. *Was there someone downstairs? Justin?*

Another sound. There was definitely someone there.

Unable to stop the sense of hope that surged up inside her, she clattered down the stairs, and flung open the kitchen door, only to have it extinguished in the next second.

Max was there, examining her larder door, plane in hand. 'Sorry, lass, I thought you were up and out already. I didn't mean to startle you.'

Feeling extremely foolish, Cassandra dismissed Max's concern and, wondering how much Abi had told the decorator about her situation, mumbled something about having a lie-in, and dashed back upstairs.

Muttering, Cassandra cursed her foolishness. 'That's it. That is the *last* time I get my hopes up over Justin Smythe. No one makes a fool of me. No one.'

Picking up her phone, she read the time. And then she checked it again. It was almost ten o'clock in the morning. *Ten o'clock!* The last time she'd slept in that long she'd been a student. Unless you counted the leisurely mornings she and Justin had spent in many hotel beds across the world... *NO. No. Those occasions I am not counting. Not any more.*

Glad the thought of Justin made her feel cross enough to harden her heart enough to get moving, Cassandra began to formulate a plan for the day. She had no idea if any of it would help, but if she didn't do something positive she'd be lost. 'Time for some damage limitation!'

Within an hour Cassandra had an appointment to see Donald Clearer, had checked Max was happy for her to go out, and had written a thank you letter to Abi.

As she watched the envelope disappear through her neighbour's letter box, a sense of shame Cassandra was beginning to become familiar with washed over her. It had been a long time since she'd said thank you to anyone for putting themselves out for her. *But then*, she thought with a hint of self-pity, *it has been a long time since people were nice to me without an agenda. Which is partly my fault. Time to do something about that.*

Climbing into her hired car, Cassandra set off towards Penzance. She had an hour before meeting her solicitor. That was enough time to grab an espresso, find a good phone signal, pray for a healthy dose of good luck, and somehow rediscover a hell of a lot of the City girl backbone she'd been developing over the last eight years, but had been seriously squashed over the last seventy-two hours.

Dan surveyed Dora's living room with disbelief. It was stacked almost to hip height with full, and in some cases overflowing, cardboard boxes.

'I know you've been at Chalk Towers a while, Dora, but how did you accumulate this lot!'

Chuckling, Dora shrugged. 'Some of it came with me, but the rest sort of happened.'

'Where on earth are you and Stan going to find space to put it all? It's not like you have an attic to shove it in.'

'Apparently Stan's wife, Mary, was an avid collector

128

of everything and anything. He tells me he's used to clutter.'

'Which is just as well!' Dan picked up the nearest box, only to drop it straight back down again. 'What the hell is in here? Rocks?'

Dora fluttered her eyelashes. 'And there I was telling that lovely city girl that you were a strong young man.' She held open the door so Dan could carry her belongings down the landing to her new home with Stan. 'And yes, it *is* rocks. But they're very pretty rocks! I've collected them since I was a girl.'

'Oh, that's alright then!' As Dan stretched his arms around the first box that was to be transported to Dora's new life with more care, a grin played at the corner of his lips. Perhaps the city girl had asked after him. He hoped so, because she had formed a very definite part in his dreams last night.

***

Donald Clearer listened carefully to what Cassandra had to say. She'd told him about what Abi had found out; admitting it was largely speculation as she went. Then she'd described how she had spent the last half an hour on the telephone to as many of her employees – or ex-employees – as she could.

The only option she could see, Cassandra told Donald frankly, was total honesty. She'd explained everything, only stopping short of telling the tutors and governesses that Justin had been her lover for years.

The majority of the nannies, she told the lawyer, had appreciated her candour, and although most had already secured new work, they were now unlikely to sue her for wrongful dismissal. Many of them, she'd been touched to discover, had been horrified by what had happened on her behalf now they were in the picture.

Making a few notes, Donald said, 'If I may say so, Miss Henley-Pinkerton – sorry – Cassandra, you have been wise to speak openly to your staff. I wasn't sure you would.'

Not sure she liked what that said about the lawyer's first impression of her, Cassandra smiled sadly. 'You may well have been right before this week, but a lot has happened in the last few days.'

'Indeed it has, my dear. What I have to say now is, I'm afraid, going to be another bitter pill to swallow. I have taken the liberty of arranging tea to be served as soon as we're done to take the taste away a little. Are you ready?'

Cassandra nodded, clasping her hands together in her lap. She couldn't stop the feeling that it was going to take a lot more than a cup of tea to make this situation taste better.

'Whether it was Mr Smythe or Mrs Smythe, or possibly them both together, who acted against you, The Pinkerton Agency has gone. The rumours of a sale were false. You have been dismantled, not sold on.'

'But how?'

'I'll try and explain that in a minute. There is a glimmer of hope, albeit rather fog-bound. This illegal dissolving of the company is far better than a third party being involved because it means we can try and claw back the money you are entitled to, or take steps to reboot the agency. At this stage I am not sure which would be more cost effective. That decision has to be yours. You may not want to restart it now your personal situation is a little different.'

Cassandra felt her throat go dry. No words would form as she listened. Her brain was too busy trying to process what she was being told.

'Finally we are left with the question of the terrace on Miners Row.' Mr Clearer pulled a document from the pile on his desk. 'That I think we can say is yours. The payment was cash, and when Mr Smythe dealt with the estate agent in St Just, he operated under your name.'

Cassandra frowned. 'Are you telling me that Justin has destroyed my business, but at the same time bought me a house in Sennen?'

'That is very much what it looks like.'

'But that's crazy. Why would he do that?'

Smiling his thanks as his secretary arrived with the teapot and two cups, Mr Clearer said, 'My only guess at this time is that he feels guilty. He doesn't want you broke, Cassandra, but he also wants you as far away from London as possible. Let's face it, although the world runs from the Internet these days, it's much harder to save a business when you aren't there in person to make a lot of noise.'

'Guilty? After doing all that?'

Mr Clearer dunked a Rich Tea biscuit into his china cup. 'I've been a lawyer my whole working life, Cassandra, and the illogical things men and women do out of guilt never cease to astound me.'

Dan stood in the middle of Stan's living room and

131

surveyed the cardboard boxes which had been transposed from one flat lounge to the other. Sweat ran down his back as he took the offered glass of iced water, 'I hope you know what you're doing, Stan mate?'

The older man laughed. 'It is a bit like a postal depot in here, isn't it?'

'To put it mildly.' Dan laughed in return. There was something about this place. The hours were unconventional, there was often illness and sometimes death to deal with, but the optimism of Chalk Towers' residents was unlike anything Dan had come across before. Of all the things he'd done as a care worker, he'd never yet had to help arrange a pensioners' wedding, and he certainly hadn't expected to be helping two residents to shack up together.

'Is Max coming over later to help me move the furniture?'

'About half six apparently.' Stan winked mischievously. 'Hoping he'll bring Abi and her pretty new neighbour, are you?'

'Stan Abbey, I have no idea what you are talking about. Now, where do you want Dora's rock collection?'

'She has a rock collection?'

132

Chapter Fifteen

Cassandra laid out the large spreadsheet Donald Clearer had allowed her to print while she was at his office on the patio table.

The house in Sennen, once it was done up, would be worth almost as much as her place in London. It really was as if Justin had been trying to compensate her for being such a git.

Resting her elbows on the table in an uncharacteristically slovenly fashion, she took a collection of pens and began to mark in the names of the employees she had spoken to, their new or previous employers, and how receptive they had been to the thought of continuing to work for her should she reboot the business.

It had only taken a couple of minutes thought before she knew she didn't want to save the business in the form it had been. Any and all connections to Justin had to be terminated.

Cassandra sighed into her gin and tonic as her heart contracted. She had loved him. Did love him. *Perhaps I'm wrong? Perhaps he'll still come…*

After shaking her head sharply, she took a sip of the ice-cold liquid and was glad she'd purchased a stock of groceries on her way back from Penzance. The fact she was staying here for the foreseeable future had spurred her on to buy some home comforts.

'So,' she ran a red fingernail down the first column of the spreadsheet, 'of the twenty-five tutors I had on my books who weren't up for contract renewal in January, I have seven who haven't decided to stay in direct private employment or taken the opportunity to change direction.'

She ran her other hand absentmindedly across the wooden tabletop. 'This could do with sanding down.'

Cassandra sat up straighter. Where had that idea come from? 'I'm supposed to be concentrating on the future of my business, not contemplating the state of my garden furniture!'

The thought of Jo's shop floated into her mind's eye. The restorer's generous offer of future help made Cassandra smile. It would be good to have a project to discuss with her. Maybe restoring the tired patio set that had come with the house could be a good excuse to visit Jo?

Pulling her thoughts back to the task she was supposed to be tackling, Cassandra turned to a blank sheet of A4 paper in her notebook, and wrote 'To Do List'. Then she wrote the number 1 at the side of the paper, and hovered her pen next to it with no idea what to write first.

Closing her eyes, Cassandra tried to picture herself sitting at her study desk in her flat. She had always thought clearly there. 'You are sat on your usual leather chair. You are facing a staffing problem. How do you sort it out?'

Letting the thoughts form in her brain, Cassandra pictured herself in her favourite navy business suit, her hands dancing over her laptop's keyboard. The mere idea of indecision wouldn't have even dared knock at the front door of her flat, let alone entered her head. Breathing slowly, she immersed herself in the feelings of being in her small study with its minimalist shelves and cool grey walls, fixtures and fittings, and Cassandra wrote.

1. Ask Mr Clearer if he'd like to be the lawyer for my new business.
2. Decide what that new business is to be.
3. Write to each of my staff personally and reinforce what I have said to them on the phone.
4. Find Justin and discover the absolute truth.
5. Do up this house – sell it?
6. Get everything in writing.
7. Go back to London and start again.

As she wrote the last item on the list Cassandra sagged. The whole idea of starting all over again seemed a colossal task. When she'd launched the agency at the age of twenty-two she had felt unstoppable. In fact, now Cassandra thought about it, she had felt invincible even only a week ago. Then Justin had pulled the rug from under her feet, and in the space of a few hours everything she'd spent her life creating was lost.

Suddenly the life she lived felt worthless. *It was all a lie.*

Pouring another gin and tonic that was almost all gin, Cassandra tugged a jumper over her T-shirt as the sunshine began to fade. Her eyes fell on the dividing wall between her and Abi's gardens. The compassion of her neighbour almost made it worse.

Abi's story had been so much worse than her own. Justin hadn't died, nor had he treated her as if she was an embarrassment. He had taken her for a fool though, hadn't he? *Or had he?* Was it Jacinta? But if it was Jacinta, then why was Justin letting his wife destroy her?

Conscious that the gin was having more of an effect on her than was wise if she wanted to be able to function properly the following day, Cassandra tried her mobile phone once more.

'Answer, Justin! Answer, for goodness' sake.'

***

The sound of Abi arriving home made Max hang up the phone with a quick 'thank you' to the hotel receptionist, who'd patiently assured him that they would have roses and champagne waiting in the room he'd just booked.

'Max?'

'I'm in the kitchen.' He sat down hastily, not wanting her to know he'd been on the phone in case she worked out he'd been sorting an anniversary surprise. Getting up again as Abi walked in, Max automatically switched on the kettle.

'Actually, I think I'd rather have a glass of wine.'

'You alright, lass?'

Abi snuggled into Max's side, taking comfort in the feeling of safety he always projected. 'I'll be better in approximately four hours' time.'

'Four hours? That's eleven o'clock tonight.'

'Which is after Stan has arranged for me to Skype Sally.'

'Ah.' Max pulled an open bottle of wine from the fridge. 'How about you have wine and coffee? Dutch courage, but not too brave – if you see what I mean? Drunk in charge of a Skype link is probably some sort of weird criminal offence.'

Grateful for Max's attempts at lightening the mood, Abi sat down, soon cradling a cup in one palm and a glass in the other. 'Stan called as I walked home. What on earth am I going to say to Sally?'

'How about the truth?'

Abi smiled. 'So reassuring her, but with no promises of a guaranteed happy ever after?'

'It's all you can do. Tell Sally that you like Dora. That she isn't after her dad's money, and that Stan is happy. That's all true, isn't it?'

'Sally always manages to make me feel guilty that I'm in England and she's not.'

'No she doesn't, love. You make yourself feel guilty because you're here and she isn't. It was Sally's choice to take herself and the children to Australia. '

'I guess so.' Abi nodded. 'I'll still be glad when it's over. The next few hours are going to drag.'

'Then we should fill the time profitably, don't you think?' Max wiggled his eyebrows suggestively, making Abi laugh out loud.

'Max Pendale, are you trying to seduce me with comical facial expressions?'

'Yes.'

'OK!' Abi grabbed his arm, was about to tow him towards the stairs when there was a knock at the front door. 'On the other hand…'

'Typical.' Max let go of Abi and headed to the door. Listening out to see who it was, and to discover whether to get out more wine glasses or not, Abi heard the unmistakable sound of Beth and Jacob walking down the hallway.

'How lovely, we were just considering getting a takeaway, weren't we, Max?' Abi looked pointedly at her partner, hoping he'd get the hint that she wanted to talk to Beth alone about Skyping Sally, and would volunteer himself and Jacob to go and fetch the food.

Her real intention, which was to discover how her friend was feeling now that the doctor had confirmed her pregnancy and if she'd plucked up the courage to tell the head at her school, was thwarted as Jacob produced two bottles from behind his back: one of champagne, and one of elderflower cordial.

Max stared at the bottle of cordial, then Jacob, then Beth, and back again before the penny dropped. He took his best friend's hands. 'You're not?'

'I am!' Beth allowed herself to be engulfed by Max's arms. 'But I can't quite take it in.'

Abi beamed, and hugged Jacob. 'Oh my God, you really are going to be a daddy!'

The pizzas had been consumed, the champagne bottle was almost empty, and Beth had refused to drink any more elderflower-flavoured liquid ever again. Sat around the patio table in the back garden, the four friends chatted and laughed their way through the evening, until Abi thought her sides would ache.

'I can't believe you want me to be a godmother! Does

138

this mean I have to buy a magic wand and a tutu?'

'Ohh, I can picture you in a tutu. Pink and frilly presumably?'

'Max!' Beth smirked. 'You used to be such a good boy.'

'I am. Mostly.' He stretched his hand across the patio table and took Abi's palm in his. 'And I promise I will be the pillar of respectability when my little godchild is about.'

Cassandra took a step back from the bedroom window, and let silent tears run down her face. She knew she'd cried more since she'd got to Cornwall than she had in the whole of her life.

'Self-pitying bitch!' She took another mouthful of gin, and rested her back against the cool bedroom wall as she listened to the sound of happy conversation floating up through the open window from Abi's back garden.

Feeling utterly miserable, knowing that the only reason she didn't have the sort of friends you could chat over a glass of wine with was because she'd sacrificed every one of the few spare minutes she'd had to spend with Justin, Cassandra slammed the window closed, and stumbled downstairs into the back garden so she could use her phone.

She angrily called Justin's number and shoved the mobile to her ear. 'Oh, what a surprise! The bloody answerphone. Well, I *am* shocked. If you are listening to this, Justin Smythe, you had better pick up right now. Show me you have the tiniest ounce of decency in you.'

Cassandra paused, giving her erstwhile lover the chance to pick up. 'Oh well, there you go. Another surprise – not! No decency, then. Why should you have when you have sent me to the back of beyond, left me here, destroyed my business, and then gone and hidden behind your wife like a coward?'

She was shouting now, the words echoing around the narrow terraced garden, the gin that remained in the glass slopping over her hand. 'I gave up my whole life for you! I thought we were getting married. Married, you bastard! Have you *any* idea what you've done?'

Slumping onto the bench, Cassandra stopped shouting, her voice dropping as it became strangled with emotion. 'I don't understand. What did I do wrong? Why are you hurting me like this? I love you. Please…please, Justin. Please…' The sobbing started again then, and Cassandra found she couldn't stop.

Hanging up, she sat still for a few minutes before her brain registered she was cold. She ran back inside, banging the back door behind her, and picked up the remaining gin.

Abi, Max, Beth and Jacob stared at each other, each feeling awkward and embarrassed to have unexpectedly overheard the desperate, drunken pleas of the new inhabitant of Miners Row.

Chapter Sixteen

'Do you think we should go round?'

Max had been expecting Abi to ask the question, and already had his answer ready. 'No, lass. By the sounds of it Cassandra has had a skinful. We will check on her in the morning, though.'

Beth and Jacob, their excitement on hold for a second, looked questioningly at each other, before Beth said, 'I take it that was the new neighbour you've been worrying about?'

'Yes.' Feeling uncomfortable about talking about Cassandra behind her back, especially when she was evidently so distressed, Abi stood up. 'Come on, it's beginning to get chilly, let's go inside.'

Leaving the men outside to finish the lager they'd moved onto after the champagne, Beth sat at the kitchen table and failed to stifle a yawn. 'Seems as though we have far more to catch up on than I thought.'

'Max is right, isn't he; we shouldn't disturb Cassandra until she's sobered up.' Abi was as much talking to the kettle she was filling as she was to Beth. 'Her manner is rather unfortunate, but she sort of reminds me of how I used to be. I feel sorry for her.'

'It seems this Justin guy has taken her for a right old ride.'

'Cassandra helped me take the quilts down while

you and Jacob were out the other night. By the sound of things there's a very complicated knot that needs unpicking before she gets her life back.'

'Do you think she'll stay?'

Abi gave a hollow laugh. 'No. That's the only thing I'm sure of! She made it very clear that she was *not* a seaside person, not in the slightest. Anyway, more importantly, what did the head say?'

'Nothing. I mean … I haven't told her Yet.' Beth smiled. 'I know it sounds like I'm putting off the evil day, but I'm not. I just wanted to enjoy the moment with you guys and Jacob for a while. I've arranged a meeting with the head on Monday.'

Abi nodded. 'That makes sense. And you're feeling OK in general?'

'Fine. Bit queasy in the mornings, but nothing much else considering I'm three months gone already if the doctor has done her sums right. We have our first scan next week to make sure.'

'Wow! That's so soon.'

'I know. It's weird. I feel I've sort of missed out by not knowing before.'

'On the other hand, you haven't had to worry about it, and so you're probably more relaxed, and that has to be good for the baby.'

'That's what the doctor said.'

Abi headed to the calendar that hung on the larder door. 'If my calculations are right, I think you're due around New Year's Eve?'

Beth put her hand over her belly. 'I can't decide if that's good planning or bad planning. I suppose it gets all the present-giving for the year over in one month!'

'Planning? There's a joke!'

'Charming!' Beth stuck her tongue out, and checked her wristwatch. 'It's half ten already. What time are you Skyping Sally?'

'Oh, hell. In half an hour. I was having such a good time and then, what with Cassandra's outburst, I'd forgotten all about it,' Abi groaned. 'I wish I knew what to say.'

'I'll stay if you like. Moral support.'

'I appreciate the offer, but you're already yawning every time you think no one is watching. Jacob should be taking you home and tucking you up in bed.'

'Home.' Beth sighed. 'That's another problem, isn't it?'

'What do you mean?'

'I love my flat, but it's hardly big enough for a family.'

Abi frowned. 'You've got a little spare room.'

'Which would be good for a cot, and even a starter bed, but babies don't stay baby-sized for long. We'll have to move before we know it.'

'I hadn't thought that far in advance, and nor should you. Not yet. One step at a time. Go home and get some sleep.' Abi manoeuvred her friend to her feet. 'You're sleeping for two now after all.'

'Normally, I'd argue, but I'm wiped out. I've had a great evening though. Max will stay over, won't he?'

'I hope so. He's decorating next door from tomorrow anyway, so it makes sense for him to be here.'

'It makes sense for Max to be here anyway. You know, you two should really…'

Abi spoke firmly, holding her hand up with a gentle smile. 'In our own time, Beth. When we're ready.'

'Of course. Sorry.' Beth stood up as Jacob and Max came into the kitchen. 'I hope your neighbour is OK. It sounds like life on the other side of this wall is a hell of a lot more complicated than we first thought.'

Max was sure Abi hadn't slept much, if at all. The Skype call had not gone well. Although Abi had neither lost her temper nor burst into tears, Max was still silently seething over Sally's unfair behaviour.

Kissing the top of her head, Max lifted Abi up onto his lap as they sat on the sofa in the kitchen, the only relic of her time in Surrey. 'You feel like you've let Stan down, don't you?'

'Yes.'

'You haven't. Logically you know that, don't you?'

'Logically, yes.'

Abi felt exhausted. She'd replayed the Skype call over and over again all night. Perhaps it wouldn't have been so bad if it hadn't been a video call. Then at least she would have been spared the expression of disgust on Sally's face as she accused Abi of being the gold-digger, rather than Dora.

Sally's final words wouldn't stop echoing around her consciousness. *You must be delighted. This is the moment you've worked so hard to reach. The point when you find out all about Dad's finances – and not just his, but this wealthy woman he's got mixed up with. What's your next move, Abi? Become indispensable to her as well? Steal this Dora's home and money, hmmm?'*

Abi had been more hurt than shocked. When she had first got to know Stan she'd worried about Sally's reaction. Although it had been awkward for a while, they'd come to an understanding once Sally learned that Abi was never going to need Stan's money: Luke may have made Abi's life unhappy, but he'd also left her a fortune.

Now it was as if all the suppressed resentment Sally had ever felt towards her father's young friend had exploded in that one call. Abi hadn't had the chance to say that Dora was a lovely woman, or that she hoped Sally and her children would be at the wedding. Nor had she had the opportunity to say that she had major reservations herself, but the fact that Stan was happy was undeniable. The whole call had snowballed into a mass of Sally's bad feelings.

Max held her close. 'You do know it was Sally who was venting her guilt, don't you? She feels bad that you're here and she isn't. That's all.'

Abi laid her head on his shoulder. 'It was her decision to move away. I admire her for having the guts to take her children to a foreign country in search of a better life with no one to help her.'

'It was brave of her to do that. But that doesn't give her the right to talk to you like you've committed a crime by being kind to her father. I wish you'd let me Skype with you.'

'Next time I will.' Abi curled up into a ball on Max's lap. 'Don't you wish you could just run away to the hills sometimes?'

Max gave a gentle laugh. 'Frequently! And I'm sure

you'd like that too, wouldn't you, Sadie girl?'

Picking up on Abi's low spirits, the retriever had been sat at their feet since they arrived in the kitchen, and now she laid her chin on Max's lap.

'It's OK, Sadie; I'm a bit worried about telling Stan, that's all,' Abi gave the dog's fur a friendly ruffle, 'but I'll go and see him after work, and sort it all out. I expect you'd like to come with me, wouldn't you?'

Sadie obediently wagged her tail, making Abi smile at Max. 'We're sort of like a family, aren't we? The three of us, I mean.'

As soon as she'd said it, Abi wished she hadn't, in case Max saw it as a hint in the light of Beth's news, but instead her partner appeared delighted. 'Abi my darling, we are a family, and one day, perhaps our little tribe will grow.'

'It's just with Stan getting married, and Beth and Jacob moving towards parenthood, it all feels…I don't know, like…'

'Like we ought to rush and catch them up?'

'Yes.' Abi studied her boyfriend's face, trying to gauge whether he was experiencing the pressure as well, or just saying the right things because she was feeling fragile.

'I feel it too, but we have to do what's right for us, when it's right. Our circumstances are our own.'

Abi smiled. 'I love you, Mr Pendale.'

'And I love you too, but right now I have to face last night's other issue.'

'Oh God, I forgot for a moment! I bet Cassandra has the hangover from hell. I wonder if she's got any painkillers? Do you think we should go over to check on her together? I know you have a key, but I'm not sure what state you'll find her in this morning if you just walk in.'

'Good point. She could be collapsed half-naked on the sofa or something, and that's a sight I could live without seeing.' Reluctantly getting up from his comfortable position with Abi on the sofa, Max said, 'Do you have time to check on her with me?'

'I'm sure Beth will understand if I'm a few minutes late.' Abi picked up her bag, not sure she really wanted to find a half-naked Cassandra either, and searched through the cupboard where she kept medicines. 'I think I'll take her some hangover-busting tablets in case she needs them.'

Cassandra didn't dare move. Everything hurt. Inside and outside. Even opening and closing her eyelids made her ache. *Why am I on the sofa?*

With mortifying realisation, Cassandra relived the previous evening in a painful flashback. Ending with how she'd realised that her emotional rant down the phone had been rather louder than the whisper she had been convinced she was speaking in at the time, and with the stillness of the Cornish air, had probably been carried to the ears of her neighbour and friends.

She could picture Justin's face screwed up in disgust at how feeble she was for leaving a message on his machine. It was probably just as well she couldn't remember precisely what she'd said, but she certainly had a clear memory of pleading with him for answers.

147

Cassandra tried to sit up. Moving very slowly, she was unsure she'd ever be able to deal with the shame of it all when she heard a key in the front door.

'Hello?'

Bloody hell. 'Abi?' Cassandra could barely get the word out.

As her neighbour crouched in front of her, Cassandra wanted to disappear, wanted to yell at Abi to go away, wanted to run away and hide, but all of those things would have involved using more muscles than was advisable at that moment.

'Max is here to start sanding down the walls. Shall I ask him to come back in an hour?'

Cassandra tried to nod, but it felt as if her teeth were about to fall out, so she just murmured a tiny, 'Thank you.' The mere thought of having to listen to the scrape of sandpaper on the walls was enough to shrivel her insides.

'I'll sort it. Here, see if you can drink this.'

Cassandra hadn't noticed the glass of water Abi was holding. Her neighbour gently placed the glass in her hand, wrapping her palm and fingers around it, making sure it wasn't about to slop all over the floor.

'It's water with Alka-Seltzer in it. That'll kick the hangover.'

Once Abi had gone, Cassandra glanced at the glass, and her body instantly recoiled at the thought of consuming any sort of liquid. Straightening up so she could drink without spilling it all down her front, Cassandra wasn't sure what hurt more: her head or her pride.

After calling Beth to let her know that Max was coming to unlock the gallery that morning, and that she'd be there as soon as she could, Abi returned to Cassandra.

'Well done. I didn't think you'd have drunk that yet.'

'I didn't want to.' Cassandra took some comfort from the fact she was no longer slumped in a stupor – not on the outside anyway. 'But nor do I want to feel this awful all day.'

The lingering smell of juniper was strong enough for Abi to guess that Cassandra had continued knocking back the gin last night after they'd heard her in the garden. 'I'm ever so sorry, but I think you ought to know – we heard some of your conversation last night. We didn't mean to, but…'

'I know.' Cassandra felt herself go crimson. 'You must think me a fool.'

'No.' Abi's reply was so emphatic that Cassandra believed her sincerity. 'I think you've been hurt by someone you love.'

'I'm so embarrassed. I knew you and your friends were there, but it didn't register until later how much the sound travelled here.'

Abi smiled. 'You're used to the continual hum of noise in London. It takes some adjustment to get the hang of real silence.'

'You're probably right. Thank you.'

'Not at all. Now, without wishing to sound rude, you smell awful. Do you think you can make the stairs to the shower, or do you want some help?'

Cassandra looked so surprised that Abi laughed as she

went on, 'Well, you can't help me out at the gallery if you stink like a gin palace, can you?'

'I'm coming with you today?'

'I'm not leaving you here on your own. Go and get clean. There's no rush, I'm not in a hurry. Max is keeping an eye on the gallery, so we have as much time as we need.'

'But…'

'Oh, stop with your buts and go and get washed. I'll make a mug of tea.'

'Why?'

'Because I'm British, and it's what we do in a crisis.'

'No, I mean … why are you helping me?'

'I told you the other day, I suffer from chronic niceness syndrome. I tell you, it's a real pain in the arse sometimes. Now go and get clean before I have to tell you how much I hate the smell of gin and make you feel even worse.'

Chapter Seventeen

Dora fluttered her eyelashes at Dan as he arrived at her new front door with the final suitcase full of her clothes.

'Don't you flirt with that young man, Mrs Henry,' Stan called through from the kitchen.

'You can't even see me, what makes you think I'm flirting?'

'You're still breathing, aren't you, girl!' Stan called playfully as he walked into the room. 'Morning, Dan. Thanks for bringing this lot over.' Gesturing to the jungle of boxes and suitcases, he added, 'Although if you'd like to stay for a drink I can only offer you a perch on top of a box or a spot at the kitchen table.'

'I ought to be sorting out a feud between Lionel and Geoff in the living room. Apparently their usual pre-bed match last night turned into some form of ninja dominoes – but if you're offering a cuppa, then I'm happy to put off the evil hour for a bit.'

Dora laughed. 'Those two couldn't play their way out of a paper bag!'

'Just because they haven't yet built the casino you couldn't shark your way out of!' Stan wandered back into the kitchen followed by Dora and Dan. 'Perhaps you could explain to me and Dan how our flat is going to

151

absorb all this stuff.'

Chuckling, Dora said, 'It does appear to have expanded a bit since it was on my shelves. I think we'd better do a car boot sale.'

Dan raised an eyebrow. 'Without a car, or indeed any sort of boot?'

'That's it!' Dora smiled, 'Actually, I was thinking that I'd have a big sort-out and see if either the lovely Abi, Beth or Cassandra would like a few bits and pieces. The rest can go to charity.' She reached a hand across and laid it gently over Stan's. 'I have all I'll ever need in this lifetime.'

'You know,' Dan said as he picked up his cup, 'sometimes it is very difficult not to envy you two.'

'Us? With our wrinkles and the joint life expectancies of a fruit fly?'

'Yes. Your contentment is something many would envy.'

Dora studied the care manager's rugged face. 'Are you alright, Dan? I didn't have you down as discontented.'

'I'm not. Not at all.'

'But someone to be contented with wouldn't go amiss?'

'Do you know what, Dora, sometimes I wish you weren't quite so shrewd.' Dan turned to Stan, determined to change the subject. 'Do you know if your daughter and the children are coming for the wedding? If they are, then I won't get the cleaners to come and disinfect the hell out of Dora's flat until afterwards; that way they can stay there, and save on hotel money.'

Stan shook his head. 'I'll know later. Abi Skyped them

152

last night.' His smile faltered. 'I did think she would have phoned me by now to let me know how it went.'

'Won't she be at work?' Dan said. 'You told me she ran the Art and Sole place in Sennen.'

'She does. Maybe she'll call me afterwards.' Stan tried to keep the nagging doubts in his head hidden. He knew all too well that if Abi had good news she would have called him whether she was at work or not. 'I'll let you know about the flat. That's very kind of you, Dan.'

'Not at all.'

'Well, sort of kind.' Dora winked. 'I'm not sure about the insinuation that my home requires disinfecting by some sort of decontamination squad!'

'I hope you don't mind, but I had a look around while you were upstairs.'

Cassandra noticed Abi had gone around opening windows, releasing the stale air. 'Not at all.' Still moving slowly, she took the mug of tea her neighbour was holding out to her.

'I wasn't sure how you had your tea, so I've made it white without sugar for now.'

'Spot on. Thank you. Again.'

'No problem. Again.' Abi gestured around the kitchen, leaning against the old table. 'Actually, I have a confession to make.'

'You do?'

'This place; it's nothing like I imagined. Max told me I was worrying over nothing, but I couldn't help feeling protective of the place.'

Cassandra frowned. 'You've lost me.'

153

'I thought you'd ripped the heart out of the house. I saw the mess out the front and assumed you were taking your obvious unhappiness out on the house. But that isn't the case at all. I shouldn't have made assumptions based on my knowledge of the executive wives I knew in London.'

'It might have been the truth if I hadn't found that restorer's shop in Truro.' Cassandra winced as she sipped her tea and promptly burnt her lip. 'It was strange; the place seemed to have a calming, positive effect on me. And Jo was sympathetic to my situation.' She paused. 'Everyone I've met here has been. I've never come across anything like it before.'

Abi smiled. 'That's the first thing that hit me when I arrived. Friendly people – that, and how cold it is when it rains!'

'Rain? I thought it was supposed to be sunny all the time in Cornwall?'

'Let's say that's a small tourist board fib.'

Cassandra managed a weak grin. 'Everyone seems to be happy to have me here, even if they've never met me before. It's a bit weird.'

Abi smiled back. 'It takes a bit of getting used to.'

'You're telling me!'

'Not every person is lovely. The place has its fair share of misery guts and worse, but in comparison to London... let's just say that the air of grumpiness isn't so condensed.'

Cassandra laughed, and instantly regretted it. 'Ouch. Whatever happens, please don't let me drink gin ever ever ever *ever* again.'

154

'That's a no gin policy, then.'

'I'll even get my new solicitor to put it in writing!'

'Now that is serious!' Abi checked her watch. 'You ought to eat something. Can I get you some toast or cereal?'

Cassandra felt nausea rise in her throat. 'No thanks.'

'Not even some dry bread?'

'No, really. Thanks though.'

'Come on, then.'

'You weren't serious, were you? About me coming with you to the gallery? I have so much to do and, to be honest, I don't think I want to see anyone this morning.'

Abi spoke softly. 'I know, but if you don't come, you'll sit here and start over-thinking, and end up feeling sorry for yourself. If you come with me you won't have time.'

'You sound very sure about that. You don't even know me.'

'Been there, done that, bought the T-shirt, and wore it so much it went threadbare. And I have a feeling I understand something of what you're going through, although I'd never claim to know how you feel.'

Cassandra rose very carefully to her feet. 'You're right. I'll get a few things. I'd like to see the gallery in daylight anyway.'

As they walked down the hill towards the village, Abi tried to squash down the guilt that she hadn't phoned Stan yet about her failed conversation with Sally, and said to Cassandra, 'You know you liked Jo's shop?'

'Yes?'

'She runs classes on how to do up furniture. I know I've sort of mentioned it before, but why don't you do one? I know it's a bit more homespun than you're used to, but it could be fun.'

Cassandra stared across the horizon, so she didn't have to see Abi's expression. 'I don't come across like someone who is comfortable with homespun, do I?'

'No, hun, you don't.'

'And I'm not. At least, I wasn't, but do you know what, I think I might be now – a little bit, anyway. It's probably only a temporary reaction to everything that's happened, but I'm craving the chance to do something that isn't, ummm…'

'London?'

'Exactly. Something not London. I'll see what Jo offers when I go back to Truro. I'll just be looking, but maybe… Thanks, Abi. Thanks for everything.' Then, feeling rather awkward, Cassandra gave her neighbour the briefest of hugs. 'Thanks.'

Surprised to find that it wasn't Max but Jacob who was propped up on the stool behind the counter, a rival potter's catalogue open in front of him, Abi said, 'Hi, where's Max?'

'Gone to fetch some paint.' Jacob beamed as Cassandra walked in behind Abi. 'Hello. You must be Abi's new neighbour. I'm pleased to meet you.'

Cassandra took Jacob's outstretched hand. Taking in his short ponytail and casual clothes, she forced herself not to dismiss him completely, as she would instinctively have done in London.

'Jacob lives upstairs with Beth. He is Cornwall's very best potter.'

'Why thank you, Mrs Carter,' Jacob gave an exaggerated bow before pointing to the catalogue, 'but this guy is pretty good as well.'

'So what are you up to, sussing out the competition?'

'More assessing how good this guy's brochure is. I'm going to have to change my range once the baby comes, so I'm contemplating a new catalogue for my work.'

'Baby?' Cassandra blanched and her head thumped with a cruel reminder at the level of hangover she was suffering. 'You were in the garden with Abi last night?'

'Yes. We were celebrating the forthcoming arrival of the next generation.'

Mumbling, 'Congratulations,' Cassandra was extraordinarily grateful that Jacob hadn't mentioned her fraught phone call, although his curious expression told her he had definitely heard it. Making sure they continued to steer away from the subject, she asked, 'Do you have any ceramics here? I'd love to see them.'

'Not right now. I'm in the middle of swapping studios, so most of it's in storage. I can show you sometime if you're interested?'

'I'd love to. I'm doing up the house next door to Abi, and a few unique pieces of art would be most welcome.'

Jacob gave another mock bow. 'You are clearly a woman of taste.'

'That's a debatable point right now.' Cassandra gave the bemused potter a quick smile and wandered over to the newly hung watercolours, to divert the tears that were threatening.

Abi gave Jacob a barely perceptible shake of her head so that he didn't follow their visitor. Starting to unpack her art supplies for the day, she said, 'Hang on, Jacob, why do you need to change your range for when the baby comes?'

'I want to do my bit. Beth loves her job, so I don't think it's fair to ask her to give it up. Once her maternity leave is over I'll be a stay-at-home dad. That means doing as much of the complex arty stuff as possible now, before moving over to mugs, plates and all the quick stuff once he or she has arrived. I can do that at weekends and in the evenings.'

Abi laughed. 'I can see you at the potter's wheel with Jacob junior in a sling on your back.'

'Oh, that's a thought! I must get one of those.' Jacob grinned at the prospect as he climbed off the stool. 'Anyway, if you two beautiful young ladies will excuse me, I must go and see how much space there is at my new studio to store unworked clay.'

Once Jacob had gone, Abi gave Cassandra a proper tour of Serena Browne's watercolours, before asking, 'I'm not intending to hold you hostage or anything, but if you want to use the counter as a desk for a while, then feel free. Wi-Fi is good in here.'

Cassandra had been working at the counter for an hour. Three strong coffees had been drunk, a few visitors had come and gone, and as she sat, the artwork on the walls screaming out to be taken home with her and soft, calming music playing in the background, she found herself relaxing for only the second time since her feet had crossed the Tamar.

While Abi sat across the room, working quietly, ideas

for a new business venture had begun to form in Cassandra's head. *You can't. Don't be absurd. The idea is ludicrous. It's just because you are surrounded by so much creativity.* But the more she tried to dismiss the thought, the more the idea refused to leave her. She knew, as the comforting environment of the gallery soothed her troubled thoughts, that the moment she gathered enough courage, she'd be throwing the plan to save the remnants of her agency in the bin.

'Are you OK, Stan?'

Coming into the kitchen to take his leave of the old man, after helping Dora carry the things she wanted in the bedroom, Dan found Stan staring out of the window.

'Oh hello, Dan. Yes, thanks.'

Not convinced, Dan pointed to the seats around the kitchen table. 'Tell me.'

Stan crossed his arms. 'Seems to be all one-way traffic with the sharing where you're concerned, young man.'

Dan couldn't help a smile crossing his face. 'It's my job to care for you, Stan.' He tapped his identity badge. 'See, it says "Dan Millfield, care manager". I'm paid to be nosy.'

'Even if I don't want to talk about it?'

'That's your choice, naturally, but you look worried, which is not like you at all. However, I'm not going to make you talk, especially as I've left my portable torture kit in the office. You know where I am if you need me.'

Stan nodded. 'Sorry, Dan. I didn't mean to sound ungrateful.'

'You didn't.' Dan smiled. 'I'm very fond of you and

Dora. I want you to be happy. So if there's anything I can do, you will let me know, won't you?'

'Thank you.'

Dan acknowledged the thanks, and headed for the door to go and sort out the truculent domino players.

'Dan?'

'Yes.'

'Where was it? Afghanistan?'

A brief flash of something that could have been pain crossed over Dan's eyes. 'How did you know?'

'I'm eighty-nine, Dan. How do you think I know?'

Chapter Eighteen

Dan put the phone down and returned to the stack of emails that awaited his attention. The amount of paperwork associated with caring for the elderly was teetering on the insane. Still, at least some of the emails that required his time were of a more optimistic nature than the frequent requests he got for end of life or respite care.

The first he addressed was from the florist whom Stan and Dora had asked him to contact with quotes for four small bouquets of flowers. The next email concerned a sit down reception at the Queen's Hotel in Penzance, which Stan intended to take the form of the county's biggest ever cream tea.

Dan knew he should hand all this wedding administration over to Abi or Max, yet he felt strangely connected to Stan and Dora, and wanted to help them with their special day. He told himself very firmly that his keenness to stay involved was nothing to do with the fact he might get to see the aloof Cassandra again.

Checking his watch, Dan saw he had half an hour before Max was due to pop by the flats. With an effort of will he dislodged the image of the laughing blonde from his mind, and settled down to tackle as many of his emails as time allowed.

'I'm sorry this facility is currently full of residents, but if you'd like to put a name down on our waiting list…' he wrote. These were messages he hated sending, as they basically meant, 'If you'd like to hang on until one of my friends dies, then you can have their home.'

***

'Max. Thank you so much for doing this.'

'No problem at all.' Max passed Dan the dog lead he held in his hand as Sadie jumped out of the van, from where she'd been sat on the passenger seat, very much enjoying the view. 'This old girl could do with a proper walk, and as you said on the phone, Stan could probably do with some Sadie time.'

Dan stroked the retriever affectionately. 'I appreciate you telling me about the Skype call. I knew something must be wrong, but I had no idea what it was.'

Max, joining the fussing of Sadie, said, 'Abi hasn't told Stan how badly it went yet, but the fact she hasn't will have spoken volumes to him. You will make sure Stan understands that she had another problem to sort out this morning won't you?'

Dan frowned. 'Cassandra?' He didn't like to think of the woman who he'd caught in the midst of such joy being as sad as Max had described over the phone.

'Yes. Obviously it isn't my place to tell you what happened, but Abi is doing her best to make Cassandra feel better this morning and well, there is only so much Abi to go round. Plus, she feels guilty.'

'Why should she feel guilty that Sally was angry?'

Max smiled through a sigh. 'Because Abi, clever though

she otherwise is, believes that she is responsible for every trouble in the world.' Giving Sadie a 'see you later' pat, he fixed her lead in place, and handed it to Dan as he climbed back into his van. 'I'll collect her after work if that's OK?'

Dan looked at Sadie fondly. 'I'd change the rules and let Sadie live here if it was in my power. Thanks for finding the time to bring her, Max. Stan is in dire need of some canine support, I think. See you tonight.'

Hoping he was doing the right thing, and knowing his attempts to make Stan feel better were going to make him sad first, Dan let Sadie walk on ahead. She'd be able to find the way to her owner with her eyes shut.

Dora swung the front door open. 'Dan and Sadie! How wonderful, and talk about good timing. Stan is very subdued today. He's denying it, but I know something's up.'

'That's why I got Max to bring Sadie over. I got that impression as well. Would it be OK if I stole Stan away for a while, Dora? I think letting Sadie take him for a walk would be ideal for raising his spirits.'

'You're a good man, Dan. Thank you. Come on; let's put a smile on my daft ole boy's face.'

Dan wasn't sure he'd ever forget the expression on Stan's face when he caught sight of his faithful dog wagging her tail madly at him. 'Hello, gorgeous.' Greeting Sadie with an enthusiasm that was mutual, Stan looked at Dan suddenly. 'Max and Abi are alright, aren't they?'

'They are. Max is just rushed off his feet and wondered if you and I could do Sadie's lunchtime walk today. Sound OK with you?'

Stan was already taking his jacket off the coat hook by the door. 'Are you joking? Come on, girl, walk time!'

Giving Dora a kiss on her soft pink cheek, Stan regarded Dan. 'But if you think I'm talking to you while we walk, and not getting any information back in return, m'andsome, then you are in for a disappointment! Sadie and I are capable of chatting without you, you know.'

Not sure if she was confused or excited by the feeling of hopeful expectation that fluttered around her mind, Cassandra drove back to Truro, a borrowed CD of calming music from the gallery filling the car with gentle rhythms.

Talking to herself, something she noticed she'd been doing more and more since she'd arrived in the south-west, Cassandra started to formulate her afternoon.

'First, go to the garage and increase my car rental period by a month. Then go and see if Jo has a list of her courses – assuming her shop has the same effect on me as it did before. Get some lunch, and only then will I turn on my mobile phone.'

It had been a strange feeling not having her mobile on all morning. Cassandra couldn't remember a time when she hadn't had her phone on. This morning, however, she hadn't been able to face the sound of it beeping at her when she passed through a Wi-Fi zone, and more honestly, she knew that if, by any chance, Justin had responded to her pathetic dip into alcoholism, she didn't want to hear it.

Thanks to Abi, the hangover had cleared. Having soaked up the excess alcohol with way too much coffee,

Cassandra was determined to have one final try at calling Justin.

'But this time, you are going to be cold, businesslike, and in total control.'

Stan was smiling widely as, lead proudly in his hand, he and Sadie shuffled down the path towards the village of St Buryan. It felt a shame to disturb his joy at being outside with his faithful friend, but Dan could feel the weight of what Max had told him hanging over them, and he knew it wasn't going to go away.

Pointing to a bench a little further down the road, Dan said, 'Let's give Sadie a break, and take the weight off a minute.'

Stan did what he was told, and promptly turned to his human companion. 'So, what did Max tell you? I think I know Abi well enough to know she'd have called me earlier if she could. So?'

Dan laughed. 'There are no flies on you, are there?'

'Not one.' Stan was uncharacteristically serious. 'I assume my daughter wasn't delighted to hear from Abi, then?'

Staring out over the field before them, Dan said, 'I don't know the details, but from what I can gather, Sally was less than thrilled by Abi's attempt to reassure her. I think Abi was quite shaken by the incident, and doesn't know how to tell you without upsetting you. Although she would have phoned if another issue hadn't got in the way this morning.'

'Another issue?'

'She found Cassandra very upset this morning. Abi's

taken her under her wing.'

Stan looked proud. 'That's my Abi alright.' And then he sighed, 'Perhaps I was wrong asking Abi to help convince Sally I wasn't going mad, or that Dora wasn't after my money. Sally has never actually accused Abi of stealing me away, but I'm sure she must feel like that sometimes. I had hoped Sally would be able to give Dora and me her blessing, though.'

Sadie, her timing as perfect as ever, got to her feet and laid her chin on Stan's knee, making the old man smile. 'You understand, don't you, old thing.'

Dan, not knowing that there wasn't anything he could say to make things better, gazed into the retriever's big brown eyes. 'It was Afghanistan.'

'Cassandra! How wonderful.' Jo put down the sandpaper, and rubbed her palms free of dust on her paint-spattered apron. 'How goes the house renovation?'

Relieved that Jo remembered who she was, Cassandra's nerves calmed a little. 'At snail's pace sadly. A few work issues have been getting in the way.'

Jo pulled a sympathetic face. 'Real life's not all it's cracked up to be sometimes. Coffee?'

Cassandra was surprised. 'Are you sure you have time?' She drew closer to the workshop area of the shop, to see that Jo had been tackling a chest of drawers, which was midway between jumble sale junk and shabby chic perfection. 'It looks as if you have your hands full.'

'I've always got my hands full, but I always have time for a chat too!' Jo tilted her head towards a small table,

166

which looked out of place as it was so worn and knocked with age. It held a huddle of mugs. 'I don't suppose I could be cheeky and ask you to do the honours. Only instant today, I'm afraid, my machine is on the blink.'

Not commenting on how long it was since she'd last made a cup of coffee for someone else – and not sure she could actually remember the last time she'd drunk instant coffee – Cassandra happily put the kettle on.

Her first question had been answered. She still felt as though she fitted in this shop, as if she could be content here. Spooning what she hoped was the correct amount of granules into two mugs, Cassandra called over her shoulder, 'My friend Abi says you teach furniture restoration.'

A small shiver of something that could have been pleasure tripped up Cassandra's spine as she spoke. *My friend Abi. Was she a friend?* Cassandra hoped so, and there and then decided to make further amends for her previous behaviour.

'I most certainly run classes. Just small numbers of people at a time, although I also do one-to-one sessions for those who want home visits.'

'Home visits?'

'Some people like advice on doing up furniture that's too large to bring here. I had an amazing time tackling a kitchen dresser that needed a bit of TLC at Lanhydrock House near Bodmin a few years ago. Have you been there yet?'

'No.' Cassandra poured a little of the long-life milk that was on the table into Jo's cup, and decided to have her coffee black. 'I haven't heard of it.'

'Seriously?' Jo looked genuinely shocked. 'Then I feel a trip coming on. It's open to the public; fancy it?'

'I'd love to.' Cassandra couldn't keep the surprise from her voice. 'But – you hardly know me?'

'True. But it's early days yet.' Taking a sip of coffee, Jo pulled a face. 'I don't suppose you'd do me another favour?'

'Sure.'

'Nip out and get us a couple of takeout coffees. You are crap at making instant!'

'How long were you out there?'

Stan's respect for Dan was growing by the second. He had known his care manager had been in the forces, but he hadn't realised that Dan had been a Staff Sergeant Combat Medic in the specialist intensive care and hospital facilities at Camp Bastion, tending to a non-stop procession of wounded soldiers and civilians alike.

'Two years, on and off.' Dan closed his eyes for a brief moment, trying to dismiss the images of suffering that he'd lived with on a daily basis. 'How about you, Stan?'

'The Army as well. Five years. Korea for a while, but general duties on the whole.'

'Does it ever go away? The feeling you never did enough, I mean?'

Stan smiled at his friend. 'No, Dan. It never goes, but it fades, and becomes something that was rather than is. May I ask why you left?'

Dan exhaled slowly, and looked down at Sadie who had, thankfully, had enough of being still and wanted to get walking again. 'Looks like we're on our way again, Stan. Come on; let's enjoy the fresh air and the view.'

Cassandra hadn't felt offended by being asked to go and get coffee. It had only struck her once she was carrying the two takeout cups back to the shop, that if she'd been asked by anyone to fetch coffee for them in London, she'd have been seriously annoyed. She ran her own business for goodness' sake – or used to…

The rest of the afternoon had dissolved into laughter and a lesson in sanding wood.

'If Justin could see me now he'd never believe it!' Cassandra brushed a dusty hand through her hair, leaving a streak of light silver speckles in its wake. 'He'd never consider that I was capable of getting messy, let alone that I'd actually delight in physical work.'

Jo shrugged. 'Well, I don't know the ins and outs of your situation, but from what you've told me so far, this Justin seems a total shit. Leave him.'

Cassandra, sandpaper still in hand, felt her jaw drop. Partly from hearing Jo swear in her defence about a man she didn't know, and partly because it hadn't occurred to her that she had the power to do the leaving.

Surely he'd already left her? Except he hadn't really, had he? Justin had never said anything; he'd just stolen her life from her – and now, in this place, with Jo smiling and sticking up for her without asking any questions, Cassandra began to think that perhaps Justin had actually done her a favour.

'Are you alright, Cass, you've gone a funny colour?' Jo waved a packet of biscuits under Cassandra's nose.

'What? Oh, yes. Yes I'm fine.' Taking a cookie from the offered pack, Cassandra sat down on a chair that was patiently waiting for Jo's attention. She hadn't been called Cass since she'd been with the boyfriend before Justin. He'd been lovely, and thoughtful, and had always called her Cass. She'd given him up for Justin. *Idiot!* Quietly smiling, she added, 'I didn't expect to be fine. Not for a long time, but I am. Thank you.'

'Whatever are you thanking me for? I've made you work like a Trojan since you walked through the door.'

'Which is precisely what I needed.'

Jo glanced up from where she was dusting the top of a recently smoothed shelf. 'We have about an hour before I call it a day and throw you out onto the streets. Do you want to talk about Justin, or shall we file him as a waste of time and energy? I'm easy either way.'

Cassandra laughed. 'I take it you don't have a bloke in your life messing you about?'

'I don't have a bloke of any sort right now, but if I did, then I would not be letting him come between me and my smile.' Jo winked at Cassandra's astonished expression. 'You have a great smile and a lovely laugh. You should use them more often.'

An image of Dan telling her she had a great laugh flittered though Cassandra's memory as she muttered, 'Thank you, Jo. I...'

Cassandra got no further, for she was interrupted by the buzz of her phone.

'Oh, hell. Typical.' She stared at the ringing mobile in disbelief.

Jo frowned. 'You OK?'

'I don't know yet.' Cassandra felt her whole body stiffen as she answered the call, 'Justin. Good of you to bother to call. I think you owe me an explanation – a lot of explanations actually. And I should warn you, the answers to all the questions I am about to ask had better be phenomenally good.'

Chapter Nineteen

Getting the thumbs-up from Jo in recognition of the fact she was managing to retain a cool businesslike exterior, Cassandra mouthed 'I'm OK' to her new friend as Justin began to bluster excuses down the line.

Watching as Jo switched the shop sign to closed rather earlier than planned, before taking herself into the storeroom at the back of the shop, so that she could have some privacy, Cassandra waited for her erstwhile lover to stop talking long enough for her to get a word in edgeways.

'JUSTIN! Will you please shut up!'

Instantly, Justin's muddled ramble of apologies and excuses ceased.

Even though she felt churned up on the inside, Cassandra actually felt much calmer than she had expected to now Justin's phone call had finally arrived. Speaking each syllable deliberately, and with a subtle hint of menace of which she felt quite proud, Cassandra said, 'You have two minutes to explain why my business has disappeared, and, worse than that, why you lied to me. Start talking. Now.'

'Darling, it wasn't…'

'Justin, I am not your darling. The clock is ticking. Talk.'

She heard him draw a breath of surprise, before he began to speak even faster than before. 'First, the business; I was conned, as you well know. Secondly, I had no idea what was going on. I didn't knowingly lie to you at the time.'

'Implying that you are lying to me now? For fuck's sake, Justin, I rented out my flat for you, making myself effectively homeless for the next six months.' Cassandra looked at her free hand. She hadn't noticed she'd been deflecting her anger and hurt by digging her fingernails into the palms of her hands again. There was a neat line of crescent-shaped marks in her flesh.

Sounding shocked, he snapped, 'I phoned to find out if you were OK, and what was happening with the agency.'

'Is that so? Then perhaps we can start with you telling me what you intend to do to compensate myself and my staff for the hurt you've caused?'

'Me? I told you, I'm the one who's been conned.' Justin was getting angrier with each word. 'I had a sizeable financial interest in that company, and you've destroyed it.'

'*I've* destroyed it?' Cassandra's blood raced in her veins. 'Don't you dare blame this on me, when it was you who sent that bloody letter to everyone. It's very tiresome listening to you getting angry when you feel threatened or guilty, Justin. I bet you didn't even know you did that. Each time you know you're in the wrong you go all belligerent and defensive. It's so see-through.'

'That's low even by your standards! I do no such thing. And I haven't seen any bloody letters. All I know is that Crystal was instructed to send out end of business messages by *you*.'

'I wouldn't waste your breath arguing that one, Justin.' Cassandra's chest began to tighten. The knowledge that part of her still loved this man, however much she didn't want to, was beginning to batter its way through the defences she'd managed to create over the day. 'Justin, please. Will you bloody well man-up and tell me the truth. What happened to make you destroy my business? My whole life was caught up in the agency.'

As if sensing that perhaps Cassandra's heart hadn't hardened towards him as much as she'd first suggested, Justin softened his tone. 'I miss you, baby, but I've been put in an impossible position.'

'*You're* in an impossible position!? Have you been dumped in the middle of nowhere, with no friends, nowhere to go, no decent Wi-Fi connection, and no clue as to why the man you love has stolen your life?'

The sound of Justin swallowing carefully came down the line. 'I'm sorry about the Wi-Fi. I didn't know it was so bad there, but you can make friends, can't you? And the seaside is beautiful. I know how much you love it.'

If she'd been hurt before, that was nothing to how Cassandra felt as reality hit her between the eyes. 'You don't know me at all, do you?'

'What?'

'I can't stand the seaside. I have never liked it. Ever.'

'Oh.'

'Oh indeed.' Cassandra sucked in an audible breath. 'Now, your two minutes are up. Were you calling to tell me something worth hearing, like why Crystal is telling everyone you are in the States, when you clearly aren't?'

'I wouldn't be so sure about that!'

'Justin, you idiot, you're at Waterloo Station. I can hear an announcement for a train to Guildford playing in the background.'

Not commenting on being caught out, Justin said bluntly, 'Crystal and Jacinta are friends.'

'You don't say.' Cassandra felt an acute desire to end the conversation. It was all so obvious. Crystal had been lying to both of them. Playing them off against each other. *Of course she has.* Crystal had always hoped to grab Justin for herself, so what better way to get revenge on the mistress by siding with the wife? 'Justin, I have been waiting for you to call me for days. Why phone me now if you aren't going to say anything worth hearing?'

'I miss you, darling, and I got your call last night.'

Feeling her cheeks colour, Cassandra snapped, 'That was more gin-inspired than anything else. Perhaps you could at least tell me the name of your lawyer so that I can get mine to talk to him or her directly, so I can discover what we can do about your wife and PA. I presume that if you had no hand in it, then they are behind the letters?'

'What bloody lawyer? I'm your lawyer.'

'No, Justin, you *were* my lawyer, and then you stole from me. I could have you struck off. Arrested, even.'

'Don't be foolish. That would kill your reputation as much as mine.'

'What reputation? I don't have one worth saving thanks to the letters you had sent to my employees.'

'I told you! It was Jacinta. It wasn't me!'

'Actually, you didn't say it was Jacinta. First you denied all knowledge and blamed me. Then, just now, you said it was your PA. Make your mind up!' Pausing for breath, Cassandra added, 'Give me one good reason why I should believe you haven't planned all this with your wife, and that my being here isn't your way of getting me conveniently out of the way?'

'So Justin wasn't the one who crashed your company?' Abi wasn't convinced, but tried her best to sound objective as she talked to Cassandra across a wooden table in the Old Success' pub garden.

'That's what he said.' Cassandra took a sip from her cola. 'And the way he said it made me trust him.'

Trying to make sense of what she'd heard, Cassandra frowned into her meal. 'The remainder of the conversation with Justin was a load of non-answers and bluff, but the idea that I believed him capable of deceiving me seemed to floor him. He kept saying he'd been conned, and that it wasn't him, but someone else, possibly his wife, who had screwed up my business. All he was sure about was that I'd blocked him from being able to access the remaining company information, but he couldn't find out why without phoning me. But, of course, I'd only done that after I had discovered my business was being attacked.'

'This is all so complicated! So has Justin's silence has been because he was embarrassed about not escaping his marriage as quickly as he'd planned after he'd got you down here?'

'I think so – although I'm not one hundred per cent sure about anything.'

Abi pulled a face; the more she learned about Justin,

the less she'd be inclined to have faith in anything he said. 'The letters came from his company's office, didn't they? He must have known. I thought you said he'd signed them?'

Cassandra sighed as she looked around the pretty pub garden. She may have hated the beach, but her assessment of the seaside resort as a whole was very definitely taking an upturn. 'It has to have been his PA. She's been forging his signature with his permission for years.'

Stabbing a forkful of salad, Abi asked, 'And if it was Jacinta using the crush Crystal has on Justin to her advantage, what can you do? You've been cheating with her husband for years. This revenge is extreme, but if you fight it, everyone will know.'

Cassandra pushed the remaining food around her plate. 'That's why it's so clever. I'd take my hat off to her in different circumstances. No one knows about the affair. At least, I thought they didn't. My family certainly don't know. They all think I'm married to my work. They'd be so disappointed in me.'

Abi had been surprised by Cassandra already that day, mostly because of her invitation for a meal out to say a belated thank you for being so welcoming, but the fact she had family seemed even more surprising somehow. The slim blonde seemed so self-sufficient, so much a self-contained unit, that it was weird to associate her with parents. 'Are they in London too?'

'No, they don't approve of the city. They live in a village in Oxfordshire. My father is the local vicar.'

'No way!'

Cassandra smiled. 'It's OK, you're allowed to laugh. I

know it is an unlikely scenario.'

'It is! Sorry, but it is.'

'So you see why they don't know about Justin.'

'Quite.' Abi contemplated a solitary piece of chopped tomato before impaling it on her fork. 'Did Justin reveal what he was going to do next? I mean, forgive me if I seem nosy, but is he leaving his wife and coming to Cornwall, or not?'

Wishing that she hadn't been quite so sensible, and had added a shot of Bacardi to her cola, Cassandra said, 'Leaving his wife? I don't know, but I doubt it. Being thrown out by her, maybe; but I doubt Jacinta has made him suffer enough for her own satisfaction yet. As to whether Justin is coming to Cornwall, I'm not sure. He said he'd come down here to sort things out face to face soon.'

'Do you believe that?'

'I want to. Is that mad, after all this? Surely I should never want to lay eyes on Justin again?'

Abi gave her companion a compassionate smile. 'That very much depends on whether you love him or not. Do you?'

'I shouldn't.'

'But?'

'But, well, perhaps it's habit, but Justin has been part of my life for years. I don't feel I can give up on him until I know for sure what's going on. He made no sense during the phone call, contradicting himself every five minutes. Plus, he did the stupid huffy defensive thing he does when he's dug himself into a hole and isn't sure how to get out of it, but otherwise he seemed as confused as I am.'

'You think Justin wants to live with you down here?'

Cassandra's voice was small now, reminding Abi of a wounded animal. 'I don't know.'

'I'm sorry. I haven't met Justin, and I shouldn't judge, but I can't help but ask, do you want to be with someone who treats you like this?'

Cassandra knocked back a swig of cola as if she was drinking a tequila shot. 'It's been so long. Who else would want me? I'm soiled goods, as they used to say.'

Abi shook her head sharply. 'You are no such thing!'

'Well, at least I've made one decision today.'

'You have?'

'Yes, I'm not going to fight to reform the agency, I'm going to let it go. I will instruct my lawyer in the morning to take steps to dissolve the company – or what's left of it legally.'

'Are you sure? That's so brave after you started it from scratch. What will you do instead?'

'It's too soon to say, but it isn't going to be in London.'

Abi beamed. 'Well, I hope that whatever it is, it will keep you down here. You may not like the seaside very much, but I think it might like you!'

Chapter Twenty

Although she'd been a resident of Miners Row for two weeks now, Cassandra still hadn't got used to living in an environment where neighbours chatted to each other and where people wanted her company because they liked her, rather than because they needed her business acumen. 'Are you sure you want me to come?'

'*Everyone*, that's what Stan said. And *everyone* includes you.' Max opened the door to his van. 'Hop in. Abi is driving over with Beth and Jacob. We'll see them there.'

'But I'm not part of "everyone".' Still hanging back, Cassandra held her Gucci handbag in front of her like some sort of social shield.

Max grinned. 'If you think I'm letting you escape the horror of wedding planning when I have to sit through it, then you are very much mistaken. Anyway, Dora's issued a three-line whip. You're required to be there.'

'Why?'

'She wants your brains and beauty apparently.'

Cassandra, feeling two spots of pink heat on her cheeks, realised she had probably blushed more since her arrival in Cornwall than she had in the whole of her life. 'Dora said that?'

'Word for word.' Max got into the driver's seat and

patted the place next to him. 'Resistance is futile!'

Laughing, Cassandra obeyed. 'Is that so?'

'Yep.'

***

As the van pulled into the car park at the Queen's Hotel, Cassandra realised she had been so engrossed in exchanging plans and ideas for decorating the house with Max that she hadn't noticed they'd turned, not towards St Buryan and the Chalk Towers flats as she'd expected, but into Penzance.

'I thought we were going to see Stan and Dora?'

'This is where they're holding the wedding. It's only two weeks until the big day, so we're meeting here for an on-the-spot sort out. There is a surprising amount to do, even though it's only a little affair – I mean wedding.'

Cassandra smiled at Max as he moderated his language. 'It's OK, I'm not that sensitive. But thank you anyway.'

Not wanting to pursue that line of conversation, Max pointed to Jacob's car 'Looks like we're last to arrive.'

'How about Dora and Stan?'

'Dan drove them over earlier.'

As they walked towards the hotel's once grand entrance, now aged and weather-worn, Cassandra tried to make her voice sound curious rather than hopeful. 'Dan's here?'

'I expect so. You know what Stan and Dora are like. Letting them loose alone would be like sending two naughty schoolchildren out without a teacher! They'd probably march straight into the kitchen and sample the cakes at source.'

Cassandra had been expecting the inside of the hotel to be as worn as its exterior, but as soon as she stepped over the threshold she gasped in delight, her eyes scanning the perfectly proportioned marble columns and the crystal chandeliers. 'It's so beautiful.'

'It was Mary's, Stan's first wife's, favourite place.'

Cassandra raised her eyebrows. 'And Dora's alright with them getting married here?'

'Dora isn't in competition with Mary. She sees this as a mark of respect to her memory.'

Feeling embarrassed, Cassandra mumbled, 'Sorry. I wasn't thinking.' *Am I ever going to get used to this level of consideration?*

Abi, Beth, Stan and Dora sat in front of a large bay window, gazing out across the palm tree-lined promenade and beyond the sea wall to the sea itself, which, despite the calm of the summer's afternoon, was doing its best to see how far it could crash up the defences.

Seeing Max and Cassandra arrive, Abi got up and waved across the busy dining room. 'Jacob and Dan are getting some drinks at the bar, if you don't want champagne, Cassandra, then this is the right time to dash over and say so.'

'Are you kidding? Champagne is always welcome.' Trying not to feel as though she'd only been invited out of pity, Cassandra gave Dora and Stan her best smile, 'Thank you ever so much for inviting me. You're so generous.'

Dora chuckled. 'Don't you believe it. It's all a plot. We think Dan has the hots for you, so we thought we'd kick things off a bit.'

'Dora!' Abi and Beth exclaimed in unison, each stunned at Dora's bullish approach, which had sent Cassandra bright pink.

'Well, it's true,' Dora carried on regardless, 'you need to dump that Justin, and get some good people in your life. Even if they are bossy, interfering good people like me!'

It was impossible not to feel affection for the old lady whose mischievous eyes twinkled at her across the table. 'I appreciate the sentiment, Dora, but I suspect that I'm not Dan's type. And to be honest he isn't mine. I tend to avoid tattoos, I prefer a proper haircut and, if I'm honest, southerners. And even if Dan was my type, I'm not looking for anyone. Too much mess to sort out myself before I inflict my baggage on someone else.' Not wanting to think about all the worries that awaited her once she returned to the house, Cassandra said, 'Anyway, let's not worry about my car crash of a life today. This is all about you and Stan.'

Jacob arrived with a tray of glasses and a jug of orange juice, followed by a preoccupied-looking Dan holding a bucket of ice and a very good bottle of champagne, and Max, who was bringing up the rear with a pile of menus.

Sitting next to Beth with as big a smile as she could muster, suddenly Cassandra couldn't escape the feeling that she was somehow separate from everyone else at the table. It was as if she wasn't actually there, but was watching them all from the wrong end of a telescope.

As Jacob poured Beth a generous serving of orange juice, Cassandra tried not to peep at Dan, who had been creeping into her thoughts far more often than anyone with tattoos and a services haircut had any right to do. Instead she added her belated congratulations to Beth.

'Thank you. It's so exciting, although having to drink juice and not champers is a bit of a blow!'

Stan pushed a glass in Beth's direction. 'I'm sure you could have a very weak Buck's Fizz, Beth.'

'Do you think it would be OK?' She looked at Jacob, who shrugged. 'Isn't alcohol a total no-no when you're pregnant?'

Dan picked up the champagne bottle. 'Well, speaking with my medic's hat on, a tiny amount as it's a special occasion won't hurt. I can do the honours if you like.'

'Medic?' Cassandra was surprised; even though he was in care work, the last thing she'd seen him as was a doctor or nurse. Had she got Dan wrong as well? Were the people skills she had always been so proud of, her ability to read people's business requirements on sight, all been wrong?

'I was a medic in the forces. Midwifery wasn't exactly my field, but I've done the basics.'

Cassandra caught Dan's eye, and for a second she saw that Dora could be right. There was a flash of something that could have been interest. *A medic in the forces.* She couldn't help speculating on which one, and had to physically stop herself asking by clamping her lips together. The idea of Dan in uniform was doing things to her insides that were shockingly inappropriate for taking afternoon tea in a posh restaurant.

Oblivious to Cassandra's internal battle, Beth, who could see Jacob was about to launch a whole heap of baby-related questions at Dan, put her hand up in the nick of time. 'Before you drown Dan in a gory medical inquisition, Jacob, remember it is Stan and Dora's afternoon. We're supposed to be planning the perfect wedding.'

Jacob laughed. 'I hadn't said a thing.'

'No, you hadn't, but you were about to.'

The potter rolled his eyes. 'Stan, mate, you'll have to watch it. Live with them for five minutes and they can read your thoughts so well that speech is often rendered unnecessary!'

Opening his afternoon tea menu, Stan laughed. 'You don't have to tell me that, m'andsome. This old biddy had me sussed from the off!'

'Cheek!' Dora wagged a finger affectionately at her fiancé before she addressed the table as a whole. 'I don't know about you folk, but planning stuff makes me hungry. Do we go for a massive cream tea or do we go for the little bits of loads of different sorts of cakes on those three-tier stands, *Miss Marple* style?'

Cassandra read her own menu; her mouth was watering at the prospect, her stomach informing her she hadn't eaten since a slice of toast at breakfast. 'It's like being in Claridge's! Better, even; have you seen this list of cakes?'

Abi felt an unexpected flash of affection for her new neighbour. Two weeks ago she would have made the comparison sound inferior. There was no doubt that Cassandra had changed a great deal in a short time.

Beth's eyes were wide at the choices available. 'We ought to have a cream tea if this is to be a practice for your cream tea wedding reception, but…boy, I do like the sound of the tiramisu cake slices.'

'They do sound delicious.' Cassandra ran her polished fingernails down the food list. 'Although a cream tea sounds good. I've never had one.'

The shocked silence around the table was so abrupt you could have heard a pin drop. Stan shut his menu with a decisive slap, making them all jump. 'Never had a cream tea! That's it sorted then.'

'It is?' Cassandra took a sip from her perfectly cooled champagne.

'We will each have a single cream tea, just as a taste tester; plus we'll have two tiers of cakes to share between the eight of us. Agreed?'

A chorus of 'agreed' floated around the table.

'And,' Stan went on, raising his glass of bubbly in a toast, 'our new friend Cassandra will taste the scones first! Never had a cream tea! Honestly, girl, why didn't you say? We'd have sorted that gap in your life ages back.'

Cassandra found tears prickling at the corners of her eyes as every friendly eye fell on her, and glasses were raised with Stan's toast: 'To Cassandra, a proper welcome.'

As the friendly waitress took their food order, along with a request for two giant pots of tea to dilute the alcohol a fraction, Cassandra gazed at the people around the table. *Eight of us. Four couples.* She experienced a dart of sadness. *Except we're not. And whatever Dora says, I have nothing to offer Dan.* The spectre of Justin flared up again. Until she had got to the bottom of what was truly going on, then she would never be a part of any couple. Not with Justin, Dan, or anyone else for that matter.

Max raised a toast to the happy couple, and as everyone joined in, a ripple of laughter bounced around the table.

Cassandra looked at them all again. Her neighbour and her decorator, a care worker, a schoolteacher and a potter, a retired miner and, if Dora was to be believed, some sort of MI5 agent. And they'd taken her under their wing, even though she'd been far from friendly at first. Hostile even.

The sensation of being swamped began to grow again. Suddenly Cassandra wanted to run away, but if she left, all these good people would never understand why. *Even they must have a limit on how many times they'll be forgiving.*

Stan was on his feet now. 'Before the food arrives, I have one more favour to ask of you, my friends.'

All eyes were on Stan as he reached out and held Dora's hand. 'Sadly, my daughter Sally and my grandchildren, Pippa and Craig, are unable to make the trip from Australia to come to our wedding. And so, we would consider it a great honour if you, Abi, Beth and Cassandra, would be Dora's bridesmaids, and if you, Max, would be so kind as to be my best man? And could you, Jacob, be a stand-in father of the bride, and Dan our usher – with Sadie's expert help, naturally. Only if you'd all like to. There's no pressure if you don't fancy it.'

Cassandra felt her head begin to whirl. *Bridesmaid?* She hardly knew these people. This didn't make sense. People weren't this generous in real life – they just weren't. She felt as though she was drowning, albeit pleasantly, in sugar.

She could hear the others agreeing and glasses being raised again, but her hand wouldn't grip her glass, and her jaw wouldn't open. She was vaguely aware of Max asking Dan if he'd rather live out of Chalk Towers on his day off, rather than in the on-site flat, and Dan agreeing that an escape was on his list of things to tackle, when suddenly the world was covered in little dots of pale green light.

And then there was nothing.

Chapter Twenty-one

'Well, that's one way of getting to see Dan's medical skills in action.'

Behind closed eyelids, the world began to stop spinning, and Cassandra was vaguely aware that it was Dora speaking, but she felt too embarrassed to open her eyes to see for sure.

'Although personally I think I'd have gone for something less dramatic than swooning.'

Through the haze, Cassandra heard Stan respond to Dora, 'Rubbish, woman. You'd have done something madly overblown that needed his direct attention; possibly even the kiss of life.'

'True!' Dora chuckled. 'Ah, look. I saw an eyelid flutter.'

Cassandra could hear them clearly now. *Did I really faint?* She realised she was no longer sitting down, but was lying down. *Where? Am I still in the dining room, or has Dan carried me to a bed?*

Wishing she was back in the uncaring anonymity of London, where the chances of anyone even noticing she'd fainted in the first place were slim, Cassandra wanted to disappear. If a genie had arrived at that very moment, her first wish would have been to become invisible.

A smooth northern accent took command. 'Dora, Stan,

some space please.'

Dan. He was very close. Cassandra could feel his breath on her face. The fingers of one hand were stroking her fringe from her eyes, while the other picked up her wrist to feel her pulse. 'Cassandra?'

Part of her wanted to stay there and let him keep stroking her forehead, the other part wanted to open her eyes and stare straight into his. Her semi-conscious romantic notions were cut in half by Stan saying, 'How about we use a cream tea as smelling salts? We could waft clotted cream under her nose.'

Patience oozing from his tone, Dan said, 'Dora darling, Stan, I love you both dearly, but right now I'd like you to go and sit with your other guests, eat your tea, and sort out your wedding. I will care for Cassandra.'

The sound of a door closing told Cassandra that the pensioners had done what they were told, and a few seconds later, Dan whispered, 'It's OK, Cass, they've gone, you can come back now.'

'How did you know I wasn't still out for the count?' Cassandra opened her eyes, her face flushed with embarrassment that her deception had been so transparent.

'Experience.'

'At the risk of sounding clichéd, where am I?' Pulling herself up on her elbows, Cassandra looked around, to discover she wasn't lying on the four-poster bed of her dreams, but a rather worn beige sofa.

'The hotel staff room.'

Swinging her legs around so she could sit up, Cassandra buried her head in her palms. 'I don't think I've ever been so ashamed in my life! What must they all think of me?'

'They're worried. I'll go and tell them you're OK. Abi was all for calling an ambulance.'

'She was?'

'Dreadful overreaction, of course, but you gave her a fright when you hit the table. I suspect you'll have a bruise soon. Does it ache?'

'A bit.' Putting her hand to her forehead, she winced. 'Worse if I touch it.' Closing her eyes again, Cassandra muttered, 'I have caused nothing but trouble since I got here. They are good people, and they're all better off without me. Could you call me a taxi please? I'll get out of the way, and then you can eat your tea in peace.'

Dan got to his feet, a cloud of anger crossing his usually serene face. 'Will you sit down and stop feeling so bloody sorry for yourself.'

Cassandra sat down with a shocked thump. She had no chance to argue as Dan continued. 'You will sit there until I say otherwise. I am going to reassure your friends that you are alright, and then you and I are going for a gentle walk on the seafront.'

'But…'

'But nothing. Do what you're told for once.'

The July sunshine shimmered against her bare arms as the sea breeze played against her face, and messed up her hair.

'Here you go.' Dan pulled a foil-wrapped parcel from the small backpack he habitually carried with him and passed it to Cassandra.

Unwrapping it, Cassandra she found herself holding

her very first cream tea. Her mouth opened as she examined the scone heavily laden with clotted cream and jam, but then she closed it again. Every vestige of her businesswoman persona seemed to have deserted her. Nothing she could say would be adequate to thank the man sat next to her as he produced a flask of tea and two plastic mugs.

'Not exactly the bone china we would have had in the hotel, but I don't suppose there's anywhere better to experience your first cream tea than to eat it while looking out to sea.'

'I –'

'Why don't you just eat for a minute. Get some fuel inside you before you tell me what the hell is going on. I know I'm a total stranger, but as Dora, in her gloriously unsubtle way, is determined to get us together, then we might as well accept we're going to be thrown together at every opportunity she gets. So if we do the getting to know each other bit now, then we can tell her to forget it and admit defeat. Yes?'

Cassandra agreed; not sure if she felt sad or relieved that Dan had basically informed her he didn't find her attractive.

'So,' Dan launched in with his potted biography, 'I'm thirty-five, born and bred in Manchester. I was a medic in the Army until five years ago. My last posting was in the combat hospital in Camp Bastion, Afghanistan.'

Dan didn't so much as glimpse in her direction as he spoke. Cassandra wondered if it helped him to address the sea, as it crashed over Battery Rocks, rather than her. She was certainly regarding him with steadily increasing

194

respect as he went on.

'I should have stayed until the end. Until Britain pulled out of the region. I could have, but then…' He dragged a head over his shaved head as if in exasperation, but whether it was with her or himself, she wasn't sure, 'you get to the point when you think nothing will touch you, nothing will ever break through the hard shell you encase yourself in so that you don't go mad with grief for the soldiers and civilians that you treat every day, every night, all the time, endlessly…'

Not knowing if she was allowed, but instinct forcing her to anyway, Cassandra laid a hand on Dan's leg.

Although he glanced at it, Dan didn't remove her hand as he carried on talking, and Cassandra hoped he took some comfort in her touch. 'I didn't stay. People were in need of my help, but I didn't stay.'

Dan was quiet for some time. The silence between them was only punctuated by the seagulls overhead and the crash of waves. Eventually, Cassandra said, 'You are still caring for people though, Dan. Dora, Stan and the others would be lost without you. I haven't been there much, but it's obvious that you help make Chalk Towers a happy place.'

He turned to look straight into Cassandra's eyes. 'Even though I have tattoos, shave my head, and talk with a northern accent?'

Cassandra was mortified. 'You heard me?'

'I heard you.'

Swallowing her mouthful with difficulty, she asked, 'Then why are you even talking to me? I'm horrible.'

'You can be horrible. But anyone who has a laugh like

195

yours can't be bad through and through.' Dan gave Cassandra a half-smile. 'And anyway, I may have tattoos, a shaved head and a northern accent, but, on the other hand, you have extremely dubious taste in men, you're always saying the wrong thing, and you are so posh you could give the Queen a run for her money.'

Cassandra didn't know if she was supposed to laugh or get angry, but she was sure she wasn't able to argue. All she did know was that Dan hadn't moved her hand away. 'May I ask you a question now?'

'You can ask. I may not answer.'

'Fair enough.' Cassandra focused her gaze on a seagull that was hopping across the top of the sea wall opposite the bench upon which they were sitting, hopeful for scone crumbs. 'What happened to make you leave the Army?'

Dan paused. 'I'll consider answering that if you tell me why you're here. I've heard bits and pieces from Dora, but, with the best will in the world, she is not a reliable witness. Although,' Dan sounded thoughtful, 'I'm sure some of that is Dora lapsing back into her cover. She lived under it for so long after all.'

'Her cover?'

'Yes, you know. The eccentric daft biddy act. She was a spy. Didn't she tell you?'

'Well, yes, but…'

'You didn't believe her.' Dan nodded. 'I can see it would be a leap. OK, you talk first. Then I'll tell you my bit.'

Abi glanced out of the window again as she sank her teeth into a succulent slice of raspberry tart. She could see

196

Cassandra and Dan as they sat together on the opposite side of the road. Neither of them was looking at the other, they were staring out to sea. 'Do you think she's alright, Max?'

'I don't know, but I'm sure Dan can handle whatever Cassandra throws at him.'

Dora gave Abi a reassuring nod. 'Don't worry. It'll do them good to have some time to chat.'

Beth couldn't help but smile. 'You're a bit of a matchmaker, aren't you, Dora?'

'Yep.' Dora poured herself another cup of tea. 'When I was fourteen years old my mother told me that life was only worth living when you helped make other people happy. I believed her then, and I believe her now.'

'Which is why I love you.' Stan beamed at Dora. 'Don't worry, Beth; Dan is one of the good guys.'

'But is Cassandra one of the good girls? I can't decide.' Max laid a selection of cakes on the two empty plates at the table. 'Either way, we should save them some cake. Let's get on with the planning, shall we? I don't think Cassandra would like us talking about her.'

'I was right, then.' Dan packed the flask away and put his hand over Cassandra's, squeezed it, and then quickly let go as he stood up. 'You do have dubious taste in men.'

Cassandra got to her feet, wishing Dan had kept hold of her hand. 'I wish I could argue with that, but I can't. Even at the age of thirty I can't spot a good one.'

Dan had listened quietly to Cassandra's story, how she'd come to be in Cornwall, and why she felt like a fish out of water, and now, not commenting on her poor boyfriend-spotting, asked, 'And the fainting was because?'

'I'm not sure. I've never done it before'

'Have you been eating properly?'

Feeling a bit embarrassed by her lack of cooking skills, Cassandra shrugged. 'I don't tend to cook. I always ate out in London. I've not been starving myself though.'

'No proper meals. Just snacking?'

'I suppose so. I hadn't thought about it. I don't think it's a lack of good food though.' Cassandra shrugged. 'It's hard to explain. I was sat at the table, everyone was happy and laughing, and I felt so overwhelmed. So much has happened to me so fast in the last few weeks. Since I arrived in Sennen, I've been robbed of my pride, my business acumen and my self-confidence, along with my agency, and possibly my partner.'

'Possibly your partner?' Dan frowned. 'After everything you've told me, you're honestly still thinking of Justin in terms of being your partner?' He'd been about to take her hand, but now Dan gripped the handle of his rucksack instead.

Hating that it sounded as though she was making excuses, Cassandra said, 'Six years together is a long time. I have to hear what Justin has to say face to face.'

'You weren't together for six years.'

'We were. I told you, we –'

'No, Cassandra. You were together for a few hours every week and the occasional overnight stay for six years. Add it all together and it probably adds up to way less than a year.'

'How dare you! You know nothing about our situation at all. If it wasn't for Justin's vindictive wife I'd still have a home and a business to call my own.'

Then, Cassandra strode across the road in front of Dan and stalked back to the hotel, wishing she had brought her car with her so she could drive straight back to Miners Row on her own.

For a split second Dan was inclined to let her stride off on her own, and drive back to Chalk Towers, but somehow Cassandra had got under his skin. She was a challenge that needed tackling. *Bloody woman!* 'You didn't really want to know, then.'

Cassandra whirled round to see Dan was standing a few feet away from her, a let-down expression on his face, his hands on his hips.

'Know what?'

'Unbelievable. If the conversation doesn't revolve around you and your problems, then it's not important, is that it?' Not giving Cassandra a chance to bite back a reply, Dan went on, 'I've met plenty of women like you in the past. Usually the higher-ranking officers' wives. All materialistic and designer, who think they are oh-so in control of their lives. Then when something doesn't go their way for a change it's everyone else's fault but their own. Listen to yourself, woman!'

'I haven't blamed anyone!'

'Is that so? Not even Justin's *vindictive wife*! Who, may I remind you, you've been figuratively screwing over for years.'

Cassandra stared hard into Dan's blue eyes for a second, before spinning round and staring out to sea. She didn't want to acknowledge he was right. 'Thank you for your earlier consideration, Dan. I apologise again for

199

fainting and preventing you from enjoying your afternoon tea. Perhaps you should return to Stan and Dora. If you could pass on my apologies, I'll take a taxi back to the house.'

'Not bloody likely. You can come back inside and prove to me that you aren't a heartless bitch who turns her back on the first genuine offers of friendship she has received in six years.'

Cassandra tilted her chin up and pushed her shoulders back. Her false bravado crumbled as she abruptly remembered what it was that she'd asked him, then not waited for an answer.

Why Dan had left the army was obviously a subject he usually kept closed, and wouldn't normally volunteer information about. He had almost told her, and then she'd started thinking about Justin and Jacinta and what she'd lost, and forgotten all about it.

Her shoulders sagged. 'Oh, God! I'm sorry, Dan.' She glanced towards the bay window of the hotel. She could see Dora and Abi waving happily in her direction. Waving back, she risked a peek at Dan.

'I can't excuse my behaviour, but please, perhaps for now, could you accept that I feel a bit lost. I'm truly sorry for my outburst. If you feel you could trust me, then I would genuinely like to know why you left the army.'

Dan spent so long staring straight into her eyes that Cassandra started to feel awkward, until at last he said, 'Did you know that there are flecks of peppermint in your irises?'

Chapter Twenty-two

Cassandra wasn't sure if it was the glint in Dan's eyes, or the welcoming beckoning of the people on the other side of the hotel's bay window that convinced her that running away was not an option. Not only would it be cowardly, it would be rude, and from that point, there would be no going back to this benevolent group of people. With each step across the car park the truth came into sharper focus. She had one last chance to have friends here.

With a long exhalation of breath, Cassandra climbed the first of the stone steps up into the hotel, and turned to see if Dan was following her, or if he'd walked the other way, got in his car, and driven back to Chalk Towers.

'You thought I'd gone?'

'I wouldn't have blamed you.'

'I thought you were going to get a taxi?'

'So did I – when I was over there.' Cassandra pointed back across the road to the sea beyond.

'But now you're going back inside.' His eyes smiled, even if his mouth wasn't giving way.

'I don't want Abi to worry. She's been very good to me. They all have.'

Something about the relaxation of Dan's shoulders told Cassandra that, this time at least, she hadn't disappointed him. 'You should talk to the girls more. Share with them.

201

It'll make you feel better, I promise.'

It was all Cassandra could do not to cry as she was hit with a wave of concern and questions about her welfare when she sat back down at the round table. 'You saved us cake!'

'Of course we did,' Dora said. 'A nibble of scone out of a napkin is one thing, but you haven't had a real Cornish cream tea until you've eaten one off proper china plates, with tea from a teapot, and a silver teaspoon with which to ladle on your cream and jam.'

'Is that so?'

'Go on.' Stan pushed a small pot of cream and a glass pot of homemade strawberry jam in Cassandra's direction. 'That lot will keep your strength up. Are you sure you're OK, girl?'

While walking across the plush thickly carpeted floor, back towards the round table, Cassandra had decided to treat the next hour as if she was bringing a particularly tricky business meeting back to order. Now, however, with six sets of concerned eyes, and one set of eyes belonging to someone who had stared into her eyes so hard that they had picked up flecks of pale green, something that Justin had never done (unless he'd simply not thought to tell her), she couldn't do it.

'I'm fine now, thanks, Stan. It was my own fault. I haven't eaten much over the last day or two.' Aware of being watched, Cassandra hesitated as she approached the cream and jam. 'Umm, which is it first? I know Devon is one way and Cornwall is the other. But which is it?'

The chorus of 'jam first' made Cassandra burst out laughing, and the weight on her shoulders seemed to evaporate. There was no need to explain, no need to make a thing of what had just happened. She could just move on, a fact that was underlined for her as she caught sight of Dan out of the corner of her eye. There was no doubt he liked her laugh.

Max, who'd been watching Cassandra closely for signs of tension that might ruin the afternoon for Stan and Dora, also felt the atmosphere lighten as he said, 'Did you know that the original Cornish cream teas weren't on scones at all?'

'Really?' Beth chuckled. 'I assume this is pub quiz information?'

'Oh, do you like pub quizzes?' Cassandra asked as she tried to dollop half the over-generous portion of cream back off her silver spoon.

Abi answered before Max could. 'He is a general knowledge wizard! The only time I've ever been in a winning pub quiz team was with Max before we started going out together.'

Beth, who was now helping Cassandra scrape the cream off with her own spoon, laughed, 'Go on then, Max, I can see you're bursting to tell us. If cream teas weren't on scones, what were they on?'

Picking up his pint, Max said, 'Well, traditionally they were served on a Cornish split.'

Abi was trying not to giggle as Cassandra gave up trying to be delicate with her cream and pushed it off with her finger. 'I assume a Cornish split isn't a local gymnast with a weird fetish?' Cassandra asked.

Laughing at the Londoner's unexpected humour, Max explained, 'It's a sweetened white bread roll, a little bit like a plain brioche. The split would have been warmed slightly, and then buttered, before the jam and then cream – clotted, obviously – was added.'

'Buttered as well?' Cassandra could feel the delicious calories jumping directly onto her hips as she took her first mouthful.

'Yes. You can imagine how gorgeous they would have tasted, but also how many heart attacks must have come as a result of a lifelong addiction to them!'

Dora, who'd been unusually quiet as Cassandra tackled her first cream tea scone construction, watched with satisfaction as the city girl took her second bite. 'Better than Claridge's?'

'Ummm…' Unable to answer properly, Cassandra chewed her mouthful as Dan filled her teacup with tea, just as Jacob topped up her champagne flute with bubbly.

Once her mouth was empty, Cassandra looked at both of them. 'Are you trying to fatten me up?'

'Yes!'

Again the answer was unanimous, and Cassandra shrugged in defeat, before taking a deliberately massive bite of the scone to the rapturous applause of her comrades.

'Flecks of peppermint?'

'That's what the man said.' Cassandra passed Abi a drawing pin to stick a poster onto the gallery's notice board while Beth lounged on the sofa, rubbing the very first glimpses of her baby bump.

'That's a very strange reaction, considering he'd just been shouting at you.' Abi pushed the last pin into place and stepped down from the stool she'd been balanced on.

'To put it mildly.' Cassandra smiled, running a hand over her stomach in a similar fashion to Beth. 'I'm still stuffed from yesterday!'

Cassandra had been stood outside the gallery in time for Saturday morning opening, a bunch of flowers in one hand, and a packet of fudge in the other. Rather than actually say sorry again, she had taken the unusual step of sharing what had happened between her and Dan, and was pleasantly surprised to find having girlfriends to talk to was as much fun as he'd told her it would be.

'Well, I think it's romantic.' Beth stretched her legs outwards and then stood up. 'He obviously likes you. And you said he called you Cass?'

Abi propped the galleries front door open, relishing the brief hit of sunshine on her face. 'I must say, I think Cass suits you. It sounds more relaxed than Cassandra.'

'I like it too.' Cassandra felt another effortless smile cross her face. 'I always liked it, but Justin said it was common, so I didn't use it. I think I will from now on though. Cass it is.'

Beth rolled her eyes. 'I know I have never met Justin, but he sounds a total arse.'

Cass had to agree. 'And I've wasted quite enough time thinking about him. Time to start again.'

Abi tilted her head to one side, her yellow fringe flopping over her eyes. 'And does this new life include living by the seaside?'

Cass suddenly felt awkward. 'That's unlikely. I am happier down here than I was, thanks to you guys, but I think a road to Damascus experience beach-wise is probably pushing it.'

Beth was almost as stunned as Abi had been when Cass had first confessed she didn't like the seaside. 'You seriously don't like going to the beach?'

'Nope. But, I have to say, I do like Cornwall. I like the pub gardens and the little shops, and cream teas are every bit as good as Stan said they'd be, and this gallery is fantastic, but the beach – no. Sorry.'

Unlocking the till ready for the day, Beth said, 'Each to their own, I suppose. There's heaps of Cornwall that's inland. Personally, I love the villages a little way back from the coast best of all. Have you been to Zennor yet? If you go with Max though, I should warn you he'll tell you about the mermaid, and every other bit of Cornish village folklore he knows.'

'Which is a lot!' Abi added.

'That sounds quite nice actually, but I wouldn't expect Max to schlep around villages with me, especially as he's up to his elbows in painting my house.'

Abi beamed at her neighbour. 'You said "your house". I think that's the first time I've heard you sound happy about that.'

'I've done a lot of thinking since I spoke to Justin. And, if I'm honest, even more since yesterday afternoon.' The women were staring at her with such open curiosity that Cass couldn't help but laugh. 'Should we put the kettle on for this?'

Beth clapped. 'Now you're talking our language!'

As Beth pottered about making coffee and tea, Cass explained about her last trip to Jo's shop in Truro, and how much she loved her bumblebee furniture. 'I know it's a totally new – not to mention uncharacteristic – direction for me; and I have no idea if it'll work, or if once I discover how much hard work it is, I'll go off the idea, but I'd like to restore my own furniture.' Cass braced herself, half expecting Abi and Beth to laugh.

Abi however was clearly thrilled. 'I think that's a brilliant idea.'

'You don't think I'm being silly?'

'Not at all.' Abi took the mug of coffee Beth passed her. 'Are you going to do one of Jo's courses?'

'I'm on the waiting list. She is so booked up.'

'I don't doubt it.' Beth sipped her tea after blowing on the surface. 'Max has always held Jo's skills in high regard.'

Cass sat on the edge of the sofa next to Beth. 'A situation that is obviously mutual. It was Jo who recommended Max as a decorator to me before I knew he was Abi's partner.'

Turning the page of the large pad of paper propped on the easel, Abi asked, 'What are you going to tell your lawyer to do? You aren't going to let Justin or his wife just steal your life's work, are you?'

A little shamefaced, Cass said, 'To an extent I am. I did cheat with her husband.'

'I suppose so, but she has still stolen from you. Plus Justin lied to you – a lot. He never had any intention of divorcing her, did he?'

'I don't know.' Perching on the edge of the gallery sofa, Cass felt the wave of sadness she'd been keeping at bay edge closer. 'Justin said he was coming to talk to me in person, but I doubt I'm going to believe a single word he says any more.'

207

'Probably wise.' Abi's mind filled with a vision of her brother-in-law, whom they all referred to as Slimy Simon. He'd managed to lie with so much style that he had people believing Abi was insane with grief after Luke's death. He'd always come across as perfectly plausible.

Not wanting to let thoughts of Justin darken the mood, Cass said, 'I've decided to ask Donald, that's my lovely lawyer, to do a little more digging. Whatever the truth of the situation turns out to be, I want to make sure my staff are compensated, and see what recompense I can get.'

'But won't you lose a fortune?' Beth asked as she dunked a biscuit into her drink.

'I'll be out of pocket, but I still have a flat in London I'm renting out and, if Donald is correct, then number two Miners Row is mine and not Justin's.'

'Really?' Abi was openly surprised.

'Yes. Donald thinks it was guilt that made Justin put it in my name. Which sort of implies he knew what Jacinta was up to fairly early on, doesn't it?'

'It sure does.' Abi pulled a face. 'He probably thought he'd be able to use your place as a bolthole if Jacinta decided to take direct revenge on him as well.'

Cass groaned. 'That's the worst thing. The feeling that I've been such a fool. That Jacinta – or worse, Justin – are laughing at me. That I was merely a convenient mistress for him. That I wasn't loved at all.'

Beth put her arm around Cass's shoulders. 'Forgive me, but Justin is a shit. You're much better off with Dan.'

Cass blushed. 'Dan is lovely, but he could do much better than me. I'm sure he was just being kind yesterday. Everyone here is kind.'

Abi and Beth exchanged glances, before Abi said, 'For goodness' sake, woman; he noticed the flecks of peppermint in your eyes!'

Chapter Twenty-three

'At least if Dan and Cass do get together then they won't be so bull in a china shop about it as you and Jacob were!' Abi winked at Beth.

'We weren't that bad!' Beth stuck her tongue out at her friend. 'Jacob just knew a good thing when he saw it.'

Having had an unusually heavy trickle of customers and browsers in and out all morning, the gallery was empty now. Cass had left to see how Max was getting on some time ago, and Abi had been toying with the idea of sharing her concerns about her own future with Beth, but there hadn't been time. And with each new day now bringing with it an increase in the number of holidaymakers as the season crept towards mid-July, and the school summer holidays, the chance to talk before and after school was getting leaner outside of weekends.

'Talking of having a good thing,' Abi wasn't sure she should say anything, but the thought that she and Max would be stuck as they were for ever refused to go away, 'I don't suppose Max has said anything to you about me?'

Beth frowned, immediately concerned for her two best friends. 'You guys are alright, aren't you?'

'Oh yes. Great.' Abi glanced down at the pixie community she now had dancing around a maypole on the page in front of her. 'I'm probably being silly but, well…Max seems happy to keep things as they are now. He stays at my place sometimes, but I hardly ever go to his flat, and he hasn't mentioned moving in or anything else.'

'What? Never?' Beth, who'd known Max since primary school, could easily believe he'd got too comfortable to move things along. Or was too nervous to do so…

'Never. I thought perhaps, with you and Jacob expecting, and Stan and Dora showing it's never too late to find happiness with someone, he might have felt the urge to ask me if we should live together.'

'You could ask him.'

'No I couldn't.' Abi was adamant. 'One of the reasons I love Max so much is that he's old-fashioned. Chivalrous even. I think he'd hate it if I was the one who asked first. He'd see it as if I was hassling him, or worse, it would make him feel as though he'd failed me in some way.'

'Bloody Lucinda.' Beth, who had never forgiven Max's ex-wife for robbing him of so much of his confidence when it came to relationships, said. 'It was always going to be a slow job with Max, hun. He does love you. Truly he does.'

'I know. He's great, and I love him too. I'm probably just feeling a bit left behind.'

'You'll be great parents when the time comes.'

'Thanks, Beth, I hope you don't think I'm being all begrudging of you and Jacob, or Stan and Dora come to that. I'd hate you to think that. It's only that…'

'You'd like it to be you and Max as well.'

'Yes, I would.'

212

Beth was now even more determined than ever to make the anniversary of the gallery's opening in September a celebration of Abi's arrival in their lives. 'I'm sure Max feels the same. He needs to take his time, that's all. Maybe...' But Beth never got to share her thoughts with Abi, because a very jolly group of American tourists burst into the scene, with wide white-toothed smiles and, luckily, even wider wallets.

For the first time since she'd arrived in Cornwall, Cass thought, the time seemed to fly, rather than drag from minute to minute. Having been delighted with Max's progress – the kitchen and hallway already gleaming and fresh in an enlivening shade of butter yellow paint – she had occupied herself with rearranging the living room. Clearing out the few pieces of furniture that the previous occupants had left behind, she began to visualise how she'd like the room to look if she was to live there herself. 'Not that I'm going to, but if I like it, then there's more chance someone else will be willing to pay a decent price to stay here.'

A few happy hours later, Cass sat in her garden drinking a glass of Pinot while scrolling through websites for new sofas and an armchair. The dining and kitchen furniture she was determined to either get from Jo or restore herself. She looked at the bottle. Justin would not have approved of the supermarket label. The thought made her smile.

Every now and then the aroma of fresh paint hit her nostrils as a light breeze blew across the garden. Max had completed the decorating, and having declared the larder door a lost cause, had replaced it with a suitably in-keeping new one.

Torn between ordering a battered but gorgeous second-hand leather sofa and matching armchair, or a brand new sofa and a tartan wing-backed chair, Cass decided to order neither pair for a minute, but saved the pages so she could examine them at her leisure later. First she had a new plan to make. A proposal to present to Donald first thing on Monday morning.

Now Monday had arrived, Cass found herself unaccountably nervous. She'd never been unsure of her business actions before, but this was such a massive change of direction. In every possible way.

An image of her parents in their little village in Oxfordshire flitted through her mind. Would they be pleased? Proud of her, even? She hoped so. Building a few bridges in that direction was a task long overdue.

After parking her little hire car in the town car park in Penzance, Cass gripped her handbag and walked to Donald's offices with her throat dry and her palms sweaty. Trying to focus on the trip to Lanhydrock she was looking forward to that afternoon with Jo, Cass walked into the lawyer's domain.

Donald, to his credit, appeared neither shocked nor disapproving as she explained that, having spoken – at last – to Justin, and after a great deal of thought, she had decided not to keep her somewhat depleted business going.

'Did Mr Smythe shed any further light on the situation? Do you know who was behind what happened?'

Explaining as much as she understood from what

214

Justin had confessed about Crystal and Jacinta, Cass added, 'I suspect from what I learned that the rumoured US company trying to buy the business out is another fable. An extra twist of the knife from Mrs Smythe.'

'Or Ms Scott-Thomas, as she calls herself.' The lawyer nodded sagely. 'Letting you suppose there might be financial remuneration from the buyout, only to discover that it was a fake agreement?' Donald shuffled some papers on his desk. 'I was coming to that conclusion. I could find no trace of any agreement. This leaves us with old-fashioned revenge then.'

'I'm afraid so.'

'And you aren't going to fight it?'

Cass frowned. 'I've thought hard about this. For myself, I'd like to get some money back, but not as much as I'd like to make sure all my employees get the wages they are due, plus the redundancy they are legally entitled to. Is there a way to make Jacinta provide that? Seeing as she was the one who dissolved the agency via forgery.'

'There should be. However, you would have to press for a criminal prosecution, and Justin would have to testify that he did not order the signatures or the distribution on the letters of dismissal on your say-so.'

'Ah.' Cass felt the colour drain from her face. 'He'd never do that.'

Donald frowned. 'You think it would come down to Jacinta's word against yours?'

'Sadly, yes. I have got to see a rather different side of Justin since I came to Cornwall. I honestly don't think he has got the guts to stand against his wife.'

'I see.' Donald sat back in his chair. 'Do you have

215

enough personal funds to pay your ex-staff what they are due?'

Hoping it wouldn't come to that, but knowing it might, Cass inclined her head a fraction. 'If I sold my flat in London I could cover the wages and possibly nominal redundancies. If I have to.' She lifted up the delicate bone china cup of tea she'd been presented with on arrival. 'I have been very fortunate. Now that I've spoken to all my nannies again, and they have calmed down enough to see that I've been the victim of a fraud, not one of them has demanded anything of me beyond some help in finding re-employment – which I have gladly given. They all have, or will have when I have finished working through my list, the best references. I only employed the best in the first place.'

'What have you stated in the references as the reason for them seeking new employment?'

'Change of business circumstances. No blame has been laid at my staff's door. Let's face it, it's my fault. I'm not having them suffer because I was foolish enough to fall in love with the wrong man.'

The lawyer laid down his pen and studied his client carefully. 'Would you like me to pursue things further? I have to say, it appears you didn't need my help at all. You've worked it all out yourself.'

Donald's expression was full of pride, and Cassandra warmed to the lawyer even more.

'You've given me the confidence to know I was searching in the right places. Can we say that I'll pay you for services to date, and that if I decide to proceed with a criminal investigation, then I will be back in touch?'

Stretching a hand across his desk to shake Cass's,

Donald beamed. 'I wish you luck, Ms Cassandra Henley-Pinkerton.'

Cass put out her hand. 'Just Cass now, I think.'

With a twinkle in his eye, Donald shook her hand. 'I'd be glad to know how things work out for you, Cass. Good luck.'

'Would you like to take the guided tour, or would you prefer me to show you around and chat about each room as we go? Your call entirely.'

Cass stared at Lanhydrock House with awe. She'd been to dozens of ancestral homes, some private, some public, but this one seemed to be calling out to her. The geometrically pleasing building took her breath away as the sunlight bounced off the many conical decorations on the corners of the roof. Its precision appealed to her tidy business brain, and as she followed a smiling Jo up the main driveway towards the entrance, it was all Cass could do not to rush eagerly towards the grey-haired attendant who was standing by to take their tickets.

As she turned however, and surveyed the formal garden, Cass stopped walking. 'Wow.'

'Quite a view, isn't it?'

'And look at that gatehouse. Its turrets remind me of Maleficent's tiara.' Cass felt a tingle climb her spine as she took in the stunning free-standing folly-style gatehouse, behind which swept the Cornish countryside, with not a grain of sand or pebble in sight. It was the most beautiful view she'd ever seen. And she wanted to see more.

Jo regarded the gatehouse with a new, delighted

curiosity. 'I've never noticed that before, so it does. You wait until you see what it's like inside. It's quite a contradiction.'

'Really?'

'There was a fire here in 1881. It ripped through the original Jacobean house. What you can see now is the Victorian rebuild. The chap that had it rebuilt, Thomas Charles, was ahead of his time. Into modern gadgets – well, modern for then. At every available opportunity he had the latest technology installed here. You'll see as we go round.'

Cass regarded Jo with increased respect. 'I don't think I'm going to need an official guide. It'll be more relaxed going around on our own. If that's OK?'

Jo winked. 'I was sort of hoping you'd say that. Come on.'

It wasn't long before Cassandra saw what Jo had meant. The house was full of contradictions. The sparse nature of the servants' quarters, the luxury of the family rooms, and the comforts of 'upstairs' living made her think of Victorian Christmases despite the heat of the summer sun peeping through the chinks in the blinds, which had been drawn so the sunlight wouldn't fade the furniture.

The house had, what must have been at the time, state-of-the-art central heating, ovens and even fire hydrants. Jo was a wonderful guide. She moved neither too fast nor too slow, and her passion for what she saw was infectious.

'I'm dying to see the dresser you restored. Is it in the kitchen?'

'It is. Come on, let's go there next.' Weaving past the other tourists, Jo led Cass into the kitchens, and pointed with pride to a gigantic scrubbed oak dresser which was covered in pewter and bronze cooking pots and plates.

'That's incredible. You're so clever.' Cass peered a little closer to the furniture. 'Just checking for bumblebees.'

Jo laughed. 'You have no idea how tempted I was to pop one onto the back, but I chickened out in the end. I'd like them to employ me again one day.'

By the time they'd visited every room, Cass's head felt like it would explode with the variety of new sights, aromas and information, and her feet were killing her. 'I think I owe you a pot of tea.'

Sat at a table on the edge of the brightly coloured garden, Cass and Jo stared out across the view for a while before Jo said, 'The gardens go on for miles. You can walk along the river, or ramble in the woods forever if you wanted to.'

'And not a wave in sight.'

Jo smiled. 'I guess that's its only drawback. No seaside.'

Cass laughed. 'That is no drawback. I had no idea Cornwall was so beautiful. I'm not keen on the seaside itself, but this? This is incredible.'

Jo clapped in delight. 'You're not? Nor am I! Oh thank God, I was beginning to think I was the only freak in the factory! Well, that settles it.'

'Settles what?'

'How would you like to be my apprentice? Only part-time, but we could work out a deal. I could teach you all

219

the restoration techniques I know in return for a percentage on any interior design work that I can pass your way?'

Cass was stunned. 'How did you know I'd been toying with the idea of interior design?'

'I didn't! I just saw the way you looked around the house, and listened to your comments, observations and judgements as we moved from room to room. That's why I brought you here. I had a feeling you had a good eye. I wanted to check before I asked you. So, how about it?'

Chapter Twenty-four

This was not a great time to be stuck behind a tractor.

Cass eased her little car out a fraction to see if she could squeeze by, but it was hopeless. 'How quickly you've changed!'

It was only now there was a danger of being late for her appointment with Dora to view a wedding dress, that Cass realised how relaxed she'd become about time in the last few weeks.

She'd spent a gloriously indulgent morning with Jo, learning how to apply gel stain onto restored furniture to 'fix it', and chatting about her fledgling plans for a small interior design business, which she hoped would be more of an advisory service to begin with.

Cass smiled as she recalled how impressed Jo had been with her plans to approach the larger houses in the area and offer design and redecoration advice along the lines of 'Classic Designs for Busy People'.

Perhaps she'd get her own office in time, but for now she wanted to keep things very low key. Sort out the remains of The Pinkerton Agency first, and then think of the future.

Every morning she woke up now, Cass had the urge to pinch herself. Things like this didn't happen, did they? People you hardly know don't offer friendship, and they certainly don't offer job opportunities. Except they do; because they had, and it was happening.

'Maybe it all feels unlikely and extreme, because I spent so such a long period living in a competitive selfish environment? And let's face it, Mr Tractor, I was one of the most selfish and competitive. I'm damn sure I don't deserve all this luck.'

Cass had wanted to tell Dan about her new opportunity, but as she had no real reason to see him, and not wanting to tempt fate, she'd decided not to say anything. She badly wanted the chance to ask him about the Army again, not to mention to discover if he had forgiven her for being so ungrateful. But she was so afraid he wouldn't want to so much as catch a glimpse of her that she'd avoided Chalk Towers completely; telling herself she'd talk to Dan the moment she'd sorted out her mess with Justin once and for all. That way, at least she would have something positive to say.

Finally pulling up outside Abi's house, Cass could see that the others were waiting for her.

'I'm sorry I'm cutting it fine; the traffic between here and Truro was very tractor-ish today.'

'Not to worry.' Dora, who insisted that Cass was the right person to help her handle the very bossy woman who ran the boutique where she was intending to buy her wedding outfit, smiled at Max, who immediately ushered Sadie into the boot of Abi's estate car. Cass and Abi got in the back, while Max helped Dora into the passenger seat.

'Are you still sure you and Stan don't mind us bridesmaids picking our own dresses?' Abi leaned towards Dora as Max drove them to the village of Zennor.

'Of course we don't. It's not like you're all five years old and dying to play little princesses for the day!'

'Ugh!' Abi pulled a face. 'I didn't even do that when I was five! Thanks, Dora.'

Cass, who decided to keep to herself that she had been exactly the sort of five-year-old who'd dreamed of marrying a prince and living happily ever after, preferably in pink, said, 'I hadn't expected it to be such a big wedding. You and Stan must know a lot of people.'

'Stan's been here most of his life, and since he moved into Chalk Towers he has got back in touch with all of those folk from his past who are still with us. Then there's the whole of the Chalk Towers crew as well. We can't invite some and not others. It's worse than a primary school on that front. If we missed some folk out it would be Zimmer frames at dawn!'

Once again finding herself laughing in conjunction with Dora's infectious chuckle, Cass said, 'And you want me to come with you this afternoon because you're scared of the boutique woman? I don't buy that, Dora.'

Still chuckling, Dora swivelled around in her seat. 'You wait till you meet her. I think your city slicker persona might be required, so I come out with the outfit I want to have, rather than the one she wants me to have.'

'That woman looked terrifying!' Abi bit back the words *I wouldn't want her sorting out my wedding dress*.

As Cass and Dora disappeared into the confident clutches of the rather scary boutique owner, Abi felt an atmosphere of unspoken words fill the air between herself and Max.

223

'Do you know the story of the Zennor Mermaid?'

Suspecting that Max could feel the slight tension too, and wanted to deflect the situation, Abi stared at medieval church to their left. 'Only that there is a legend about a mermaid, I don't actually know the tale. Are you going to tell me one of your local stories?'

Slipping on Sadie's lead, and taking Abi's hand, Max began to take them past the quintessentially Cornish cottages. 'Once upon a time, many years ago, a mysterious beautiful lady occasionally attended the church behind us. Nobody knew who this richly dressed woman was, but her stunning appearance and her heartbreakingly lovely voice made her the focus of much village gossip and speculation.

'As you can imagine, a woman who – if it's possible – was even more gorgeous than you had no shortage of men trying to court her.'

Abi was immediately thankful that Max always knew how to break an awkward atmosphere. 'Even more lovely than me? Fancy that!'

'Don't get cocky, woman, especially when we have the breathtakingly lovely Sadie with us!'

Poking Max playfully in the ribs, Abi said, 'Go on, what happened next?'

'Well, one of the local young men, a handsome fella called Mathew Trewella –'

'Like you,' Abi interjected.

Max rolled his eyes at Abi as he carried on, 'With the best singing voice in the village…'

'Not like you after all then!'

Looking at the retriever, Max said, 'Sadie, lass, shall I

tell you the story instead?'

Abi laughed. 'OK, I'll be good. What did this devastatingly handsome singing guy do?'

'Young Mathew decided he wanted to find out everything he could about the enigmatic stranger, so after a church service one Sunday, encouraged by the fact that the lady had smiled at him, Mathew Trewella decided to follow her as she left the church and walked towards the cliffs.

'That was the last time anyone in Zennor saw Mathew. Years passed, and gradually the villagers forgot the young singer's unexplained disappearance. Then, one Sunday morning, a ship cast anchor off Pendower Cove, which is just over there.' Max paused to point backwards across the village towards the coastline. 'The captain of the ship was sitting on deck when he heard a beautiful voice calling to him from the sea. Peering into the water, he saw a beautiful mermaid, with her long, blonde hair flowing all around her.'

'Why are mermaids always blonde?' Abi flicked a hand through her own yellow hair.

Max pointed back at the equally golden Sadie. 'You'll have to ask Sadie that one. The secrets of blonde women are a mystery to me, lass. I never understand what they actually want.'

Sitting on a bench that gave them a view along the length of the little village towards the church, Abi took the opening he'd offered her, and, speaking carefully, said, 'Max, am I a mystery to you? Do you honestly have no idea what I want?'

Staring directly ahead at the medieval architecture,

225

Max took his time before replying, 'I think I do, but then...then, well, I know it isn't exactly dynamic of me, but I start to wonder if I've got it right. I was so wrong last time, and I love you so much more than I loved Lucinda. I couldn't stand it if I was mistaken again, and...'

Abi placed a hand over Max's giant fist as it gripped Sadie's lead. 'You haven't got it wrong.'

'Not even a little bit?'

'Not even a little bit.' Abi kissed him gently. 'I don't want to put pressure on you or anything, and we aren't Beth and Jacob, we aren't even Stan and Dora, but we *are* us.' Her forehead crinkled into a row of attractive lines as she added, 'Did that make any sense at all?'

'Perfect sense.'

'Good. All I am saying is, when you are ready, I am ready. Abi's House is *our* house, not *my* house. OK?'

Max's smile was so big it gave the impression that all his freckles had joined up. 'I love you so much, Abi Carter, and I promise I am almost ready.'

'Good. Now,' not wanting to push the point, or make Max feel he had to start making her promises there and then, Abi said, 'so what happened on the ship then?'

'The mermaid asked the captain if he would raise the anchor of his ship as it was resting upon the doorway of her house. She explained she was anxious to get back to her husband, Mathew, and her children. The beautiful stranger from the church was one of the daughters of Llyr, king of the ocean, and she was a mermaid called Morveren.

'The captain, who had heard many legends about

226

mermaids bringing bad luck to sailors, upped anchor and moved his ship as far away as he could. Some years later, however, he returned to Zennor and told the people of the village what had become of Mathew.'

Abi stood up and pointed at the church. 'So Mathew and the mermaid lived happily ever after under the sea?'

'So that version of the legend says.'

'There are other versions?'

'A few. That's the most popular one. Do you want to see her?'

'See her?'

'Sure, the image of Morveren is carved in wood in the church.'

'Come on then!' Abi towed Max after her in her hurry to take a glimpse at the Zennor Mermaid. 'You must tell Cass the story.'

'She does seem to be settling in at last. Do you think she'll stay at number two?'

Abi shrugged, 'I'm not at all sure. She isn't fond of the seafront, although she seems to be mellowing towards Cornwall itself. I don't think she'll decide anything until she has been able to cut all ties with Justin once and for all.'

'I hope she does stay.'

'You do?'

'Sure. I think she'd be a good neighbour for us.'

'For us?' Abi looked at Max hopefully.

'If you'll let me, I'd love to move in. Is that OK?'

Abi jumped up into Max's arms, leaving a bemused Sadie staring up at them. 'I thought you weren't ready yet?'

'Honestly, woman! That was a whole five or six minutes ago!'

'I have an ulterior motive.'

Dora poured the tea as Cass collected a carton of milk from her fridge.

'I would have been disappointed if you hadn't.' Cass regarded the old lady as she sat on the opposite side of the kitchen table at number two Miners Row. 'You wanted to talk to me about Justin, didn't you?'

'My goodness, if I'm that see-through these days, then it's just as well I retired!'

Cass, who was still unconvinced of Dora's past employment claims despite what Dan had said, smiled through a sigh. 'You have been so good to me, Dora, please don't think me ungrateful. But I feel I've come so far in the last few weeks, mostly thanks to you and Abi, and Jo over in Truro, and…'

'And now you have made peace with being here, the last thing you want to do is talk through what brought you to Cornwall in the first place.'

'Yes.'

'And yet, despite your evident skill with make-up, you aren't sleeping properly. You need to tie up the loose ends, Cass. You know you do, and if you would like me to help, I have an idea how to get that young man to give you what you're owed.'

'How much has Abi told you?'

'Nothing. Abi hates gossip, but I'm not daft, and you did say quite a lot when you came over the first time. Dan was worried about you after the cream tea as well. He spoke to Stan.'

Seeing a cloud pass over Cass's face, Dora quickly added, 'We aren't being nosy, nor are we all enjoying a good natter at your expense.'

'I know. It's just I'm not used to all this, and I feel bad about being so mean to Dan.'

'He didn't say you were mean.'

'Because he's a good guy. I, on the other hand, am not so nice. Although I'm learning. I hope.'

Taking a sip of tea, Dora regarded Cass with unexpected seriousness. 'Tell me from the beginning. If losing my husband at such an early age taught me anything, it's that life, whatever it throws at you, has to be faced sooner or later. And sooner is the better option.'

Chapter Twenty-five

Abi punched Beth's phone number in fast, desperate to tell her the good news. 'Guess what?'

'You OK, Abi? You sound out of breath.'

'I'm very alright.' Abi stretched out her bare legs, letting the sun bounce off her skin as she sat on the bench in her garden, watching Max and Sadie chasing each other as though they were both child and puppy.

'Tell me, woman!' Beth leaned back against the head of her bed, looking at the bridesmaid's dress she had picked for the wedding, hoping that her bump, which seemed to be getting bigger by the hour, wouldn't prevent her from putting it on.

'Max is moving in!'

'Oh, that's fantastic.' Beth felt a huge hit of relief. She'd begun to worry that Max might lose the best thing in his life through inaction and fear of reaction. 'I'm chuffed to bits for you. How did you pull that off? I bet you asked him and not the other way around.'

Abi laughed. 'Well, it was sort of the Zennor Mermaid's doing.'

'Excuse me?'

'I'd say it wasn't as weird at sounded, but that would be a lie.'

'I can imagine! So when's he moving in? Do you want

Jacob to help shift stuff? Is Max putting his flat on the market?'

'Hold on, Miss Bull in a China Shop! We only got back from Zennor ten minutes ago.'

'That's the second time you've called me that!'

'Well I can't think why!' Abi laughed again. 'We haven't discussed it beyond the fact that Max isn't planning to go back to sleep at the flat again.'

'We have to celebrate! Do you feel better about things now?'

'So much better. Suddenly I feel as though I have things to look forward to again.'

Beth, whose eyes were still running critically over her cornflower blue dress, said, 'So did Dora get fixed up with an outfit?'

'She did. I'm about to pop next door to hear all about it. I must admit, I'm glad I didn't go to the fitting. The boutique woman appeared to be every bit as daunting as Dora said she was, and all I did was see her open the shop door. I never even heard her speak.'

'I'm sure Cass could handle her though. Have you picked your wedding outfit yet?'

'I thought I'd go shopping tomorrow. You want to come?'

'I might need to. I got myself a dress last week. I happened to spot one in a charity shop in Penzance that I loved, but although it fitted then, it's already a bit of a stretch across the belly. Another few days and I may well explode out of it.'

Seeing Cass through the kitchen window at the back of

the house, Abi waved.

'Come on over, Dora can tell you about our wedding dress experience before I take her home.'

It felt strange hopping over the wall into her neighbour's garden. Only a few weeks ago that would have been an impossible scenario. 'Hey, Dora, sorry I didn't ask about the dress on the way home. I got a bit carried away by my own news.'

'Not a bit of it! You didn't just have news, you had extremely exciting news.' Dora appeared as happily thrilled by life as ever. 'Stan is going to be over the moon when I tell him Max is moving in. He always pictured you two with a family in Abi's House.'

'Thanks, Dora. Was the boutique woman as scary as you claimed?'

'Not so much scary as daunting. I'd met her on my own before. She came to Chalk Towers for the initial consultation, but this visit was decision time, fittings. I could have handled her, but sometimes it's helpful to have a friend onside, isn't it.'

'Absolutely.' Abi was pleased to see how comfortable Dora and Cass appeared to be in each other's company. She hoped they could be friends like she and Stan were. 'I'm dragging Beth bridesmaid shopping tomorrow, we wondered if you fancied it, Cass? You are a hell of a lot better at clothes than we are.'

'I'd love to!' Cass held up a mug as if to ask Abi if she'd like tea. 'It's crazy that you guys don't like clothes shopping when you both wear clothes so well.'

'Do we? Thanks.'

Dora nodded agreement to a top-up of tea. 'I thought

Beth already had a frock?'

'She did, but her bump is developing fast, and she doesn't think it will still fit by the wedding day.'

'Crumbs, do bumps grow that fast then?' Cass was scandalised. The idea of her body being beyond her own control disturbed her slightly.

'They can sometimes. My sister-in-law seemed to go from being flat-bellied to a pumpkin overnight, and then back again just as fast,' Abi said. 'What colour is your outfit, Dora?'

'Joyce, that's the boutique lady, says it's vanilla, I say it's cream. Honestly! As if anyone wants to walk down the aisle thinking they're dressed as an ice cream.'

Abi laughed. 'Is it a dress or a two-piece?'

'You'll have to wait and see.' Dora winked. 'But as it's cream, then it means any colour you girls go for will work.' She put down her cup. 'Anyway. Now you're here, Abi, I wondered if I could ask you a couple of questions about London.'

Noting the abrupt change of mood, Abi's mood went from carefree to uneasy in less than a second. Was this going to be about Sally?

'Cass tells me that the information she managed to get about Justin's dubious exploits came as much from your contacts in the City as from Mr Clearer.'

Not sure if she was relieved or not that Stan's daughter was not to be the topic of conversation, Abi said, 'I didn't do much. I gave my late husband's PA a call. She and her staff are well connected amongst the City types' wives.'

Dora looked solemn. 'I could do with checking a few

things with her. Would Luke's PA mind, do you think?'

'I suspect not; Sasha likes a bit of gossip. What are you up to, Dora?'

'As if I'd be up to anything!'

'Don't flutter those eyelashes at me! I'm not Stan.' Abi wasn't sure what to do. 'I can't give out her number without asking, but I could call Sasha and ask if she'd mind you talking to her.'

'Thank you, that would be very helpful.' Dora looked at Cass, who seemed rather less comfortable on her seat than she'd been before. 'Don't worry, lass, I'll be discreet. Despite all the evidence to the contrary I can be the soul of discretion.'

Cass held her mug of tea to her chest. 'The thing is, Dora, I'm just not sure I want to know. Well, I do want to know, but…' Cass took a deep breath. 'Look, if I can get my money back that would be incredible, but…Knowing in your heart you're been played as a fool is one thing, having to face it in big bold black and white letters is something else entirely.'

Abi came out of the kitchen's back door and stopped and watched at the vision before her. A smile spread all over her body as she saw Max quietly pottering in and out of Stan's old shed. Seeing him there, heaping together items for disposal and items to be saved, Abi had a sensation of feeling complete. They were Mary and Stan all over again.

Not wanting to disturb his contented sorting, but at the same time wanting to fling her arms around him, Abi decided to give Max a few more moments' uninterrupted

235

pleasure while she went upstairs to her bedroom – their bedroom – and emptied out two drawers in the chest nearest the bed. She wasn't entirely sure what she'd do with the winter jumpers she was evicting from their home so that Max had some space for his clothes, but that didn't matter. Smoothing out the lining paper at the bottom of each drawer, she pictured them full of her partner's things.

My partner? A glowing warmth started in Abi's chest and spread through her whole body. She'd always referred to Max as her boyfriend, but now, if they lived together, he had to be her partner. Not even the spectre of her conversation with Sally could dampen Abi's happiness as she plunged into the wardrobe to denude a handful of hangers of their contents so that Max's meagre collection of shirts could hang un-creased.

Finally, she went into the bathroom and, moving up her own towels on the heated rail, added two for Max.

Returning to the bedroom and glancing out of the window, Abi could see Sadie lying out in the sunshine next to the piles of shed stuff. Then Max came out of the shed. At some point he had pulled his shirt off, and stood now in his shorts and trainers, his ginger hair gleaming in the sun as his permanently tanned skin spoke of muscles honed from a life of hard work. It was all Abi could do not to yell out of the window for him to get up the bedroom right now. Instead she immersed herself in the view. *My partner in Abi's House*. Even in her childhood, when she'd fantasised that Abbey's House would one day be Abi's House, she hadn't dreamed she'd be this happy. It was all thanks to Stan.

Stan. 'I must call him.' Abi swallowed. 'Or maybe I should try and talk to Sally again, for Stan's sake?'

Checking her watch, Abi knew it was far too early to Skype Australia, but perhaps she could leave a message, saying all the things that she had wanted to say last time but hadn't had the opportunity.

Heading to the kitchen, she turned on her laptop, ignored all her work emails and switched on Skype, already mentally composing what she'd type. Much to her surprise, Abi found she had three missed calls from Sally, one only a few hours after their failed conversation.

'Perhaps she regretted her outburst?' Abi said to herself.

'Who did?' Max came in through the back door, and immediately passed his sun-warmed arms around Abi's shoulders.

'Sally.' Abi pointed at the screen. 'Do you think she wants to talk to me to say sorry or to rant further?'

'To say sorry, I expect.' Max kissed the top of her head. 'What are you doing on Skype anyway? They'll all be sound asleep over there.'

'I know, but I was feeling so happy, and it's all thanks to Stan. I know he hasn't said anything, but I know he is upset about Sally not approving of his wedding. I owe it to him to at least try and make it right.'

'Did I ever mention you were a good person, Abi Carter?'

'Once or twice.' Feeling bolstered by Max's support, Abi began to type. She wrote about Dora, about the wedding, about how much Stan would like his daughter's blessing. Abi didn't mention their last conversation; that wouldn't help anyone. At last she paused and said, 'What do you think? Too much? Not enough?'

Max scanned the message. 'Looks good to me. Hopefully she'll check her Skype when she wakes up. At least you've tried. That in itself will mean a lot to Stan.'

'Fingers crossed then.' Turning off the computer, Abi swivelled her desk chair around so she was eye to eye with Max's delicious torso. 'You looked so happy outside playing with your new shed.'

'Are you teasing me, Mrs Carter?'

'A bit.'

'You didn't mind, did you? It's such a jumble in there, and I know it's been on your list of things to sort out since you moved in, so I cracked on a bit.'

'I don't mind at all. And anyway, it isn't my shed, it's our shed. It made me happy to watch you.'

'Truly?'

'Truly.' Abi stood up and kissed Max. 'It made me think of the young Stan and how many happy hours he would have spent in his garden when he was with Mary here.'

'You little romantic, you.' Max kissed her gently, and then suddenly pulled back. 'What did you do with Cass and Dora? They aren't about to walk in or anything are they?'

'I left them in Cass's kitchen with Dora plotting revenge on Justin.'

'Then God help Justin!' Max ran a palm through Abi's hair.

'They've probably started plotting another celebration by now.'

'Celebration of what?'

'You moving in!'

'Oh, that!' Max smiled suggestively, before picking Abi up off the chair. 'Celebrating? Umm? Sounds a good idea to me.'

Chapter Twenty-six

'Abi gave me Sasha's number as a starting point, and I did some digging. It didn't take me long to work out how to unearth information about Jacinta or Justin's PA. There's always someone who knows more than you think they do. The trick is to find them.'

Dan stared solemnly across his desk at Dora, who was clutching a notebook and biro with the look of a private detective hot on the trail of something that smelt bad. 'You found out more than you expected?'

'Pretty much exactly what I expected, actually. It's all a bit textbook. Clichéd, even.'

'I think you should elaborate.' Dan, fighting off the urge to pour them two fingers of whisky each, crossed his arms and leaned back in his chair. 'Am I going to have to swear off my decision to never punch another human being ever again?'

Dora's professional expression slipped a fraction as her eyes drifted towards her care manager. 'You really do like Cass, don't you?'

'Whether I do or not is hardly the point. What I do not like is someone – anyone – being ripped off or taken for granted.'

Watching him in silence for a second, Dora took an unnecessary glance at her notebook, before saying, 'If my

241

assessment is correct…'

'Which it is?'

'I am ninety-nine per cent sure.'

'Tell me.'

Dora laid her notes down. 'It appears that Justin hasn't just been cheating on Jacinta, but on Cass as well. With Crystal.'

'Shit.'

'Quite.'

Dan felt the muscles in his arms twitch, unconsciously balling his hands into fists. He hadn't worked out why he felt so protective towards the high-maintenance city girl, but listening to Dora describe how Justin had started to see Crystal some time ago, prior to any plots against Cass, made him feel like he had to do something.

The care manager began to play his mobile phone between his fingers in agitation. 'When did Jacinta ask Crystal for help in starting this plot, or was it the other way around?'

Getting up from her chair, without waiting to see if Dan wanted one or not, Dora poured two cups of coffee from the machine in the corner of his office. 'I spoke to Sasha's assistant, who put me in touch with a friend of hers in the administration department of Family Values. It seems that Crystal rules that place with a rod of iron, and is neither liked nor respected. She has something of a reputation for being self-serving.'

Passing Dan his coffee, Dora went on, 'If Crystal had learned about Justin planning to buy a property in Cornwall – which as she is his PA is a reasonable

242

hypothesis – I suspect she feared he was leaving London, and therefore leaving her as well.'

'You think she was aware of his affair with Cass then?'

'Oh yes. I have no doubt, having spoken to the woman myself, that she would think it a victory to be the youngest of Justin's mistresses. To suddenly discover that perhaps he actually cared for Cassandra, rather than her just being someone to have sex with, made her even more jealous than she already was.

'I suspect that, until that moment of discovery, Crystal was having fun pulling the wool over two powerful women's eyes. Suddenly it must have dawned on her that, in fact, she was the one being used.'

Dan began to see what Dora was saying. 'So you think that Crystal decided to get her own back on Justin for humiliating her and on Cass for meaning more to him than she did by siding with his wife?'

'It would seem so.'

'How the devil did you find that out? You can hardly have asked her outright if she was sleeping with the boss.'

Dora laughed. 'When I first started working undercover, there was none of this wonderful bugging technology you have today. You merely had to ask the right questions as carefully as you could.'

'So you did just ask her?'

'No.' Dora grinned. 'I arranged for some old friends in London to meet with Sasha. They told her what sort of questions to ask, how to ask them, and showed her how to use a gadget or two.'

Dan shook his head, as much in disbelief as respect, at

Dora. 'Gadgets? I assume we are talking the latest in discreet Dictaphones here?'

'Something in that area, yes.'

'And Sasha did what was asked, just like that? Against a friend?'

'Friend?' Dora scoffed at the notion. 'There are no friends in the City. There are merely people who have the jobs you want. Sasha is a highly intelligent young woman. She would excel in a company like Family Values, and what's more, she is approachable, and knows the value of treating her staff with respect.'

'She did it because she wants Crystal's job?'

'I suspect it was partly ladder-climbing, but partly because I told her it would help Abi. I made sure that news of how Luke really treated her while they were married hit the gossip circuit; they're all feeling a bit guilty about that now. I took advantage of that and rubbed in how much it would please Abi if Sasha helped, as well as how much it would help her career-wise to uncover a company fraud.'

'You said that? A company fraud?' Dan was amazed. 'Dora, remind me never to piss you off!'

Dora chuckled. 'I'm not so hardnosed as I was, but I had to be when I was young. The things I saw...' She broke off and was quiet for a while; lost in memories that she tried hard *not* to remember.

Understanding all too well, Dan remained silent for a while, before pulling his friend back to the point.

'To clarify then, you got Sasha's number via Abi. Sasha was intrigued, and agreed to meet a friend of yours to learn how to use secret recording equipment. Then she took Crystal out, or met her by "accident" or something, and got her talking about work and men and such?'

'Pretty much. Obviously I sent Sasha lots of info on my ex-colleague, Harold his name is. I didn't want her thinking she was being set up on some weird stalker-type date. She was very keen, as I said. That girl is a loss to MI5!'

'Sounds like it!' Dan sipped from his coffee cup thoughtfully. 'Was it Crystal who approached Jacinta after fearing she was about to lose a wealthy lover, or was it Jacinta who found out about Cass and approached Crystal for help?'

'The latter. You should have heard the gloating in Crystal's voice. The pleasure she took from the fact that Jacinta had approached *her* for help.'

'You don't think Jacinta knew about Crystal's affair with Justin then?'

'No, I don't. I think Jacinta approached Crystal because she is his PA, and therefore the person with the most direct influence over her husband. We will be able to use Crystal's – and therefore Justin's – double deception as leverage against him. Justin is, as I feared, a worm of a man, and worse, a coward. He won't want his wife knowing about his second affair.'

Dan spoke with open hostility now. 'Justin was never going to be faithful to Cass, even if he did marry her. I can see it all now. Cass would gradually adopt Jacinta's role, and Crystal would replace Cass as chief mistress to brighten up his business trips. Until the next pretty young thing with blonde highlights and killer ambition took her place.'

Unable to argue with Dan's logic, Dora added, 'There's one other thing I discovered that is significant. Jacinta has significant shares in Family Values. And if Crystal's boasts to Sasha were truthful then Justin doesn't know about them. It seems that Jacinta was in no small part responsible for making sure her husband got the partnership in that firm in the first place. She pulled strings.'

'You make her sound like some sort of puppet master, or mistress I suppose.'

'That is precisely the impression I got. My understanding is that when Justin told Jacinta he was leaving her she threatened to take away his new job and everything that went with it if he divorced her.'

'How do you know all this, Dora?'

'Contacts, Dan my love!' Tapping the side of her nose with a sly wink, Dora added, 'I've had them for generations, and I have never cut them. One never knows when information might be required.'

'What I don't understand, is why a woman as obviously well connected as Jacinta would want to stay married to a creep like Justin, when she knows he's cheated on her at least once?'

'Status, pride, and money.'

'Oh, those things.' Dan ran a hand through his short hair. 'So, do we tell Cass, or not?'

'I didn't think it was supposed to rain down here!'

Cass sheltered under a shop awning after, with much giggling, the three friends discovered they couldn't all fit under Beth's massive umbrella.

Abi huddled closer to her friends. 'It was raining the first day I arrived. I was so cold. I felt so cheated that it wasn't hot. Luckily it is mostly sunny in the summer.' Hitching her bag further up her shoulder, wishing she'd worn a skirt and tights rather than her jeans, which were now clinging to her legs, unpleasantly damp, Abi pointed to the department store on the opposite side of Penzance's raised pavement. 'We've exhausted all possibilities for bridesmaids' dresses everywhere apart from in there, and that posh wedding boutique around the corner.'

Beth, who was beginning to feel tired and hungry, pointed towards the department store. 'Let's try there. It's close and has a coffee shop.'

Cass rolled her eyes. 'You two wouldn't be obsessed with taking coffee breaks, would you?'

'Yes.' Beth and Abi laughed as they spoke in unison.

'Although,' Beth added as they crossed the road, 'I'm more of a hot chocolate person these days. Can't get enough of them.'

Abi scanned the list of what was on each floor. 'And we're in luck, the cafe is on the same floor as the bridalwear. Trying on uncomfortable dresses can be rewarded immediately afterwards with hot chocolate. And if you're a good girl, Beth, I might let you have a biscuit.'

Regarding her new friends with affection, Cass couldn't help remember what Dan had said about how much fun it was to share things with other women. He'd been right. He'd been right about a lot of things. A flush of shame at how she'd initially behaved towards these people coloured her cheeks.

'You OK, Cass?' Abi asked as they boarded the first escalator.

'Fine, thanks. I've gone a bit hot after coming in from the rain, that's all.' Cass forced her expression into what she hoped would be a convincing smile. She hadn't told them what a strange shopping trip this was for her. She felt so out of her comfort zone. In the world she was used to, Cass only went to boutiques. She'd never ordered clothes off the peg, and the mere idea of going to a department store for wedding clothes was completely unthinkable.

'Over there.' Beth pointed towards a small section of wedding clothes in the far corner. 'We're bound to find three outfits that fit OK together.'

Cass was bemused. 'I've never shopped like this. How can you be so laid-back about it? Don't you want to look incredible at the wedding? You're both so pretty. It wouldn't take much to make you drop dead stunning for Stan and Dora's big day.' Realising that she'd sounded bossy, Cass added, 'If you wanted to, that is.'

'You're fairly pretty yourself.' Abi gave her a quick hug to show she hadn't taken offence. 'This is weird for you, isn't it?'

'Good weird, but yes. I haven't bought clothes from a department store since I was a student.' Cass winced as she heard the sound of her own voice. 'God, I'm such a bloody snob.'

Beth smiled. 'You were conditioned by the world you lived in. We'll have great fun bringing you down to our level.' She winked before pointing at a rack of variously coloured bridesmaids' dresses. 'Now go and hunt through that lot quickly, before my need for refreshment reaches boiling point!'

With three hot chocolates steaming before them on the table, and a packet of ginger biscuits propped in front of Beth, Cass couldn't stop marvelling at the fact they'd all found something to wear.

'If the girls from my old agency could see me now they'd never believe it. They'd think you'd drugged my drink or something.'

'You like your dress though, don't you?' Abi hoped so, she adored her own snug-fitting, tastefully low-cut dress, which was almost identical to Cass's.

'I love it. I love them all.' Cass looked down at the oversized carrier bag laid carefully over the fourth chair at their cafe table. Inside it were three mocha-coloured matt silk bridesmaid dresses. Hers and Abi's were sleeveless, with neat straight skirts that stopped short of sweeping the floor, whereas Beth's was a two-piece, with a forgiving panelled skirt that had plenty of 'baby-give' in it, and a short-sleeved top that flattered her pregnancy-enhanced breasts to perfection.

'That's good. I think Dora will like them as well.' Beth crunched into another biscuit and, uncaring of where she was, kicked her shoes off. 'It's such a shame Sally is being so difficult. Even if she can't be here, she could have joined us via Skype or something.'

Abi slapped her forehead dramatically. 'I totally forgot to tell you, what with Max moving in and buying the dresses and everything. I sent a new Skype message to Sally explaining the situation properly, and she replied.'

'Is she coming over?' Beth cupped her hot chocolate as if it was freezing outside and not just a damp summer's day.

'No, but she has definitely mellowed towards the idea of the marriage.'

'Well, that's something.' Cass smiled. 'Dora was telling me that Stan has been very low about it.'

'Max said the same. Even a walk with Sadie only cheered him up for a while. I'm going over this evening to tell him the news in person and to Skype Sally with him.'

Beth was about to ask about how Stan's grandchildren had taken the news, when Cass's mobile burst into life.

'Oh, it's Dora. Probably checking up on our dress status.' Cass answered, 'Hello, Dora, you caught us toasting our successful dress shopping with a hot beverage.'

Abi and Beth exchanged glances as a cloud passed over Cass's face.

'You want all my handwritten correspondence about the agency...and with Justin?...Well, yes, but why do you want it?'

Cass talked for a long time, while Abi and Beth looked at each other, not sure whether they should stay there or leave their new friend in privacy.

Eventually, Cass hung up.

'Are you alright?' Abi asked cautiously.

'I'm not sure. Dora says she has found out what happened to my agency. She wants all my business records and any handwritten letters I have from Justin.'

Beth was confused. 'Why would she want those?'

'I haven't a clue. She's sending Dan over for them this

evening. Apparently it is very important. Dora wants to make sure all her facts are right, I suppose.'

'Right for what?' Abi frowned.

'I'm not entirely sure about that either. And why does she have to send Dan to fetch them. You could take them when you see Stan later, couldn't you, Abi, if you didn't mind of course?'

Beth put down her empty cup. 'Well, that bit is obvious.'

'It is?'

'Dora is desperate to get you on your own with Dan again.'

'Dan?'

'Yes, Dan. You know, tall bloke, tattoos, cute. Saved you at the hotel the other day.'

Cass blushed, awareness of her surroundings coming back to her. 'Oh yes, that Dan.'

Chapter Twenty-seven

'How do you think Cass will take it?' Dan passed his office phone to Dora. 'I still don't think she's accepted Justin isn't going to leave his wife for her. Not deep down.'

Dora sighed. 'I'm honestly not sure. We don't know her that well yet. One thing I'm sure of though. Cass has a strength about her. You have to, to survive running your own business in the City, especially one that deals with the parents of private school children intent on sending their little darlings to Oxbridge from the moment they're born.'

Double-checking the phone number that Sasha had given her, Dora looked Dan straight in the eye. 'She's going to need her new friends. Most of all she is going to need you, Dan.'

'I'm not the sort of guy she wants, Dora.'

'No, you're not; but you're the sort of guy she needs.' Regarding him like a benevolent professor, Dora added, 'And please don't insult my intelligence by telling me you aren't interested, because it's clear that you are. Which is why you are going to go and fetch the documents from her for me this evening. It is also why it is best that you leave me to make the next few calls on my own, because they are liable to make you cross.'

'Abi, my girl!'

Engulfed in Stan's arms, Abi was nosed out of the way by Sadie, who didn't appreciate not being the first in the queue to be greeted by her former owner.

'Alright, Sadie! I'm pleased to see you as well.'

Sitting on the sofa while Sadie was fussed, Abi dived in. 'I'm so sorry I haven't been over much lately, Stan. What with finding bridesmaids' dresses, the start of the tourist season in the gallery, looking after Cass, and Max moving in, it's been non-stop.'

'Never apologise for having a full and happy life, my girl.' Stan sat next to her with a small puff of relief. 'Good to take the weight off! Dora has been playing spy all day, and I've been trying to tidy up enough of my stuff to squeeze a bit more of her stuff out of boxes and into cupboards.'

Abi nodded. 'I understand that completely. For such a self-sufficient guy, Max has way more stuff than I anticipated. It's a good job he only has a small flat.'

'Will he sell it?'

'I think so. We haven't got that far in our plans.'

Stan couldn't have been happier if he tried. 'I am so pleased for you, Abi. This is just what I wanted for you; for your childhood dream to come true. A family in Abi's House.'

'Well, there's no family as such, but Max is a start.'

'There will be a family. I know there will.'

Abi blushed. 'I hope so. Anyway...' she drew a sustaining breath, determined to get to the reason for this visit before they went off at a conversational tangent

'...talking of family, I have been back in touch with Sally.'

Stan's pale face coloured. 'I should never have asked you to talk to her in the first place. Max explained what happened.'

'That doesn't matter now. Sally was worried, frustrated she wasn't here, and confused. You have to admit, the news of your marriage did come out of the blue. You hadn't even mentioned Dora to her before, after all.'

Looking at his wrinkled hands, Stan spoke with regret. 'I've handled it all very badly where Sally is concerned. I'm sorry you were caught in the middle of that.'

'Well, I'm pleased to say that the situation is much better now. Sally wants to chat to you tonight.'

'Tonight?'

'Yes.' Abi reached out and took Stan's hand. 'She is pleased for you, but reassurance is required. Oddly, it's Sally who feels she has let you down because she isn't here to care for you.'

'But that's ridiculous; she had to put her own family first.'

'Logically, she knows that, but real life is rarely logical. Not where emotions – especially guilt and worry – are concerned.'

'You're right.' Stan sat up, his usual optimism returning. 'What time do we do that Skype thing then?'

'About ten o'clock. How about we watch rubbish on television until then?'

'Now that is a plan,' Stan looked a bit sheepish, 'although I'll probably drop off.'

'No problem. I miss the sound of your gentle snoring sometimes.'

Stan patted Abi's hand. 'You'll wake me at ten won't you?'

'Of course – unless I've dropped off as well!'

Cass wasn't sure if she should put the kettle on or get out a bottle of wine. What sort of evening was this? A serious chat? A friendly get-together? It certainly wasn't a romantic moment, so perhaps tea and coffee and not alcohol?

Don't flap! Cass could feel herself getting cross at her own indecision. It was as foreign to her as buying a bridesmaid's dress off the peg.

She decided they'd be better off in the kitchen, looking at each other across the table rather than squashed side by side on the sofa feeling awkward at their close proximity. The last thing Cass wanted was Dan thinking that she was interested in him. Even though she was...

A crush on someone new would not make life any easier right now. Anything more than friendship would just muddy the already churned-up waters of her heart. It was irrelevant that images of Dan in his Army uniform kept popping into her head at the most inappropriate moments – that was merely old-fashioned lust, a different issue altogether.

Dan was just a friend. Plus, he was a friend to all her friends. He *had* to remain an interesting outlet for her daydreams alone.

Knocking together the three piles of paperwork on the table, Cass couldn't begin to imagine what Dora wanted them for. The more she thought about what Dora was up to, the more Cass was inclined to believe that the soon-to-be Mrs Abbey really had lived the life she'd claimed to have; that it wasn't just a fable woven together by a lonely old woman.

Cass found herself speculating how she might have coped if she'd married as young as Dora did, and then had her happiness snapped away from her by war, when an overriding relief that Dan wasn't in the Army any more swept over her; its strength took her by surprise. The thought of anything bad happening to him... *Anything else bad.* He still hadn't told her what had happened to him in Afghanistan to make him leave the Army when he did.

'Perhaps I'll ask him tonight, if the subject comes up.'

Cass was considering how she could steer the conversation in that direction without seeming too intrusive, or downright nosy, when the doorbell rang. The sound of Dan's arrival was doing strange things to her pulse rate and she rushed with less calm than she would have liked to let him in.

'Good evening.' Dan smiled, but Cass's honed business antennae sensed there was something rather awkward about his expression, as if he had something difficult to say, and wasn't exactly sure how to say it.

Rather than letting an atmosphere build, she said, 'Thanks for acting as Dora's messenger. I thought we'd sit in the kitchen. Maybe have a drink to help wash down whatever bad news you have for me.'

'What makes you think I have bad news?'

'Instinct.'

Sighing as he followed Cass down the narrow corridor that joined the front door to the kitchen, Dan said, 'I'd love to say that your instinct was wrong. However, you're no fool, and you must have worked out that anything Dora has unearthed is likely to make you sad. I wish it were otherwise.'

Determined to remain in business mode so that she didn't break down in front of Dan, Cass sat at the table and beckoned to him to do the same. 'Tea or coffee now, and alcohol after?'

'No offence, but I'm awash with hot drinks after having Dora in my office most of the day. She doesn't seem to be able to operate without a cup of tea or coffee to hand.'

'Wine now then?'

'Unless you've got a beer?'

Inwardly cursing that she hadn't thought that he'd probably want a lager or something, not wine, Cass apologised, 'I'm afraid not. I don't drink beer, so I didn't think to buy any.'

'There's no reason why you should have. A glass of wine would be very welcome.' Dan pointed to the papers in front of them. 'Is this the correspondence Dora wants to see?'

'I think so. I've split the piles into agency accounts, business mail, and that one is the handwritten stuff. There isn't much of it. Most of my work, and my more private mail, is on the email or text message list. I printed out what I could at the library. There's probably far more there than she needs. Why does she want to see it?'

'May I look?'

'Go ahead.' Cass poured two full glasses of wine as

she watched Dan flick through her paperwork. She felt strangely vulnerable as his eyes passed over her private letters. He was working too fast to be actually reading them, but it was still a disquieting sensation seeing him sort through her piles and extract occasional papers. 'What are you searching for?'

'Dora wants as much handwritten stuff as possible.'

'It's all in that third pile.'

'Anything from Crystal?'

'Crystal? Why?' The unease she'd been trying to keep under wraps began to show in her voice.

Dan pushed Cass's glass of wine closer to her. 'Here, you might need this.'

'Stan,' Abi whispered, gently rocking her friend's knee, smiling over at Dora who had returned to the flat half an hour ago, and was already snoozing in the armchair, 'it's almost ten. Wake up.'

'What? Abi?' Stan sat up slowly as he came to. 'Is it time already?'

'It is.' Abi put her finger to her lips and gestured towards Dora, whose snores were beginning to resemble the snuffling of a burrowing woodland creature.

'Bless her.' Stan looked affectionately at his fiancée, 'All that espionage has worn her out. We'd best set up the laptop in the kitchen so we don't wake her up.'

Trying not to show that she was nervous, Abi was glad Sadie had woken up with them and would be coming through to the kitchen too, so that she could ruffle her fur if things didn't go to plan. There was nothing like her presence to keep things calm.

'You ready, Abi girl?'

'As soon as you are.' Abi fired the laptop into life, and Stan settled himself into a chair.

The second the Skype icon appeared, it was obvious that Sally had been waiting at her end for them to come online, for the line rang instantly. Sitting out of view of the webcam, Abi gave Stan the thumbs-up. 'There you go, just press the video call button.' Smiling, she added, 'It'll be alright, Stan.'

With a brief nod, Stan prepared to talk to his daughter.

'I have been the biggest fool.' Cass wasn't sure where to look. The more Dan explained about what Dora had discovered, alongside what she suspected, the more her confused attraction to him increased.

'No, you're not a fool. You've been taken advantage of by the man you were in love with. He used your feelings to make you an easy target. The question now – a question that Dora wants these letters to help answer – is did Justin know the extent of the corruption, or was he partly innocent in the con as he claims.

Cass didn't want to meet Dan's eye. She felt sick as she listened to Dan explain the full extent of Dora's discovery – including the involvement of Justin's PA.

Crystal?

They weren't friends exactly, but as Crystal had risen through the ranks alongside Justin, going with him from the last job to his new one, Cass had got to know her well in a professional capacity. Although, she had obviously got her level of ambition very wrong.

'And Jacinta thinks she is in control of this, but in fact

260

it's *Crystal* who is playing with the strongest hand?'

'Dora said it's like cards, and that, for now, both women have the best poker faces she's encountered since the sixties.'

Cass gave a rueful smile. 'That sounds like Dora.'

'Doesn't it.' Dan wanted to reach out a hand and comfort her, but Cass had pulled herself inward. Her arms were on her lap, and she'd hunched her shoulders inwards, as if she was trying to make herself smaller. 'Cass, I'm so sorry.'

'You have nothing to be sorry for. I was the fool, not you.'

There was silence as they stared into their own wine glasses. Until, out of the blue, Dan said, 'It was a child.'

'A child?'

'The reason I left Afghanistan. I couldn't save a child.'

Chapter Twenty-eight

'A child?' Cass forgot her decision to be reserved, and found her hand was holding Dan's before she'd considered that he might not want comforting.

Reassured, as he put his free palm over hers, Cass immediately felt his body heat spread up her arm and fill her up. Trying to dismiss the sudden acceleration in her pulse rate, and hoping he was too distracted by what he had started to tell her to notice, she gently said, 'Go on.'

'As you'll know from the reading the newspapers, civilian casualties were as frequent for us in the Camp Bastion hospital as military casualties. And I saw so many children with limbs blown off, too many…enough for a lifetime…'

Cass squeezed his palm tighter. She wasn't sure if he was talking to her or just to the room in general now. Dan's eyes had dulled, and his face was pale as he articulated the words that had formed the basis of his nightmares for years.

'A few days before I was due to agree to extend my stay to help treat the last wave of casualties before Britain pulled out of the conflict, a woman came in. I say woman, but she wasn't much more than a child herself. Nineteen at the most. I never did find out for sure…'

Cass felt a lump forming in her throat. Dan was so capable, so strong. To see him like this, touchingly vulnerable and even afraid, made her feel privileged and humbled.

Taking a small sip of wine, Dan seemed to come back to himself and turned back to Cass, looking directly at her green eyes. 'She was pregnant. A mortar had hit her village, and she'd been trapped under rubble for hours before they got her out. Many more hours had passed before she reached us at the hospital.'

'Oh, Dan...' Cass could already see where this was leading, and a single tear ran down the side of her face.

Wiping the tear away, Dan flipped his hand over and grasped Cass's hand properly, weaving their fingers together. 'I was the medic who prepped her for surgery. Her English was fractured, but then, so is my Afghan. Between us we made each other as clear as we could. She told me if the baby could not be saved, then she didn't want to live.'

The image of a small, frightened pregnant woman flashed before Cass's eyes and refused to leave.

'I went with her into surgery. She came out. The baby didn't.' Dan's voice cracked, and Cass could see he was fighting not to cry now, and Cass wondered if he'd ever told anyone this before. 'Her face when I had to tell her...I won't forget. Not ever.'

'But it wasn't your fault. You didn't drop the bomb and you weren't the surgeon.'

'Makes no difference. I have no idea which side the mortar belonged to, nor does it matter that I know that the surgeon did everything in her power to save them both. It

264

was me who'd had to promise her I'd let her die if the child could not be saved.' He shook his head sharply. 'It was the only way to get her into theatre. I knew it was a lie when I said it. I assumed she did too.'

Cass was fairly sure she knew what the answer to her next question was going to be, but she had to be sure, and sensed that Dan actually needed to say the words. 'What happened?'

'I had a day off the next day. My first in weeks. When I got back to the ward the following the day I was met by the news that she had stolen tablets while there had been an emergency elsewhere. She took them all. There were over sixty of them.'

The silence in the kitchen seemed to wrap itself around Cass. She could feel the air against her skin as her lips dried and her eyes coated with a fresh film of tears. She had no words. What could anyone say?

Stretching her other hand out, she felt the slight shake in Dan's body as he took it, fighting not to let go of the grief he'd held in for so long.

Not sure why she did it, why her dislike of excessive displays of emotion suddenly didn't matter, Cass said, 'Let go, Dan. It's time.'

Stan wrapped Dora in a big hug as Abi closed down the laptop, her shoulders almost sagging with relief.

Sally had been beyond apologetic. Her regret for aiming her hasty anger and guilt at Abi was clear, and after listening to Stan, and hearing all about Dora, seeing for herself how much joy twinkled in her father's eyes when he spoke about his fiancée, and being introduced to a now wide-awake Dora via Skype, she had given them her blessing.

Dora was still beaming as Abi got up to leave. It was almost eleven thirty, and suddenly Abi felt very tired.

'Thank you, Abi.' Stan kissed her cheek as she roused a reluctant Sadie into life, 'I don't know what we'd do without you.'

'I have no doubt you'd manage just fine.' Abi yawned. 'But you are very welcome. I'm so relieved Sally has come round.'

Dora sank onto the sofa, as if her body had also just realised how late it was. 'Oh, and thanks again for giving me Sasha's details. They were very useful.'

'I hadn't dared ask, to be honest.' Abi gave a half-smile. She still wasn't sure if she'd been helping Cass or not by passing on Sasha's information.

'I discovered a great deal. Dan went over to Cass's a few hours ago to tell her what I'd found out, and hopefully to find some evidence to back my theories up. I suspect he's home by now, but he hasn't reported how she took the news yet. He probably assumed we were asleep by now.'

Not wanting to gossip about her neighbour, Abi simply nodded. 'I'll go and see if she is alright in the morning.'

'You're a good girl.'

'I try.' Abi stifled another yawn. 'Come on, Sadie, let's go and see if Max is still awake.'

'Can I get you something stronger?'

Dan smiled weakly as Cass pointed to the bottle of very expensive whisky that she'd originally bought for

Justin. 'I'd love to, but I have to drive back to the flats.'

'You could stay.' Cass quickly added, 'I have a spare room.'

Dan looked down at their still entwined hands. 'See! I said you were a lot kinder than you thought you were, didn't I?'

Sighing, Cass followed his eye line and fixed her own gaze on the vision of their locked palms. Her pale fingers, tipped with long red nails, fitted so perfectly over his larger tanned hands. His fingernails were neatly clipped and clean, his hands free of blemishes, unlike his right wrist, which now she looked closely didn't just have a small rose tattooed on it, but a scar. A scar that had become the stalk of the yellow rose.

She looked up at him questioningly.

'Sometimes we had to collect casualties from the front. I was injured. Many got worse.'

'Why the rose? If I were you, I'd be proud of that scar.' Cass had an irresistible urge to kiss it. Tenderly, just to make him feel better. She'd done it before she'd registered what she was doing, and then, flushed with embarrassment at the move, lowered her eyes back to the piles of documents Dan had come to collect several hours ago.

'Yellow roses signify friendship. I lost friends out there. I made the scar into a small memorial for them.'

Thankful that he hadn't commented on her kiss, Cass tilted her head in appreciation of his gesture towards his fallen comrades. Then, with a sigh, she said, 'It seems petty to even ask this now, but do you think Dora knows what she's doing?'

'Honestly, I have no idea. But she's convinced she is

on to something, and listening to her on the phone, sorting out her enquiries…well, she sounds so professional. All my doubts about her past have gone. Whoever it is she is talking to in London now is way beyond Sasha in influence.'

'He took me for a ride. That is never going to happen again.'

'You'll have to face him, though. To get closure, or you'll always wonder. Plus, if you don't, all the work Dora has done today will have been in vain. Not to mention the massive phone bill she's run up in my office will have been money down the drain!'

Cass reluctantly unclenched her fingers and slowly pulled her hands free. 'You have all been amazing. I'll never forget it.'

Dan frowned. 'You say that as if you're going away?'

Shrugging, Cass said, 'Once this is over I have no reason to stay. I have a business idea to start afresh. I could do that anywhere. This house will always be the one I was supposed to share with a man I thought I knew, but didn't. I can't stay here.'

'You don't have to go far.'

Cass said nothing for a few minutes, then, looking at her watch just to break the tension between them, was surprised to see it had gone midnight. 'Bloody hell, it's tomorrow. Do you want me to make up the spare bed?'

Dan placed his palms flat on the table and pushed himself upright. 'I don't think so. I have to be at the flats for breakfast anyway.'

Not sure if she was sorry or relieved he was going, Cass passed him the paperwork he'd come for.

'Thanks. I'm sure Dora will be in touch very soon.'

'Thank you for telling me about Afghanistan. I feel privileged.'

As Dan stepped through the door, he turned and gave Cass a gentle kiss on her cheek. 'I'm not staying because there is no way I'd have been able to stay in the spare room. I'll see you soon.'

The following morning Cass woke to the ringing of the front doorbell.

A delivery man was stood on the doorstep with a bunch of yellow roses.

The attached note said was, *Yellow is for friendship.*

Chapter Twenty-nine

Beth sat back with satisfaction. The kitchen cupboards had been scrubbed to within an inch of their lives, and now, as the last plate had been slotted back into place, she felt a tremendous sense of achievement.

'I knew you had nesting tendencies in pregnancy, but I never dreamed you'd turn into the world's most gorgeous Miss Mop.' Jacob leaned against the kitchen doorframe and watched Beth as she wiped a grubby hand across her cheek, smearing her face with sticky dust.

'Let's hope the feeling lasts long enough to give the whole flat a spring clean. It's weird. I've never felt such an urge to be tidy before.'

'You're telling me!' Jacob winked. 'I don't suppose you fancy giving the new studio a good wipe over as well?'

Beth threw her dishcloth at him. 'That is your problem, Mr Potter!' She eased herself to her feet, more aware of her belly with each passing day. 'How is the new place shaping up? I want to come and have a nose round. Somehow I don't seem to have a minute. There is so much I want to do before I can't any more.'

Jacob frowned. 'You make it sound as if your life is coming to an end.'

'Well, love, it sort of is. Not in a bad way; in a very

exciting way. But there will be massive changes to every aspect of my life. Our lives. Most of all my immediate freedom will be gone. I want to make the most of being able to leave the house without having to check a million things before I even have time to tie my own shoelaces.'

'I hadn't thought of it like that.' Jacob was quiet for a while before asking, 'Is there anything you'd like to do? Anything special, I mean, before the first baby Denny arrives?'

Beth laughed. 'The first? You're anticipating a tribe of small Dennys?'

'I'd love loads of kids, wouldn't you?'

'Probably.' Beth looked down at her stomach. 'But shall we have this one first?'

'Good plan.' Jacob patted his girlfriend's belly. 'Why don't you come with me to the studio, I'd love you to see it now I've got the work station set up. You can help me choose what to exhibit at your gallery in August.'

'August! Oh my goodness, I'd forgotten.'

Jacob gave a playful laugh. 'You forgot there was going to be August?'

'No, silly, I'd forgotten all about the anniversary of Abi's arrival before then, and then the gallery anniversary in September, afterwards.'

'I thought we'd decided to leave Abi's anniversary celebration to Max?'

'We were, but that was because Max wanted to have private time to ask Abi about him moving in with her. Now he's moved in, shouldn't we do something to mark the day?'

'Beth, love, we are doing something.'

'We are?'

Jacob laughed. 'I think all the disinfectant has gone to your head.'

'What do you mean?'

'The wedding.'

'What about it?' Beth clapped a hand to her mouth. 'Oh my God, I'm such an idiot. I never made the connection. They're on the same day aren't they?'

'They are. Plus Max is taking Abi away that night. She doesn't know yet. It's an anniversary present, so for goodness' sake don't tell her.'

'I don't think you have to worry about that. Recent evidence suggests I'll have forgotten by lunchtime!'

Cass put her weight behind her elbow, and gently pushed the sandpaper block across the top of the small bedside cabinet Jo had declared was an ideal piece of furniture to practise her fledgling restoring skills on.

There was something wonderfully soothing about the rhythmical motion, and of seeing the results of your hard work appearing before your eyes, she thought. While she made sure she got each run of the sandpaper in exactly the right place, there was no room in her mind for anything else. Which was a welcome relief after last night...

'You're quiet, Cass, everything alright?'

Cass picked up the mug of coffee Jo had placed in front of her. 'Just concentrating. I love how fast you can see things happen.'

'Wonderful, isn't it?' Jo leaned against the wall, rubbing her own dusty hands down her apron. 'It's like being paid to give yourself therapy all day.'

'Your apprenticeships should be on the NHS! You'd save the mental health department a fortune.'

'You may be onto something.' Jo chuckled into her cup. 'Does this mean you've decided to take me up on my offer of an apprenticeship stroke partnership?'

Stretching out the ache in her arms that came from using muscles so unaccustomed to hard physical work, Cass sighed. 'I want to say yes.'

'But?'

'Last night I learned what was behind the collapse of my business.'

'Justin?'

'Yes, but not in the way I'd assumed. My friend Dora has several contacts in London and has unearthed a situation which was based purely on jealousy and not on any sort of financial greed. At least, that's how it started. I'm not convinced that Justin didn't decide to make the whole theft financially viable once he'd realised what was going on. But I don't really know about that – that's more of a hunch.'

'And until you know for sure you don't want to make me any promises?'

'I don't want to find myself in a position where I let you down.' Cass looked at the furniture around her with an expression of regret. 'I'll understand if you'd like to make the offer to someone else.'

Jo threw a rag at Cass. 'Don't be silly. I'm happy to wait.'

'You are?'

'For a confident woman you don't half lack self-confidence!' Jo put down her cup as the ring of a bell indicated a customer had come into the shop. 'I asked you because you're good. You have a good eye.'

As Jo left her speechless to go and deal with her customer, Cass stared at her dust-smudged hands. She knew her face would be streaked with dust as well. Suddenly she started to laugh. She couldn't stop, as hysteria gripped her.

Justin would hate this. He might not even recognise her: no salon haircut, faded nail varnish, and no make-up on. She felt oddly pleased that she'd left the house without even contemplating her appearance.

With Jo's words still warming her, and the memory of Dan telling her he had to go home because he'd never be able to sleep in her spare bedroom, Cass wrenched her shoulders back and, taking her mobile from her pocket, called Dora.

'This has gone on quite long enough.' Cass told the phone as she waited for her friend to pick up. 'It's getting boring, and holding up my whole bloody life! Enough already, it's time I...Hello, Dora. I wanted to thank you for working so hard on my behalf. Dan has the documents you asked for. It's time I invited Justin down here for a little chat. What do you think?'

Abi had just finished highlighting the sparkle of a rainbow, when Max arrived at the gallery, armed with two rounds of sandwiches.

'What's this? Waiter service?'

Passing Abi some lunch, Max pointed at the currently customer-free sofa. 'Don't you be getting used to it, lass.

Come and join me.'

Abi laughed. 'Fear not, I don't picture you as a waiter somehow. Your big hands would snap the bone china!'

'Cheek!' Max unwrapped his cheese and ham roll. 'And there I was being nice!'

'Nothing to do with wanting a bit of company while you wait for the coat of paint you put on Cass's living room wall to dry, then?'

'That was but a bonus, honestly.'

'Yeah, right!' Abi came and sat down next to her partner, and gave him a quick kiss. 'Thanks for lunch. You are very kind.'

'True.' Max stretched his legs out, enjoying not being cramped up after a morning of painting the skirting boards. 'Have you seen Cass today? She was out of the house before I got there this morning.'

Abi frowned. 'But you were there before nine, weren't you?'

'I was, but there was no sign of life. Although there was a fresh bunch of roses in a bucket by the sink.'

'Really?' Abi chewed her lunch thoughtfully. 'From that toad Justin, I suppose, trying to wangle his way back into her affections.'

'I'm not so sure.'

'You didn't read the card did you?'

'No way. A card would be private. It's just that the roses were yellow.'

'So?'

'From what I've heard about Justin, he would send red roses.'

'You're right.' Abi nodded. 'I think our time with

Dora has rubbed off on us!'

'Yes, this is indeed spy thinking. I bet James Bond considers the colour of roses all the time.'

'I'd bank on it.'

Max rolled his eyes at Abi. 'Dan didn't leave until late last night. I heard the car drive off. Then the florist's van was on the door at eight this morning. Cass left pretty much straight after that.'

Abi laughed. 'You really have been spending too much time with Dora!'

'Our very own Mata Hari.' Max smiled. 'The truth is far less interesting. I couldn't sleep, and was up and about sorting the van about eight.'

'Why, you don't have to drive to work for a bit longer, do you?'

Max shifted slightly on the sofa. 'I was making room for some of my furniture from the flat. There are a few bits I'm like to keep if that's alright. Not much, just a few things I had from my parents. I'll sell the rest.'

'What are you talking about? You don't have to sell anything. Bring it all, we'll find room. Max...' Abi felt a small stab of sadness; she'd thought he was feeling genuinely at home with her in Miners Row. 'This is your home as well now. You don't have to get my permission to bring in some furniture. I want you to have as much of your stuff as I have mine. I want it to be our stuff now.'

Putting an arm around Abi, Max pulled her close. 'Are you sure, lass? Abi's House is well, *Abi's* House. You fought so long to make it that way. I don't want...'

'Max! We've been through this. It's our house now. Our future. You do like living with me, don't you?'

Abi felt sick. She'd been so happy, but now every doubt she'd ever had about Max's ability to commit to another woman after Lucinda came racing back to the surface.

'I love it! Of course I do.'

'You were about to add a "but" to that sentence. What is it, Max, please tell me?'

'I don't know; I feel a bit like I'm just on holiday, or a lodger maybe.'

Abi felt as if she'd been doused by a bucket of cold water. 'A lodger?' Her words came out so quietly that Max barely heard them. 'That's why you should have your things, why we should get rid of some of my stuff and get things we have chosen ourselves.'

'You don't mind then? Me changing round things at your place?'

'OUR PLACE!'

Abi shouted so loud she shocked not just herself and Max, but the small group of tourists who instantly backed away from the threshold of the gallery.

Chapter Thirty

Beth was exhausted. Her cleaning was getting out of control. She'd only been home for the school holidays for one day. If she kept on like this she'd have no energy left for the whole summer.

Jacob's new studio was looking fantastic. As soon as they'd walked in together Beth had felt as if she was in a comfortable and familiar space. Although she'd miss the studio in Hayle, she knew she'd always have the memories of their time there together. A smile crossed her face as she remembered her first trip to Jacob's studio. They'd gone to choose pottery to be displayed at her gallery, and had ended up having the best sex of her life on the studio floor.

Beth rubbed her belly, unable to take in that she was almost four months pregnant already. 'How things change.' She couldn't prevent the small stab of disquiet that was nudging her as she wondered if they'd ever do anything like that again.

Walking through the village towards the gallery and her flat, Beth yawned; she was going to have to have an afternoon nap whether she wanted one or not.

Waving to a family walking on the opposite side of the road that she recognised from school, Beth felt her fears calm. *It doesn't matter if we don't have a wild sex life any more; we're going to have something better: a family.*

An image of Jacob pushing a pram across the beach, while she held the hand of a toddler wearing a little swimming costume, warmed her from the inside. Suddenly Beth felt very lucky. If she hadn't happened to have discovered Jacob's ceramic website when she was first looking for artists to display at Art and Sole, then they'd never have met. With this thought keeping her smile firmly plastered to her face, Beth stepped inside the gallery to say hello to Abi before she went upstairs to her flat for a rest.

Expecting to see the gallery's manager either happily chatting to a visitor, or busy working away on her latest book, Beth was surprised to find her friend sat alone on the sofa, her knees tucked under her chin.

'Abi?' Walking around to the front of the sofa, Beth was confronted with an Abi who appeared completely defeated, as if she was trapped in dark thoughts. 'What's wrong?'

Snapped out of her introspection by Beth's arrival, Abi unhooked her legs. 'Actually, nothing. It's nothing.'

Beth examined her friend more intently. 'You were just admiring the watercolours then?'

'Yes. That's exactly what I was doing. Serena has a skill all of her own, don't you think?'

'She has.' Beth sat down, 'Abi, hun, I'm not convinced you were looking at anything at all.'

'Perhaps I did drift into space for a while. The paintings have that effect, don't you find?' Abi's voice was uncharacteristically harsh.

'You sounded like Cass then.'

280

'I suspect her city ways have awoken my own.'

Now Beth was worried. This didn't sound like Abi at all. She'd been in the room five minutes now, and not once had Abi asked how she was – not that she should have to, of course, but it was just what Abi did. 'The self-confident part or the hard-nosed businesswoman part?'

Abi continued to stare straight ahead for a while, and then stood up. 'A bit of both, perhaps. Long overdue maybe. I feel as though I've been a doormat for far too many years. And do you know what,' Abi turned to Beth now, her expression full of sadness, 'I've had enough.

'I know it took a lot of courage for Max to have another relationship after his divorce, and that it was a big step for him to move in. But it wasn't exactly easy for me either after Luke. And now...' Abi's steady voice caught in her throat, but she quickly gathered herself '. . . now Max tells me he sees himself as some sort of lodger at Abi's House. A lodger! Insulted isn't even close to how I feel. I should never have let anyone close to me again, not after it took me such an age to get my self-confidence back, feeble though it is.'

'What are you talking about?' Beth was openly shocked now. 'Max hasn't said he feels like a lodger, has he?'

'He has.' Abi felt her fight already dissolving in the face of her friend's shock. Sinking back down onto the sofa again, her tone softened. 'I hate feeling like this, Beth. I don't know who I am any more. I thought if I acted stronger; if I put my survival suit of armour back on, then maybe I wouldn't feel anything.'

281

'Like you used to when you lived with Luke?'

'Yeah. I used to hide inside myself, safe in an invisible protection of my own making. It kept me sane, kept me going. But now…'

'Now it doesn't work because you love Max and anything that goes wrong hurts, whereas with Luke it worked. It was different because you stopped loving Luke long before he died. Right?'

'Pretty much.'

Still confused, Beth said, 'Have you two ever argued before? Assuming you have actually had a proper row this time?'

'No. No, I don't suppose we have.' Abi was taken aback by the thought. 'And this was, well, I suppose it was an argument, but not a shouting row or anything. It was more a circular conversation with several dead ends, which ended in Max heading back to his flat.'

'What?' Beth was stunned. 'Max has moved out. He's gone?'

Her indignation totally gone now, Abi felt the wave of hopelessness she had been absolutely determined not to allow enfold its way around her. 'I think so.'

All thoughts of how tired she was disappeared. 'Bloody idiot!'

'But I thought, if I could use some of Cass's survival techniques, I might…' Abi's voice wavered.

'No, hun, you're not the idiot, Max is! Just when I thought he knew what a good thing he had. I'd lay money on him having a delayed attack of cold feet.'

Hope sparked inside Abi. 'You think so?'

'Sounds like it, although I think you'd better tell me

exactly what happened in case I'm leaping to conclusions here.'

Abi asked Beth, almost mumbling, 'You don't think he's left me then?'

'Not for a minute. Come on, what happened?'

With a sigh, Abi explained how she and Max had gone from happily chatting to talking about what to do with his flat and furniture, to Max announcing that didn't feel he could make Abi's House their home after she'd fought so hard for it to be hers. Eventually, having got into a stalemate, Max had groaned, ran a hand through his hair, and without another word, left the gallery, got into his van and driven off.

Keeping to herself her thought that it sounded like a misunderstanding between two people who weren't cut out for arguing, Beth asked, 'Is Max working at Cass's today?'

'He should be, but the van wasn't there when I came in this morning.'

'What happened when you tried to phone him?'

'I didn't. I don't know what to say.' Abi raked a hand through her own blonde locks, echoing Max's gesture from the day before. 'I don't want to be the one who does all the running. Max would hate that anyway. He's so old-fashioned.'

'I'm not so sure that's true any more, but you could be right.' Not convinced, Beth said, 'Do you want to go home, Abi? I can keep an eye here, or we can close early.'

'I'm OK. I'll stay here thanks.' Abi smiled at Beth, as if seeing her friend properly for the first time since she walked into the gallery. 'You should go upstairs and put your feet up. We can't have you too tired for the wedding next week.'

'Are you sure? You don't want to go and talk to Max or anything?'

'No. If he isn't happy at Abi's House I'll sell it so we can get a place we both like. But I don't really want to. Is that selfish of me?'

Beth was horrified. 'Not at all. It's not like it's any old house. It's your childhood dream home! And Stan would be so upset. Can you imagine his face?'

'I know. Telling Stan would be worse than moving out. He was so thrilled when he thought Max and I would start a family in his old home one day. He'd be crushed if we left before even the possibility of the patter of tiny feet. But if Max won't live there with me…That's what I was trying to work out when you came in. How to tell Stan I'm going to be selling the house he moved out of so I could live there. He'd hate me.'

'You love Max that much? You'd leave your dream home for him?'

'I do. I don't want to lose him.' Abi groaned as she strolled over to look at the mess she'd made of the picture on her desk, 'And if Max had stayed last night, I'd have told him so.'

Chapter Thirty-one

'Any wedding nerves yet, Dora?' Cass sat at the now familiar kitchen table in Dora and Stan's flat. She was trying not to feel disappointed that she hadn't bumped into Dan on the way in, despite the fact she'd lingered in the car park and walked up the stairs and past his office door deliberately slowly.

'Nope. I doubt very much if I'll get any.'

'None at all?'

'Not one.' Dora chuckled. 'Only be nervous about things worth being nervous about, Cass. Life is short, as Stan and I know only too well.'

Cass's eyes fell on the papers on the table before her. 'Thanks for doing this for me, Dora. I don't know why you're helping me like this, but I am more grateful than you'll ever know.'

Dora patted Cass's hand affectionately. 'I should thank you actually.'

'Really?' Cass was openly surprised. 'But I've given you all this stuff to do when you should be getting ready to get married.'

'I am sorry that you've had all this happen to you, and I wish you hadn't, but it has been wonderful to feel useful again.'

Cass was so astonished that Dora chuckled again.

'There's no reason to be so shocked. Stan coming along has turned my rather dull life around, but he doesn't need much looking after, and if I don't keep my brain moving I quickly get bored.'

'Hence the poker?'

'Hence the poker, bridge, crosswords, and all the other games. You have given me the best puzzle to work out that I've had in years. Not only was it good to be challenged again, but I had the added bonus of knowing that I was doing it to help someone I care for. It's been a privilege.'

'You've only know me two minutes.' Cass felt mildly overcome, and this time put her hand out to hold Dora's. 'I don't deserve all this.'

'Cass, you are hardly the first woman I've come across who's been naive in the name of love. No one deserves to be taken advantage of.'

Pausing for a moment, Cass took a deep breath and asked the question she wasn't sure she wanted an answer to. 'Dan said Crystal was behind all this because she has designs on Justin herself. Is that right?'

Keeping back the full extent of Crystal's betrayal, so not to hurt Cass further, Dora said, 'I'm afraid so.'

'So was this Justin's plan all along? To have a few years indulging in my bedroom services, reel me in like some sort of willing fish, then let me fall in love with him, while he worked out how to take advantage of my business?'

'I don't think so, dear. If you think about it, Justin didn't make any money out of destroying your agency. No one did; it was the destruction of all you'd worked for that

286

was the only aim here. I am sure it was to make *you* look like a failed businesswoman. It was, and I quote, "To take Ms Henley-Pinkerton down a peg or two.'"

Nausea rose in Cass's throat. 'Who said that?'

'Crystal.'

'How do you know? What have you done, Dora?'

'I called in a few favours from some friends from the past. I used a few of the contacts Abi has in London, and found out a few useful pieces of information thanks to old-fashioned groundwork and the wonders of modern technology.'

'Modern technology?'

'Mobile phones are virtually bugging devices if you know how to use them properly these days.'

'Oh my God! You didn't bug Justin?'

'No, but I arranged for a listening-in on a conversation with Crystal. Best for you to know as little about that as possible!'

Cass was stunned. 'But you could get into so much trouble.'

Dora smiled. 'I'm an old woman, who on earth is going to bother about me? And to be honest, can you see Justin, Crystal, or Jacinta admitting to anyone that they'd been outsmarted by an octogenarian?'

'Do all three of them know then?'

'To my knowledge none of them know about my investigation.'

Her forehead crinkled in confusion, Cass said, 'Can you start from the beginning, Dora? I'm not totally sure what you did, or what's been going on. Is Jacinta involved in this, or is it just Crystal? And for that matter, is Justin the innocent bystander – in a business sense – just as he claimed?'

Dora was thoughtful. 'I think we'll have to persuade that man to come down here. You need to ask him that, face to face. You have to see his expression, to read his eyes while he tells you what's going on. Until then, until you actually see his face, you're always going to have that voice at the back of your head asking if he did love you or not. The other stuff isn't so important, is it?'

'It isn't. It ought to be, but I hate the idea that he tricked me into loving him more than his jealous women taking my business.'

'So,' Dora pointed at the mobile phone that Cass had placed in front of her on the table, 'call him. You have to get this sorted before you can restart your life.'

'What will I say?' Her hard, professional mode completely deserted her as the prospect of discovering the truth edged closer. 'Now I know he cheated on me as well, I'm not sure I'll be able to see him without throttling him.'

'You will say that you want to see him because you'd like to clear the air. You will not let on that you know about Crystal's involvement. That is going to be your leverage.'

'It is?'

'You make that phone call, and then I'll explain everything.'

'Are you totally insane, Maxwell Pendale?'

Max grunted. 'Took you longer to get here and shout at me than I thought it would.'

'I'm pregnant, everything takes longer.'

'Already?'

'Yes!' Beth hadn't been to Max's flat for several months, but she was sure that the last time she'd been it hadn't looked like a box storage area. 'You've packed up?'

'On the button as ever.' Max brandished the kettle in her direction. 'If you've come to tell me off then I'd like a cup of tea. You?'

'Please. But that doesn't mean I'm not going to tell you off. What the hell are you playing at? Abi is crushed. I caught her deciding how she is going to tell Stan that she is selling the house.'

Max flushed, his freckles suddenly standing out even more than they normally did. 'You're not serious?'

'Deadly. If you don't feel comfortable in Abi's House, then her solution is to sell up and find a house together with you.'

Max was already fishing out his mobile phone as he said, 'But I love Abi's House.'

'Then why did you tell Abi you felt like a lodger?'

'I didn't! That's what she said. I needed to sort furniture and stuff.' Forgetting all about making tea, Max rang Abi's number, speaking to Beth as he did so. 'I love Abi to pieces. I've been doing all this for her.' He gestured around the flat, which had all the hallmarks of a place that was about to be vacated. 'I've been up half the night packing and sorting what to sell and what to take over to the house. Damn, she isn't answering.'

'If she's at home, but not in the garden, then she won't have a signal will she.' Beth sat down with a tired sigh. 'Be careful you don't screw this up, Max. Abi has grown up a lot since we first met her. She isn't going to be a doormat like she was with Luke, no matter how much she loves you.'

A flash of panic crossed Max's face. 'I thought she'd still be at the gallery.' Throwing his keys at Beth, Max came to a decision. 'Could you lock up for me? I want to get to Abi's House before she does anything stupid.'

'If I can have a kip on your sofa first, then you've got a deal.'

Cass couldn't prevent her hands from shaking, and hated it.

Passing her a small glass of wine, Dora said, 'Mr Smythe is coming then?'

'Yes. Tomorrow apparently. Although I won't truly accept it until I see him standing right in front of me.' Taking a sip of her drink, Cass closed her eyes, letting the darkness soothe her for a second before opening them again. 'It feels so strange to think that, after all these years, Justin has no idea that I've rearranged my life without him.'

'That young man has no idea about a lot of things. You're going to have to be strong tomorrow. I know you are a very controlled and capable woman, Cass, but just in case Justin doesn't take to hearing you speak the truths that he didn't want you to know – or, in fact, that you know more than he does – then I'd like Dan to be hidden

290

upstairs while you talk. That way, if you want help, he can be there in seconds.'

With the mention of Dan's name, Cass took hold of herself. 'Thank you, Dora, but no. I'll see if maybe Max and Abi will be around. Dan has done enough for me already. He's supposed to be here for the residents.'

Not probing as to why Cass didn't want Dan there, especially as she was convinced she knew the reason why anyway, Dora agreed. 'Fair enough.'

Cass swallowed. 'What if Justin decides that my house is his after all? I know that Donald said it's mine, but Justin still paid for it. He only put it in my name as if it was a gift to avoid tax.'

'Therefore the house *was* a gift. It is yours. Justin can make all the fuss he wants, but that won't change anything on that front. He's a lawyer, he knows that.'

'Right.' Cass took a bigger drink for her glass. 'You'd better tell me the rest. It's time we turned this into a proper campaign meeting.'

'Abi?'

'Hello, Max.' Abi didn't get up from the rocking chair next to her bedroom drawing desk. 'I didn't hear you come in.'

Max's heart sank as he took in her closed-off posture. He'd been so determined to surprise her, to make Abi happy by dashing off to his flat to get sorted so he could pick which things to move in here with her. He hadn't thought that by not explaining himself he wasn't surprising Abi, but upsetting her. And worse, planting seeds of doubt within her.

291

Unsure of what to do, fishing round for something to say, Max asked, 'Where's Sadie?'

'At Stan's. I'm going to pick her up later.'

'We could both go.'

'If you want.'

Frustration rising inside him, Max snapped, 'Abi, please. I am trying to tell you something.'

Doing her best to fight the anxious knot in her chest, Abi said, 'Go on then.'

Kneeling down in front of her, Max took her tiny hands in his. 'I know I went about it the wrong way, and frankly cocked it right up, but the reason I disappeared wasn't because I was leaving you. Quite the reverse.'

'The reverse is moving in, and you told me you didn't want to live here.'

'No I didn't, you daft woman. I told you that I wasn't sure my stuff would fit in here. I went home to sort my stuff out and pack it all up.'

'Then why the hell didn't you tell me that?'

'It was supposed to be a surprise.'

'It was more of a shock.' Abi squeezed his hands. 'Talk to me, Max. If you want me to sell up so we can buy a home together, then I will.'

'Now listen to me, Abi Carter. No way would I ever ask you to leave this house. Got it?'

Relief spread across Abi's face as Max put a finger over her lips so he could finish what he wanted to say without interruption.

'I went home to say goodbye to the flat, I suppose. It doesn't even feel like home there any more. This is where I want to be. I don't clean out people's sheds on a whim you know, lass. That space is mine!'

Laughing now, Abi threw herself onto Max's lap. 'Are you sure? I want you to be happy here.'

'I am happy. I'm very happy, but every now and then I get scared it'll all go away. Is that OK?'

'So do I. But it won't go away, will it, Max?'

'No, love. It isn't ever going to go away.' Max put a hand into his large dungaree pocket. 'Here. What do you think?'

Abi found herself faced with a list of rented flats. 'Why are you looking at flats to rent?'

'Wake up, Abi! I was thinking of renting mine out rather than selling it. We could have a steady extra income to pay for any future little Pendales' university fees. We'd rent to someone local, not one of those awful incomers…'

'Maxwell, I am one of those awful incomers!'

'Ummm.' The rest of Max's answer was muffled as he picked Abi up and threw her onto the bed. 'Truly dreadful…'

Chapter Thirty-two

Cass wasn't sure she recognised the woman looking back at her from the bathroom mirror.

Her hair had begun to grow out of the bob style she'd treated herself to on her very first trip to Truro, although it still framed her face with featherlike wisps. Justin had never seen her with short hair. Nor had he seen her without varnish on her fingernails or make-up on her face.

Lifting her hands to her face to inspect them more closely, Cass took in her blunted nails. Her skin wasn't quite as soft as it had been either. Sanding furniture had taken its toll. Only a few weeks ago she'd have been horrified by this, but now she felt a long-forgotten sense of achievement. Every scratch on her previously flawless skin meant she'd done something worthwhile. She was creating – not only a work of art out of a piece of old furniture, but a new life for herself. A life that didn't revolve around a man.

Still slim and undeniably angular, her frame appeared softer in her T-shirt, jeans, and trainers, rather than a crisp white shirt, business suit, and high heels. She had put weight on, and her curves, which had been little more than token gestures before, were certainly more defined. Cass was struck with the idea that Justin might not recognise her when he finally arrived.

The muscles in her shoulders tensed. He would be getting into Penzance railway station in twenty minutes. Cass knew that if she didn't do this alone her pride would be even more dented than it was already, but that didn't stop her wishing she'd asked Dan to be there to hold her hand. It was reassuring to know that Max and Abi had agreed to sit in their garden while Justin was there, so that if she needed reinforcements, then all she had to do was shout over the wall.

Shoving a stray hair from her fringe into place, Cass tried to channel her inner businesswoman. She had no illusions. Much of her current situation was her own fault; she'd allowed the wool to be pulled over her eyes, and she'd been so caught up in herself, her agency, and her lover that she had closed herself off to the rest of the world around her.

She had been unbelievably lucky that the house Justin had pushed upon her happened to be next door to such good people. No one in London would have offered to miss work so that they could be around to support her.

'Or maybe they would have, if I'd taken the trouble to make real friends...'

Cass picked up her lipstick, and then put it down again. 'No. No mask today.'

The sweeping look of disbelief that Justin gave Cass as she opened the front door confirmed for her that, should they have met for the first time that day, he wouldn't have given her so much as a second glance.

Determined to remain fully in control of the coming conversation, and not to let how much he'd hurt her show, she greeted her ex-lover formally. 'If you'd like to head down the hall to the kitchen, Justin, we'll talk in there.'

'In the kitchen?'

'You were expecting me to have found the time to build a study over the past few weeks, perhaps?' Cass followed him down the short corridor and into the kitchen. Then, as agreed with Max and Abi, she opened the back door;: the signal which would tell her neighbours that Justin had arrived.

'Please, sit down.' Cass gestured to the pine chair opposite her. 'I've made tea. Would you like one?'

'Not particularly.' Justin's frown seemed to be growing more furrowed in front of her eyes, and Cass found herself wondering if he had always had so many lines on his forehead, or if they'd developed since her departure from London. *Dan doesn't have that many*. The thought of Dan increased Cass's determination to stay strong – at least on the outside. Even if nothing ever happened between them, she still wanted Dan to be proud of her.

Keeping the knowledge that she was aware of Crystal's designs on Justin to herself, precisely as Dora had advised, Cass began, 'I have no interest in going over old ground, Justin. I merely require answers for my own peace of mind, so I can do right by my ex-employees, and move on, by myself, with no questions hanging over me.'

'Move on? By yourself? Cassandra, what are you talking about?' Justin laid his briefcase on the table before him and clicked it open. 'We're a couple, and we had a deal. You are here to do up this property, before we rent it out as a holiday let.'

'Please, Justin, it's Cass now. Cassandra has gone.' Clenching her hands together in her lap, hoping her surprise at his opening gambit of total denial didn't show in her eyes. 'A deal which started with you telling me, when we were in London, that you had rented this house. Then, on arrival, I discovered that in reality you had purchased the property outright, putting the deeds in my name.'

'For tax reasons, and to keep it away from Jacinta, so she couldn't claim it back when we got divorced.'

Now Cass was truly thrown. 'But you aren't intending to divorce her. I don't think you ever were.'

'What?' Justin's voice rose into a shout, but he quickly pulled himself together. Getting up and moving around the table, Justin stood behind Cass; draping his arms around her shoulders, just as he'd used to when she was sat at her old study desk.

Trying not to stiffen, Cass was taken aback at how wrong it felt to allow him to touch her now. *How could I have been planning a life with this man?*

'Please sit back down, Justin.'

'Oh, come on! I haven't seen you in weeks. I was expecting far less boardroom and a lot more bedroom.'

'Excuse me?' Cass could feel the disbelief in her voice. 'You have got to be kidding me? You didn't honestly think you could seduce your way out of this, did you?'

Banging back onto his seat like a truculent teenager, Justin pulled some documents out of his briefcase. 'You aren't still maintaining that I am behind ruining the agency? That is so childish! I lost money on that.'

298

'Childish?' Cass could feel her hackles rising, and had to bite down hard on the expletives that were forming in her throat, forcing herself to remember what Dora had told her to say.

'Whatever has got into you? And why do you look so homespun? Would you like me to take you up to Bristol for a makeover?'

'I beg your pardon?' Cass scraped her chair back and stood up, her hands on her hips, indignation fuelling every word she uttered. 'First of all, I am perfectly happy with the way I look, thank you very much, and second, if I wanted a makeover of any sort, I'd decide, and I wouldn't have to go further than the village!'

'My God; you've changed fast. And not for the better.'

'Of course I've bloody well changed! Have you any idea what it's been like? You sent me here to update a house under false pretences, my business has been destroyed, and because I rented out my flat in London, I can't go back unless I were to live in a hotel. I had to adapt or sink.

'You left me on my own, Justin. *Alone*. Just so that you could step up the ladder and tell your wife you were leaving her without me in the way.'

'For your own safety! So you didn't get caught in the crossfire.'

'No, Justin. It was so you could get rid of me in the most cowardly way possible. There is only one thing I'm unsure of. Were you in on the destruction of The Pinkerton Agency from the start, or did you learn of it from Jacinta later?'

Justin stared straight into Cass's eyes, and it took all

her strength not to turn away. 'Later.'

'Thank you for not lying to me this time. Now, did you ever intend to divorce your wife and marry me, or was that holding tactics? Keeping me as part-time holiday entertainment perhaps?'

Justin regarded her as though she'd gone mad. 'I think the sea air has gone to your head, Cassandra.' Examining her appearance more closely, Justin began to smile with blatant suggestion. 'Perhaps it has done some good, though. Your bust is bigger.'

Automatically crossing her hands across chest, Cass listened as he kept talking.

'I blame myself for leaving you on your own for so long. You've had far too much time to think.' Reaching out his hand, Justin tried to take hold of Cass's as she gripped her mug of tea, only for her to pull it away. 'For heaven's sake, Cassandra, I'm trying to be friendly.'

'No you're not. You're trying to get your leg over. It won't work, Justin. Not any more. And I told you, I'm Cass now.' Exhaling slowly she met his eye. 'Last chance. You tell me the truth or I will have to ask you to leave my house.'

'Your house?' A cloud of concern passed over Justin's face, only to disappear again as he shrugged it off. 'My house.' He flourished the paperwork he'd taken out of his briefcase in her direction.

The knowledge that Max and Abi were only a few feet away gave Cass courage as she tried again. 'Justin, I wanted to give you the chance to come clean. For old times' sake, I suppose. However, you clearly aren't interested in being honest. Too long in the City perhaps.'

300

'What on earth do you mean?'

'Shut up, Justin!' Cass grabbed the paperwork that he still held in his hands, and scanned them briefly. 'I see. This *is* my house, unless I sign these forms. Which I have no intention of doing.'

'You have to sign them!'

'I told you to be quiet!' Deliberately shouting so that her neighbours would hear, Cass then moderated her tone a fraction. 'If you think I've been here sitting on my hands waiting for you then you're very much mistaken. I've already told you I contacted a local lawyer about the agency. I have also made investigations into what you've been up to. So, this is your chance, Justin; bearing in mind I know far more than you think I do. Your final chance to show me some backbone and get your wife and Crystal to give me back the monetary value of the business they destroyed in a mutual, although separate, fit of jealousy.'

'Crystal?' Justin paled, but it was such a subtle change to his blond complexion that if Cass hadn't been looking for it she would have missed it.

'Don't tell me you've forgotten about your stunningly attractive, young, and most capable PA?'

She could see angry denial forming across her ex's lips before the words even escaped. 'The agency's collapse was nothing to do with me.' Continuing to noticeably steer the conversation away from his PA, Justin added, 'You have obviously had some sort of personality transplant since you came here, Cassandra. I'm glad I haven't got around to asking Jacinta for a divorce yet.'

'Oh my God, Justin! You are the limit. I would like you to leave now.'

301

'Leave? You're the one who asked me to come here! I thought we were going to discuss our future together.'

'*Our* future? As in, you and me?'

'Naturally, you and me. Who else would I want to do this with? I thought we'd get this place up for a holiday rent and reboot your agency in Chelsea or somewhere more upmarket.'

'Chelsea?' Cass looked at Justin in open disbelief.

'Do you really have to repeat everything I say, Cassandra?'

'I think I do, otherwise I might not believe you're actually saying the words I'm hearing.

'Are you honestly telling me that you want me in your life, even though your wife plainly knows of my existence, but you haven't asked for a divorce.' Anger formed in Cass's throat. 'How arrogant are you? What makes you think I'd want you after you instructed Crystal to tell me you were in the States when you weren't? After you told me your new boss hadn't taken the news of your divorce well last time we spoke at length, and yet you have just informed me you haven't mentioned divorce to Jacinta yet?'

Cass didn't dare stop talking now she finally had Justin's full attention. 'And to add the cherry to your deceitful cake, it was *your* PA and *your* wife who conspired to destroy my life's work – and they succeeded. Why would I have asked to see you today for any other reason than to reassure myself that my past employees were going to be well compensated for being caught in the middle of their spiteful crossfire?'

Like a bemused goldfish, Justin opened and closed his

mouth for a few moments, before he said, 'This house is mine, and I will be keeping it. You have until Saturday to get out.'

'I think you were brilliant. I'd have punched him!' Abi passed Cass a slice of chocolate cake, as Max read through the documents Justin had left for her to sign, releasing all her rights to number two Miners Row.

'I almost did. Arrogant git.' Cass let some of the tension in her shoulders escape with a protracted sigh. 'I know he can't take the house from me unless I sign, which I won't. But if I don't, he's going to keep on hassling me. And I am still no nearer to getting back the money his wife stole from me. Although Dora said she still had a trump card to play, in case he pulled a stunt like this.'

'She isn't daft, is she?' Max glanced up from what he was reading. 'However clever a lawyer Justin thinks he is, he can't afford an adultery scandal if he wants to keep his new job, right?'

'Quite. That's why he sent me here in the first place. I think? I'm getting a bit confused.'

'Then, if he doesn't play fair by you, a scandal is what he'll get. And I can't see him liking that. It would mean Jacinta would have won.' Abi was thoughtful; she knew Cass didn't want a scandal herself, as she was so protective of her family.

Max knocked the papers together on the table. 'Do you think he knew for certain, beyond the seeds of doubt you'd obviously already planted, that Crystal and Jacinta were working together against you?'

'No. That rattled him. I think he assumed it was just his wife.'

'Good.' Max put the papers in his inside pocket. 'If it's alright with you I'm going to take these to show Dora when I collect Sadie, I'll drop them back later.'

'No problem, but why?'

'Because Dora has another plan.'

Cass smiled for the first time that day, 'I think I rather love Dora. She makes the team from *Mission: Impossible* look like total slackers.'

Chapter Thirty-three

'Are you ready?'

Dora's countenance was more serious than Cass, Max, or Abi had ever seen it.

'I think so.' Cass felt far from convinced that what Dora was proposing would work. 'The business world in London made me a good bluffer, but I'm not sure about this, folks. Justin is no fool.'

Max nodded reassuringly. 'You'll be great, and we'll be on hand if he cuts up rough.'

'Thank you, but I hope it won't come to that. In fact I hope that I can sort it before you guys arrive.' She frowned. 'If I can't, are you sure you want to do this, Dora? Tonight is your poker hen night with your friends. You shouldn't have to be over at my place laying a trap.'

'There's no *have to* about it. Justin's a slug, and I never did like slugs. Nasty slimy creatures.' Dora smiled across their kitchen table at Stan, who nodded approvingly. 'Anyway, I'll be back here in plenty of time to fleece my fellow old crocks out of their hard-earned pension money, fear not.'

Stan grinned. 'I'm glad I'm going out on my stag do with Max and Jacob tonight. I dread to think what chaos you'll cause. I feel sorry for Dan having to work tonight!'

The hands of the kitchen clock were moving awfully slowly. Still unconvinced Dora could persuade Justin to cough up the money he owed her, Cass had been practising what to say to Justin on and off ever since she'd returned from Chalk Towers.

With Justin's return imminent, Cass knew Dora was in place at Abi's House with Stan. Cass had heard her distinctive chuckle drift over the garden wall a few times. It came as a comfort to know that, even if all this went horribly wrong, at least Dora had enjoyed her unexpected revisit to the world of espionage. Plus, right at that moment, she was doing something she'd wanted to do for a while. Dora was visiting the house where her future husband had spent so much of his life.

Cass could picture the old woman helping Abi get the spare bedroom ready for Stan, who was going to be sleeping there after his stag night with Max and Jacob, and the following night as well – the night before the wedding.

A stab of regret shot through Cass. For a few hours, only a couple of weeks ago, she had been thinking about planning her wedding day. *Better no partner than the wrong partner.* Doing her best to think only about the new opportunities that awaited her, thanks to her friends in Sennen and Jo in Truro, Cass shoved her shoulders back and had another go at rehearsing her lines with the vase of fading yellow roses that still sat in the kitchen windowsill.

'I hope Cass is alright.'

Dora, who was as relaxed as ever, saw the worry on Dan's face. 'She can do this. As soon as we get the signal,

306

I'll go round and be a proper nuisance as planned.'

Sat next to Dora on the bench in Abi's back garden, Dan couldn't help but smile. 'You're loving this, aren't you, Dora!'

'You bet I am! Not much happens at my age you know.'

'Apart from weddings, poker tournaments, and spying.'

'Apart from all that.' Dora waved across the garden at Stan, who was in his element exploring the improvements Max had made to his old garden shed with Sadie at his side, just as she used to be. 'I'm glad you're here, Dan. I know Cass thinks that Max and Abi will be the cavalry if she needs one, but I have a feeling your arrival will have more impact.'

'Max is a hefty bloke, Dora. He'd have been fine.'

'He would. But Cass doesn't look at Max the way she looks at you.'

Dan groaned. 'Dora, honestly I've told you before, Cass and I are friends, beyond that we aren't going to happen.'

'Oh for heaven's sake, allow me to have some fun matchmaking. Hadn't we established that nothing exciting happens when you're old?'

Rolling his eyes, Dan got up to watch for the arrival of Justin's taxi outside number two Miners Row. 'You haven't told Cass I'm here, have you?'

'No. She'll be glad you are, though. Trust me.'

Wearing a business shirt and heels, albeit with jeans, and hoping the outfit would install her with some extra courage, Cass walked slowly to the front door as soon as the bell rang. She didn't want to appear rushed or flustered by Justin's arrival. She had to be the woman in control now more than ever or she'd lose her house.

Her house. Cass wasn't sure at what point she had accepted that the old terrace was her house, but as she looked at the freshly decorated walls, with its tasteful artwork care of Art and Sole, and the snug shag-pile rugs beneath her feet, she knew that the place it was more hers than she'd ever imagined it would be. *But is this my house, or is it my home?*

Refusing the offered seat, Justin stood next to Cass's kitchen table. 'I assume you have seen sense, and have signed my documents.'

'I assume *you* have seen sense, and arranged with Jacinta a means to provide me with the compensation I am owed for the illegal disintegration of my business?'

'Don't be ridiculous, woman, of course I haven't. I've already explained; I didn't know about it until the wheels were in motion.'

'And yet you didn't try and stop it once you found out, did you? You could have told me straight away. You could have used your legal knowledge to put an injunction out to prevent more damage. You could have done all manner of things to help save my life's work, but you did nothing except protect your own hide. I am embarrassed to have loved you.'

Evidently stunned, Justin frowned. 'You *will* sign those forms, Cassandra.'

A cold chill ran down Cass's spine at the expression on his face, and she fervently hoped Max was ready to intervene.

With a greater show of bravado than she felt, Cass said, 'Oh for goodness' sake, Justin. I may have been foolish enough to be taken in by you before, but not now.'

'If you don't sign then Jacinta will wonder where the £300,000 spent on this place went.'

'Jacinta? Why would that bother you if you're divorcing her?'

Justin shifted slightly, his discomfort obvious as his mistress called his bluff. 'It's not that straightforward.'

Cass snorted. 'I think it is very straightforward. Your wife and her friend conned me. Jacinta probably gloried in telling you what she had done to The Pinkerton Agency. I bet she used it as a weapon to prevent you from leaving her for me. What's more, I think she did all this simply to preserve her position in society. And, just maybe, if you leave her, your new business partnership will become rather less secure? Perhaps you have discovered that Jacinta has more connections than you were ever aware of?'

The scarlet flush that covered Justin's face told Cass that, not only had she hit the nail on the head both times, but that soon, his temper was going to explode.

'It's no good yelling at me, Justin. You know I'm right.'

Struggling to bite back the avalanche of anger that wanted to burst from his throat, Justin growled, 'I am not going to dignify that with an answer. Now, I suggest you sign my paperwork and I'll leave you to rearrange this new life of yours. I have no doubt you can find a place to rent using the money you're being paid by your flat's tenant in London.' He dropped a couple of estate agents' flyers on the table. 'I thought these might help. I am not unreasonable. I will give you until the end of the month to find somewhere else to go.'

Cass was incredulous. 'You have collected house particulars for me? I'm not leaving, Justin. You gifted me this house. My lawyer double-checked the point.'

Taking a step away from her ex, suddenly a little afraid of him, Cass gave a private sigh of relief as the doorbell rang.

'If you'll excuse me.' Without hanging around for Justin to comment, Cass dashed for the door.

'You OK?' Dora whispered as she came in.

Whispering back, Cass said, 'No. He's insisting on keeping the house and is getting angry.'

Putting a hand on her young friend's arm, Dora winked. 'Dotty old lady to the rescue.'

Supporting Dora's arm, as if she were a rather doddery pensioner, Cass walked back to the kitchen. 'Justin, may I introduce you to my next-door neighbour, Dora. Dora, this is Justin who purchased this house for me.'

Pointing to the kitchen table, Cass settled Dora down at the table. 'I have been so lucky with my new neighbours, Justin. Dora and I have already got into the habit of having a weekly game of cards. She has been teaching me poker.'

'Has she? May I have a word in private, Cassandra?'

Allowing him to draw her to one side, but not out of the room as he evidently would have liked, Cass muttered under her breath, 'Before you start, it is important for the future of the house, whoever lives here, to have a good relationship with the neighbours.'

'I suppose that's true, but if you sign my papers I could leave you to your game.'

'No. And if you want further discussion, you'll have to wait.'

Annoyed their meeting had been interrupted and prolonged, Justin bit his tongue. His intention to threaten Cass into signing was going to have to be delayed as he reluctantly followed her back to the table.

Evidently amazed as Dora dug a pack of cards from her handbag, Justin leaned against the kitchen door, resigned at having to observe a game of cards before he got what he wanted.

From behind her fanned-out hand of cards, Cass watched Justin with curiosity. It was strange. She felt as if she was face to face with a stranger, and yet Dora had worked him out without even meeting him. She had told Cass he'd be arrogant enough to think old meant stupid, and she'd been right.

As the late afternoon became evening, Dora began to play on that assumption; outstaying her welcome on purpose by taking ages to make every single move. Then, having finally persuaded Justin he may as well join in, Dora compounded the crime of being old by beating him at poker.

Cass could feel the tension in the air building with each new hand. *Any second now he's going to snap.*

'For heaven's sake, this is insane.' Justin threw his cards on the table.

Saddened by Justin's predictability, Cass snapped, 'It's only a game.'

Acting as though Dora wasn't there, he rounded

311

on Cass, his face crimson, his voice menacing. 'What the fuck am I doing playing cards with a stupid old woman who should be in some sort of home? More to the point, what are *you* doing, Cassandra? This isn't you at all!'

Battling with embarrassment, Cass was offended on Dora's behalf, and ashamed at how right Justin *almost* was. A few weeks ago she would never have been able to picture herself even talking to Dora, much less playing cards with her. Dora, however, merely grinned.

'Tell me, Mr Smythe,' the old lady's smile stayed in place, but it was suddenly devoid of warmth, 'if I'm so stupid, how is it I can tell, after only a few minutes reading those documents,' Dora pointed to the pieces of paper Cass had left unsigned on the table, 'that they are not legally binding.'

'What? How dare you read our private papers?'

'You don't deny they aren't legally binding then?'

'They are binding! What would you know about it anyway?'

Dora's expression hardened. The effect was startling, as she switched from her daft old lady act to a woman very much in control of the situation. 'I know because no lawyer can represent himself. I know, having studied Cass's business documentation and a few items of her personal correspondence, that a number of the official papers you have used in the past have not only been signed by one Crystal Templeton, but drafted by her in the first place. Including these, I think.'

Enjoying the stunned expression on Justin's face, Dora carried on talking. 'And if my instincts can be trusted, the

312

amount of Ms Templeton's input means that, in a court of law, it would be easy to wave the word "forgery" around just long enough to cause a great deal of embarrassment.'

Cass looked from Justin to Dora. Her heart was thumping hard and she found herself gripping the edge of table, wondering whether it would be Justin or Dora who broke eye contact first.

It was Justin.

As soon as the lawyer opened his mouth to argue, Dora put up her hand to stop him. 'The question is, Mr Smythe, which woman put you up to all this in the first place? I am confident you were in it from the beginning despite your claims to the contrary. Although, and I'm only acting on a hunch here, I suspect you had little choice in the matter. You certainly appear to have no backbone, so you wouldn't have been able to stand up to either Jacinta or Crystal.'

Justin blanched at Crystal's name. Dora's steely gaze read every line on his face as she said, 'Ah, so it was Ms Templeton. Yes, she struck me as clever when we spoke on the phone.'

'You have spoken to Crystal?' Justin was incredulous.

'Yes. It's unbelievable what skills we pensioners have picked up. We can use telephones and everything since rationing stopped.'

Sitting down with a thump, Justin said, 'You have honestly spoken to Crystal? Why?'

Taking a sidelong glance at Cassandra, who was gripping her glass of wine so hard the stem was in danger of cracking, Justin said, 'Go on then. I'll go along with this charade. What did Crystal tell you?'

'The truth.' Dora folded her arms. 'You have a choice now, Mr Smythe. You can be the one to tell Cass what you have done, or I can. You choose.'

The silence went on and on. When the doorbell rang, the relief to hear a sound sent Cass to her feet with far more speed than decorum.

Expecting to see Max arriving to check that everything was alright, as arranged, Cass felt confused at the sight of Dan on the doorstep.

'I was worried. You've been ages.'

Shocked to have found that Justin and Dora's confrontation had slipped from her mind for a second, as her attention strayed towards the care manager, Cass hurried back down the hallway. 'Come on. I don't want to leave her alone with him.'

None too pleased to have another stranger present to hear his conversation with Dora, Justin took in Dan's tattoos and spiked hair with disdain.

'Your choice in friends has clearly nosedived further than I thought.'

Cass had had enough. 'Dan is twice the man you'll ever be, Justin, so keep your snap judgements to yourself and tell me the truth, now.'

'Or you'll get your gorilla to attack me?' Justin's snide comment at Dan's expense hit Cass where it hurt, especially as she knew she'd made similar assumptions about him herself at first.

'I would rather you didn't insult my friends in what we've established is my house.' Cass, finding strength in Dan's unexpected presence, crossed her arms and stood up. 'What is it that Dora thinks you

314

should be telling me?'

Justin's eyes narrowed. 'OK, but they leave.'

'No need.' Cass could tell he was feeling hemmed in. 'They already know. I'm the only one who doesn't. Tell me.'

'If they know they would have already told you.'

'They could have; but they believe in fair play. They don't want to put words in your mouth. It's called *justice*, Justin. You may have come across the concept in court.'

He scowled. 'Jacinta will never agree to a divorce. She has, as has been discussed, the power to...remove my new position from me. She thinks the idea of destroying the agency was hers.'

Glad to be sitting down, Cass somehow managed to keep her voice steady. 'And when did Jacinta discover our affair?'

'Crystal told her.'

'Crystal *again*. Your right hand. How?'

'Too many hotel receipts with two breakfasts went through the books.'

'You idiot!'

Cass stared at the table. She could hear Dan stepping closer, and the thought of turning to hug him, to let him make all her worries go away was increasingly compelling. Remaining where she was however, Cass said, 'If it wasn't Jacinta's idea, then who first put the idea into her head?'

'Well. The thing is…'

'It was Crystal's wasn't it?'

Justin suddenly looked so defiant that, in that second, Cass saw how blind she'd become. Hot and cold at the

315

same time, she whispered, 'You really are sleeping with Crystal?'

Justin's lack of comment said it all.

Dora, seeing the pain on Cass's face, decided to wind things up. 'Cass, love, I'm sorry. I was hoping to spare you from that extra hurt. Crystal found out about you. She was jealous. She thought you were going to drag Justin away to Cornwall.'

'But I didn't want to come here.' Cass's voice was pleading, but every note also dripped with confusion at her own feelings.

'Justin told Crystal you were the one who wanted to start a new life down here.' Dora fixed their visitor with a gaze made of ice, daring him to deny it. 'You see, Cass, it is *Crystal* Justin has been trying to get shot of, not you. I think she got wise to his plans and tried to get rid of you first by feeding you to Jacinta.

'Don't forget that Crystal is a very clever woman. She got Jacinta to believe she'd come up with the plan to destroy your agency herself; a way of making you less attractive in Justin's eyes. After all, your agency gave you position in society.

'In the end Justin was caught in the middle, and suddenly he saw he was going to lose everything. Wife, job, and both mistresses, all at once. You were sent here, not to avoid the wife while he got a divorce sorted, but the third woman, while he left her.'

Dora turned to the lawyer. 'You did love Cass, didn't you.'

'Yes. And I *did* want her away from London to keep her safe. I *did* intend for this to be a holiday home, but then...'

The former spy finished the sentence for him, 'Then, separately, Crystal and Jacinta threatened you with exposure from different angles. Rather than do the right thing, you sat back and let them dismantle everything Cass had worked for.'

Justin looked ashamed. It was such a foreign expression on his features that Cass didn't recognise it for what it was at first.

Fishing in her handbag, Dora pulled out a stone and laid it on the table. 'This is a piece of crystal from my rock collection. You can see that, despite its beauty, it is cloudy. The edges are sharp despite its stroke-able appearance. It is formed by being squashed, but when it emerges from the earth, it is very hard, and in certain lights it is enchantingly beautiful. Beguiling, even.'

Letting her words sink in, Dora pushed the rock towards Justin. 'Keep it as a reminder to never trust anyone named after something so hard, something that can become sharp when its edges are chipped.'

Dan couldn't hold back any longer. Coming behind Cass's chair, he passed his arms around her, and hugged her gently. 'We would like you to leave now, Justin.'

Justin stared at his former lover. 'Oh, I see, Cassandra. You really have moved on.'

Standing up, the frail biddy act completely gone, Dora faced Justin. 'I suggest that, before you go, you write Cass a cheque to cover the cost of her ex-employees' redundancy pay.'

'I will do no such thing.'

'I think you will.' Dan's voice was so quiet, but so commanding that only a fool would have disobeyed.

317

'And what exactly are you threatening me with now, Cassandra? His fists?'

'Not at all. Like all military folk, Dan is a man who prefers peace. You will write a cheque now, or I will personally phone your wife, your partners at Family Values, and then the press, and tell them about your life as a multiple adulterer, and how you were outwitted by a little old lady,' Dora said sweetly.

In the grip of Dora's pokerface, Justin muttered multiple expletives. He wrote a cheque quickly and dropped it to the floor. 'How did you discover so much about me anyway?'

'I could tell you, but then I'd have to kill you!' Dora winked at Cass as Justin disappeared out of the house. 'I have always wanted to say that!'

Chapter Thirty-four

Cass hadn't thought she'd sleep, but emotional exhaustion had managed to conquer the combined sensations of hurt, betrayal, relief, and gratitude, along with whatever the hell it was she was feeling for Dan.

Her gaze landed on the cheque that sat on her bedside table. Cass had deliberately placed it there in case she felt the need to see it if she woke up in the night. A tangible thing to look at. Reassurance that she hadn't dreamed Justin's begrudging act of compensation towards her staff.

A small tug at her heart sent a bruising feeling through her slim frame. He had loved her. But not enough. Not enough to not give in to his male vanity and sleep with Crystal, and certainly not more than his career.

With Justin gone, Cass knew she was finally free to start a new life. She would instruct Donald to get the redundancy money to her ex-staff, and start planning her own future. It was time to claw back some level of control over her life.

The thought of how gullible she'd been made Cass shiver beneath her duvet. It was that feeling which was stopping her feeling guilty about extracting money from Justin rather than directly from his wife – she didn't even want to consider Crystal.

Torn between wanting to leap out of bed and start the

rest of her life, and hide under the covers in shame, Cass started thinking about Dora and Stan.

She hoped Max and Jacob had given Stan a good stag night, and that Dan had got Dora home in time to bluff her way to victory in her poker hen night.

In the discomfort of the evening before, Cass hadn't stopped to wonder why Dan had been there rather than Max and Abi. As she watched the sun's rays peeping through the small triangular gap at the top of her bedroom curtains, logic began to make its presence felt, and she realised Dan had been there for purely practical reasons. Max had obviously had to stay with Stan while they waited for Jacob, and their night out to start, and Abi would have been keeping Beth company. Dan was the only person left. Anyway, it was his job to look after Dora. He hadn't come because he wanted to, but because it was part of his job.

For a moment, when he'd slipped his arms around her shoulders, Cass had hoped it was because Dan cared for her a bit. The morning light was making things much clearer.

Cass realised that she was already dangerously close to being taken in by a man again; and all thanks to her physical attraction to him. A man who, whichever way she looked at it, was as far away from her type as it was possible to get.

She wasn't going to be used again. Ever.

Dan was a good person, like all the other people she'd been lucky enough to meet in Sennen, but he was just a friend. The roses had been yellow after all. End of story.

* * *

'How's the head?'

Jacob grimaced as Beth drove them into the car park of the West Cornwall Hospital, on the outskirts of Penzance. 'I must be getting past it. I only had three pints so I didn't let you down this morning, but my head is thudding the same as if I'd downed a brewery's worth of beer.'

'Old age and impending fatherhood already taking their toll then.'

'Cheek.' Jacob took a swig from a bottle of water, washing down some paracetamol. 'Stan had a good time though. He can still drink a fair bit, you know.'

'I don't doubt it.' Beth smiled at the thought of Stan chuckling his way through the evening. 'Is he looking forward to tomorrow?'

'Very much.'

Finally spotting a free parking space, Beth turned off the engine and breathed out slowly.

Jacob frowned. 'You alright?'

'Nervous.'

'I thought you'd be excited. We're going to see our wee one for the very first time. Sort of anyway.'

Beth rummaged through her purse for some change for the pay and display machine. 'I am. I can't wait, but at the same time…'

'At the same time what?'

'I'm scared. What if there is something wrong? I'm not sure I'm strong enough for that. Aren't you a little bit worried about what lies ahead? And what if I'm a badly prepared parent.'

Jacob scooped the loose change from Beth's palm to go and fetch a parking ticket. 'I'd be lying if I said I wasn't a bit apprehensive, but it's so exciting. The very best of adventures.'

'Really?' Beth stared lovingly into Jacob's eyes.

'Really. And whatever happens, we'll have the adventure together. Look, love, you are fit, healthy, you don't drink much, and you don't smoke at all. There is no reason anything should be wrong, is there.'

'I suppose not.' Climbing out of the car, Beth heaved the holdall she'd brought off the back seat.

'I'm still not sure why you've got so much stuff with you, though.'

'Well, the doctor said we could be here ages while we wait for our turn, so I've got us some puzzle books and snacks. Plus, because our first scan is potentially a bit late, they could want to do a more thorough examination. I've got my dressing gown and stuff in case I have to strip off. Not to mention a urine sample.'

Jacob laughed. 'What were you saying about being a badly prepared parent?'

Max cursed under his breath. Why did Beth's scan appointment have to be this morning, just when he could use her help.

The suitcase was open on the bed, and his half was already packed. It had been easy. Some clean underwear, a spare T-shirt, a shirt for the evening, clean jeans, and a jumper in case the temperature dropped.

Abi's clothes drawers had been open for over half an hour, and still Max didn't know where to start.

Muttering, he decided to tackle the problem methodically. 'Obviously she will need clean knickers.'

Having always appreciated Abi's underwear when she wore it – or at least when she took it off – being faced with a mound of mixed-up satin and lace left Max totally confused. 'So, the main rule with women's underwear is that the knickers match the bra. Where are the bras?'

Bemused as to why they weren't next to the knickers in the drawer, when her socks were, Max pulled out three pairs of socks, three of his favourite black panties, crossing his fingers that they were ones Abi would have chosen herself, and began an exploration of the next drawer down for bras.

'Oh, good grief.' Max found himself face to face with a bewildering array of bras, mostly black or white but with many other colours thrown in. Some had straps one way, some another – some had no straps at all. 'What the hell would I have found in here if Abi was the sort of woman who actually cared about clothes?' He had the sudden thought that Cass probably had an entire chest of drawers full of bras, colour-coded neatly into all shades of the spectrum.

Selecting two black bras, and crossing his fingers he'd got that right, Max steeled himself for guessing which outer garments Abi might want to wear during their trip away.

Last night, discussing the night away he'd got planned with Jacob and Stan, he'd told them he was going to tell Abi today so that she could pack herself, and therefore they wouldn't start their anniversary with an argument about missing T-shirts. Both of the other men had been adamant he should do no such thing. That the whole point of a surprise was to keep it until the last possible second.

And anyway, they had reassured him, Abi wasn't the sort of woman who was in the least bit worried about clothes, as long as she was comfortable and happy.

Last night, with a pint of Tribute in front of him, Max had believed his friends. Now, with the wardrobe doors wide open, and the realisation that he might have to return to the perilous arena of the underwear drawers to find some tights if he packed a dress for Abi, he was having doubts.

Going cold as he remembered how close he'd come to messing things up with his partner only a few days ago, Max bravely entered the dress domain, and after picking one he'd seen Abi wear before, he kept packing, trying to banish thoughts of what shoes went with what.

'Elizabeth Philips?'

Beth gave Jacob an anxious glance as they got up from the plastic seats, which they'd been sat in so long it felt as though they'd been welded to their backsides.

Following the midwife into a small side room, Jacob slipped his hand into Beth's. 'I don't think I've ever heard anyone use your proper name before. I thought she was calling someone else for a minute.'

Glad to be able to dispel her anxiety by talking about something else other than the forthcoming scan, Beth said, 'Grandad used to call me Lizzie, but no one ever used Elizabeth, not even my parents. I'm not sure why they didn't call me Beth in the first place.'

'It must be lovely to have a name with an element of choice. I mean, Jacob is just Jacob. Well, I suppose it could be Jake. But Elizabeth can be Beth, Liz, Lizzie,

Bess... I think we should pick a name for Denny junior which gives them scope to adapt it, fit their own personality. What do you think?'

'I think I'd like a pee!' Beth smiled at the midwife who was now giving them all her attention.

'Not long until you can go and get comfortable, I promise.' She patted the paper-covered bed, which was positioned next to a computer monitor and some equipment Beth decided not to look at. 'I'm Sue, and I'm going to introduce you to your baby.'

Beth felt a tremor of excitement edge ahead of the nerves that had been somersaulting around inside her all morning.

'Do you have a sample for me?'

Jacob rummaged in the bag and produced the phial for Sue's inspection.

'Excellent. I'll test that while you undo your trousers for me, Elizabeth. Just rolling them down a little will be fine for today.'

'OK.' Doing what she was told, Beth gave Jacob a look which told him clearly that she wanted him to hold her hand.

Seconds later, Sue was pouring the sample down the sink and scrubbing her hands. 'Well, that was perfect. Now, are you ready?'

'As I'll ever be, and, um, it's Beth.'

'I like that. Suits you better than Elizabeth.' Sue smiled at the almost parents before her. 'Let's have a peep.' She gave the bottle of gel a shake and squeezed a little onto Beth's mini bump.

'Oh! I expected it to be cold.'

'We're less cruel to our new mums these days; it's all warmed in advance!' Sue placed a plastic scanner over the gel. 'You have a little bump already. I see from your notes that you're almost four months pregnant, so we should get a clearer picture than if you'd only been three weeks. Have you drunk plenty of water while you waited?'

'Gallons. I am in danger of wetting myself.'

Sue laughed. 'You wouldn't be the first. But fear not, there is a toilet through that door. As soon as I'm done you can run through at speed.'

A moment later, however, Beth had forgotten all about her desperation to visit the bathroom. She'd also forgotten about how scared she was about being a mum.

'Oh, wow.' Jacob squeezed Beth's hand, tears pricking at the corner of his eyes as they watched the computer monitor burst into life.

'Is that really our baby?' Beth's voice was full of wonder.

Sue moved the ultrasound probe through the gel. 'It is; and I'm pleased to report that all limbs are where they ought to be.' Sue pointed to four points on the screen which looked like blurry lines to Beth, but she didn't care. It was the little face that captivated her. That, and the heart. It was beating so fast it seemed impossible.

'My baby is alright?'

'You and your baby are in fine health. However, I suspect you are nearer four and a half months gone than four. Would you like me to print off some photographs for you to take away?'

'Yes, please.'

Thirty seconds later, clutching the photos as if she still

couldn't quite believe what she was seeing, Beth dashed to the bathroom. *Grandad, it's real. I'm having a baby!*

Chapter Thirty-five

Abi stared at the photo in her hands, a knot of emotion forming in her throat. 'These are so beautiful. How are you feeling?'

'Elated but odd covers it.' Beth passed a photograph to Dora, who shared it with Cass as they sat in the garden of the Lamorna Wink pub, having a last planning meeting before the wedding. 'It's like looking at something that isn't real – and yet it is.'

Dora gazed in wonder. 'I can't get over how clear these pictures are these days. They used to be grey and black smears on a piece of paper. This is incredible.'

'I wasn't sure what to expect. I was so nervous that I hadn't allowed myself to think about what was going to happen. I just wanted to hear that my baby was alright, nothing else really mattered until I knew that all was OK.' Beth put a protective hand on her stomach as she spoke. 'You should have seen Jacob. He was blown away.'

'I can imagine.' Abi swapped photographs with Cass, as she privately wondered how Max would react in that situation. 'When do you have to go back for your next scan?'

'Not for two months. They can tell us if it's a girl or a boy then, but we've decided not to find out.'

Dora nodded with approval. 'Quite right. Some things

aren't meant to be known until they are meant to be known. Happy and healthy is what you want.'

Cass laughed. 'You old-fashioned thing you, Dora.'

'I am,' Dora picked up her glass of wine, 'in some ways at least. In other ways I am bang up to the minute. Why else would I be sat with three under-forties for my last evening as a single woman since 1950?'

'Because you are young at heart!' Abi raised her glass in Dora's direction as the waiter arrived with a tray piled impossibly high with cheesy chips, steak and salad.

'I certainly hope so.' Dora winked at the young waiter, who obligingly winked back, making them all laugh.

Cass picked up a chip and watched as a loop of melted cheese clung on with dear life. 'I never used to eat these in London.'

Abi picked up a chip of her own. 'Nor me. Luke thought eating anything with unnecessary fat was the first step on the road to ruin.'

Relishing the taste of her first mouthful, Cass said, 'I was so paranoid about putting weight on. I thought Justin would leave me. Ironic, huh.'

'About as ironic as Luke dying of a heart attack despite being a health freak.'

'God, really?'

'Yep. So eat what you like, do what you like, but keep things in moderation.'

Dora clapped. 'Wise words, Abi.'

'I'd like to claim credit for such wisdom, but it was Stan who told me that.'

The bride-to-be played her fork in her liver-spotted hand. 'I loved my Gordon very much. It took me many

330

years to allow myself to even consider that when I went home from work he wouldn't be there.' She looked Cass square in the face as she carried on talking. 'For over a decade I never went home properly. Sometimes I wonder if I ever truly accepted my loss until I was in my seventies and had no choice but to retire. Then, like a miracle, Stan came to Chalk Towers and saw me. The *real* me. Not Dora the poker wizard, or Dora the life and soul of the party, but me. The one on the inside.'

The girls were quiet, each feeling their respect for the woman before them grow even higher. Beth broke the tension by starting to talk about how much her grandad Jack had liked Stan, but Cass wasn't listening. An image of Dan sat next to her on the bench near the hotel where they were due to return for the wedding tea the following day. *Does Dan see the real me? The one inside? The one I'm only just discovering myself...*

'So are you and Stan ready for tomorrow then, Dora?' Abi topped up everyone's wine glasses with either alcohol or orange juice.

'As we'll ever be. Dan has been a total star helping to organise everything. Very much going above and beyond his remit as a care manager.'

Cass looked up at the mention of Dan's name. 'That sounds about right. He was very kind to me when I felt ill at the hotel.'

Dora gave Cass an assessing look. 'He is a good man. Not too many like him.'

Catching the undertone of what Dora was saying, and seeing that Cass was feeling uncomfortable, Abi kept the conversation moving. 'Has Dan got transport organised for the Chalk Towers crew, or do you want Max and myself to do a few trips ferrying folk back and forth?'

'Bless you, but Dan has a minibus booked. He was going to drive it himself, but I've persuaded him to hire a driver so he can stay for the reception.'

'Sounds good.' Trying not to feel nervous about her role as chief bridesmaid, Abi asked, 'I don't have to do anything apart from stand there and hold flowers, do I? You aren't going to drop me in it and demand a speech or anything?'

'As if I would!'

Beth rolled her eyes. 'Yes, you would. Don't you dare do that to any of us!'

Dora chuckled. 'Fear not, Jacob is giving me away, so he'll be doing a quick speech, and then it's over to Stan's best man. I dread to think what he'll say.'

'Who is the best man?' Cass was trying to stop herself from daydreaming about what Dan was going to look like in a suit.

'Didn't Stan say? It's Max. If Beth's grandfather, Jack, had been alive, it would have been him of course. They were best friends at school.'

Beth looked at Abi. 'Has he written a speech yet?'

'He's been very quiet these last few nights, and he keeps making lists of things to say. He won't let me read it though.'

Before Dora could speculate on what might be in the speech, Beth's mobile burst into life. 'Oh, I'm sorry, Dora; I thought I'd switched it off.'

'No worries. Who is it?'

'Max. Maybe he's been trying to reach you Abi. Is your phone off?'

Abi immediately reached for her phone, but there was no missed texts or calls. She frowned as Beth answered her call, hoping everything was alright.

Pulling away from the phone for a second, Beth said, 'Max is fine, Abi. He assumed you'd have your phone on silent. The gallery has got busy and he can't find the price list for the paintings.'

Abi laughed. 'Sounds like Max.'

Taking the phone and wandering away from the table, Beth whispered into the mobile. 'Max, what do you mean you can't find Abi's tights? What the hell are you doing? I never had you down as a cross-dresser.'

'It is my day off!'

'Max! I have told Abi you're at the gallery and can't find the price list. What are you really doing?'

'I told you. I'm searching for Abi's tights. I'm trying to pack secretly for our trip while rehearsing my speech.'

'Of course! Sorry, I forgot about the trip. I take it Abi has no idea?'

'Not a clue. But packing for women is a nightmare. What do I take?'

Beth laughed. 'OK Maxwell. Count to ten, grab a pen and paper, and we'll write another list. Ready?'

Abi had made serious inroads into her steak and chips before Beth came back. 'Has he found the price list?'

'Yes. Max is very much with list now.'

Dora chuckled. 'I bet Stan is asleep on the gallery sofa. Can't see you'd have many customers with him there. You've heard his snore, Abi; it could curl paint off the walls, so I fear for your watercolours.'

Beth laughed, only feeling a little bad for her white lie, for in fact it was Stan and Jacob who were holding the fort that afternoon.

Cass stabbed her last chip into a pot of peppered mayonnaise. 'Nonsense, I bet Stan's charming everyone who comes in. Sales will be up.'

'Will you close the gallery on the day of the wedding, or will you get someone to open it for you?' asked Dora

'I was considering taking the day off, and staying closed,' Abi said. 'What do you think, Beth? Beth?'

Beth had gone pale and very still.

Abi reached out a hand. 'Beth?'

'I'm OK. Oh, my goodness.'

'What is it?' Cass and Dora exchanged anxious glances.

'I think the baby just kicked. Oh, wow. That was weird.'

'So early?' Abi automatically put her palm out to see if she could feel, 'May I?'

'Please do, although it seems to have been a one-off. The midwife thought I was four and half months already rather than almost four months, so it's about right according to the baby book Jacob picked up yesterday. I tell you, I have never seen him devour a non-pottery related book so fast and so thoroughly. I might have imagined the kick…oh! Or maybe not.'

Abi smile wider as a tiny flickering hit her palm through Beth's T-shirt. 'That is incredible.'

As the feeling subsided, Beth relaxed. 'I can't even

334

begin to describe how that felt.' She picked her mobile back up. 'If you'll excuse me once again, Dora, I have to call Jacob.'

Chapter Thirty-six

Jacob bounded into the bedroom, a cup of tea and a pile of hot buttered toast on a tray, wearing nothing but an apron. 'Breakfast is served, madam.'

Beth burst out laughing. 'Oh my goodness! You look incredible, but I hope you'll at least stick a pair of boxers on before we go to the hotel!'

'Possibly. It's hot out there though, so I could go like this!' Jacob sat down on the bed next to Beth. 'Open wide, I've got to feed you up. We're going to need all the energy we can get today. All three of us!'

Beth kissed Jacob. 'After today you can feed baby and me as much as you like but if I can't fit into my bridesmaid outfit then there'll be trouble.'

'No there wouldn't!' Jacob grinned. 'Anyway, you could always wear my apron instead.'

Max's freckles looked particularly obvious as he sat at the kitchen table, which Abi recognised as a sign that her partner was nervous.

'Don't worry; you'll be a fabulous a best man.'

'It's been years since I did any public speaking. Perhaps it's just as well I gave up teaching to be a decorator, I'd have been permanently tongue-tied.'

'You'd have been an excellent teacher. I'm glad you

are a decorator though.' Abi pushed a mug of tea across the table.

Max smiled. 'Because you get to wash a load of paint-spattered overalls every weekend?'

'Because, if you'd been a teacher you wouldn't have been in the pub in St Just when I first came to Cornwall, you'd have been in another town or village and we would never have met. Unthinkable.'

Looking Abi straight in the eye, Max reached out to her. 'Unthinkable.'

Coming around the table to sit on Max's lap, Abi snuggled against his chest. 'Do you want to rehearse your speech with me?'

'No. I want to help you get into your wedding clobber.'

'But Stan might get up any minute!'

'He knows where everything is!'

Cass stood in front of her wardrobe. It was an act of habit. She already knew what she'd be wearing for the majority of the day. For the job she had to do first, any clothes would do.

Pulling on her jeans and the oversized T-shirt she'd purchased on her first trip to Truro, Cass picked up the cheque from Justin, slipped it into her handbag, and headed for the little hire car she had already decided she'd buy if she could.

Donald Clearer was expecting her at ten o'clock to arrange the compensation of her ex-employees. Alongside the cheque, Cass had written a personal note of regret and explanation to each of her governesses; with a fervent promise that if any of them wanted a reference at any time, then all they had to do was ask.

With the knowledge that once she had seen Donald the London chapter of her life would be over, Cass experienced a lightness she hadn't felt for a long time.

Standing outside the lawyer's office, Cass watched the flow of people moving up and down Penzance high street. She chuckled to herself. Compared to London this wasn't busy at all, but now, to her, it was.

In a few hours' time she'd be wearing her bridesmaid outfit, helping launch friends she never dreamed she'd have step into a new chapter of their lives.

In a few hours' time she'd be free.

'Are you alright then, Stan?'

'Right as ninepence, thanks, Abi girl.' Stan was tucking into the full English breakfast she'd cooked for him. 'Fabulous bacon this. Local?'

'Farm shop on the outskirts of Penzance. Good, isn't it?'

'The breakfast at Chalk Towers is good – if you want to have the communal breakfast, that is – but it isn't a patch on this. I'll get Dora to ask Dan to get the cook to buy this instead.'

'And why can't you ask Dan yourself?'

'Because Dora is far better at making things happen.'

Abi laughed. 'I can't argue with that. I haven't seen Cass yet, but Dora seemed satisfied that she'd be ready to move on with her life this morning.'

Stan chewed his toast thoughtfully. 'The future Mrs Abbey is, without doubt, one of the most remarkable women I have ever met. I can't believe how lucky I am.'

Abi sat down next to Stan as Max came in, his ginger hair wet from the shower. 'Oh, this looks marvellous. If one of Abi's fry-ups doesn't set you up for the day, Stan, then nothing will.'

'My Mary used to make a wonderful breakfast.' Stan smiled as he gazed at the kitchen sink where his first wife had stood so often. 'I hope she would be pleased for me. I know she'd be pleased that you two are taking care of her home so well.'

'Mary was something special; she'd be happy for you.' Everything she'd heard about Stan's first wife over the past year convinced Abi she was right about that. 'And the fact that Dora respects her memory enough to get married at the Queen's speaks volumes.'

'Dora surprises me every day.' Stan nodded into his mug of tea. 'I'm one lucky old duffer!'

Dan examined his reflection in the mirror. He still wasn't sure about this, but Stan had insisted. He'd said that Dan should wear his uniform, because it was time to be proud of the lives he'd saved, and accept that there'd always be lives he hadn't been able to save.

Looking back on the walk he'd orchestrated to cheer Stan up after Sally's hostile reception to the wedding, Dan saw that it had in fact been him who'd had the pep talk from Stan, not the other way round.

It had been a long time since Dan had worn his dress uniform, and he hadn't been sure it would still fit. Rather than being too small for him, it was a little loose if anything, a reminder that he didn't knock back as much beer now as in his Army days.

To his relief, Dan didn't feel the revulsion he'd expected to as he examined himself critically. Talking to Stan, and then confessing to Cass, had obviously done him good.

Cass.

The city girl was occupying more of his waking thoughts with each passing day. Instinct, however, told him to hang back. No matter what Dora said, he was convinced Cass wasn't ready for commitment with anyone new yet. But maybe, if they could become better friends…That would be a start.

'Stan, you are so handsome.'

'Thank you, Abi girl.'

'Honestly, you look the cat's whiskers.'

Stan laughed. 'That's such a strange old saying.'

'It is a bit.' Abi laughed too, as the door to the kitchen opened and Max came in, wearing his suit. 'Wow. You're gorgeous.'

Max beamed. 'Less disbelief in your voice would be preferable, Abi Carter!'

'Sorry.' Abi gave him a look that told Max in no uncertain terms that she very much approved of how good he looked in his shirt and tie, before saying, 'Well, if you'll excuse me, I'd better go next door, it's time Cass and I got changed.'

Abi gave Max and Stan a kiss each. 'Good luck, Stan. See you at the hotel!'

'Ready, girls?'

Jacob smiled at the three bridesmaids as Abi and Cass carefully adjusted their dresses so they could sit in his car, where Beth was already waiting. 'You look like a round of the most delicious coffee mochas ever!'

'Cheeky sod!' Beth gave Jacob a friendly slap on the leg. 'Now, drive!'

'Ready, Stan?'

'As I'll ever be, m'andsome.' Stan pointed to the van, which Max had cleaned in honour of the occasion. 'Wagons roll!'

'Ready, Dora?'

'Oh, my!' Dora regarded Dan with approval. 'If I was forty years younger, then Stan might have a bit of competition! Cass is going to have her eyes knocked out.'

'Dora, it's your wedding day! No matchmaking! Anyway, I'm the one who is supposed to tell you how amazing you look. Which you do. That lady in Zennor may be a bit scary, but she sure knows how to fit a wedding dress.'

'Why thank you, soldier boy.' Dora curtseyed. 'Alright then. Come on, chauffeur! Let's go get me married.'

Pulling the car into the hotel car park, Dan pointed to a minibus. 'Looks like the Chalk Towers crew are here already.'

'And so are the others.' Dora spotted Max's van and Jacob's car. 'I hope there are plenty of people with cameras. I want someone to capture the moment when Cass sees you in that uniform.'

'Dora!' Dan felt himself blushing. 'You promised. No matchmaking today.'

'I won't have to do or say a thing. All she'll need to do is look at you in that outfit.'

Helping Dora from the car, Dan sent a text to Abi as arranged to let them know they'd arrived. Half of him didn't want to see Cass. He knew she'd look gorgeous, and he wasn't sure how she'd react if he told her so. After all, he had tattoos and spiked hair…

The thought died the second the bridesmaids walked towards Dora. All three of them were smiling widely. Radiant didn't even begin to describe them as the summer sunshine shone on the soft fabric of their dresses and lit up their perfectly dressed hair and natural make-up.

Dan had told himself he wasn't going to search out Cass, but he couldn't help himself.

'Oh, my…' He spoke so softly that only Dora heard.

'Beautiful, isn't she?'

'Beautiful but lost.' Dan whispered back to the bride-to-be as they waited by the car for her escort, who came not just with smiles, but with a small arrangement of flowers for Dora to carry.

Cass hadn't been prepared. She had assumed Dan would be in a regular suit. Until then, she'd thought that going 'weak at the knees' was a fiction made up by romance writers. Now she knew different.

As Dan took Dora's arm to escort her to the door, Abi took up her place directly behind them, while Cass and

Beth linked arms and followed on.

When they got to the hotel's wedding room, Dan stood back so that Jacob could walk Dora down the aisle, when the potter whispered, 'Change of plan. Are you alright with Dan giving you away, Dora?'

Beth frowned. 'Everything OK?'

'Perfect.' Jacob winked. 'OK with you, Dora? Dan?'

Dora looked at the potter shrewdly. 'What are you up to?'

'You'll see,' Jacob shouted, as he dashed to the front of the room.

Dan, who stood a little straighter as he found himself thrust into the limelight, rather than perching on a chair at the back of the room as he'd intended, took a deep breath.

With a thumbs-up to Max, who stood with Stan and Sadie at the front, Jacob waved to the registrar, who gave the signal for the music to start.

Dan looked at his companion. 'Best foot forward, Dora?'

'Always.'

As they walked down the aisle that had been fashioned between the rows of chairs, all of which were occupied – by Chalk Towers residents and many of the inhabitants of Sennen Cove who'd known Stan for years – Abi could see precisely why the potter couldn't give Dora away as planned.

Jacob was next to the registrar, a large-screened tablet open and on, showing Sally, Pippa and Craig, all up despite it being the middle of the night in Australia. Dressed up to the nines, they were waving madly as they prepared to watched Stan and Dora tie the knot.

Thank goodness for Skype! Abi wondered if Stan was crying as he saw his family cheering him on.

Chapter Thirty-seven

The hotel dining room had been arranged perfectly. Stan, his new wife Dora, Max, and Abi sat side by side at a small rectangular table in the round of a bay window. Groups of circular tables were laid out before them, with seats placed three-quarters of the way around each one, so no one had their backs to the happy couple.

The Skype connection was still running, and with a brief apology to Sally and her children, Jacob blurred their view as he carried them through from the ceremony room to the dining room, ready to hear the speeches.

Vast arrays of scones, jam, clotted cream and butter sat on each table, with an accompanying selection of finger sandwiches, bottles of champagne, and jugs of iced water.

The staff, attentive throughout, were circulating with colossal pots of tea and coffee, as the atmosphere of happy chatter wrapped itself around everyone present.

Waving to Max, who was sat at the far end of their table next to Dora, Abi watched as he read some prompt cards he'd extracted from his suit pocket. 'You'll be great.'

'Thanks, Abi. Spot of stage fright.'

Dora turned to their best man while Stan was talking in a happily animated fashion to his family in Australia. 'Do you think Dan has worked out that he has to do the father

347

of the bride speech as well?'

Max glanced at Dan, who was sat next to Cass, obviously trying not to look at her, just as much as Cass was trying not to look at him. 'I suspect not. I'd better have a quick word. Maybe Jacob could tell him what he'd been planning to say before the Skype thing worked out.'

Approaching Dan at the same time as beckoning Jacob, Max crossed the room. 'Dan, mate, you know you have to make a speech, don't you?'

'Hell, I hadn't thought of that!' Dan turned to Jacob, who was approaching with a large glass of champagne in one hand and a heavily laden cream and jam scone in the other. 'What were you going to say as pseudo-father of the bride? Can you still do it? I'm not sure speeches are my thing.'

'No can do, I'm afraid. I've promised Sally I'll hold up the Skype so she can watch proceedings.'

'I could do that.' Dan grimaced. 'I've never been comfortable with public speaking.'

Jacob studied Dan for a second. 'Stan and Dora would like it if you did; you know they would. You know them both better than I do.'

'That's emotional blackmail.'

'True.' Jacob shrugged. 'All I was going to do was thank everyone for coming, wish Stan luck for taking on the poker queen of Chalk Towers, raise a toast, and hand over to Max.'

'That was all? Really?'

'Yep.'

Cass watched as Jacob went to check the Skype connection was behaving before the speeches started.

Despite being determined not to even glance at Dan in case her expression gave away how attractive she found him, she knew he could do with some reassurance.

Dan would reassure you, now he needs you to reassure him.

Swallowing hard, ignoring her resolve not to let the effect of being so close to Dan show, Cass turned to Dan as he anxiously fiddled with an empty teacup. 'You've done far harder things than this.'

'I hate this sort of thing.'

Cass smiled back, trying not to look into Dan's eyes and failing. 'I can't imagine you getting nervous about anything.'

'You are very kind.'

'Am I? You weren't so sure a few weeks ago.'

'Perhaps we've both changed a bit lately.'

'For the better?'

'I think so.' Dan got no further. He felt his throat go dry as Max stood and tapped the side of his glass to bring the room to order.

Risking rejection, Cass put a hand on Dan's leg under the table. 'I know you can do this. Stan and Dora will be so proud. And it all fits.'

'Fits?' Dan slid a palm on top of Cass's hand, soothed by its presence.

'Dora's husband was a war hero, so was Stan as far as I'm concerned. And so are you.'

'I was no such thing.'

Cass whispered fast under her breath, so that only Dan could hear her, 'Daniel Millfield, you have saved *lives*! You have done more good in the world than I could ever strive to. Don't you dare tell me you aren't a brave man.'

Stunned by the passionate yet muted outburst of the woman next to him, whose eyes were telling him so much more than they could have said there and then, Dan inclined his head a fraction. 'Can we talk? Soon I mean. After the ceremony.'

'I'd like that.' Cass gave his hand an encouraging squeeze. 'Go on, you're up.'

As Dan stood in front of everyone, resplendent in his uniform, Cass thought her heart would burst with pride. She knew she'd fallen for him. *Crap timing, Cass. How very you.*

Sliding back into his seat, Dan let a silent rush of relief escape from between his teeth. Cass muttered a quick, 'well done', and then placed her hands on the table so that she wasn't tempted to hug him in case she couldn't let go again.

Max waited just long enough for the clapping to subside before he got to his feet. 'Ladies and gentlemen, I've thought very carefully about what to say to you this afternoon. How to sum up what Stan and Dora mean, not just to me, but to my beautiful partner Abi, and our friends...' Max glanced across at Beth, Jacob, Dan and Cass '. . . isn't easy, their lives have been so full of love and adventure and, above all, compassion.

'Compassion. It's a word that's often seen as rather clichéd, a weak word even. But it isn't, and Stan and Dora are the proof of that.

'Some of you will know that it was exactly one year ago today that I was lucky enough to walk into a pub –

350

nothing unusual in that! – but on that day I saw a young woman looking a little bit lost. There was such a determination about her however that something about her caught me right in the heart.

'That girl was Abi Carter. A girl who I discovered was searching for a house. A very special house.'

Abi felt tears prick at her eyes as she risked a glance at Sally listening so intently from the other side of the world; who raised a glass to her. Abi didn't dare look at Stan, for she knew she'd break down if he was looking as choked as she felt as Max continued.

'With the help of my best friend Beth, Abi and I found the house, and there we came across the most extraordinary man I've ever met. We met Mr Stanley Abbey.'

Dora put down her glass and reached out a hand to Stan, who had his eyes fixed unwaveringly on his best man.

'Stan may be a fraction older than me in years, but in his heart he is young, he is brave, and he always has a go. Last year Jacob and I took Stan to an auction at Christie's in London, we helped him move to Chalk Towers, we have seen him take steps that a younger person may never have the guts to take. Abi and I learned early on that Stan has a "grasp life with both hands" mentality. A view we thought no one could better.

'Until we met Dora.

'Dora.' Max stopped and looked at the bride with an expression of stunned affection that made everyone laugh. 'Dora has been working quiet miracles all her life. Undercover, underground. She has seen so much, done so much, and helped keep this country and the people in it safe without them having any idea.

'Coming to live at Chalk Towers soon after it opened, Dora didn't take a minute to whip the place into shape.' A chuckle from the residents rippled across the room. 'And I understand from Dan that nearly everyone in the place has fallen victim to her skill with a pack of cards...'

General choruses of agreement were made as Max turned to the Skype screen. 'And so when Max and Dora met, it was only a matter of time before two such happy souls should find each other.

'We have many of Stan and Dora's friends here today, but we also have, via the magic of technology, Stan's daughter Sally, and his grandchildren Craig and Pippa with us. I'd like you all to raise a glass to Australia now, and take your hat off to them for getting up to drink champagne at three o'clock in the morning so they could join in this special occasion.'

A moment later, his throat refreshed, Max resumed. 'I mentioned compassion.

'Stan didn't *have to* welcome Abi and myself into his home, a home which was to become ours. He could have turned us away. But he didn't. If he had, we wouldn't be here today.

'Dora didn't *have to* help a good friend of ours free herself from an unpleasant man who was making her life difficult. But she did.'

Cass swallowed, before raising her glass to Dora with a personal nod of thanks.

'Stan and Dora make time for people. They care. A rare thing in this modern world.' Near the end of his speech, Max pivoted on his toes to face the bride and groom. 'Stan and Dora care. Not just for each other, but for everyone and everything, and I for one am privileged to know them, to love them, and to be able to call them my friends.

'Please stand and raise a toast to the brand new Mr and Mrs Abbey.

'Dora and Stan.'

Beth washed her hands, and was just checking that her hair was still being held in the butterfly-shaped hairclips that were struggling to hold it in position, when Abi and Cass came into the ladies' washroom.

'That was some speech from Max, did you know he was going to say anything about your anniversary.'

'Not a clue.' Abi stared at her own hair in the mirror. Blonde strands were poking out at all sorts of odd angles. Taking the clips out instead of readjusting them, Abi let her hair down and shook it free. 'With the wedding and everything, I'd forgotten it was exactly a year today since Max found me in the pub. It's been one hell of a twelve months, hasn't it?'

'You aren't kidding.' Beth, following Abi's example, freed her own hair, and stood side on to the mirror; her bump was evident beneath her skirt. 'Do you think women ever get used to being pregnant? It's such a leap to think there's a person growing inside me.'

'I doubt it. It's pretty amazing though.' Abi attempted to tuck a bit of her fringe that had escaped Cass's heavy hand with the hairspray into place. 'I bet you can't wait until it's born.'

'I can, and I can't. If you see what I mean.' Beth yawned. 'Sorry, as well as being constantly hungry, I'm tired all the time. Thank goodness this is an afternoon do and not an all-nighter.'

'Won't be long until we go now. Stan has already booked himself and Dora into the honeymoon suite upstairs.'

Beth laughed. 'I love that. Late eighties and heading for a night of passion in the honeymoon suite. Those two are unstoppable!'

Having corralled the tired, mildly tipsy, and boisterous residents of Chalk Towers into the minibus, Dan made his way to the reception to make sure the staff had his number if there was a happy couple related emergency, before walking through the car park to take his leave of Max, Abi, Beth, Jacob, and have his promised talk with Cass.

Sadie snuggled against Max's legs, as the bridesmaids, duty done, laid their mini bouquets in the back of Max's van, and jointly wished they'd thought to bring flat shoes to change into after the ceremony.

Just as Dan joined them, Max loosened his tie, and passed Sadie's lead and a set of keys to Cass. 'You sure you'll be OK with this old girl?'

'Of course.' Cass knelt down as much as her fitted outfit would allow, and cuddled the retriever. Sadie seemed to accept her temporary ownership with the same grace she accepted everything. 'We're going to put the world to rights together, aren't we, Sadie?'

Max smiled. 'Well she's very good at that, aren't you, old girl?'

Abi, who'd been having another go at trying to convince Beth that she had plenty of time to worry about finding a bigger place to live once the baby was actually in the world, registered that Sadie wasn't coming home with them. 'What's going on?'

Max pulled his van keys from his pocket and held them up. 'We're escaping! Happy meeting me anniversary.'

A broad grin spread over Abi's face. 'We're going away. Tonight?'

'Not tonight. Right now. Come on, lass.' Max hopped into the van, and started the engine.

'But I haven't packed. I can't spend three days like this?'

'The suitcase is packed and in the back of the van.'

'You packed my clothes?' Abi was amused but suspicious.

'Well. I did, but then I panicked and phoned Beth, and she showed me how to repack.'

With a mouthed 'thank you' to Beth, Abi jumped into the van next to Max.

As they waved to their friends and Sadie, whose tail was wagging with its usual gusto, Abi asked, 'Where are we going, Max?'

'You'll see when we get there.'

Chapter Thirty-eight

Cass clutched a takeout coffee cup, putting an arm around Sadie's comforting bulk as they sat side by side on the sand. A fresh summer breeze brushed its way around them in the quiet of early morning Sennen.

'Do you think Abi would believe me if I told her I sat on the beach without being forced to?'

Sadie gave her temporary carer a look that told Cass quite clearly that Abi would be *most* surprised by this massive turn-around.

Only a day had passed since the wedding, but for Cass so much had happened. Or at least, so many corners in her life had been turned.

After Abi and Max and been waved off to a secret location, she had quickly taken her leave of Beth, Jacob and Dan with the excuse of getting Sadie settled at her place.

The urge to stay, to talk to Dan, or simply to hold his hand, had been strong, but Cass knew if she'd spoken to him there and then, emotion and lust would have taken the lead over common sense. If they were to have any sort of friendship, it had to develop away from the blurring of the guidelines caused by how well Dan wore his uniform, and the glances of approval he'd kept throwing her way when he'd thought she wasn't looking.

'I did the right thing just leaving after the reception, didn't I, Sadie?'

The retriever kept quiet on the subject of Cass's self-imposed seclusion, so she just hugged the dog tighter as they watched the waves curl up the beach together. Trying not to wish that Dan had tried to get in touch with her, Cass spoke up to the sky and a group of circling seagulls. 'No more time wasting thinking about things I can't control. If Dan is interested, he will come and find me.'

Sadie gave her another look.

'OK, I'm being contrary, aren't I?'

The dog put her head on Cass's knee, making her laugh. 'That'll be a yes then, will it?'

Stroking Sadie thoughtfully, she mused, 'At least I know Donald Clearer is on the case.'

The cheque from Justin had been paid in, and the money was already poised to be distributed to the one-time employees of The Pinkerton Agency, which had now been officially, and legally, dissolved. There was no need for Cass to have any contact with Justin Smythe again.

The news of his affair with Crystal, once the initial shock had subsided, was somehow inevitable. 'Once a cheat, always a cheat, isn't that what they say, Sadie?'

Taking a final draught of coffee, Cass put down her cup, and tucking her knees under her chin, stared at the clifftops where distant moving shadows denoted other early morning dog walkers taking the air. 'Perhaps I could get to like the beach if I could always have it all to myself.'

Tilting her head to one side, Sadie gave Cass such an old-fashioned stare that she couldn't help but laugh. 'I can see you're not convinced by that either. Maybe you're right. I'm not really a seaside dweller, am I?'

Brushing some offending sand off her palms, Cass got to her feet. 'Come on, Sadie, we have about five hours before Abi and Max get home, and a great deal to do before then.'

On hearing the names of her owners, the dog's tail began to wag.

'So, will you help me get on with my plan then, Sadie?'

Nudging Cass's legs in encouragement, the retriever led the way towards the car Cass had purchased the day before, having finally returned her hire car.

'Good girl. Let's go then. Time to implement the second part of my rebooted life.'

Jacob parked outside Abi's House, and let Stan and Dora out of the back seats.

Dora was laden with handfuls of pastel-coloured fabric bunting, while Stan carried a bag stuffed with groceries for Abi and Max to find on their return, and a large bunch of flowers. Getting out of the passenger seat, Beth joined Jacob by the car boot, where he was getting out a box of beer, wine, and some orange juice.

'You got the key, Stan? This lot weighs a ton.'

As Stan opened his old front door, Beth relieved Dora of some of the bunting. 'Ready?'

'For anything!'

Beth laughed. 'Right, let's get this place ready for the

best welcome home party ever.'

Cass tethered an obliging Sadie to a lamp post outside the estate agency and pushed open the door, where she was greeted with a broad smile from Maggie.

The agent hadn't expected to see Cass again so soon. It had only been yesterday that she'd come in to the office, apologised for her behaviour the first time they'd met, and explained her plans to a forgiving Maggie.

'Decision made then, Cass?'

'Yes. Decision made.'

Standing on the balcony of their hotel room, Abi stared out over the beautiful Wye Valley. Max couldn't have chosen a more romantic hotel for the anniversary of their first meeting. The woodland scene before her presented itself in a blanket of treetops, the twist of the River Wye to one side, a path leading into the forest on the other way.

The hotel itself was idyllic, the room perfect, and the locally sourced food delicious. They'd had the most wonderful time, enjoying each other's company without having to worry about anyone else but themselves. But...

The question that hadn't been asked had hung in the air between them the whole time.

Staring across the horizon, Abi could hear Max moving around their bedroom behind her, double-checking that they'd repacked all their clothes. She knew they couldn't leave before she'd said something; not if they wanted to move on with their lives. One of them had to put a pin in the bubble of uncertainty that had begun to inflate a little more each day since the news of Stan's engagement.

It had been many months now since the ghost of Abi's husband, Luke, had haunted her thoughts with his taunting put-downs, and yet she could hear him now, just on the edge of her consciousness.

You haven't got the guts, have you? Neither of you. You're pathetic.

Abi watched as a lone kestrel danced gracefully around the distant skyline. She'd been sure that Max would hate it if she was the one who brought up the question of marriage. Old-fashioned was his way, and if she mentioned it first, then she feared he'd feel he had failed in some way.

Another flash of Luke's gloating face floated through her mind. Marriage had not been a happy time for her, nor had Max's marriage been good for him. Abi's husband had almost instantly changed from a caring man to a nightmare during their honeymoon, and from what Beth had told her about Max's wife, the same could be said for her. *So, perhaps...*

'Are you alright, lass?'

Abi jumped. She had been so submerged in thought that she hadn't heard Max come up behind her. 'I was thinking.'

'Me too.' Parcelling her into his arms, Max drew Abi close, so that her back rested against his chest, as they stared out over the scenery. 'I love you, Abi.'

'I love you too, Max. It's been the most amazing year.

'And this month has been quite something as well, hasn't it?' Abi kept her eyes locked on the kestrel. 'With

Beth and Jacob starting a family and Stan and Dora proving love has no age limit. Well…it makes you think.'

'I know. Look…' Max paused, embracing Abi more firmly. 'I'm sorry if I seem a bit slow in moving things on. It's just…'

'It's OK.' Abi swivelled round and stared directly into Max's eyes. 'You told me before. We have to live at our own pace, not Beth and Jacob's, or even Stan and Dora's.'

Max bent down and kissed Abi gently on the lips. 'I want to spend the rest of my life with you.'

'And I you.' Abi began to laugh. 'Sorry, but I've just remembered that awful last scene from *Four Weddings and a Funeral*. You know, when it's pouring with rain and Hugh Grant asks the American woman to agree to *not* marry him.'

'Oh, I know the one you mean! They were both soaked to the skin. It was so corny. Dreadful scene. Almost killed a great film.'

There was a hushed silence, and then, acutely aware of every nerve in her body, Abi asked, 'Max, tell me honestly, because I feel like this is coming between us. What do you truly feel about marriage?'

Max tilted up his partner's chin. 'If I ever marry again it will be to you. And what about you? How do you feel about it?'

'The same.' Abi's heart soared as the gap that had been building between them began to close. 'I'm not ready to go that way again yet. Luke changed overnight when we married. I know you wouldn't, but at the same time…' Abi stopped as Max smiled in understanding ' . . . I do want to move on with *our* life, Max. A life together.

362

With a family perhaps?'

'No perhaps about it.' Max scooped Abi up in his arms, the expression in his eyes clearly showing his intention to start trying for a baby there and then.

Abi giggled. 'We can't now! We have to check out of the hotel in half an hour!'

'And I plan to make the most of every single one of those thirty minutes.'

Dan hung up his phone and laid it on his desk. He hadn't heard from Cass since the wedding. She had disappeared so quickly with Sadie that he hadn't even had the chance to tell her how much he'd like to get to know her properly now Justin had been extracted from her life.

It had been while he was giving his speech as he'd watched Cass watching him, willing him on with those incredible peppermint eyes, that Dan had decided he'd ask the city girl out for dinner as soon as the wedding was over. But somehow the time hadn't been right; there had been residents to help with food, and bathroom trips, and guests to chat to, and suddenly the wedding was over, and then Cass had made her excuses and gone without having their promised chat.

Dan fiddled with his mobile. Dora had been very definite about the fact his presence was required at Abi's House after his shift finished in an hour's time. Although he hadn't been able to see her face, Dan was convinced that it had her poker expression on it.

He hadn't been in Abi and Max's lives a year ago, so it made no sense at all for him to be invited to their mini anniversary party. Dora was matchmaking. Again. Cass,

363

as Abi's neighbour, was bound to be there.

Tilting his seat back so he could stretch out his long legs, Dan groaned at his own feebleness. He wanted to see Cass; but until she gave him some sign that she wanted to see him too, then Dan was determined not to go anywhere near either her or Miners Row.

Chapter Thirty-nine

'They are coming home today, aren't they?'

Beth looked at her watch for the third time in as many minutes.

'Oh, course they are!' Jacob sat down on the doorstep of Abi's House and stretched his legs out. 'It's a beautiful day, they're probably making the most of every minute.'

'Do you think I should text Abi?'

'I thought you wanted this to be a surprise?' Jacob took a swig from his bottle of lager. 'They're probably stuck in the holiday traffic. You know what a nightmare it can be driving through Cornwall this time of year.'

Beth, who was trying to ignore her rumbling belly, and not start eating until Abi and Max got home, nodded reluctantly. 'Sadly that's probably it.'

The gentle sound of Dora, Stan and Sadie all snoring on the living room sofa drifted through the open window. Beth smiled. 'They are so content together. I hope we're like them when we're older.'

Tapping the step to indicate he wanted Beth to join him, Jacob put an arm around her. 'We'll be even madder than them probably. Actually, there was something I wanted to ask you, but we don't seem to have had a minute's peace lately.'

'What's that then?' Beth laid her head on Jacob's

shoulder, closing her eyes against the late afternoon sunshine. 'If you are about to tell me that you want to name our child something weird I will elbow you in the side right now.'

'As if I would curse us with a little baby girl Strawberry or a bouncy boy called Nintendo?'

Beth shuddered. 'Oh don't joke! It's only a matter of time.'

Jacob laughed. 'Don't worry, Beth; I've listened to your lecture on why it is important to give your child a real name many times.'

'Sorry. I know I go on about that. It's seeing a growing yearly supply of children with made-up names or surnames as Christian names that has done it. They always have lower IQs than kids called Emma or Daniel or something normal.'

Jacob laughed. 'Not into generalisations or anything then?'

'Maybe a bit.'

'Anyway…that wasn't what I was going to say.' Jacob twisted his position so he could look at Beth properly. 'I would like to ask, if you would like – and you are allowed to say no – it won't change how I feel about you, but…'

Beth's heart started to beat faster. *Is Jacob about to ask what I think he is?*

'I would like you, Beth Philips, granddaughter of Jack the Lad, and teacher of this parish, to be my wife.'

Her eyes shining, Beth was about to give a positive answer, when Jacob put a finger to her lips and added, 'I am not asking you because of the oncoming arrival of young Strawberry or Nintendo. And I am certainly not asking so you appear respectable in the eyes of the less enlightened villagers and members of the teaching profession. I am asking because I am very much in love with you, and I want you to be the one I snore next to on the sofa when we're in our eighties.'

Gently taking his hand from her lips, Beth leaned forward. 'Yes, please. I love you, Jacob. Grandad would have loved you too. I think you are every bit as eccentric as he was for a start!'

'Actually, if we had a boy, I wondered if we could call him Jack. What do you think?'

Cass saw the van, with *Max Decorates* emblazoned across the side, pass her house and pull into an empty parking space at the side of the road.

That was her signal to act.

Sat in the living room's window seat waiting for her neighbours to get home for the last hour, Cass had been partly reading, partly failing not to think about what she was going to say to Dan when they inevitably bumped into each other at Chalk Towers. Now she picked up her handbag, nipped out of the back door and walked into the village as fast as she could.

Max pulled the van's handbrake and turned off the engine. 'I think we should do that every anniversary. Just take off and be on our own. Or does that sound dreadfully anti-social?'

'It sounds wonderful to me.' Abi was about to climb out of the van when she spotted the row of bunting flags draped across the front wall of Abi's House. 'However, I have a feeling you might have to be social any second now.'

'What? Why?' Max winked. 'I thought I'd take you inside and finish off our non-honeymoon in style.'

'Depends how much you like an audience while you perform?'

'Excuse me?' Max followed the direction of Abi's gaze. 'Ahh, I see. Did you know about this?'

A hand-painted banner had been tied between the open upstairs windows of their home, saying, *Welcome Home Abi and Max. Happy Anniversary*.

'Not a clue. I suspect it's Beth's handiwork.' Abi gave Max a quick kiss. 'Hold on to that honeymoon thought though!'

Climbing out of the van, Max's smiled dipped a fraction. 'They aren't expecting us to come back engaged are they?'

'I've no idea.' Abi slipped her hand into his. 'Don't worry about it. This is our life, not theirs.'

As they crossed the road, Max said, 'Can you hear snoring?'

Beth and Jacob rushed towards their friends. 'Welcome home! Hope you don't mind this invasion.'

'Of course not.' Abi embraced Beth. 'But what's all this in aid of? I've had my anniversary celebration.'

'Not with us you haven't!' Beth laughed. 'There should be more of us, but, as you can hear, two of our party passed out waiting for your return!'

'That will be Stan and Dora having forty winks, will it?' Max looked up at the banner. 'Thanks, guys. What a great welcome.'

Jacob pointed to the front door. 'Even better is to come. There's wine, beer, and fresh bread and butter inside. And Cass will be here with a bumper round of fish and chips in a minute.'

Max grinned. 'Fantastic. They don't do such good fish and chips in the Wye Valley.'

'Honestly, Once a Cornishman…! Our meals were all lovely.' Abi laughed. 'Come on, let's go and wake up the oldies, suddenly I'm starving.'

Sat in the garden at Abi's patio table, swaddled in throws to keep the growing evening sea breeze off their shoulders, the friends tucked into salt- and vinegar-covered fish and chips, straight from the paper they'd come wrapped in.

'This is another thing to add to the list of things I'd never have done in London.' Cass stabbed a particularly thick chip with a tiny wooden fork. 'A dinner party where you eat off paper rather than plates or slates, without real cutlery!'

'Nor me!' Abi waved her own wooden fork at her neighbour. 'Luke only allowed fish and chips if they were served in a restaurant, with the chips neatly placed in a separate fake mini chip pan, and the batter so thin it may as well not have been there.'

'Sounds like your ex and mine have a lot in common.' Cass took another mouthful of their fish supper, and then asked, 'Forgive me if I missed this when I got back from the chip shop, but have you guys come back engaged or anything?'

Max almost choked on some batter, but Abi laughed.

'No, we talked it over, but we're happy as we are, aren't we, Max?'

The decorator reached a hand out 'We are, lass.'

Dora's shrewd eyes shone approvingly. 'Good plan.' She raised a glass. 'That's absolutely the right decision for you two. Here's to finding the right person, and simply enjoying being with them.'

Abi laughed. 'I do declare you're psychic, Dora; but I'll drink to that.'

As they raised a glass of wine, Beth caught Jacob's eye, silently asking him if they should share their own news. On receiving the smallest of head tilts in return, Beth said, 'Actually, there is some news in that direction.'

'There is?' Max's smile widened as he guessed what Beth was about to say.

'Jacob and I have decided to get married.'

'You have?' Stan was amazed. 'When did that happen?'

Laughing, Jacob confessed, 'When you guys were asleep. Aren't I the romantic, proposing to the gentle background music of you, Dora, and Sadie snoring?'

'Sadie was snoring as well?' Max cuddled the retriever.

As the chorus of 'Congratulations,' had died down and hugs had been exchanged, Sadie got up and stood at the door.

Recognising that as a sign that someone was at the door, Stan lifted his hands for hush.

'Yes. There it is again. Someone's knocking on the front door. Good old Sadie, if she hadn't been in my life I'd never have heard the front door when I lived here.'

Abi felt a new rush of affection for the elderly retriever. 'And if you hadn't heard me knock on the door last year, we wouldn't all be here today. Thank you, Sadie!'

Max got up. 'Well, we ought to answer it, before whoever it is goes away.'

'It can't be the neighbours complaining about the noise, because we're all here.' Stan ruffled Sadie's fur. 'Shall we go and open the door and find out, my girl?'

Stan was already on his feet, when Dora put out a hand. 'Actually, I think it'll be for Cass.'

Instantly on her guard, Cass said, 'What have you done, Dora?'

Unrepentant, the old lady said, 'Well, everyone is here except for Dan. It has to be him, doesn't it?'

Cass immediately studied her remaining dinner, so she didn't have to see everyone looking at her. 'Oh, Dora, please tell me you haven't invited him?'

'Well, naturally I have. He's my friend. Anyway, I know he wants to see you as much as you want to see him. You're obviously both too damn stubborn to make the first move, so I've meddled a bit.'

Shooing Cass to the front door, Dora said, 'Go on, or he'll go away again.'

Feeling self-conscious, Cass turned to Beth and Abi for support; but although her friends were keeping quiet, their facial expressions told her quite clearly that they thought Dora was right.

'Dora Abbey, you are a pain in the backside.' Cass sighed as she returned indoors to Abi's kitchen with Sadie as her chaperone.

'You'd better believe it, Cass. Just think of me as your fairy godmother.'

'A fairy godmother that uses trickery rather than fairy dust?'

'The most effective sort, I think you'll find.'

Chapter Forty

The sight of the solid outline of Dan through the small glass window in the front door made Cass's stomach knot in an oddly appealing way.

Does he know I'm here? Cass wouldn't have put it past Dora to have called Dan with some made up emergency to get him there, just so they had the chance to talk, without actually mentioning her presence.

A prickle of nervous perspiration dotted the back of Cass's neck as she opened the door.

'Dan.'

'Oh, hello. I wondered if you'd be here.' Dan looked at his watch rather than at Cass. 'I'm a bit late. I was invited.' Staring at a point at the back of the hallway behind Cass instead, Dan asked, 'Any fish and chips left? I'm starving.'

'I'm afraid not.' Cass felt a bit awkward. 'Dora didn't tell me you were coming. I could go and get you some.'

'I didn't think she'd tell you. She didn't tell me you were here either, but I suspected a set-up.'

'But you still came.'

'I wasn't going to, but then, well…I did.'

Seeing an opportunity to escape and grab some time and space to think, Cass put her hand in her jeans pocket, relieved to find she had enough cash in her pocket to buy a portion of fish and chips without having to back inside to get her handbag. 'If you go into the garden, you'll find the others. I'll fetch you some supper. It won't take me long.'

The doorway felt alight with static electricity. Edging past Dan, Cass took care not to brush his arm in case any accidental contact gave away how much her body wanted to touch him with rather more specific attention.

'Running away again?'

The words stung, and Cass immediately spun on her toes to face Dan properly, snapping, 'I don't run away, I...' Her words died away as Dan's face broke into a smile.

'Yes you do. But then, so do I.' Dan reached out and offered Cass his hand. 'May I accompany you to the chip shop? I'm not sure I'm up to the third degree from Dora until I've had the chance to talk to you alone. She'll only give us a lecture on how we're as bad as each other.'

Cass thought her heart was going to actually thump right through her chest as she slipped her palm into Dan's and began to walk down the path, rather slower than she had planned to only a few seconds ago.

Emboldened by the fact Cass hadn't rejected the offer of his hand, Dan said, 'Can I ask you something?'

'OK.' The heat of Dan's hand was doing weird things to Cass's insides, and she found she had to concentrate hard on simply walking in a straight line.

For goodness' sake, woman, he's only holding your hand. What on earth would you be like if...? Cass forbade her thoughts to go any further.

'Why did you disappear so fast after the wedding? It

374

wasn't so you could settle Sadie into your place, was it?'

'No. No it wasn't.' Cass was silent for a moment before she tried to explain. 'I'm sorry. I promise I didn't want to be rude, or even appear to be rude, but so much has happened. I was afraid, I suppose.'

'Afraid?'

'Of saying the wrong thing. Of giving out the wrong signals. Or, more accurately, that I'd misinterpreted signals again. After all, I have proven I'm not as good at reading people as I previously supposed.'

'When you say people, you mean men.'

'Yes. Sorry.'

Dan stopped walking and studied Cass's face carefully. Two points of pink had appeared on her cheeks, and her eyes had clouded with anxiety. The pulse he could feel beating so fast in her wrist, however, was telling him its own story. And so, Dan knew, was his.

'You were worried the fact we have a serious case of the hots for each other might mess up any friendship or possible future relationship.'

Hearing Dan saying what she'd been thinking in such a matter-of-fact way made Cass blush from ear to ear. 'Uh-huh.'

Dan gently took hold of her shoulders. 'Do you know how many people I've told why I left the Army, Cass? The real reason I mean?'

'Umm. No.'

'Two. Stan is one. Mostly because he asked me outright, and because he has been there. A generation or two before me admittedly, but even after all this time nothing has changed that much sadly. And you are the

375

other one. No one else.'

Cass felt a lump form in her throat. 'I don't know what to say.'

Dan ran a finger across her cheek. 'What I mean is, I don't trust easily. And I certainly don't love easily. I've witnessed too much death, too much loss, to want to risk feeling that much pain for someone I care about. To love someone means to accept that one day you'll lose them. But somehow you've broken through. Believe me, I tried to stop you.'

Cass felt her heart beat faster. 'But, Dan. I'm a nightmare. '

'True.' Dan moved so close that Cass could feel the softness of his breath on her face. 'But you're a nightmare with the most incredible peppermint eyes.'

Cass lifted her head off Dan's shoulder and stared out across the bay. 'Do you think they'll all still be at Abi and Max's?'

'I suspect so, although Dora and Stan could be snoring on the sofa.'

'Again!' Cass laughed.

'Again?'

'Beth told me that they were sound asleep there before Abi and Max got home.'

'Married life is obviously exhausting!' Dan checked his phone. 'Although, maybe they have all gone? I hadn't realised the time. We've been here for hours.' Crumpling up his chip papers and scanning the immediate area for a bin to put them in, Dan said, 'Come on you, it's almost midnight. I'd better get you home before you turn back into a pumpkin.'

'That's hardly Prince Charming talk, is it!' Cass couldn't stop smiling. 'Is it really that late?'

They'd just talked at first. Listening and sharing each other's fears and shortcomings; agreeing they had to see each other again, but that they had to make sure this wasn't merely lust. 'Although', Dan had added hurriedly, 'I'm up for a bit of lust anyway if you are.' The mere thought had made Cass smile even wider.

They had gone on to discuss plans for the future, including Cass's ideas for a continued life in Cornwall. Plans that Dan had declared to be perfect from his perspective. Somehow the minutes had turned into hours, which had melted away in the face of their happy conversation. A conversation that had been punctuated by some lingering kisses.

'This is the second time today I've sat on the sand voluntarily.'

'You weren't kidding, were you? You aren't a beach bunny.'

'I'm not. Although this sort of beach activity with you is the exception!' Cass couldn't believe she was sat there, with a man who was struggling to keep his hands off her. And vice versa.

Tugging Cass to her feet, Dan said, 'But we ought to at least go and apologise for disappearing without a word. If they are all still awake.'

'Oh they'll be up. Dora will be dying to see if her matchmaking has worked.'

'Good point.'

'Anyway, I want to tell Beth and Abi my plan.' Cass felt

a wave of uncertainty come over her. 'It is a good idea, isn't it?'

'It is a wonderful idea.' Dan tucked her slim frame next to his as they walked back up the hill towards Miners Row. 'I'm glad you felt you could discuss it with me.'

'And I'm glad you wanted to listen.'

'Of course I did.' Dan looked so surprised that Cass felt she had to explain.

'I'm not used to people listening to my ideas without immediately working out what they can get out of it themselves.'

'I see. City syndrome. Well, you can come and talk to me about anything. Anytime. Ever. OK?'

'OK.' Cass knew her expression was radiant with happiness. It was new sensation, and one she hoped wouldn't fade too quickly. 'If they are all awake shall we tell them tonight, or wait?'

'Tonight. I think they'll all be delighted, although there is a drawback.'

Cass frowned, 'There is?'

'If Stan and Dora are there, I'll have to offer to take them home.'

Cass felt her cheeks begin to glow again. 'And you'd rather have stayed to continue our conversation in private at my place?'

'Indeed.' Dan put on his most serious expression. 'Over breakfast.'

'We'll give them ten more minutes then we'll call a taxi to take us back to Chalk Towers.' Stan was stroking Sadie's back while she slept gently at his feet.

Abi laughed. 'You'll never get a cab this late. You're welcome to stay in your room, Stan, the bed's made up still from before the wedding.'

'Thanks, Abi girl.' Stan yawned. 'I am getting a bit tired.'

Dora chuckled. 'No stamina, Stan, that's your trouble. I do wish they'd come back though, I'm bursting with curiosity here.'

'The fact they disappeared together is a good sign though, isn't it?' Abi started to clear away the tea and coffee cups they'd been using since they'd come in from the garden a couple of hours ago. 'Isn't that what you wanted, Dora?'

'Yes. I'm just impatient to know if my meddling worked. It could be that my magic wand needs polishing up a bit!'

Beth gazed at the old lady in wonder. 'You're like a character from *Scooby-Doo*! All that meddling.'

'I always thought I'd make a good Velma!'

A general chorus of agreement that Dora would have made a brilliant meddling kid in *Scooby-Doo*, which turned into a gentle argument when Stan and Jacob insisted Dora was too attractive for Velma, and would have been more like Daphne, was interrupted by a knock on the front door.

'Ah, the wanderers return.'

Chapter Forty-one

'Are you sure, Cass?'

Beth had asked the same question three times now, wondering if tiredness was making her hallucinate entire conversations.

'Beth, love, Cass doesn't have to explain all over again does she?' Jacob put his arm around his stunned fiancée's shoulders. 'What brought all this on, Cass? You really are offering us this house?'

'I am. At first it came from desperation to break every connection I have ever had with Justin. But I couldn't see how to do that. My mind was a mess. It wasn't until Dora did her James Bond thing that I allowed myself to start thinking about my future with more than just the odd flight of fancy.

'Then when I was on my own with Sadie we got to thinking more constructively. She's a wise old thing that retriever.'

'She most certainly is.' Max rested his weight on his elbows on the table. 'But we thought you had grown to like living next door.'

'I do. It's great, but it''s mostly great because I've met all of you guys, as well as Dora and Stan.' Cass pointed down the hallway, in the general direction of Stan and Dora who had retired to bed in triumph, now they knew that Dora's interference had worked.

'And Dan?' Abi asked.

Blushing appealingly across the kitchen table at the man in question, Cass said, 'And Dan,' before turning back to Beth and Jacob. 'The thing is, try as I might, I'm not a beach person. And as I'm planning a completely new start, with a new business enterprise, thanks to the wonderful Jo in Truro, then I'm going to require somewhere in a town, preferably with a workshop big enough to paint furniture in.'

The sides of Cass's mouth were beginning to ache from smiling so much, and she was surprised all over again at her own excitement at the prospect of a new adventure. 'It makes perfect sense to offer this place to you and Beth first – but only if you want to. There's no obligation, no pressure. I heard you saying to Abi, Beth, in the hotel car park, that you were going to need a bigger home once your baby has arrived.'

Abi, seeing Beth and Jacob were having trouble digesting what Cass was offering, stepped in. 'So, what you're saying, Cass, is that now you're free of your links to London, you're going to kick-start a whole new life. Like I did, but with way more confidence.'

Cass laughed. 'Most of the confidence is fake or forced to be honest, but yes, that sounds about right.'

Pouring himself a glass of water, Max asked, 'What is this big new life plan then, Cass?'

'I'm going to take a course with Jo in Truro doing furniture restoration. She has already offered me an apprenticeship in exchange for free interior design advice. I've always had a flair for colours and seeing what goes with what. Until I'd met Jo I hadn't seen it as interior design. Just something I did.' Cass sounded as bemused as she felt. How had she not noticed this whole creative side to her world that presumably had always been inside her, waiting to be fulfilled?

'Eventually I want to open an Interior Design workshop. Somewhere to do up the furniture Jo can't find time to do – and isn't too complicated – and where people can come for advice or to book me to redesign their living spaces.' Cass turned to Max. 'Can I recommend you as the decorator to go to when people ask for more than I can provide?'

'Hell yes.' Max beamed. 'Thanks, Cass.'

Beth stifled a yawn, her curiosity greater than her desire to sleep despite the fact it was past midnight. 'Where will you do all this? I mean, it would be easy for you to put a shed in your garden like Abi has, and work from there.'

'True, but I have to start fresh.' Cass looked at Dan who gave her a reassuring wink as she went on. 'As much as I like it here, and as lucky as I've been with my incredible neighbours,' turning, Cass smiled at Abi, 'I have to live a tiny bit more inland to satisfy the part of me who'll be forever a city girl.

'Sadie and I have been to see Maggie at the estate agent's. She thinks she has found the right sort of place for me on the other side of Penzance. A small shop-cum-studio, with a tiny office downstairs, and a flat above. Dan and I are going to take a look tomorrow afternoon.'

Reaching out for Beth's hand, Jacob asked, 'If we said yes to your incredible offer, how would it work?'

'You could either buy number two, or rent it, while you rent out your own flat, I guess. Up to you.' Cass held up her hand as Beth and Jacob exchanged glances, obviously not at all sure what to do. 'I don't expect a quick answer. This is a big decision. Why don't you have a think about it for a few days? It's so late; we should all get some sleep.'

Pushing her spare house keys across the table, Cass spoke to Beth. 'My meeting with Maggie is at ten tomorrow morning. Go take a look if you like while I'm out. If you don't want to take the place then I'll see if Maggie can rent it out for me.' Standing up, Cass said, 'Thanks ever so much for a lovely evening, Abi, but I have an appointment with my bed.'

Dan got up as well. 'And I ought to go back to the flats. Thanks, all.' Kissing Cass on the cheek, he quickly disappeared out of the house.

Cass was about to follow Dan, when Abi and Beth laughed, speaking in unison. 'Spill the beans, Ms Henley!'

'Honestly! I think you two have been picking tips up from the new Mrs Abbey!' Cass laughed. 'Let's say that the next time Dan sends me roses they may be nearer red than yellow. Orange, perhaps? I'll give you all the news tomorrow! Now it's bedtime.'

Cass got to her front door, to find Dan sat on the doorstep.

'Did you get lost on the way to Chalk Towers?'

'Nope.' Dan's eyes shone with desire. 'I'm exactly where I intended to be.'

'Good. Then you'd better come in.'

384

The four friends stared at each other across the kitchen table, not one of them quite believing what had just happened.

It was Beth who spoke first. 'What do you think, Jacob? I mean, I love Grandad's flat – it's so full of memories – but we really will need more space in time, won't we? But could we afford to live here if we rented the flat out? The rent won't be cheap, will it? I know we could never afford to buy it.'

Jacob was doing rapid calculations. 'We could probably afford the rent if you kept working like you said you would, but you might not want to any more.'

'I do want to. For my sanity's sake really. But only part-time. No point in having a child if you never see them.'

Max picked up Cass's spare keys, and passed them to Beth. 'Go and have a look tomorrow. Just the two of you; on your own.'

Finally alone with Max, Abi was trying hard not to show any form of excitement on her face at the prospect of their best friends becoming their neighbours in case Beth and Jacob decided not to take up Cass's offer. 'We could help with babysitting.'

'We could,' Max said. 'And we wouldn't have to worry about not getting on with the neighbours, or having people to Sadie-sit if we wanted to have another romantic weekend away.'

'Which we would.'

'Which we would.' Max got up and held out his hand.

'Bedtime.'

Allowing herself to be escorted to the king-sized bed that was just large enough for Max, but massive for Abi, she said, 'They could say no.'

'Will depend on the rent, I suppose.'

'Cass wouldn't make it too expensive, would she?'

'No idea, but I doubt it. She probably won't insist on a deposit either. That's usually the sticking point with renting.'

'It's funny,' Abi sat on the edge of the bed and pulled off her T-shirt, 'half an hour ago I was sure our new neighbours would be Cass and, eventually, Dan. Now I want our neighbours to be Beth and Jacob. I like Cass and everything, but wouldn't it be wonderful if...'

'Out of our hands, lass. Out of our hands.'

Max had just returned from delivering Stan and Dora back to Chalk Towers, and Abi was getting ready to go and open the gallery, when Sadie got to her feet seconds before the humans heard the knock on the front door. 'They can't have looked around already?'

Following Max into the kitchen Beth and Jacob's faces were flushed with excitement, as Abi, desperate to hear the verdict said, 'You can't have decided already?'

Jacob laughed. 'We only got as far as the living room and kitchen.'

'Why, what happened?' Abi was confused. 'You can't have got lost. The house is a mirror image of this one.'

Beth's eyes were wide with joy. 'Basically, we got to the kitchen, looked at each other and simultaneously wondered who we were kidding. Of course we want to live there.'

'You do?' Abi's face lit up. 'For real?'

'For real.'

'Forgive me, but can you afford it?' Max asked. 'And what about your flat? Will you rent it?'

'Cass left a note with the expected sale and rental price. We can't buy it, but we can rent it.' Jacob oozed delight as he spoke. 'In the meantime, I know someone who might want to rent our place.'

'You do?' Abi had to fight back a childish urge to jump up and down with excitement.

'Dan.'

'Oh, yes!' Max clapped his huge palms together. 'Dan was only saying the other day he wanted somewhere to live out of Chalk Towers, so he could have time away from the place when he was off duty.

Abi began to rummage in her coat pocket. 'Come on!'

Beth and Jacob were confused. 'Come on where?'

'Into the garden.' Abi rushed to the bench where the best phone signal could be found. 'I know we're supposed to be opening the gallery, but it can look after itself for another hour or two.'

Following Abi with bemusement, Beth, Jacob and Max watched as she hammered a number into her phone. 'Chalk Towers first, then we'll call Cass.'

Beth rubbed her bump as she looked at Max for an explanation, but he just shrugged as Abi's call was obviously answered.

'Stan!'

Beth smiled as she understood; nodding her approval at Abi, she hugged Jacob and Max at the same time.

'Stan, guess what? Beth and Jacob are going to move into Miners Row. They are going to be our neighbours! Are you and Dora free this afternoon? I can feel an enormous Cornish Cream Tea coming on.'

THE END

If you loved *A Cornish Wedding,*
why not read

A Cornish Escape

Abi's life is turned upside down when she is widowed before her thirtieth birthday. Determined to find something positive in the upheaval, Abi decides to make a fresh start somewhere new. With fond childhood memories of holidays in a Cornish cottage, could Cornwall be the place to start over?

With all her belongings in the boot of her car but no real plan, a chance meeting in a village pub brings new friends Beth and Max into her life. Max soon helps Abi track down the house of her dreams but things aren't as simple as Abi hoped.

Can Abi leave her past behind and finally get her happy ending?

ACCENT

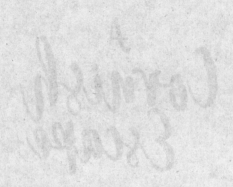

The *Another Cup of …* Series
Jenny Kane

Bookends

When one book ends, another begins...

Bookends is a vibrant new reading community to help you ensure you're never without a good book.

You'll find exclusive previews of the brilliant new books from your favourite authors as well as exciting debuts and past classics. Read our blog, check out our recommendations for your reading group, enter great competitions and much more!

Visit our website to see which great books we're recommending this month.

Join the Bookends community:
www.welcometobookends.co.uk

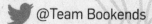 @Team Bookends   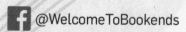 @WelcomeToBookends